Redemption Grove
David Rawding

Redemption Grove
A Red Adept Publishing Book
Red Adept Publishing, LLC
104 Bugenfield Court
Garner, NC 27529
http://RedAdeptPublishing.com/

Copyright © 2018 by David Rawding. All rights reserved.

Cover Art by Streetlight Graphics

No part of this book may be reproduced, scanned, or distributed in any printed or electronic form without permission. Please do not participate in or encourage piracy of copyrighted materials in violation of the author's rights. Thank you for respecting the hard work of this author.

This is a work of fiction. Names, characters, places, and incidents either are the product of the author's imagination or are used fictitiously, and any resemblance to locales, events, business establishments, or actual persons—living or dead—is entirely coincidental.

For my brother, John, and my sister, Heidi.

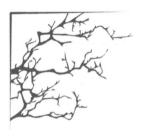

Chapter 1

The squeaking brakes of a garbage truck wrenched Chris Olson from a shallow sleep. He shaded his eyes with a grubby hand against the morning sun. Lying on his back on a patch of sunburned grass in the park, he watched the green rig's clunky progression among the subdued houses across the street. Chris brushed aside the hood of his gray sweatshirt, reached into the black backpack that he used as a pillow, found his ball cap, and slipped it on his head. He fished out one of the two pills from his jeans pocket and examined the little blue circle cradled in his palm. Oxy, blues, 30s... there were plenty of street names for oxycodone 30 mg, but Chris liked to think of the painkillers as his little blue buddies. With his tolerance, thirty milligrams didn't even get him high anymore—it just made him feel normal. He popped the pill, crunched down with his molars, and chewed the shattered bits.

Down the sidewalk, an old man pushed a cart stuffed with a bedroll, pieces of cardboard, plastic bags, and random knickknacks. With his flaring white beard, deep-set blue eyes, and pilled red sweater, the old guy resembled a homeless Santa Claus.

As the old man approached, he tipped his leather ball cap. "Morning, young fella."

"Hey." Chris heaved himself to a sitting position. "You know what time it is?" He slid his chilled fingers into the front pocket of his sweatshirt.

The old guy stopped his progression down the sidewalk and regarded the rays of light that poked through the row of palms and the neighborhood beyond. "I'd guess around seven o'clock." He pointed

1

a crooked finger at an area across the shrinking pond on the other side of the park. He shook his head. "LAPD are making their wake-up calls. I got to get my breakfast before they fill up at the mission. I'll be seeing you." The old man pushed his cart, but one of the wheels refused to budge. He kept trying to get it moving but had no success. "What the heck is wrong with this thing?"

This could be me one day. Chris drifted over to the old man, squatted down, and inspected the offending wheel. Fishing line had gotten wound around the small axle. "There's your problem." Chris produced a lighter from his pocket and used the flame to burn through the tangled mess. Then he yanked out the many broken strands that clogged the wheel. He stepped back. "Should be good now."

The old man pushed his loaded cart, which moved freely. "I'll be damned. What was it?"

"Fishing line. You some kind of fisherman?"

"Used to be when I was your age." He rubbed his long nails through his beard. When the bleary-eyed man smiled, he offered an upper deck of uneven yellow teeth.

At his age, the guy ought to have been in a senior home instead of living on the streets. Chris was twenty-one and could hardly handle the sore bones, sickness, and chronic empty belly that came with being homeless.

"Seems fine now. I'll be seeing you, old-timer." Chris collected his ratty backpack and thought again about how the man resembled Santa Claus. "And Merry Christmas."

The old man cocked his head and said, "It's May."

"I know." Chris chuckled and headed in the opposite direction. "Enjoy your breakfast."

As Chris strode along the sidewalk, he yawned and smacked his chapped lips. On any other morning, he'd follow the old guy to get in on that free church grub, but he had plans. His sister, Aida, had reached out through email, since he didn't have the money or the credit for a cell phone. Using the library computer, he had arranged to meet her on her trip down from Alaska to Los Angeles. He hadn't seen her in over a year. She'd given birth to his niece six months back, and he'd made no effort to fly up there. She'd been barraging him with emails to try to lock down a date to visit. He missed his sister, but keeping up with his addiction had become his first priority. Aida, as persistent as ever, had gone and booked a flight to see him without even checking to see if he was free. He'd thought of tossing her an excuse, but the image of Aida wandering around LA alone made him feel guilty, so he'd reluctantly agreed to meet her.

Morning commuters cruised the streets, but the sidewalk remained his. He'd have to catch the bus across town to get to Aida's Beverly Hills hotel. Chris hefted his backpack and ambled toward the bus stop. After eating the pill, he'd be good for twenty-four hours. The remaining one would get him through the next full day, and the day after that, he'd be craving again. He patted his wallet in his back pocket and envisioned the thirty-two bucks from panhandling the exit ramp. At a dollar a milligram, the cash bought him another day. Staving off withdrawal was a full-time job.

Chris touched his front jeans pocket but felt nothing. *What the...?* He pulled his pocket inside out, and the solitary pill flipped out, bounced off the sidewalk, and skipped under a parked sedan. "Shit!" He rushed to the car and got down on his hands and knees. The small blue circle sat on the pavement beneath the car. He wedged his chest into the narrow space and breathed in the scent of motor oil and rubber. Extending his bony arm and grasping with the tips of his fingers, he retrieved his prize.

He blew away dirt from the pill's surface. "Almost lost you, buddy." He tucked the blue into a zippered compartment in his backpack then sighed, stuffed his hands in his pockets, and continued walking.

Chris arrived at Aida's hotel an hour late. He'd missed the bus. He wasn't used to having plans or keeping them. When he stepped into the lobby, the receptionist, a clean-cut guy with gelled hair and wire-rimmed glasses, eyed him.

Chris threw him a toothless smile and nodded. *Fuck you too, pal.* He glimpsed Aida off to the right, sitting in a white upholstered chair, staring through reading glasses at her phone. He cleared his throat.

Aida brushed aside her auburn bangs as she glanced up, then she sprang to her feet. She met him with a broad smile and a hug. "Come here, baby brother. Oh, so good to see you. It's been too long." She squeezed him tightly.

Chris caught a whiff of strawberry when he hugged her back. He tossed a wink over her shoulder to the receptionist, who took a sudden interest in his computer screen.

Aida stepped back and examined him. "Jeez, look at you... you're so skinny! Gosh, people aren't going to think we're related anymore." Aida gathered a handful of her loose belly fat. "What's your secret?"

And here come the lies. "Don't have much of an appetite." He scratched the back of his neck. Aida had a few new smile lines around her eyes and a couple more pounds on her gut and thighs, but even growing up, she'd always been on the thicker side. "You look fine. Hey, sorry I'm late."

"No worries. I still remember the LA traffic. And thanks." She brushed her teal blouse. "You're a good fibber." She put her hands on her hips. "So am I going to get to see your place this time or what?"

Aida had visited him a couple of times since she'd moved to Alaska with her husband, Frank, two years before. When Chris had first moved from their hometown of Long Beach to Los Angeles after high school, he had some money and an apartment, but he blew through most of the cash his first year in the city. Since then, he'd had some temporary places to live but nothing permanent. He'd been on the streets for a few months during his latest stretch of homelessness. Aida seemed to always show up when he was between apartments, so he had to come up with a different excuse every time she visited. He lied to her to save her the worry.

"It's getting fumigated—bedbugs."

She scrunched up her face. "So where are you staying?"

"My buddy's couch." Another lie. He had some friends among the other homeless, but none of them had couches of their own. His dealer, Jake, had a couch, but he wasn't the type to offer anything for free.

"That can't be comfortable. Here, stay with me. My room has an extra bed."

On the one hand, he hadn't slept on an actual mattress in weeks, and his back and hips were banged up and bruised because of it. On the other, accepting her offer might lead to too much family time. She would ask him questions and probably ferret out the fact that he was back on pills. Aida knew that he had messed around with painkillers in high school but probably had no idea that he still used them. Knowing her, she'd already figured out that he'd made up the *bedbugs* bullshit. She'd no doubt requested a room with a second bed.

"I'll make it easy on you: you're staying with me. Just two nights. Consider it a present for my twenty-ninth birthday." Aida squeezed his soft biceps. "It's settled."

"All right." Chris scratched gunk out of his eye. He didn't have the energy to argue. The hard-packed dirt in the park hadn't done his back any favors the previous night. Still, sleeping on the ground beat dealing with the curfews, bag searches, and occasional kicks to the head he faced in the homeless shelters.

Aida squinted and hooked her thumb over her shoulder toward the elevator. "Did you want to take a shower or anything while we're here?"

He sniffed the arm of his sweatshirt. The aroma of grass and dirt accompanied the underlying stench of oniony body odor. His unkempt ash-brown hair was greasy, but he'd stuffed it into his black ball cap. "Nah, I'm good." He fixed his stare on her blue eyes. "So what did you want to do today?"

She wanted to shop. Aida carted him around in her rental car. Since she lived in Alaska, Aida claimed she didn't have the opportunity to buy stuff from fancy places. He wasn't a shopper, but he never had much money either. The cash he managed to collect funded his pill habit.

Chris stored his backpack in the trunk of her car and shadowed Aida, who strolled down Rodeo Drive. They passed benches he'd slept on. He followed her into an upscale clothing store, where she rubbed leather jackets and patted wool sweaters. She seemed dazzled by shoe displays and grabbed a lime-green high heel from the shelf.

Chris stroked the stubble on his Adam's apple. "Where are you going to wear shoes like that? Isn't it always winter up there?"

"That's what I thought before I moved in with Frank. Alaska's beautiful in the summer and can get pretty hot. Sun's out until midnight in the summer, you know."

He'd watched a show about Alaska that made it seem like a rugged wilderness with eagles in the air and grizzlies in the woods. He and Aida had been raised on a quiet street in Long Beach. Although Chris had no particular love for his hometown or LA, they were what he knew. A good job would have helped, and four walls and a roof would have made his life a hell of a lot easier, but when faced with the choice of rent or pills, he was forced by his body and his wallet to sleep outside with blues in his pocket.

"When are you going to come and visit the rest of your family?" Aida put the shoe back on the display. "You still haven't met your niece yet. She's getting big."

Aida's marriage after college and her desire to have a baby had been the driving force behind her and Frank's move to Alaska. Frank worked for one of the Alaskan oil companies, and since he'd grown up in Anchorage, he had family there, which made the whole raising-a-baby thing easier. Chris wanted to meet his niece, Shannon. However, spending time with Aida's husband wasn't appealing. Frank didn't have much of a personality, and when he did talk to Chris, he always spoke as if he were disappointed in him.

"Need money for that," Chris said.

Aida exhaled. "How many times do I have to tell you? I'll buy your ticket."

"It's fine. I got to get my life sorted out down here before I fly off to Alaska." A steady source of income would definitely help. The last legitimate check he'd received came from a temporary sign-spinning gig a few weeks back. Since then, he'd been begging for change, which just barely covered his pill needs.

Chris followed Aida out of the store. They weaved past clusters of tourists meandering about Rodeo Drive, taking pictures and examining maps. Aida looped her arm in his and brought him close. "I could go for a mimosa. Want to grab brunch? My treat."

"I could eat." After years of being on and off the streets, he'd learned to always accept charity. There was no point in refusing what strangers offered. He figured that on some level, helping out the homeless made people feel good.

She picked a table outside a small café. They placed an order, and Aida said, "You have a job?"

Chris arched his back in his iron chair and yawned. "Not currently."

"You know, there aren't a lot of single women in Alaska, but—like I've told you before—there's plenty of work. The saying is: 'If you can't find a job in Alaska, there's something wrong with you.' Everyone's hiring, especially in the summer. I know a guy in Anchorage that would interview you tomorrow. We have a spare room waiting..." Aida extended her hand. "You just need to say the word, and it's done."

An address with free rent and a job was hard to turn down. Chris laughed. "I'll think about it, okay?"

"Your niece would *love* to meet you."

"Yeah. I mean, just for shits and giggles, what kind of jobs are you talking about up there? I only have a high school diploma."

Aida grinned and shifted in her seat. "Frank knows a ton of people in Anchorage. You could be a deckhand on a boat if you wanted to work outside—hard work, but they pay *really* well. There are a bunch of resorts and tour companies that need people. If you wanted to work up on the North Slope, like Frank, you could do just about anything. Three weeks on, three weeks off, and the oil-company pay is ridiculous. They always need young guys like you who are willing to work."

Chris sniffed. He examined his hands on his lap. They were stained, cracked, and riddled with cuts. Dirt and grime had become embedded under the nails and had spread across the rest of his body. A good job could give him a fresh start, and a new state could help him get clean. The ex-junkies he'd known over the years had all pretty much said the same thing: a person had to get away from friends, dealers, and temptation to break the addiction. Alaska was about as far away from LA as he could get. As a nurse, Aida could probably help him deal with the withdrawal. Once he was through being dope sick, he could get one of these jobs she was talking about. He could save up some money and get a place of his own. The whole Alaska idea started to make his life down in LA seem like crap.

"Oh, I almost forgot... I owe you this." She dug in her fat purse and came up with a wrapped present and a card.

He frowned. "What's this?"

"I missed your birthday. Twenty-one! That's a big birthday to miss."

He'd still been living with his ex-girlfriend Jane when he turned twenty-one. She bought him a couple of expensive suits, shirts, and ties to wear to interviews. At his birthday dinner, he blew out his candle with the wish that he could get clean, find a job, and live happily ever after with Jane. Then she found his pill stash and kicked him out. He'd exchanged the suits and clothes for cash and had been on the streets ever since.

Chris eyed Aida, who'd polished off her Cobb salad and was sipping her mimosa across the table. He glanced at the last couple of fries on his plate. Fish and chips—he'd eaten the food without taking much time to taste it. He opened the card and noticed the hundred-dollar bills fanning from the crease... three hundred dollars in all. The note was some Hallmark junk signed by Aida, Frank, and Shannon.

"That's a lot of cash."

"Well, you have to have a few drinks on your twenty-first birthday." Aida laughed. "And down here, three hundred dollars is probably... what, four cocktails?"

He wanted to tell her he wasn't much of a drinker, but instead, Chris opened the wrapped box. He found a prepaid cell phone inside.

"There's plenty of minutes loaded, and I had the guy at the store program my number in there. Email is great, but I prefer to hear your voice."

"This is... very generous." Three hundred dollars and a phone could get him a lot of pills. He didn't like that his mind immediately went there, but it did, always.

Aida pinned him with her gaze. "So what's keeping you here, anyways?"

Chris watched the people walking past their café. A Latino kid with Ray-Bans and slick black hair bent down to tie the laces of his sneakers. A skinny chick with dark-purple lipstick waited beside him. She removed her sunglasses to examine her face in the mirrored lenses. When the guy finished, she grabbed his hand and towed him back into the flow of pedestrians mingling about Rodeo Drive. Chris didn't have anything in common with that crowd. He had no love for Hollywood, the beach, or the city. He was tired of the place, but more than anything, he was exhausted with trying to keep up with his addiction. The pills had become the family that he never wanted.

"To tell you the truth, I don't know."

"So why not say—excuse my French—'*fuck* this city' and move in with us? Frank's fine with it, and Shannon would love to have her uncle close. We'll get you all set up there."

Chris cracked his neck. This might be the time to finally take her up on her offer. His growing tolerance was forcing him to use stronger doses, which would price him out of pills and push him to heroin. He'd seen it plenty of times before. If he was ever going to get clean, this was the moment. He'd have to tell her the truth. With her help, he had a shot at squashing the habit for good.

Chris gazed at the sky, which had become wrapped in a haze of smog. *Even the air is shitty here.* "Can we be real for a minute?"

Aida leaned in and lowered her tone. "Sure. What?"

Chris sniffed and swallowed in an effort to wet his dry throat. "Remember how I used to use Vicodin back in high school?"

Aida squinted. "You're still using, aren't you?"

"Yeah, except I've graduated from Vicodin. Daily doses of oxycodone 30 mg is where I'm at now."

"Well..." Aida nodded slowly. "That explains all the sniffing." She cocked her head to the side. "So how long have you been on it? Do you want to stop?"

Chris hadn't really thought to hide his sniffing—not that it mattered now. "Since high school. I—"

The waiter moved in and cleared their plates. He slid the bill between them. Aida reeled the check in and thanked him. When the server slipped away to another table, she gave Chris her attention.

"I do want to quit," he said, "but I don't know if I'm ready to deal with the withdrawals—not by myself."

Aida put a hand to her chest. "Chris, I can help you. You know that. I just wish you'd told me sooner. I remember catching you and that no-good friend of yours from high school, Jake... something, but you promised me that was a one-time thing."

Chris removed his hat and ran his hand through his greasy hair. "I thought it was, but I couldn't stop... It got away from me."

"What else haven't you told me?" Aida asked.

Here we go. The truth spewed out, purging him. He told her about his homelessness and how he popped painkillers the way regular people took vitamins. He described how he'd slept on the streets from Skid Row to the park that morning. As he gave her the truth, Aida held her cheek and listened. Her concerned frown melted to a sympathetic soft expression, and her sculpted eyebrows rose and fell as he spoke. He ended by telling her how he'd pawned all his stuff and routinely ate out of the trash.

Aida winced. "I knew you were keeping stuff from me, but I didn't think it was that much. I had no idea you were going through all this..." She wiped her misty eyes. "Me leaving you here and moving to Alaska probably didn't help, huh?"

He'd missed Aida when she moved, but that wasn't what started his habit. High school boredom had gotten him hooked. "Like I said, I was doing them before you left."

"And you're ready—I mean, physically ready—to quit? Withdrawals won't be easy. And after, you'll probably have to deal with the mental side. God, I sound like I'm talking you out of it—I'm not, but it's going to be tough." Aida spoke as if he was already her patient.

He'd started to withdraw plenty the last few years but was always able to get pills into his system before he felt too shitty. "I think I can do it—quit pills altogether."

"Have you tried checking into rehab?" Aida asked.

He'd been told horror stories about rehab that made it sound more like prison than a place to get healthy. "I don't want any part of those places. I can beat this... with your help."

Aida chewed her plump bottom lip. "You can come live with us, and we'll get you through withdrawals together. You'll have to go cold turkey, though."

Chris stuck his tongue in his cheek. "That'll suck. Well, what about some meds to help with the withdrawals? Suboxone?"

"If used correctly, sure, those kinds of meds could help, but if you had used opioids correctly, then you wouldn't be in this mess in the first place." Aida's voice remained strong. "As I said, there's always rehab instead..."

"Not an option."

"Well, then, if you want my help, I'm not going to be supplying you with any more medications. If you get dependent on something else, it'll defeat the purpose. So unless it's necessary for your survival, you're going to have to go one hundred percent clean. No drugs at all. That includes alcohol. Cold turkey is what I'm offering."

Chris nodded. "Okay."

Aida studied him. "So why do you want to quit?"

"I... well..." Chris hadn't expected the directness of her question. He depended on the pills to get him through the day. In turn, they stole his cash and put him on the street. A day without painkillers ushered in anxiety, which drove him right back into the arms of his little blue buddies. He needed to quit to feel normal—truly normal—again. Quitting was going to hurt, but he needed to get clean to start his life over. "Truth is, I'm scared. I used to be able to handle the habit. Now, when I don't get my pills, I feel like crap, and I start to panic. I'm scared of withdrawals, but at this point, I'm more worried about what will happen if I don't quit."

Aida's thumb massaged her jaw. "All right. I'll call Frank, and we'll get you on a flight back with me."

That would be the day after tomorrow. All of a sudden, things were happening. He'd started the conversation, and now he was about to fly away to Alaska. "I mean, doesn't have to be that soon..."

Her eyes became slits. "The sooner, the better, Chris."

"Okay, okay. I get it." He wiped his damp forehead. "Give me a month."

"A week," Aida said.

Chris smiled and shook his head. "You and I both know that the only way this is going to work is if I get to be the one making the choice to get clean. June first—that's in, like... three weeks. I got a couple buddies I want to say goodbye to here. I'll be ready to make the flight by then." He had some homeless friends that he could say goodbye to—it wasn't a lie—but he really needed the three weeks to mentally prepare. He could start cutting or shaving the pills down to wean himself off of them.

Her right eyebrow lifted, and creases rippled up her forehead. "Is that the truth?"

She didn't believe him, and he couldn't blame her. "Honest, Aida. You can book it for June first, and I'll get on a flight. I promise." She'd given him a way out, and he was determined to make good on her offer, but he needed to be ready, and a little time would help.

Aida closed her eyes for a minute then said, "June first, you fly to Alaska. You'll go cold turkey—no drugs at all—and I'll help you get through withdrawals. Once you're better, we can concentrate on getting you a job." She reached over the table with her right hand. "We have a deal?"

Cold turkey would suck, but being away from his dealer and having Aida's help would be his best chance to get clean. Chris balked for a second, then he grasped her hand in a firm grip.

ON THE MORNING OF HER flight back to Alaska, Aida had to leave the hotel early to catch a six o'clock plane out of LAX. Chris woke long enough to accept her hug goodbye, promised again to meet her in Anchorage on June 1, then pretended to go back to sleep while she readied her luggage. Aida had already booked the flight for him and used the hotel's business center to print the ticket. To go along with the ticket, she booked him the hotel room for the next three weeks and told him he could charge meals to the room. Aida walked out the door, suitcase in hand, and hesitated. Then she closed the door and was gone.

With Aida no longer there, he got dressed, exited the hotel, and made for Jake's place. He was out of oxycodone and needed to buy what he hoped would be his last bag. Jake had been his dealer and friend since high school, although to call him a *friend* made a mockery of the term. They would never be there for each other in a bind, unless that bind turned out to be a bag of pills and Chris had the money to pay for it.

Forty-five minutes later, he stepped off the bus and headed to Jake's house. A slight breeze brushed the stubble on his cheeks. As he strolled past a chain-link fence, a German shepherd barked at him and rushed the fence with bared teeth.

"Okay, okay, I'm going." Chris hastened his pace. He arrived at Jake's front porch and rang the bell.

Jake opened the door, through which wafted the scent of weed. His glassy hazel eyes were red at the corners. He wore baggy clothes, and his breath stank of malt liquor. "Hey, bro. Listen, I'd let you in, but I've got this girl over." He spoke with a slur and winked at Chris.

"No worries, man." Chris showed him the birthday cash.

"Look at you, Chris," Jake said with amusement. "Where'd you get three hundred dollars, huh?"

"You know me, man. I always find a way."

Jake scanned the street for a second. "Give me a minute." He closed the door.

Chris examined the quiet neighborhood. The houses were built close enough so that a person could jump from roof to roof. The aging homes were mostly single storied with fenced-in carpets of dead grass out front. The cars parked on the curb were mostly beaters, tired trucks, and two-door junkers. Still, the area wasn't that bad.

A few minutes later, Jake opened the door and handed Chris a plastic bag. "Ten blues in there." Jake brushed strands of his limp russet hair off his pierced eyebrow.

Chris hastily slipped the bag of oxycodone in his jeans pocket. "Hey, man, I was wondering. How much does a place like this cost anyways?"

"You in the market for a house?" Jake chuckled and leaned his shoulder on the paint-chipped doorframe.

Chris rubbed his thumb along his nostril and sniffed. "Nah. Just wondering. I know I'm a ways away." He examined his tired gray Converse shoes. "But one day, yeah. One day, I'd like a place of my own, you know?"

"Sure." Jake snapped his fingers. "You know, I was thinking about you yesterday. You remember our senior year when we used to hang out in my mom's basement, split a Vicodin, and drink that shitty vodka? Remember that?"

Half a Vicodin used to be enough. "Yeah. Now I got to do thirties just to feel right. Would sure be easier on my wallet if I could go back to those days."

Jake chuckled. "I know you always shoot me down, but you can get a lot more heroin for your money, bud. I can hook you up, no problem."

"Nah. Like I already told you, man, I hate needles, and there's no way of knowing what it's cut with. I'm not about to mainline something that'll kill me."

Jake put a hand over his heart. "You can trust me. Wouldn't make me good at what I do if I killed off my customers, now, would it?" Jake's phone vibrated, and he dug it out of his pocket. He squinted to read the screen.

Chris adjusted his hat and tapped his pocket. *Ten pills for three weeks.* If he cut them in half and started weaning himself off of them, that might be enough. He remembered Aida's other gift. "Hey, how many pills could I get for this prepaid phone?"

Jake glanced up. "Got a burner phone? Let's see it."

Chris hesitated then handed the cell phone over.

"This is nice." Jake curled his lower lip. "I'll give you four blues for it."

Aida might try to call, but they could always go back to email. He already had the plane ticket, so there wasn't much else to talk about, and four more pills could buy him some more time. "Deal. Let me just clear out the stuff on there."

Jake handed the phone back. "I'm gonna change the number anyways, bro."

Chris deleted Aida's number. "I know."

Jake ducked inside, came back, and handed over the four bonus pills.

"Thanks, man." Chris thought to say goodbye to Jake, but since there was a chance he'd need a refill, he didn't. It would probably be best if Jake didn't know where he was going. Better to not have a way of contacting him too. *Got to cut all ties.*

"Yeah, sure. See you next time." Jake waved him off and closed the door.

Chris made for the hotel. He ate one of the bonus four pills on the bus ride to get himself through the rest of the day. Back in the hotel room, he buried the bag of ten blues in his backpack. Chris laid out the remaining three pills from the bonus bag on the black end table then shuffled them around like a guy on the street trying to hide an ace. He let them rest and stared at his three blue buddies. It had been a while since he'd actually been able to get high from painkillers, and now he had a surplus. He licked his lips. *Might as well enjoy the birthday present.* He grabbed one and hastily swallowed it before he could feel bad. With two inside him on an empty stomach, he'd probably be able to get a good high going. He ignored the other two on the table and lay back on the bed.

After a little while, his body warmed a bit, but he wasn't euphoric. He examined the two blues on the table. *Fuck it. Let's party, boys.* Chris hastily folded a piece of hotel stationery and stuck the two blues inside the crease. He used the side of his lighter to crush the pills within the paper pocket. Next, he opened the paper and used his hotel key card to gather the powder on the tabletop. He licked the paper clean of residue before tossing it in the trash. Chris used the key card to chop and line up a rail on the dark surface. He rolled a dollar bill, put it in his nostril, and snorted the powder until he'd vacuumed every last grain of dust.

Chris coughed and massaged his nose. "Ah, there we go."

His arms and legs gradually became numb, and his lips curled into a smile while he basked in pulses of heat. Chris fell back into the soft comforter, which felt like a soft cloud that cradled him as if he were the Charmin paper-towel baby. His mind slowed, and he closed his eyes and let the drowsiness take over. *Heaven.*

When his eyes snapped open, he saw a chubby housekeeper screaming. Chris tried to get up, but his body convulsed, and vomit crowded his throat and mouth. He choked on the burning sludge but couldn't move, couldn't free his throat. He begged the screaming woman with his eyes. *Help me!*

She quit screaming and came to his side. "Sir! What do I do? What do I do?"

Help me, please! Please, help!

He shook harder. His brain shut down. Dark. *Is this it?* Light. A hand slapped his back hard, and he was on his side. Vomit passed his lips and splashed on the carpet and on the housekeeper's white tennis shoes. She kept hitting his back really hard. He gasped for breath. Hot acid lined his throat.

"Sir! Are you okay?" She stopped whaling on him and brought a warm towel to his lips.

Chris sucked air and tried moving. His limbs were sluggish.

"I'll call 911," she said.

"No." His brain moved like a banana slug as he tied thoughts together. Calling 911 would bring the cops. Cops would arrest him and take his stash. He choked, and more vomit surged out of him. A pill floated amid the puke on the carpet.

Chris moved in slow motion. He pushed himself off the bed. The housekeeper held him by his forearm, but he swatted her away. His feet were like lead, but he got them going. He grabbed his backpack and made for the door, slumped over, then grasped the handle and tumbled into the hallway. From the carpet, he spied the Exit sign. He found his feet and pushed through that door into a stairway, the housekeeper yelling at his back. He stumbled down two sets of stairs and pushed through the emergency exit. The rest was a blur of car and street sounds.

Chris tripped and cut his hands and knees on the cement. He pushed past people. Concerned, distorted faces entered and cut out of his field of vision. He kept to the sidewalk, but when he saw some grass, he abandoned the street and moved into a small park. His eyes locked onto a bench, and he collapsed on the warm wooden planks. He closed his eyes and tried to catch his breath while tears glided down his nose.

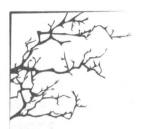

Chapter 2

M ax unbuckled his seat belt and adjusted the .44 Magnum revolver in the leather holster across his chest. He stepped out of the truck and joined Julia, who sat on the open tailgate. She punched her thumbs on the rubberized buttons of the portable GPS unit.

He breathed in the cool air. *Man, it feels good to be away from Anchorage.* He glanced at Julia. "Setting our location?"

Julia met his gaze. "All set." A spear of morning light cut through the dense draping needles of hemlocks and thick Sitka spruces and illuminated the outline of her round cheeks and curved jaw. Small bags clung below her warm clay-brown eyes.

She looks so damn cute when she's tired. "Good," Max said. "You left our route and plan with Aida and Frank, right?"

"I emailed Frank. Aida's in California, visiting her brother, remember?"

"That's right." He'd almost forgotten about Aida's brother. From what Aida had told him at work, it sounded like her brother needed a swift kick to the butt to get his life together. *She'll never give up on him, though.* Aida was by far his favorite scrub nurse in the unit. He could depend on her, which made his job as an orthopedic surgeon that much easier.

"Aida says they'll try to make the next camping trip." Julia toyed with her dirty-blond French braid, which snaked through the back of her maroon trucker hat.

"It's been a while since we could get them out for a hike, huh?" Max said.

Julia's dangling hiking boots swung like swings at a playground. "When we have kids, it'll be pretty hard too. Not everyone can spend two nights in the mountains."

"All the more reason we should get out there now, right?"

Julia had always wanted three children, while Max only needed one. Over the years, they'd met in the middle with the compromise of two. The fact that she was thirty-one and he was pushing thirty-six meant they were destined to be the old parents at school. He didn't mind, though. Kids kept people young, or so he hoped. When she had brought up stopping birth control three months back, he'd told her he was ready if she was. Spontaneous multiday treks through the mountains like this would be hard to come by once they had a couple of kids.

"Right." Julia put her feet back on the ground and leaned in to brush his clean-shaven cheek with her lips. She hefted her purple pack off the ground, clicked the plastic clips to their mates, and tightened the webbing. "You have the satellite phone, right?"

"Yup. All charged and good to go." Max slung his backpack over his broad shoulders and cinched the straps so that the firm weight settled on his hips. The pack had a heavy metal external frame and thick canvas material—no new features like Julia's. It had belonged to his dad, another avid outdoorsman driven to life in Alaska by curiosity and itchy feet.

He slammed the truck tailgate closed, and the bent lip of the burnt-yellow license plate caught his eye. Alaska's nickname, The Last Frontier, was printed in blue lettering. The expression, meant to instill pride in the ownership of vast untraveled stretches of wilderness, still rang true, but the backcountry they were entering was not as remote as some parts of the state. He and Julia had driven a couple of hours south of Anchorage and their home in Eagle River to get to the Chugach National Forest on the Kenai Peninsula, a common destination for hikers.

"Let's get out of here." Max deserted the truck at the dead-end dirt road, and Julia followed him along a narrow goat trail that weaved through a wet undergrowth of ferns. He stepped around an encroaching plant whose broad leaves were held flat like begging hands, masking the spiny stems underneath that gave it the name devil's club. Tendrils of cool air wafted up from the soft topsoil and lingered beneath the dense canopy draped in wisps of old-man's beard. An unseen thrush piped the forest's favorite high-pitched song, offering a curious mystery to the woods. The scent of mud and decay mixed with spores from moss-covered trunks. Underfoot, scattered militias of burnt-orange and cream-colored agaric toadstools were poised like miniature patio umbrellas. The forest groaned as roots stretched after a night's sleep. Mist burned under the early sun in the passing glades.

Max and Julia's hiking boots scuffed rocks and sloshed through mud puddles. Every few minutes, he had to negotiate fallen trees. Some had blown down recently and were still intact, while others crumbled at his touch. Overhead, a nervous red squirrel chattered and beat his tail. The squirrel had every right to be scared since everything out there wanted to make a meal out of him.

Max's face plowed through invisible spiderwebs. He sighed and wiped his eyes. Julia laughed and offered to lead. He followed, appreciating the curve of her butt as she balanced on the balls of her feet and hopped from rock to rock and around slicks. *Whoever invented yoga pants must have had men in mind.* She had love handles and wide hips that Max had spent many nights tracing with his fingers.

Julia had told him early into their relationship about how she'd always hated her body. He'd watched her work out to the point of exhaustion, always complaining that her butt was too big or that her chest was too small. He would console her, but she refused to see how beautiful she was, and he couldn't stop her tears. There was always something wrong with her mind, and he struggled to understand how he could help. He could remember the shameful thoughts. *Do I really want to have kids with someone this chemically imbalanced? Would she try to hurt herself?*

Therapy had saved their relationship. They'd gone as a couple, two years back, and he'd witnessed Julia cutting through her frustration as she unraveled her self-confidence and body-image issues. He stuck it out and traded shame for admiration. That veneration had grown to a deeper love than any he'd ever known. She was his. He was hers, always and forever.

A little after midday, the trail led them to a clearing beside a shallow lake. Several rings broke the surface of the water, and a heap of sticks, no doubt a beaver lodge, bristled at the opposite shoreline.

Julia dropped her pack on the grass, extricated her GPS from a canvas pocket, and stared at the screen. "We've gone six miles so far." The rattling chirps of a kingfisher cut the air, and the small bird flitted over the lake and landed in a tree at the bank. She pointed at the crest that rose high above them. "That the ridge you showed me on the map?"

Max eased his pack to the grass, retrieved the binoculars, and glassed what the map had labeled Moose Ridge. Once they passed the tree line, the exposed ridge would offer a narrow corridor with steep rockslides and gullies on either side. Patches of stubborn snow littered the ridge and the mountains beyond like paint stains. He'd examined the topographical map and figured that they could use the ridge to cross over the wall of mountains, then they could drop down the far side and be free to camp and explore the valley below. He'd hiked in the Chugach National Forest before but had never gone much farther on this backcountry trail. "Yeah, I'm guessing there's one hell of a view up there. Always wanted to see what's on the other side of those mountains."

"Let's take a break here. We've got time." Julia stuffed the GPS back in her pack.

"Sure. You still okay with camping at the tree line tonight?" Max pointed toward the ridge. She was in reasonable shape, but he didn't want to push her.

"Sounds good to me." She closed her eyes and spread her arms wide to capture sunrays. "Can you believe this is really the first week of May?"

He could believe it. The winter had been warm with little snow-fall. Typically, they would have been trudging through crusty snow-drifts this time of year, and these mountain lakes would still be capped with ice. Even the Iditarod sleds had to cross stretches of dirt, due to the lack of snowpack.

Julia leaned close and dragged a finger along his forehead and down his bushy sideburns, collecting a smear of perspiration.

"Hey!"

"What?" She offered a coy grin.

"You're a weirdo, you know that?"

"Just sweat," Julia said in a matter-of-fact tone.

"Yeah, *my* sweat."

"My sweat, your sweat—makes no difference, hon." She licked her finger.

He offered a toothy grin, brushed aside Julia's hat brim, clasped her head, and brought her face close to his. He wiped his forehead and cheeks across her lips. "You want more, huh?"

She giggled and pushed against his chest. He let his big nose mingle with her petite one and stole a warm, salty kiss. He stayed close, and they shared the same hot air between their lips.

Julia broke away and faced the water. "Care to go for a dip while we're here?"

Max ambled over to the pond's edge. Using a stick, he plunged the severed end into the muddy bottom. When he extracted the branch, the water swarmed with tiny wriggling dark bodies. "Don't want to swim here. Leeches. Loads of 'em." Max eyed the stick. Several of the centimeter-long writhing bloodsuckers were glued to the bark. "Let's catch some dinner."

He removed the collapsible fishing pole from his pack and attached the reel. He'd packed limited tackle, but experience had taught him that fish living in remote ponds usually didn't see a lot of lures. *And how could they resist a gold spoon with a red hackle tail?* His cast tossed the spinning lure into a pack of dimpled rings. In the clear water, shadowed fish appeared as they swung their heads and chased the shining metal. After a few bumps, he got a taker. He set the hook and hauled in the fish. The arctic grayling was about average size—fourteen inches long—and covered in prehistoric gray scales that rippled with green and blue hues. Max spread the large dorsal fin as though unfolding an ancient Chinese sail. The grayling, its mouth no wider than a drinking straw, gasped for air.

Max ripped the fish's gills, which produced a subtle *pop*. The tiny heart pumped a line of blood down the grayling's scaly body. He caught several more that were smaller but threw them back until he landed one that pushed sixteen inches. Although the limit was five grayling per day, he only kept the two fattest fish for dinner as they'd brought plenty of other food.

Julia joined him by the bank to gut and clean one grayling while he dragged his fingernail along the bloodline and flicked bits of leftover entrails out of the other. He caught her scanning the forest and pond, keeping her eyes peeled for bears the way he'd taught her years before. She'd grown up in Mobile, Alabama, and had come to Alaska on a whim with two friends. He met her on a hiking trail and slowed his pace so he could talk to her more. They stayed in touch after she flew back to Alabama. Eventually, he'd convinced her to come back, and that visit had ended up being a one-way trip.

When they finished cleaning their dinner, Max dropped both fish in a sealable bag and then into a plastic grocery bag before he stuffed it in his pack. After munching a few handfuls of granola and some dried mango, they resumed their trek, with Max in the lead, and made for the ridge. The trail ended, which forced them to bushwhack through dense alders and snowmelt streams. A rabbit burst through the grass and made for a grove of skinny spruces. The blurred gray feline body of a lynx trailed just feet behind. The long-legged cat bore down on the wide-eyed hare, and they were gone within the time it took to gasp. Max rubbed Julia's shoulder. He smiled at her gaping mouth and continued to push their expedition farther up the ridge. The steep grade continued, and the trees gradually thinned out.

Halfway up the ridge, among a copse of weathered trees, he dropped his pack and massaged his sides. He claimed the area as camp and set up their two-person tent while Julia lit the small portable propane stove. She opened a can of chicken noodle soup and monitored the bubbling broth. Max got a small fire going and laid a simple grill on top of two flat rocks. He cooked the white fillets over the licking flames.

After dinner, Max hung the food sack in a tree away from camp. He found his flask of honey whiskey and took a pull before handing it to Julia. Using Julia's pack as a backrest, they huddled close to the crackling fire.

She rested her head on his collarbone—her spot. A short while later, her giggling laughter echoed down and across the quiet valley below. "Want to know what Jacob Edison did this week?"

Julia always had a story about Jacob Edison, the problem child in her kindergarten class. Every year there was a new Jacob Edison causing trouble or flashing a temper.

"Let's hear it."

She hiccuped and smiled. "Little shit thought it would be funny to drop his pants and run around the classroom. Uh-huh. Little peckerwood dangling for all the kids to see."

Max grinned. "What'd you do?"

"Oh, I didn't even have to chase him this time. He tripped over his pants and fell face-first on poor Jenny Horton. She screamed—that girl can shatter glass—and she punched him, clocked him real good on the lip." Julia spoke through laughter. "So... so poor Jenny's still screaming... and Jacob, well, his face flushes, and he starts crying over his fat lip... meanwhile, his pants are still around his ankles..."

Max's laugh carried into the valley. He kissed her cheek.

Julia focused on the licking flames. "I swear, I stop sometimes, and the whole scene freezes. These are the moments when I think, 'Why me? Why didn't I get a desk job?'"

"You'd hate a desk job," he said.

"Well, I don't love chasing little streakers."

Looking down, Max cocked his eyebrow at her. "Yeah, you do."

"Yeah, I do." She beamed up at him.

"And I love hearing your stories." He massaged her neck. "You still want to have one of those little people? Even after all you see?"

"Sure do. Two of them, please." She hiccuped again.

"Two, it is." Max chuckled. "You still have the tolerance of a high schooler, you know." He laced his fingers through hers. The heat of the coals and the liquor warmed his cheeks. He whispered, "I love you."

"Good whiskey." She smacked her lips and screwed the cap back on the flask. "I love you, too, my big brave mountain man." She leaned in and kissed him hard then pecked him on the tip of his nose. She craned her neck to the dimming sky and sang "Sweet Home Alabama." In the middle of the song, she stopped to say, "Sing it with me, hon."

Max grinned. Julia was liable to break into song at any moment of the day. "You sing fine for the two of us. Go on, now. Put the bears to sleep."

Julia sang a few choruses, and when she finished, she nuzzled close to him. Max got to his feet and lifted her as if she were a piece of firewood. She giggled all the way into the tent.

THE NEXT DAY, MAX WOKE to the whipping sound of nylon. Outside, the clouds looked like whitewater from a crashing wave. Dark-gray clouds crowded the southern horizon. *Weather's moving in.* Rain and more wind were probably coming their way. That wasn't a problem in their current spot, where they had cover, but they'd have to clear the exposed ridge if they wanted to explore the next valley. The cooler temperatures on the ridge would make the wind and rain worse.

"We should get rolling, Jules, before we get socked in."

They slipped on some warmer layers and hastily packed away camp. Max led the way as they humped up the steep ridge. When they cleared tree line, he steered them around some stubborn snow. The grass ramps changed to loose gray rock, and they had to scramble up the tougher grade. An hour later, they had closed in on the crest. The wind had opened up like the choke on a motorcycle and filled his ears. A chill slithered along his spine from the sweat under his fleece. Max kept his eyes down and guided his boots among the clusters of crumbling gray rocks strewn about the top of the narrow ridge. Julia released a short yelp behind him. She sucked in a long breath through her clenched teeth.

"You okay? What's wrong?" he hollered over the wind.

She hopped to a boulder, favoring her left leg, and sat down. "Rolled my ankle. Might be sprained. Aw, damn it!" She started unlacing her boot. "Sorry."

He kneeled down with her. "Don't be sorry." Max eyed the dark-gray clouds that had slid over them. The first drops of rain hit the tops of his hands. He rifled through his pack and produced the small medical kit.

Julia had already taken off her boot and sock and slowly tested her range of motion, which was limited. Max let his fingers pad her inflated ankle. He could feel her warm blood rush underneath the swollen skin.

"I'm sorry," Julia said.

"No more of that," Max said in a stern voice. He leafed through materials in the medical kit: stacks of Band-Aids, sterile gauze in rolls and pads, bandages, medical tape, tweezers, scissors, a container of saline, alcohol wipes, ointments, a penlight, and a few over-the-counter medications. He was a surgeon, and there was plenty more he would have loved to pack in there, but like many hikers, he took pride in minimizing weight.

Max handed Julia some ibuprofen, which she swallowed, and with a practiced hand, he wrapped her bare foot and ankle with a tan bandage and added a layer of tape. "There."

She winced as she slid her sock over the wrapped foot. Julia loosened her boot, tied the laces tight, and stood. She put weight on her leg and grimaced. "Good enough to walk on."

She's tough, but she has a trip-ending sprain. "Let's head back down to where we camped. Your ankle is going to stiffen up and swell. I don't want you hurting it worse."

Julia shook her head. Her ears were scarlet, and since she wasn't wearing her hat, loose strands of hair whipped about her face. "I'm fine. I don't want to end the hike early." Her brown eyes focused on his.

She appeared determined to fight through the pain and push on, but there was no sense in it. The weather had arrived, and crossing the ridge wasn't going to get any easier on a papier-mâché ankle. He loved her for trying, but sometimes he wished she could be less stubborn.

The wind brought heavy rain, which actually helped his cause. "Time for rain jackets." Max stabbed his arms through his black jacket. "No choice now—we're heading back down. Too exposed up here." He cast his gaze across the ridge, which looked like the back of a stegosaurus, then down into the next green valley with another lake. The mountain peaks beyond jutted into the sky, hiding waterfalls and streams that flowed into bogs and valleys littered with secrets. *Save them for another day.*

Julia had slipped on her white rain shell. Under the hood, her eyebrows were knitted and her bottom lip tucked in. He hated to see her dip back into her defeated self. "We'll be back, Jules."

She spun around and started limping back down the ridge the way they'd come.

From his knees, Max hastily stowed the medical kit and cinched his pack. "Here, wait. Lean on me, hon."

She waved him off and kept going. "I'm fine. I'll take it slow." Her boot slipped on a wet rock, and her ankle buckled. She stumbled forward and tried to right herself, but the weight of her pack and her momentum brought her over the side of the ledge. She screamed and tumbled over the cliff headfirst.

"Jules!" Max hurried to the cliff edge and saw her still falling. He put a hand to his forehead and helplessly watched as her body hammered into one rock outcrop and another, flailing like a rag doll. She plunged farther down the steep face. Her backpack broke away as she slammed against jagged rocks and tumbled hundreds of feet below. She hit a boulder, then her limp body came to rest on a ledge. She was lying on her back but not moving.

His heart became heavy. "Jules! I'm coming. Jules!" The drop was too sheer for him to descend from where he was standing. His only chance at getting to her was to move farther down the ridge and traverse the scree field. He retrieved the medical kit and satellite phone. As the phone powered on, he took one last glance over the edge to where Julia lay. "Jules!"

Her jacket had been shredded, and her clothes were dirty. Her hair blew around with the wind, but the rest of her remained still. His shaking fingers dialed 911. He grasped the medical kit and removed his backpack, leaving it behind. Adrenaline ran through him like a loose sled dog. He raced back down the ridge as the wind howled and the rain stung his face.

When the dispatcher answered, Max told him what had happened to Julia and relayed their location. The dispatcher knew the ridge and told Max he'd reach out to get a helicopter crew but that it would take some time. The dispatcher promised to call back with an update. Max ended the call, stuffed the phone in his jacket pocket, and zipped it closed.

Max spied a viable route down the steep rocky slope to where Julia lay. He held the medical kit by his teeth. With his hands and his feet, he scrambled down the rocky outcrops of loose scree. The descent was treacherous, a route he'd never try in normal conditions. He caught sight of Julia's white jacket hundreds of feet down and off to the right. She hadn't moved at all. *She's just unconscious.* Max wished it to be true, but a fall like that meant severe trauma.

He shuffled down a gully, slicing his palms as he grasped sharp rocks. Gravel and loose stones clapped and skittered down the chute. He had to slide on his butt to descend the next stretch. The wind carried sheets of rain that lashed out against him. His hands quivered as he eased himself down over a wet boulder. The stones at his feet gave way, and he slid down the gully, clipping his elbow on a rock. He rolled onto his belly and dug his feet and hands into the ground to slow himself down. The gun strapped to his chest, under the rain jacket, pressed hard against his rib cage. Max grabbed hold of a jagged stone and came to a stop amid a hail of gravel. He winced and panted with the effort but kept moving. He cleared another outcropping. The slope became less intimidating, and he started traversing it toward Julia.

The phone rang in his pocket. Max maneuvered the medical kit out of his mouth and stuffed it under his armpit to take the call. The dispatcher confirmed the helicopter would be sent out but needed coordinates. Max scrolled through the satellite phone, found the GPS coordinates, and relayed them. He told him to hurry and ended the call. With Julia in sight less than one hundred yards away, he broke into a run across the clattering rocks of the scree field. *Please be okay, baby.*

His knees were banged up and his hands bleeding by the time he made it to Julia's ledge. He got down on his knees and dropped the medical kit by her side. "Jules. I'm here."

Her eyes were closed. Her pale cheeks and forehead were cut and oozing. Blood painted her nostrils and mouth and dripped from her ears—all bad signs. He probed her neck for a pulse and checked for breathing. *Nothing. Shit!*

He started CPR. His interlocked wet hands pushed against her tattered rain jacket. "Come on, baby, come on." As he gave her chest compressions, he eyed the sky. The rain and the wind were dying down. The rescue chopper was nowhere in sight. She didn't have much time. CPR was the best he could do. He had to keep moving that oxygenated blood through her body. With the fall, her injuries could be anything: fractured skull, spinal trauma, ruptured artery. The worst circumstances stuffed his head. But for the moment, the fact that she wasn't breathing and had no pulse remained the priority.

"Damn it. What the fuck? Why?" Tears welled up, and he brushed them away. *She's not going to make it.* The dreadful thought began to take over his mind. He continued to push down hard. Blood streaked from her scalp to her lips. "No, no, no. Please don't die. I'll do anything, please." Max shifted his position, used a jaw thrust, and blew in a breath through her lips. Her chest rose and fell as he filled her lungs with air. He gave her another breath and went back to compressions. He tasted her blood on his tongue. "Come on, baby. Come back to me. You want me to sing 'Sweet Home Alabama'?" He sang her favorite song as he kept up compressions.

Max continued CPR and lost track of how long he'd worked on her. He couldn't get a pulse, and he couldn't get her to breathe. His arms became heavy, but he kept pushing, kept moving her blood.

By the time the chopper broke through the clouds, it was too late. Max's arms were heavy, and he was barely able to compress downward anymore. He knew his efforts were useless. If it had been anyone else, he would have quit by then. But he couldn't. He needed her.

The chopper landed at the valley below, and two men and a woman started scrambling up the ridge, toting cumbersome packs. Max gave Julia two more breaths on cold, pale lips and went back to his pathetic compressions.

When the medics arrived, they each had ashen faces. They took over CPR, hooked Julia up to an AED, and gave her oxygen. They must have known that they were working on a corpse. Max stepped away and faced the ridge. He sobbed as numbness spread over his skin. A heavy weight dropped over his neck and shoulders.

He watched them vainly work on his dead wife. Max eyed the gun strapped to his chest. His fingers touched the rough grip. *One pull of the trigger, and I won't have to be here anymore.* He shuddered and bit down hard on the inside of his cheek. Max fixed his eyes on his pale china-doll wife. The medic looked away from the monitor and shook his head. He offered Max a grim face. Julia's body lay beside him, but she was gone.

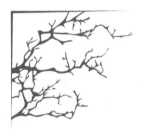

Chapter 3

M ax put his truck in park in the shadow of the hospital at 5:35 a.m. *Work. Work will help.* He glanced at the empty passenger seat. Julia had been sitting right there just two weeks before. He could still picture her beside him as if she were alive. She'd be grinning and messing with his radio dial. She'd set it to a country song and belt out the chorus while the wind coming through the open window tousled her hair. Even though Julia could barely keep a tune, he never complained. He didn't ever want to spoil what made her happy.

The truck, the carpeted halls of their house, their bed... a painful silence lingered in each place she'd once been. He wondered how the students in Julia's kindergarten class were taking the news. Her coworker had brought him a box with her things, but he'd never thought to ask her what she and the other teachers would tell the kids. He guessed they would explain it to them gingerly. The troopers who'd investigated Julia's death had deemed the incident an accident and returned his father's backpack with their condolences. The funeral and cremation were held amid a flurry of gray faces and awkward polyester hugs. When the weekend was over, his and Julia's families each flew back to their respective parts of the country.

He spent his days filling out pieces of paper—paying funeral bills, cancelling credit cards, and faxing death certificates. With every phone call, he gradually erased Julia from data banks and records. He did these tasks with numb efficiency. It gave him something to do, which was supposed to ward off the dread and emptiness. As the papers and phone calls started to dwindle, a growing panic echoed from some deep crevice within his rib cage. *What happens when I'm done?* The clock in the kitchen began to slow down.

Work was his solution. It would be his savior. He hadn't worked in two weeks. If there was a standard amount of time to be away from his job, he'd figured it would be two weeks. He found a case, a distal radius fracture—something he'd dealt with plenty of times. The patient was sixteen years old, healthy, and had injured her arm playing racquetball. The hospital had offered him more time off, but he let them know he needed to get back to work, back to living. They agreed, with the stipulation that instead of performing his usual duties as the primary orthopedic surgeon, he'd be the secondary, the assistant to Karim, a young doctor with far less OR time under his belt than Max had. Although playing second fiddle wasn't Max's preference, he was glad to be back at work.

Clutching his small duffel bag, Max stepped out of the truck and walked into the staff entrance. Inside the hospital were more forms than could ever be filled out, trainings, conversations with staff and patients, and a gulf of tasks that would require his attention. *Bliss.* On the way to the locker room, Max caught sight of Aida seated in the lounge, staring at her phone. She wore reading glasses on a beaded neck chain, one of those vintage-looking accoutrements you'd see on a grandmother cutting out newspaper articles, not a twenty-nine-year-old nurse like her. Her auburn hair was tied back in a ponytail that sat on her shoulder like a limp piece of frayed rope.

Her blue eyes shifted to him, and a grin appeared on her face. "Hey, Max, I was waiting for you." Aida shuffled over in her eggplant-purple clogs and met him with a warm hug. She squeezed him tightly. Her skin smelled like clovers. He hugged her back but struggled to put his heart into it.

Aida and Frank had visited him at his home in Eagle River twice since Julia's funeral. Both times, Aida brought him a huge dish of food and a healthy dose of her unfailing optimism. He'd managed to keep the visits short by fabricating white lies about places he needed to go or phone calls he needed to make. The more he used the word *fine*, the easier it became to usher Aida and Frank away.

"Distal radius fracture. You picked a good case to get back in the rhythm. Young and healthy patient—not much more you can ask for." Aida's enthusiasm remained undeterred.

An urgent high-pitched beep sounded, and Max nearly jumped out of his skin. "Jesus!" he whispered.

Aida fondled her pager and quieted it. She eyed the small screen for a minute. "Nothing important." She searched his face. "What? Just my pager... you okay? You ready for this?"

"I'm fine. After a couple weeks away from this place, I think I started to get used to the quiet."

"This is good, though. Your friends are here. And it's healthy to get back to work, back to our little chaotic bubble."

"You're right." Max managed a weak smile.

Aida rested her hand on her side. "My brother, Chris—you remember how I told you about him? He's moving in with us in a week. You'll have to come over and have dinner. I'd love to introduce you two."

Max put his hands on his hips. "Yeah, sure, sure."

"Well, almost time to get the room ready. It's so good to have you back, Max." She rubbed his shoulder and scurried off toward the OR.

Max headed to the locker room, where he found Karim slipping covers over his sharp leather shoes. From casual banter with Karim, Max had learned that his family had come over from Pakistan and it had been his father's dream to settle in Alaska. Karim was fit and lean and spent the bulk of his free time working out and trail running. Max had heard more than one nurse describe Karim as "hot shit."

His dark features lit up as he smiled with perfect teeth and shook Max's hand with a firm grip. "Max, we missed you around here."

"Good to be back."

Karim kept eye contact. "Hey, I know I'm technically primary on this one, but if you want to do the heavy lifting in the OR, I'm fine with it. I know I'd want to be running the show if I were you—helps you really get back into the swing of things."

"Appreciate it." Max scratched his jaw. Aida had her hugs, but this offer was probably Karim's way of making Max feel better. A good surgeon wanted to be the quarterback, and both Karim and he understood that. "Yeah, I mean, if you don't mind..."

Karim snapped his fingers. "It's settled. I'll be standby in the OR, but the surgery's in your capable hands, my friend."

"That's really kind of you."

"Don't mention it."

Twenty minutes later in the operating room, Max breathed air through his surgical mask. The five-person team surrounding the patient wore gloves, masks, coral gowns, shoe covers, and hairnets. Max gazed through his plastic eye protection at the familiar form of Aida beside him. She'd performed her scrub-nurse responsibilities by the book, setting up the tables with instruments, tools, plates, and hardware. She'd gowned and gloved Max and Karim, draped the patient, and now stood ready to hand Max any tool he asked for. Karim stood across from Max. Dr. Chung, the anesthesiologist and eldest member of the team, had already done his job and had put the sixteen-year-old patient to sleep. He remained by her head, monitoring her vitals.

The circulating nurse, Anastasia, was staring at her computer at her station close by. Anastasia was in her late twenties, and although she wore a hairnet, glasses, mask, and scrubs, Max could picture her cascading dirty-blond hair and goldfish lips complemented by her tall, narrow frame. In the past, Max had witnessed Anastasia and Karim exchanging looks that generated enough electricity to run Anchorage for at least a week.

Max eyed the trays of stainless-steel tools that gathered swaths of light. Every tool, screen, and machine had its place, and every movement served a purpose. The operating-room team and the inherent routine put him at ease.

Anastasia pressed play on the iPod. The first few notes of "Sweet Home Alabama" filled the operating room.

"No!" Max hammered Anastasia with a glare. He didn't want to hear that damn song again as long as he lived.

Everyone halted what they were doing, and Max could feel their eyes on him. Based on Anastasia's confused expression, he realized that he must have overreacted. He calmed his voice. "No music today."

Anastasia cut the music. "You always—"

"Not today."

Aida said loudly, "Moving on..."

Karim's dark eyes met Max's. In a muffled voice, Karim said, "We all good, brother?"

Max could feel warm blood flush his cheeks. He fought the initial instinct to tell Karim to shove off. He hadn't meant to snap at Anastasia. This was where he belonged. He loved his job, and it gave him purpose. "All good."

Max eyed the girl's limp arm on the table in front of him. The patient had written "YES" with permanent marker on the injured limb, and Karim had initialed below to be sure they'd be working on the correct arm. The patient's pale arm was already painted with antiseptic. Max asked for a skin marker, and Aida handed it to him. He drew a lateral line to help guide his incision.

After handing off the marker, Max said, "A number-fifteen blade, please." He swallowed and eyed his fluttering chest. *Why am I breathing so fast?* Closing his eyes, he sucked in a long inhalation and released a slow exhalation, a trick he'd learned from his mentor during residency. He opened his eyes and received the offered scalpel.

His incision was true, if a touch slow. Max became aware of the perspiration bleeding out of the pores in his forehead. He switched to scissors to help dissect more layers of tissue. Karim retracted the tendon and spread the pink-and-red muscle wide. Aida handed Max a cautery pen when he requested it. He dabbed the cauterizer's electric tip on some small bleeds to quickly coagulate the blood. He switched the cautery tool to cutting mode to slice through damaged tissue. Tendrils of smoke stemmed from the glowing tip, and Max caught the stench of burning flesh. Julia's bloody face flashed in front of him. She screamed as she tumbled over the cliff. *No! Not now.* He turned the cautery tool off and blinked a few times.

He thought to ask for assistance with the sweat building on his face but didn't want to appear weak in front of the team. *Come on. Keep your head together. No more of that.*

Aida cleared her throat.

Max drew air through his nose. This wasn't like him. For an instant, he considered asking Karim to take over. *No, I can do this.* These surgeries were routine, and the team and the hospital staff needed to see him as a leader again. He had to prove he could still do his job. *I need to do this. I'm good. Just some jitters.*

He eyed the screen. The patient's vitals were holding steady. Max slowly put the tip of the cautery tool back to work. As he started burning through more flesh, he envisioned Julia kicking and screaming as the cremation fires consumed her. The patient's hand he was standing over became Julia's. He could almost feel the fire's heat under his scrubs. Max backed away from the patient and dropped the cautery tool. The tool, anchored from the drape, swung from its cord inches from the floor like a criminal at the end of a noose.

Aida's muffled voice said, "Max?"

Karim said, "What the hell?"

Max reeled back. He was breathless, and the air refused to come, as if his throat had been replaced with a stirring straw and his lungs had shriveled to the size of raisins. "Can't breathe."

"I'm taking over," Karim said and took Max's place.

Max stripped off the mask and glasses. He was wheezing.

Aida said, "Go to PACU, Max. Anastasia, call the charge to meet him there."

Max pushed through into the corridor of the sterile core and scrambled down to the next door that led to the track and PACU. "I... can't breathe! Oxygen... I need oxygen."

The charge nurse, Kathy, was waiting on the track. She hurried Max into PACU and ushered him to a cubby. He gasped as he ripped off his restricting surgical gown and gloves and stuffed them into a bin. Kathy connected an oxygen mask to the hookup on the wall and handed it to him.

Max sat on the bed and breathed through the plastic mask greedily. After a couple of breaths, he said, "You can leave. I'm fine." Sadness panged his heart, and he didn't want her to see him break down. He was acting more like a frightened med student than a seasoned surgeon.

Kathy stood with feet spread apart and her arms akimbo. She was a short, solid woman in her fifties. She'd spent time in the army and didn't scare easily. She glared at him with narrowed eyes. "You're most definitely not fine. What happened?" Her tone was harsh.

"Go make sure my patient's okay. Please, I'm good now. Go check on her for me."

"She'll be fine. We have a good team." Kathy stepped closer and pointed at him. "You should have taken more time off. It's too soon."

"Kathy, you're a friend, but right now, you need to get the hell out of my face!"

A handful of staffers in the PACU stopped to stare, but since it was early, there were no patients to hear him.

Kathy's eyebrows jumped, and her small mouth went agape. She recovered and said, "I'll be close by—keeping my eye on you." She drew the curtain halfway around the cubby and moved to a small desk farther down the row. Several of the staff from the unit came over and started talking to her at once. They flashed curious looks at Max.

He turned away from the gaggle of concerned coworkers and peered out the window. "Damn it." The window in the room framed an overcast day. The buildings in Anchorage seemed gray and cold. He let the oxygen soak through him. *I've got to get out of here.*

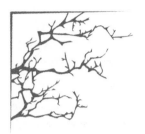

Chapter 4

Aida traveled down the Sterling Highway, a couple of hours south on the Kenai Peninsula. Alone with her thoughts and surrounded by mountains and endless spruce trees, she drove her minivan along the road in silence. Nearly a week had passed since Max's panic attack at the hospital. She and the team had acted fast, and the rest of the surgery had gone smoothly. *Thank God.*

Once the surgery was through, Aida had searched for Max. In his office, she found his hospital badge and pager on his desk and learned from some of the staff that he'd resigned. When she called him, he didn't answer, and when she went to his house in Eagle River the next day, he wasn't there. Taped to the mailbox was a note asking the postal service to forward mail to a PO box address in Sterling, Alaska. This led her to suspect that he'd taken to camping on his remote property near Sterling. Since he wasn't taking calls, she'd taken it upon herself to drive down and seek him out. Max needed to have a friend check on him, whether he wanted the company or not.

She hadn't been down there since the previous summer. Max and Julia had invited her and Frank to camp out in tents on their land a bunch of times. They spent days fishing the river, and at night, they gathered around the fire to cook salmon fillets and roast marshmallows. *Those were good times.* With Julia gone, those days wouldn't likely come again.

Aida staved off tears with rapid blinks as she veered off the highway onto Moose Run Road, a gravel drive leading into dense trees. She maneuvered the van's tires around the many potholes. Frank had wanted to join her, but she'd convinced him to stay home with the baby. If Max *were* here, he probably wouldn't have wanted a crowd. At the hospital before the surgery, Aida had noticed that Max's normally smooth brown hair was frizzled and unkempt. Tired wrinkles branched from the seams of his blue eyes. Instead of the determined, energized focus, his irises carried a dull sheen. His skin seemed dry and pale, and he'd given up shaving. She'd thought to push him into taking more time off, but Max didn't have any family in the area. All he had was his work, and she wasn't about to stop him from doing what he loved.

Aida caught sight of a moose in a clearing off the road to her right. She slowed the car to admire the brute. A thick rack waved as he swung his head to regard the van. The bull chewed leaves in a bovine manner, but he abruptly stomped a hoof on the ground and glared at her, proving he was far from domesticated and docile.

"Okay, I get it. No need to get pissy." She continued driving down the road, which switched from gravel to dirt.

She navigated the washed-out dirt road, seeing no sign of civilization, aside from sporadic shacks and boarded-up cabins amid the woods. When Aida arrived at Max's property, she steered into the rough dirt drive and parked. She spotted Max's truck sitting at the bottom of the hill. There was a cap over the back, but the tailgate was down, allowing her to see into the bed, where a pillow and blanket rested on a narrow wooden frame.

Aida scanned the woods then looked at the highest point on the property, a small cleared hill with nothing more than a campfire. She caught a glimpse of movement and spotted Max shoveling dirt into a wheelbarrow.

She got out of the van and made her way toward Max. Besides some birds calling, the dense surrounding woods were eerily quiet. All she could hear was Max's metal shovel rhythmically stabbing and tossing dirt. As she approached, he seemed to be too preoccupied in his digging to notice her. He appeared to be carving out a long trench of what she could only assume would hold the foundation for something.

When Aida got within ten feet, she said, "Max?"

He planted the shovel into the loose soil. The wooden shaft had dark patches and handprints that looked like blood. The source seemed to be his hands. Max wiped his brow with a dirt-flecked arm and faced her. He blinked a few times then licked his cracked lips. His hollow, sunken blue eyes regarded her. "What are you doing here?"

"What am *I* doing here? What are *you* doing here?"

Max pointed down the length of the trench, hesitated, then said, "Julia always wanted a cabin right here on this bluff. I'm building it for her."

He sounded mystified. He'd let his beard continue to grow, and she found it odd to see him with so much facial hair. She'd always known him to prefer a clean-shaven face.

"Are you all right, Max? You seem... tired." She stepped toward him, her shoes leaving tracks in dark upturned dirt only a few feet from him.

"I'm fine."

Yeah, and I'm the pope. He seemed skinnier than the last time she'd seen him. His brown beard and messy hair were peppered with silver. "Why haven't you answered my calls?"

"I put the phone away. Need to focus... on this."

"Uh-huh." She'd wondered at first if he'd been screening her calls, but now she understood that he'd been giving his friends and family a big *fuck you*. "So this is your solution—to become a hermit? You need people, Max. You need someone to talk to."

"I don't need to talk to anybody. I know how to grieve."

"You're a doctor, Max. You help people. If you don't want to come back to the hospital, I get it, but why not do something else? I know you did Doctors Without Borders years ago. Why not try that again? Travel to some new country and help people for a little while. It might do you a load of good. When you're ready, you can come back to the hospital."

Max stared at the dirt.

Aida started again. "Julia wouldn't want—"

"Don't!" Max yelled. His voice hung over the cleared land and was lost in the quiet of the surrounding woods. "You don't get to tell me how to deal with this."

"We both know this"—she twirled her finger in a circle—"isn't healthy."

"This is how it is."

Max was trying his best to shut her out. She had to find another way in. "My brother, Chris, is supposed to be flying in tomorrow—I still haven't heard back from him, which bothers me. Turns out he's addicted to painkillers. I promised to help him through withdrawals—get him sober and back on his feet."

Max put his hands on his hips.

He isn't even pretending to care. "I was thinking that I could bring him down here to help you out," Aida said. "Hard labor would do him some good. He could use a bit of your wisdom."

Max had a lot to offer a guy like Chris. Although he was a surgeon by profession, he could have made a living at any trade. He could build or fix just about anything and was an avid hiker, fisherman, and hunter. If some of Max's skills rubbed off on Chris, her brother would be all the better for it.

"Aida..."

Max needed someone to look after him as much as Chris needed a role model. "Chris is a good guy. He just needs some guidance."

"I'm not much of a talker these days." Max went back to shoveling dirt.

"I can see that. Listen, let me bring him down in a week or two. If you're dead set on building a cabin, you'll need a second pair of hands anyway. You don't have to talk to him. In fact, maybe it'd be better if you let him do the talking."

Max glared at her. "Are you doing this to help your brother, or are you worried about me being out here by myself?"

"For Chris," Aida replied quickly. She had to step nimbly around Max's question. Even though Max and Chris were suffering from completely different issues, she was concerned for each of them.

Max locked eyes with Aida. "You can bring him down *for a day*. Don't expect me to be his therapist, though. He's going to have to earn my respect."

"Thank you." Aida scratched her hairline. "Then I've only got one other request for you. After that, I'll let you be."

Max's expression remained deadpan.

"Can you please keep your phone on? I want to be able to call you, and it won't be easy for me to get down here when Frank's away. I've got my brother coming and the baby." Aida didn't like using her brother or her baby as an excuse, but she was betting that tactic would draw sympathy from Max.

"All right." Max sighed. "I'll try to keep the damn phone on."

THE NEXT DAY, AIDA sat in the passenger seat of Frank's truck and gazed at the Ted Stevens Anchorage International Airport arrivals terminal. She listened as luggage wheels stuttered over the cracks in the concrete. Through the front windshield, she spied a man in a paint-stained *Alaska Grown* sweatshirt as he loaded a duffel bag into the trunk of a Chevy Blazer. Family and friends greeted each other with hugs, kisses, and backslaps. Automatic doors opened, and the rhythmic squeal of a power-steering belt whined over idling engines. A couple of backpackers held phones to their ears as they spun slow pirouettes in a waiting dance.

Aida had called Chris eight times on his cell phone since leaving California, but every attempt ended with a monotone voice saying that the number was no longer in service or disconnected. She had called his hotel room at least a dozen times, but he never picked up. The receptionist said Chris hadn't checked out and, so far, hadn't charged anything to the room. The woman only mentioned that a small cleaning fee had been added for a stain in the carpet. Aida emailed Chris but hadn't received a reply yet. Short of flying down there and driving around to search for him, she had no way of knowing whether he was alive or dead in a gutter.

The flight she'd booked for him had taken off on time and should have landed. The optimistic side of her believed he'd gotten on the plane, but her churning belly disagreed. Aida glanced over her shoulder to the car seat in middle of the back bench, where baby Shannon continued to rest peacefully. She had fought to stay awake, wiping her little face against Aida's thin fleece jacket, but eventually, she'd succumbed to sleep. The truck's dash said that the time was closing in on eleven o'clock, which was well past Aida's bedtime too.

Frank shifted in the driver's seat. "I know Chris is family, but I still don't like the idea of him being around the baby."

Aida chewed her lip and returned to staring at the airport doors. Even without looking at him, she could sense that Frank was facing her. *You don't want him being around you, let alone Shannon.*

"Think we're wasting our time here? You haven't heard anything from him, right?" Frank asked.

Up until that day, Aida had still expected to see an email from Chris saying he'd lost his cell phone or some other excuse. She would have preferred an email lie to this silent treatment. She'd seen plenty of patients turn to opioids over the years. They could be manipulative, but they weren't bad people, and Chris didn't have a malevolent nature. Admitting that he needed help had taken guts. He'd been right when he said that he needed to make the choice to come to Alaska and get clean. The impetus had to come from him, not her. She'd have better luck stopping the tide than forcing him to quit.

Frank frowned. "You listening to me, honey?" That morning, he'd trimmed his scrubby dark beard to a half inch—her favorite length on him—which had to be a conscious decision on his part. He was trying to appease her. *He's a good man.* She had to remind herself of what it would be like to see circumstances through Frank's eyes.

"I share your worries, hon, but Chris has a kind heart. I have to believe that."

Frank sighed, adjusted his hat brim, and rubbed the steering wheel with his thumb.

Aida released a breath. "What other choice do I have?"

"I still think you should convince him to go to rehab," Frank said.

The familiar argument was following the typical well-trodden route. "He seemed pretty against the idea of rehab when I brought it up. We can't force him, Frank. Besides, I can get Chris through withdrawals." She sniffed and wiped her eye. "I have to make this work. I can't lose my brother too." She pictured Chris strewn across a shredded mattress, his hand clutching an empty pill bottle while dead-fish eyes stared at the ceiling. "I'm all he's got."

"You're being a martyr, if you ask me." Frank rubbed her thigh. "You know you've got my support, but I don't have to like it, babe. As long as he abides by the rules, he can stay."

"I know." She straightened her wedding ring.

A few fresh arrivals stepped through the glass doors, but Chris wasn't among them. Frank probably figured Chris was taking Aida's help for granted. When it came to his family, Frank wasn't the type of man to offer a second chance to anyone who did him and Aida wrong. If Chris didn't show, Frank might bar him from ever coming into their home. When Aida had told Frank that Chris was homeless and addicted to painkillers, he hadn't been surprised. She'd had to work on Frank for days to get him to agree to let Chris come and stay. She could still hear him saying, "You really want a junkie hanging around our baby? What about when I'm not around?" The compromise had been to set up house rules. If they caught Chris breaking even one, he would be out of their home, forced to fend for himself.

"Might as well save a little gas." Frank shut the engine off. "Hey, you never told me if they hired a new surgeon to take over for Max."

"Not yet. Francesca's taking his cases, but she's no Max."

"Can he still come back when he... um, you know... uh, gets his head right?"

"I don't know," Aida said. "After our talk yesterday, I don't think Max is too interested in coming back."

Frank released a long sigh. "You didn't push him too hard, did you? I know how you can be..."

Aida reached over and lightly grasped Frank's earlobe. "How I can be, huh?" She used her best old-woman voice. "I'll take you to the principal's office if you keep that sort of talk up, Francis."

Frank grinned. "Cut it out. You'll wake the baby."

"You and Chris going to play nice while he's here?"

Frank tossed his hand up. "It's not like I hate the kid. You and him had a pretty rough upbringing—I get that. You fixed your situation while he made his worse. I mean, I'm not going to be best friends with him, but I'm not going to be cruel either." Frank cleared his throat. "One of us has to be the hard-ass, and if it's got to be me, then so be it."

Aida pecked his cheek. With all the men around her falling short, it was a relief to have the steadiness of Frank in her life. "I'm grateful for you. You know that?"

"Yeah." Frank checked his watch. "Shouldn't Chris be here by now?"

There were only a handful of travelers lingering outside at that point. Chris's flight had arrived on time twenty minutes earlier. "His flight landed." Her shoulders sank. *He's not coming.* His fear of withdrawal must have gotten the best of him. She'd been naïve to think he wasn't going to lie to her again.

"I'm thinking he's going to be a no-show, babe," Frank said.

Aida hooked her thumb toward the airport. "I can go inside and—"

A slender guy in a black T-shirt and tired jeans stepped through the airport sliding doors. *Chris!* Brown hair escaped the sides of his black fitted baseball cap. Dark stubble stuck to suntanned skin and high cheekbones. His blue eyes scanned the vehicles.

"That's him!"

Frank smacked his lips and shook his head. "I'll be damned."

Aida opened her door and hastily wiped her eyes. She waved. Chris caught her wave, hefted his backpack over his slight shoulder, and sauntered over.

Aida lassoed his rib cage with a hug and squeezed him tightly. "Welcome to Alaska!"

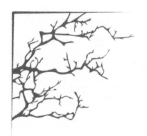

Chapter 5

At eleven o'clock at night on the first day of June, Chris was surprised to see the sun still out, easing downward toward the western horizon, even though he'd heard an old woman on the plane talking about "the midnight sun." *I hope my new room comes with good curtains.* As they drove away from the airport and made for downtown Anchorage, Aida clucked on about how good it was to see him, probed him about the flight, and talked about how new and wild Alaska had to seem. Aside from a handshake and a hello at the airport, Frank remained quiet and didn't take his eyes off the road.

"So what's up with your cell phone?" Aida said without turning around.

The sleeping baby boxed Chris in on his left. He massaged his temples. "Didn't really need a phone—gave it away." He kept his tone low to avoid waking Shannon.

"It would have been nice to have a way to get ahold of you." Aida broadcasted her frustration through her exaggerated tone.

Besides Aida, he really didn't have anyone to call. He'd gotten by just fine without a phone before. "I'm here, aren't I?"

Frank's blue eyes flashed in the rearview mirror, directed at Chris.

Chris examined his shoes.

Aida spun around and softened her voice and features. "Yes, you're here, and I'm proud of you. This is the first step to recovery."

"Thanks." In the end, he'd chosen to make good on his promise to Aida and gotten on the flight. If nearly dying alone in a hotel room wasn't enough to get him to quit, then he was in worse shape than he thought. Fear was as good a motivator as any for getting clean.

Aida surveyed the road out the front window. "You know... if you didn't want to stay at the hotel, you could have said so."

He'd spent the last three weeks sleeping in parks, too paranoid to go back to the hotel room after puking all over the housekeeper. She could have called 911, and the cops might have shown up. He wasn't about to catch a charge for possession of a controlled substance. The day after he'd puked on the housekeeper and fled the hotel, he was back to his pill-a-day habit. After he blew through the stash, he had to beg on the street again. Then he got another refill from Jake. The day before his flight, Chris had slept at the airport. Down to two pills, he'd chewed and swallowed one of them that morning. Out of cash, he'd stowed the one remaining pill in his backpack, in case things got desperate, and boarded the flight.

Chris gazed out the window. Anchorage, as a whole, turned out to be less than impressive—potato chip bags cartwheeling across the dirt-caked streets, homeless veterans holding cardboard signs at intersections, and stunted wannabe skyscrapers. The city would have been completely unremarkable, save for the fact that it happened to be plopped on the Alaskan coast.

"You guys live close to downtown?" he asked.

"We're just a few miles out," Aida said.

Ten minutes later, Frank drove into a mellow suburb outlined with hedges and fences and planted spruce trees. There was even a sign telling drivers to slow down while kids were at play. Chris followed Frank and Aida into their modest home filled with new appliances and family photos on the stainless-steel fridge.

Chris examined one photo, which had a couple of hikers with snowshoes in an outdoor winter scene. The guy held some holly and was kissing the cheek of an attractive woman who wore a mock-surprised expression on her face. "Have a Very Merry Christmas! From

Julia and Max Fitwell." It seemed odd to still have the picture up so long after Christmas.

Aida and Frank put Shannon to bed while Chris scoped out his new room. It was a decent size for a guest room, with tan walls and a flat screen mounted to the wall. He stepped over to the queen-sized bed and breathed in the scent of clovers. He dug his last pill out of his backpack and slid it under the pillow—in case he needed it that night. The dresser had all new clothes inside: a pair of jeans, T-shirts, a sweatshirt, socks, boxers... all of which made the couple of pieces of clothing in his backpack look like garbage. Aida had really put some thought into all this. She'd given him a pretty cozy room. If he planned to get clean, this would be the place and time.

When Chris glanced back at the open door, Frank was there, watching.

Chris's heart stalled. "Jeez, man, you scared the hell out of me."

"Can you come out for a minute? Aida and I want to talk to you. And bring your bag too."

"Yeah, sure." *What's he need my bag for?* Chris frowned. He scooped up his backpack and followed Frank into the living room.

"Take a seat, Chris." Aida gestured toward the gray couch, and she and Frank sank into the adjacent love seat. They'd put on stiff voices and demeanors. This was probably where they'd try to tell him how this living situation was going to work.

"Okay, let's get down to it," Frank began. "Aida and I are going to lay out some house rules for you and the general plan for your recovery."

Yup. Chris had to stop himself from rolling his eyes.

Frank pointed at his fingers, starting with his thumb. "The first one's obvious. No breaking the law and no drugs—wait till I finish. We see one thing that's drug related, and we're calling the police. As simple as that."

Chris scratched his nose and sniffed. "Fair enough." *Hopefully, the tooth fairy doesn't check under the pillow tonight.*

"That's number one. Number two is that we're going to be providing you with room and board here, which means you *will* help out when we ask. Whether that means doing the dishes or..." Frank glanced at the ceiling as though trying to figure what else would need Chris's help. "Yard work, taking out the trash, sweeping... we won't ask you to do anything other than normal upkeep stuff. That's number two."

This guy really thinks he's King Fucking Donkey Kong. "Yup." He didn't have a problem helping out around the house, but he didn't like how Frank was speaking to him, as if Chris were a grunt in the army.

Frank regarded him. "You asked for our help getting clean. Aida and I are willing to assist you through the withdrawals, but you need to be respectful toward us, and we have to know we can trust you." Frank sucked in his bottom lip and then the top one. "So Aida and I both agreed that, from time to time, while you're living here, you'll have to let us check you and your area for drugs. Starting now."

Chris crossed his thin arms. "You're talking about going through my stuff? Patting me down? I came here to get better, not to be a prisoner." Aida's house was becoming less a place of healing and more like some kind of jail.

Aida said, "This won't be an every-day thing, Chris, but if we suspect something, we'll check you and your stuff for drugs—as simple as that."

"It's nonnegotiable," Frank said.

Chris studied a coaster on the coffee table. He wanted to tell them to fuck off and just let him be. He'd expected this to be more relaxed. Aida and Frank had obviously drawn up a set of rules together, and he wondered how much of it had been Aida's idea and how much had been Frank's.

Aida's voice picked up a pleading tone. "If you really want to get clean and you don't have anything to hide... you shouldn't have a problem with this. We want to trust you, but you have to prove it to us."

This is one of those turning points. Flying away from California to break his habit had been one turning point—now he had to choose whether to follow Frank and Aida's rules or not. This probably wouldn't be the last sacrifice he'd have to make if he wanted to stay.

He sighed. "Fine."

Frank stood and motioned with his hand to the bag at Chris's feet. "Hand over your bag, please."

Chris passed the backpack to him. Frank unzipped it and got down on his knees on the carpet. He drew out the first pieces of clothes and spread them out on the tan rug.

Aida approached him. "I'll make this quick, Chris. Stand here."

He joined Aida in a clear patch of rug. Aida patted him down, starting with his T-shirt and working down his pants toward his socked feet.

He studied the crown molding. "This is so lame."

"It's no picnic for me either," Aida said. "There's stuff in your pockets. Please turn them out for me."

He rolled his eyes. "Yes, Officer." Chris handed over his wallet and lighter from his back pocket. The rest was just lint.

After Aida inspected the items, she handed them back to Chris. "Okay." She regarded Frank, who was now returning the clothes to the backpack. "We good?"

"We're good." Frank stuffed the last shirt inside and zipped up the bag. "Thank you, Chris."

Aida squeezed Chris's arm. "Yes, thank you. That helps us trust you."

"Whatever," Chris said, relieved that they hadn't decided to check his room. "So that's it for the rules?"

"Not quite." Frank handed the pack over to Chris. He and Aida sat back down.

Chris slumped into his own seat with a huff.

Frank pointed at his fourth finger. "You will be supervised by one of us if you leave the house. We'll—"

"Oh, come on." Chris glared at Aida. "Really?"

Aida straightened and said, "It's nonnegotiable."

She repeated Frank's words like some kind of parrot. It was bad enough that they'd be patting him down and rifling through his stuff. Now he had to have a chaperone as well. They were treating him like a kid.

Frank continued, "It shouldn't be for long. Just temporary. Once you're clean and get a job, you can go off on your own."

Knowing that it was temporary softened the blow. He wouldn't like not being able to do his own thing, but he'd probably be bedridden once he was in full-blown withdrawal. When he was clean, he'd be free. It was annoying to know they had him on a short leash, but if it didn't last long, he could deal.

"You should have started with that," Chris said.

"Yeah, well, we're not professionals at this, Chris. We're doing the best we can to help you. Aida's being a pretty nice sister, if you ask me." Frank rubbed Aida's leg.

Aida said, "That's it, Chris. No drugs or breaking the law, help us a little bit around the house, let us check your stuff if we need to, and until you're back on your feet, either Frank or I will be with you wherever you need to go. We're not going to be glued to your side, but we want to be close by."

Frank trained his eyes on Chris. "If you break any of those rules even once, that's it—you're out of the house and not welcome back. This isn't like California. Under this roof, it's one strike, and you're out."

"I got it."

The flannel shirt and short beard gave Frank the appearance of a lumberjack. If Aida was playing the good cop, Frank was definitely the bad cop. Chris rubbed his hands through the sides of his hair. He was too exhausted to think much about the rules. This was a nice place, and he didn't want to get kicked out. He'd have to stay at Aida's house to get clean. It still probably beat a rehab center. He shifted his back, which ached. His skin was hot even though the temperature in the room was cool.

"When's the last time you had any painkillers?" Aida asked.

He could be honest with her at that point. She could probably see he was irritated and suffering a bit already. "This morning before the flight."

"Well..." Aida checked her watch. "It's a new day. You're officially going cold turkey starting now. This is day one of your recovery."

He'd never gone cold turkey before. He'd definitely gotten to the edge of withdrawal in the past, but he always managed to scrape enough dollars together to pay for another pill. He flexed his jaw to try to loosen his gritted teeth.

Aida leaned closer. "Food's in the pantry and fridge. In the morning, we can hang out and talk about how you're feeling. I've got some junk food and movies. Distractions will help. I'm per diem at the hospital, so I'll be able to be around a lot."

Frank covered a yawn and blinked rapidly. "I'm three weeks on and three weeks off at my job, which means I won't be here as much as I'd like."

"Are you hungry?" Aida asked.

Chris yawned. "Not really. I ate on the flight." He peered toward the hall near his room. "You guys have a shower I can use? Think I'll get cleaned up and pass out."

"Of course," Aida said.

Frank nodded and mumbled, "It's late."

After he showered, Chris dressed in fresh boxers and a white T-shirt, which fit him well. Aida always paid attention to the details. He lay in bed, closed his eyes, and waded through his thoughts. *Frank thinks he's some kind of tough guy living up here in the redneck wonderland.* The only good news was that Frank would be gone for three weeks at a time.

Admittedly, this beat sleeping in parks or on benches. Free food and rent were a solid trade for some house rules. He had a shot at making a new start. The rules weren't ideal, but once he was clean, he'd be able to get a job and move out.

Chris regarded the closed door. The hallway light was off, and Frank and Aida had probably gone to sleep. He retrieved the last pill from under his pillow and examined the blue circle in the dim light. "This will be my last one." He opened his mouth and dropped the pill like a penny into a wishing well. He swallowed and rolled to his side. "That's it. I'm done now." He clung to the promise and closed his eyes. Eventually, sleep came for him, and Chris was carried into a dream like a blade of grass in a river's current.

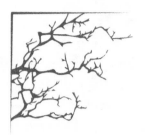

Chapter 6

Chris was momentarily disorientated when he woke up in a comfortable bed in a quiet room. The blackout shades kept the room dark, but some light was slipping in at the creases. The clock on the end table told him that it was 12:34 p.m. He couldn't remember the last time he'd been able to sleep in without a car horn or some pedestrians ripping him from his dreams. He basked in the solitude and peacefulness.

His hand wandered under his pillow, then he remembered how he'd taken his final pill the night before. *This is really it.* He sat up in bed and noticed some dull aches in his shoulders. He could feel the beat of a headache starting to move about his skull. *Sobriety starts now.* He could only wonder how hard his body would fight him.

Chris got dressed in new jeans and a white T-shirt. He made for the bathroom. He used the toilet then opened the mirror, curious to see if there happened to be any pill bottles hiding in the shelves behind. Nothing. Just toothpaste, floss, soap, and a toothbrush. *She's too smart to leave any pills out.*

He made for the kitchen. Frank was sitting at the table, feeding Shannon. Chris grinned when he saw Shannon's tiny hand grasping the bottle as she eagerly sucked away, drunk on milk.

Frank glanced up. "Afternoon, Chris. How'd you sleep?"

"Fine."

"Good to hear." Frank adjusted Shannon and nodded toward a storage closet. "Cereal and bagels in the pantry, and there's milk, eggs, and meat in the fridge. Feel free to eat whatever you'd like."

Chris avoided Frank's eyes. "Got it." He retrieved a gallon of milk and glanced at various boxes of cereal in the pantry. "Where's Aida?"

"She's in the front yard, working in her garden," Frank said. "A moose wandered into the neighborhood and wiped it out last year, but she's determined to get her vegetables up and running again. I head to the slope tomorrow. I tried to change my schedule, but it can't be helped."

"Gotta do what you gotta do."

"My family is the most important thing to me, Chris."

"Sure."

"Don't do anything to jeopardize that." Frank's voice had turned cold.

"You want to know why I don't like you, Frank?" Chris put his bowl of cereal aside and spoke slowly and with emphasis.

Shannon had finished the bottle, and Frank eyed Chris. "I don't really care if you like me or not."

Chris rolled his eyes. "It's because you always assume the worst of me. You've always looked at me like I'm a criminal. You think I'm some kind of bad guy. Sure, I've messed around with drugs, but you know what? We can't all be perfect like you, Frank."

"Keep your voice down." Frank wiped Shannon's lips with her bib.

He hadn't meant to raise his voice, but Frank's warning had gotten to him, and now Chris wanted to lay into the prick. "How about this? While I'm here, you and I don't talk." Chris licked his teeth and examined Frank's flat expression. "I appreciate you letting me stay here. I know I'm not the brother-in-law you wanted, but this is what you got."

Frank got to his feet, held the baby to his chest, and said, "If I didn't want you here, Chris, you wouldn't be here. Aida loves you, and I don't want to see her hurt. Aida and this baby"—he motioned to the wide-eyed Shannon—"are the most important things to me. I don't think you're a bad guy, but it's sad to see that you've let yourself become homeless and hooked on drugs. You can do so much more with your life."

Chris ground his teeth and wiped his sweaty palm on his jeans. "Give me some credit, man. I'm here to get clean."

"We'll see... won't we?" Frank pressed his lips together and sized up Chris. Frank never raised his voice, but he didn't seem to need to. He was probably an inch or two shorter than Chris, but he had muscle, whereas Chris was underweight.

"I'm going to eat outside," Chris said.

"Do as you like," Frank replied.

Chris brought his cereal to the back deck, where he sat at a metal table that offered a view of other backyards in the neighborhood. The best way of dealing with Frank would be to avoid him or keep their conversations short. Frank taking off for three weeks the next day was truly a gift.

"What an asshole," Chris muttered under his breath. He spooned some cereal into his mouth and scanned the green mountains in the distance. The peaceful suburb stood in stark contrast to the smog and the tide of people that washed in and out of Los Angeles every day.

Chris set aside his empty bowl and massaged his sore shoulders. Aching joints and clammy skin didn't do much to make him feel good about his decision to get clean. It would only get worse the longer he didn't have his painkillers. The sun above warmed him, and he wiped grease from his eyes and nose.

The sound of the sliding door startled him. He frowned until he recognized Aida.

She waved. "You're finally up."

"Yup." Chris reclined in the chair and tried to bite off a hangnail with his front teeth.

Aida stripped off two dirty gloves and gestured to the other chair. "Mind if I sit with you?"

"They're your chairs."

"How are you feeling?" Aida's voice and features were soft.

"Like crap." He was aware of how irritable he probably seemed. He wondered whether the anxiety was from his lingering argument with Frank or the start of withdrawal.

"That's your body fighting back."

"Guess so." Chris watched Aida as her eyes followed a Cessna plane across the sky. He breathed the cool air through his stuffy nose and patted his empty pocket. For the first time in years, he didn't have any pills to fall back on. His foot took to tapping, and he wiped sweat through his hair. *I'm really doing this.*

"You want to head out and see anything today?" Aida asked.

"I think it'll be best to lie low for a few days. This is going to be a rough week."

Aida patted his hand. "I'll be with you every step of the way."

"I don't think Frank and I are going to be talking much," Chris said.

"Maybe that's for the best," Aida said.

"Huh." Chris rubbed his sore neck. "That's weird. Usually you try to mend fences."

"I can't force you guys to like each other, and I'm sure as hell not picking sides in that battle."

Chris surveyed the distant mountains. "I do appreciate every-thing, you know."

Aida said, "I know you do, little brother."

"I think I can beat this."

"You *will* beat this." Aida brushed her hair aside. "And when you do, we'll see about getting you a job and an apartment. I visited my friend Max about a week ago—he's a couple hours south of here. I told him I'd take you down to the Kenai Peninsula for a day once you're feeling better. Max could use an extra hand. He's building a cabin."

Building a cabin was about the last thing Chris wanted to do at the moment.

Aida sighed and crossed her legs. "I dreamed about Mom and Dad last night. I don't remember much, but they were in it—Grandma too. Did you ever visit their graves when you were down there?"

The family gravestones rested beside each other in the cemetery back in Long Beach. "Last time I was at the cemetery was the same time as you—Grandma's funeral," Chris said.

He'd been to the cemetery in Long Beach to bury three family members. Dad had been first. Chris was twelve when the soldier came and broke the news that Dad had died, blown up when his Humvee hit a roadside bomb. As a civilian, Dad had been a simple accountant. As a soldier, he'd served as a staff sergeant in the Army National Guard during the Iraq War. After Dad died, Mom fell into an unshakable depression, which forced Aida, who was working on her nursing degree, to take over the role of mom on top of going to college. Grandma, who'd been living with them for years, did her best to help.

Not long after Dad's funeral, they buried Mom. After a month of falling, she finally hit earth. Mom had gotten hold of a kitchen knife, and when she was alone in her bedroom, she'd plunged the blade into her neck. Grandma had been the one to discover Mom's body. Aida and the police had spared Chris from seeing the scene when he came home from school.

Grandma remained with them for years after but gradually lost weight and the luster she used to carry in her eyes. Then one night, her organs got together and decided to shut down on her. Chris and Aida were able to say goodbye before she passed away in the hospital bed. That had been the third and final trip to the cemetery in Long Beach. Aida had taken care of everything, as always.

"Too bad they never got to meet their granddaughter." Aida cleared her throat. "Well, I think I'll go get cleaned up." She gathered her gardening gloves and Chris's cereal bowl and carried them inside with her.

Chris spent the rest of the day in his room, watching TV. Aida bought a pizza for dinner, but he could only nibble a slice at the kitchen table as his appetite had vanished. When it got late, he retreated back to his room and tried to sleep, but his muscles ached, and he sweated through his clothes. Shirtless, he tossed and turned in an effort to relieve his restless legs. His body couldn't decide whether it was too hot or too cold. He gave up trying to sleep and stared at the popcorn ceiling for hours. At one point, he crawled out of bed to search through his backpack in the hopes that he'd find a forgotten pill, or even some remnants, but there was nothing. He took a hot shower, which helped soothe his muscles and calmed his nerves a bit. After, he slipped back into bed, but his mind and body tugged at him to stay awake.

When morning broke, Chris still hadn't slept, and he was mentally and physically exhausted. Frank and Aida moved about the house, speaking in low tones. A short while later, Chris shuffled over to his window and spied Aida, with the baby, walking Frank out to his truck. They spoke some quiet words, then Frank kissed Aida and Shannon and drove off for what would be three weeks.

Good riddance. With Frank gone, Chris figured he could reason with Aida. She'd said he had to go cold turkey, but with the right pressure, she might change her mind. He just needed something to help him deal with the aches and let him sleep. She had to have some pills kicking around. If not, she could easily get him some low-dose painkillers. He'd settle down with some meds to help him with the withdrawal.

Outside, Aida seemed to notice Chris in the window. He spun away, but he was sure she'd seen him. He put on some clean shorts and a T-shirt and sprawled back out on the bed.

A few moments later, Aida rapped on his door. "You up?"

"Yeah," Chris said weakly.

She came in toting Shannon with one arm. "How'd you sleep?"

"I didn't sleep at all." He sighed and massaged his eyes.

"Part of withdrawals unfortunately," Aida said.

"Yeah. Listen, Aida, I need something to help me get through this."

"What are you talking about?" Her voice rose an octave.

"My body's aching. I can't sleep. I'm sweating through the sheets. I'm in pain here. If you let me get some pills—just a couple—to help me wean off..."

"No." Aida bit her lip and frowned. "We'll get through this. Cold turkey sucks, but I'm going to help you."

"What about some withdrawal meds? I'll even let you control the dosage. Come on, Aida, help me out here."

"We already had this conversation in LA. I told you I wouldn't do that. You have to get through this on your own." She pointed at him. "You can't manipulate me just because Frank's gone."

"I'm not. I just... I feel sick." He wiped his damp forehead and displayed his glistening finger to Aida. "This isn't healthy."

"It's withdrawal, Chris. You're dependent on those pills, but you'll break it. You're going to feel like crap, but you'll come out of this stronger."

"I don't see how that makes any sense."

"Listen to your nurse-sister." She set Shannon on his bed and grabbed his wrist and pressed her fingers to his pulse. "It's fast and high—the same with your breathing. You aren't the first patient I've helped through withdrawals."

Chris groaned. Part of him was lashing out because he was tired and irritable, but overnight, the pain had ratcheted up several levels as well. He was defenseless against his own body. He felt as if there were two candles burning in his skull, as if his head had transformed into a jack-o'-lantern. "I'm not going to be able to take this. I feel like shit. I'm in *pain*. I need my *painkillers*. It's not right."

Aida frowned. "Chris, I told you when I was in California that we aren't as equipped as a rehab facility, but we'll make it work."

"I don't know if I can handle this." He watched Shannon, who was on her back, grasping at air and kicking her tiny socked feet.

Aida rubbed his shoulder. "You're anxious. That's completely normal. We'll keep you hydrated and comfortable. You can do this, Chris. I believe in you."

Anxious was too light a term. Chris's body had changed sides and was whaling on him like a punching bag. He'd never been a fighter in any sense of the word. This was the biggest stand he'd ever made, and he could already feel his resolve slipping. He examined the light spilling through the window of his room then looked at Aida. Her eyebrows were raised.

"Did you say something?" he asked.

"I said, Can I make you some eggs and bacon? Coffee?"

"Sure."

Aida gathered Shannon and left him alone.

The window offered Chris a view of the quiet road beyond Aida's front yard. The neighborhood street connected to the main road and eventually to downtown Anchorage. The rattling sound of pills in a prescription bottle echoed in his mind—they were somewhere out there, waiting. Just one painkiller could make this beating end.

A sizzling sound was coming from the kitchen. Chris closed his eyes. *No. I can do this. I don't need pills. I gotta kick this.*

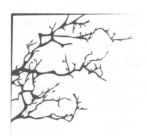

Chapter 7

M ax scratched his budding beard. He hadn't shaved since Julia's death nearly a month before. Around two weeks had passed since he'd resigned from his job and put Anchorage in his rearview, seeking sanctuary in his remote wooded property on the Kenai Peninsula. Max examined the tree in front of him. The forty-foot Sitka spruce spread its feathery canopy of blue-green needles against a backdrop of clouds. The trunk was as wide as his torso but had come down with a case of tree cancer. Two beach-ball-sized burls ballooned underneath its scaly bark. He wouldn't be harvesting this tree for firewood. Instead, he'd cut the tree down, shave the bark, sand it smooth, and lacquer the log. The burls would make for a unique porch pillar, and with some luck, he'd find another one to be its mate.

He moved on and examined a birch that bowed toward him and the cleared property at his back. He rubbed his dirt-caked hand on the papery bark, tore a piece off, and let it fall to the grass. Max picked his chainsaw up off the ground and got it rumbling with a single pull. He slid his ear protection back over his warm ears and dropped the shield across his face. Bark and pulp sprayed as he cut a notch in the narrow birch. He moved the saw to the back side of the tree and cut a line toward the center of the notch. A powerful crack split the air. Max stepped aside as a string of popping sounds followed the tree while it toppled over and crashed to the ground. He quickly trimmed the fallen birch's branches. Next, he cut the trunk into smaller logs, which he carried and stacked on one of his growing woodpiles.

Max wiped sweat off his brow with his shirtsleeve and retrieved the water. He sat on the stump seat and drank in gulps while water trickled down his chin and mingled in his beard hair. "Ah." He gazed toward the fresh upturned dirt. The digging was coming along, although he still had more shoveling to do before he'd be ready to add concrete piers for the foundation.

Max set aside the water and gazed down at his hands. Dust and sweat had worked into his palms, and blisters had burst only to form padded callouses. A surgeon who couldn't trust his own hands, or even his own mind, was no surgeon at all. He'd never felt so useless in his life. After he recovered from the panic attack, Max had stuck around the hospital to make sure his patient made it through surgery. Karim, Aida, and the team had done a fine job cleaning up his mess. If Max had lost his patient, he would never have been able to forgive himself. The girl and her family had trusted him to do a good job, and he'd failed them. After penning a letter of resignation, Max spoke to his superiors and to human resources. They tried to get him to stay, but he'd made up his mind. He exited the hospital that day without taking time to say goodbyes.

When he returned home, the quiet house reminded him of his own emptiness. After wandering around the rooms listlessly, he ventured into the attic. A box of Julia's keepsakes caught his eye, and he leafed through the pages of one of her scrapbooks: a few clippings about the school where she'd taught, class photos, the announcement of Julia and Max's marriage in the local paper, and some of her childhood photos. He paused at the sight of the picture of the wooded property they'd purchased a few years back. The remote property wasn't all that much to look at, really. The land had been only partially cleared. He'd bulldozed a small road and cleared space on the hill, but overall, it remained heavily wooded with birches, white and black spruces, and some stands of older Sitka spruces.

Their dream had been to build a cabin on the vacant land, but they'd put off the project for years. Julia would never see their cabin, but it didn't mean he couldn't still build it for her. With little else to keep him going, he latched onto the idea. He made large orders for lumber and concrete then gathered his tools and loaded the truck with food and supplies. He'd locked his house in Eagle River and made the drive south to take up residence on the land.

Max wiped his hands on his dirt-stained pants and listened. A songbird warbled in the deep woods down the hill. A cool breeze ghosted through his hair. He had to give Julia credit—she had been the one to choose this property. She'd seen the potential. If he'd had his way, they would have bought a cozier lot beside a lake or closer to town. The realtor had marched the property with them, pointing out the perimeter.

At the heart of the land was a hill that overlooked an army of spruce treetops to the west. Beyond the woods lay the Cook Inlet and a distant crown of mountains—giant snow-covered volcanoes visible on clear days like today. On these coordinates, Julia had stood and gazed at the western horizon and proclaimed, "This is where the cabin will be."

A cloud covered up the sun and cast a cool shadow at his back. *Julia...* Max began to shake. His chest tightened as if someone were trying to crumple his lungs like scrap paper. Tears ran down his nose and lips. "What's the point?" Weakness had found a way to creep in again. It had been happening more and more. The quiet of this place was suffocating, which didn't make him feel any stronger, but the noise of the city remained far worse.

"I'm a piece of shit." Max could feel himself becoming unhinged. Part of him wanted to give in to the weight of his sadness. There were plenty of ways to bookend his life. He glanced toward his capped truck parked down the hill. His .44 Magnum would be the simplest. A bullet to the temple would be the most straightforward solution.

If he pulled the trigger quickly, he wouldn't even have time to regret the decision. Deep down, he knew he didn't deserve a quick death. *I ought to let myself starve.* If Julia had to fall down a mountain, he should suffer too.

He glanced off to the woods. If he found the right branch, he could use a bit of rope and fashion a noose. That route seemed the most appealing.

He stomped his boot in the dirt. "No. It was an accident. I need to keep working, keep living. She'd want that."

Max marched over to the cabin's foundation and uprooted the shovel from the soft soil. He scooped dirt and rocks and tossed them into a homemade wheelbarrow. "Got to keep moving. Keep working. Time will help. Time will heal. It's got to." Part of him believed his words, but there was another part, a sinister part, that suspected his will to keep living was only supported by bullshit platitudes.

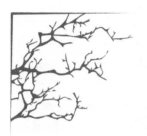

Chapter 8

Chris's mind and body declared war. He resigned himself to his bed. His appetite waned, and his skin seemed to be losing color. He suffered hourly bouts of nausea and headaches that hammered into his forehead while a team of horses tried to drag his spine through his skin. Aida cooked his meals and fed him ice chips and Gatorade. She patted his skin with cold compresses. When she came with a cup full of pills, he was washed in a wave of relief. He almost hit her when she told him the pills were only multivitamins and supplements. Chris swallowed them anyway just to have the brief sensation.

The next night, he did manage to nod off, only to be plunged into nightmares. In one, zombies ripped into his abdomen, grabbed his intestines, and sank their teeth into him as they tried to tear him open like a Christmas present. In another, he fell off a bridge over the LA River. He woke screaming as he hit the concrete flat on his back.

His eyes were too sensitive to the light, so he kept the windows covered and refused to leave the bed. He declined the food and drink Aida tried to force on him. His stomach couldn't handle anything.

She wheeled in a pole with several fluid bags and inserted an IV, saying, "It's important to keep your body hydrated. If you're going to stay in bed, you'll need to use this." She handed him a piss jug. "Unless you want me to give you a catheter."

He was too weak to argue with her. Whenever he tried to stand up, he suffered vertigo and dizziness. His brain had been replaced by a cast-iron pan and a steaming yellow pile of scrambled eggs.

I need to get some pills. Focus, Chris, focus! Where? Where can I get them? He imagined himself sneaking out of the house to try to find pills, but in his condition, he doubted he'd make it past the driveway. He curled in a fetal position, swaddled in muscle pain. His eyes darted around the room and stopped at the tray where Aida placed his meals. The cold soup smelled of carrots—rotten fucking vegetables weaseling into his nose, into his head. Chris dry heaved. He knocked the soup over, which did nothing for the smell, but at least he didn't have to see it. There was a picture on the tray—a photo taken on a film camera. He grabbed the frame and held it close. His mother and father beamed back at him. There was a softness to Mom's face as she nuzzled into Dad's Christmas sweater, her ring hand flat against his broad chest. A Santa hat sat cockeyed atop Dad's buzz cut. Two pairs of red eyes bored into Chris's skull. They burned him. His skin was on fire. *When's it going to end?* Aida must have set the picture there to torture him. He threw the picture against the far wall. The shoddy wooden frame shattered, and his parents were gone. They were both gone. He missed them. He missed his pills.

He routinely sweated through and soiled his sheets. Aida changed them daily. He'd been in bed for four or five days. With the lack of sleep and a clogged brain, he had trouble holding fast to time. Aida continued bringing him multivitamins and supplements with his meals. He imagined himself popping the smooth blue pills into his mouth, but his body didn't numb out. Instead, the headaches and the body aches only hit him harder. He slipped into a sort of fevered dream induced by sleep deprivation and nausea, in which the room and his mind became fuzzy.

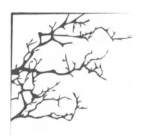

Chapter 9

Aida woke to go to the bathroom. She cursed herself for drinking too much water with dinner. After she'd spent more than a week at Chris's bedside, his vitals had finally improved. Once she quit thinking of him as her brother and simply as a patient, she found her rhythm. He'd struggled for the first four days, but on day five, he'd turned a corner. He was eating and drinking again. She'd taken him off fluid IVs, and he was strong enough to get out of bed to use the bathroom—all huge improvements. She was proud of herself for helping Chris overcome the worst of the withdrawal. The only issue remaining was his insomnia. It was a common symptom with withdrawal, and she was hoping that night he'd finally get some sleep. Next would come the mental healing. She already had a therapist lined up for him.

Chris wasn't the only man who occupied her thoughts. She'd put in a call to Max two days earlier. He picked up, and she tried to get him to talk about how he was feeling, but as with the last time, he remained terse and standoffish at best. The only thing he seemed interested in talking about was his progress on the cabin. He'd finally finished digging and had added concrete piers and set beams. Next, he'd said he would be laying out the joists. Aida had just been happy to hear his voice. Max was talking more, and Chris was getting better. She took pride in her resolve to fix the broken men around her.

As Aida headed back to bed, she stopped. She registered the sound of traffic passing by the house. The clock read 12:30 a.m. She tied off her robe and stole out of her room. She padded over to Chris's closed door, turned the knob, and pushed the door open.

Once her eyes adjusted to the dark, she peered at the bed. The comforters and pillows were tangled together. The window was open, and the screen had been removed. She stepped closer and put her hand on the blankets. Chris was gone. She stared out the window at the dimly lit street and the glow from neighboring houses. *Shit.*

Aida sat down on his bed. She had discussed this scenario with Frank, and they'd even planned for it. She would give Chris her trust, but that only went so far. Frank had suggested the idea, and Aida had eventually agreed. Frank had slipped the GPS tracker into Chris's shoe his first night there. She wasn't proud that their mistrust of him had been validated—she was sick to her stomach.

She moved into her bedroom and dressed. Using her phone, she accessed the tracking program. The map of Anchorage appeared, and a blue dot blinked. He'd made it several miles and was already downtown. *Where are you going, Chris?*

Five minutes later, Aida lifted Shannon out of her crib and eased her into her car seat and closed the cover over the top, sealing her in a cocoon. With a bulbous purse draped over one arm and Shannon's car seat in the other, she headed outside, loaded Shannon into the minivan, and drove downtown.

When she seemed close to Chris's location, she turned in to a gas station across from a car dealership. She parked in a space. The blue dot was only a couple of blocks away. She rarely visited that part of town in the daytime, let alone at one in the morning. The area had a few sketchy bars built close to a strip club and some cheap hotels and motels. Pawnshops, payday loans, and liquor stores weren't far away either.

If Chris was searching for drugs, he'd probably found the right place. She missed Frank. Though strict, he was strong when he needed to be. Aida glanced in the back seat, where Shannon rested fast asleep.

Aida sighed and rubbed her forehead. "Maybe Frank was right."
*This isn't what I should be doing—skulking about Anchorage after my
junkie brother.* She scolded herself for calling Chris a junkie, but the
word fit. Her hand slid to her thigh, and she squeezed a soft chunk
of skin between her thumb and forefinger. She felt the meat underneath respond with hot pain.

Aida pictured the zebra-stripe red scars under her jeans. A memory came into focus: the image of her as a teen, dragging the razor
blade across her delicate grapelike skin... the joyous rush that had
pulsed from her thigh to her brain as blood spilled, as sharp pain de-
livered a twisted satisfaction. Now, the scars only reminded her of
the sadness that she'd cast off in her previous life.

She would have to tell Frank about her brother's disappearance
as she'd promised she would. That would be it—Chris would be
gone. "Unless I get to him before he does anything stupid."

Aida sniffed, wiped her eyes, and swallowed hard. She put the
van in gear and started driving south.

CHRIS WAS HUFFING. A cramp chewed his right side. He hadn't
done that much walking in a while. He rolled up the sleeves of his
gray sweatshirt and dropped his hood down. He slicked back sweat
and combed it through his hair then replaced his hat, tucking the
dark brim down above his eyebrows. He'd already tramped several
miles to get to downtown Anchorage. He'd asked a guy at a bus stop
where he could find some bars or clubs, which had led him to this
seedy stretch of bars. Clusters of loud partiers bobbed outside a strip
club, so he crossed the street and headed that way.

Chris's body didn't feel as weak or sick as it had at first, but his
mind had gotten worse. All he wanted to do was sleep, but his brain

wouldn't shut down. He hadn't slept for more than a few hours at a time since the withdrawal had begun. He'd given up watching TV, and his mind raced about like a scared rabbit. There was only one way to fix all his problems: he needed to get some pills.

So when Aida left her purse hanging on the chair in the kitchen, Chris rifled through it. He found two crisp hundred-dollar bills and some twenties inside. He took a single hundred and didn't disturb the rest. When she went to bed, he escaped through his window and made his way to the city lights.

Chris zipped his sweatshirt all the way up and stuffed his hands in his jeans pockets to shake off the cool night air. He approached some smokers and drunks who lingered under the neon lights of a strip club, and he asked them in a hushed voice if they could hook him up with painkillers. After repeatedly getting turned away, Chris found two guys, Carl and Alan, who said they could get him some Percocet. Both men were in the six-foot-five, two-hundred-thirty-pound range and were all muscle. They seemed like a pair of competitive weightlifters, with broad shoulders, tight arms, and the complete absence of necks—a real pair of cement heads. Chris imagined them at the gym, spotting each other, with tank tops, weight belts, and swollen veins. Carl was the talkative one, while Alan was mostly quiet, agreeing with whatever Carl said with a brooding seriousness. Carl beckoned Chris to follow them and led him past the strip. Chris didn't like leaving the lit, occupied street, but he followed behind the two drunken linebackers anyway, with the knowledge that either man could crush him like a beer can.

Chris hesitated when they beckoned him down the back side of a motel. They were leading him to a dimly lit overflow parking lot with only a few parked cars. He scanned the area and didn't see anyone else back there. He scanned the main street, where voices hollered and cars passed, then swung his gaze back to the two men.

Carl said, "Come on, man. You want the hookup or not?" His slurred voice came across as annoyed.

"Yeah, my bad. I'm coming." Chris caught back up to the men.

They headed to a black Pontiac Firebird parked by a chain-link fence. When Carl got to the car, he spun around and said, "Money first."

Chris pointed inside the car. "I want to see the pills first."

Carl tilted his blocky head sideways, frowned, and rested his heavy arm on the top of the car. "Listen, we don't know you, so either show us the money, or we walk."

They were a pushy pair of cement heads. "All right. Here's a hundred, see? Now, let's see the—hey!"

Carl lunged and connected his fist to Chris's nose and left eye. Chris's feet flew out from underneath him. He landed on his back, scraping his elbows on the asphalt. The air ditched his lungs, and he struggled to breathe. He tasted blood on his lips. Carl stepped over him, grabbed the money, and rifled through his pockets for more. Chris kept his hands up, but when Carl didn't find anything, he punched Chris's cheek. Meteors burst into his vision. He absorbed the sting of a work boot that plowed into his ribs. Alan joined in to kick him hard on his hip and his right side.

Chris curled up in the fetal position and yelled through a split lip, "Stop. You got the money. Stop!"

To his surprise, they did. A car engine revved, and Chris peeked through his fingers to see his attackers bathed in white light. He shaded his eyes against the high beams.

"The hell?" Carl said.

The horn honked.

Chris's face stung, and his ribs and side radiated heat. He lifted his hand toward the blinding lights and cried, "Help!"

"Who the hell is this?" Carl asked and kicked Chris in the stomach.

Chris coughed and clutched his belly. He groaned and writhed on the asphalt.

"Let's get out of here." Alan was moving back toward their car.

"Wait," Carl said. "It's not the cops. Let's shut this fucker up."

Chris peered through his woven fingers. A person stepped out of the van—a woman.

Carl laughed. "Just some dumb bitch." They shaded their eyes, and Carl started walking toward her.

"Back up—I mean it!" the woman proclaimed.

Chris recognized the voice—Aida. *Get out of here, Aida.*

Carl stepped forward. "Got something to prove, bitch?"

She pulled a revolver and aimed it at Carl.

Carl froze. "Little lady with a big gun." He chuckled dryly. "Put that thing away before you hurt yourself."

There was a clicking sound as Aida cocked the hammer. *She's going to shoot him.*

Carl stepped closer to the gun, too drunk or stupid to care. He started laughing. "Do it, huh. Do it, lady."

"Chris, come here!" Aida yelled.

As Chris pushed off the sandy pavement, Alan kicked him back down and rested his boot on his neck. "We ain't through with your little druggie yet."

Alan pressed down harder, and Chris smelled the rubber tread. He moaned as his face and mouth ground into the pavement. "Just go, Aida," Chris said with one eye trained on her.

"Get off him. I'll shoot—both of you." Aida's raised voice rang firm.

"You won't do shit." Carl was ten feet from Aida. "You would have already done it by now if you were going to. Alan and I learned to spot the cowards in prison. This little druggie"—Carl pointed at Chris—"he's a chicken shit. And you, little lady—you may talk tough, but you got some coward in you too."

Aida let the hammer slowly fall back to position and put the gun back into her purse. She was shaking and seemed so small against Carl.

She wasn't going to be his hero that night. Chris's heart dribbled against the ground. *I have to get her away from here.* He struggled, but Alan used all his weight to keep him pinned down. Aida ducked into her van.

Carl said. "See, you stupid—ah, fuck! Ah!"

Aida stepped back into view and held something in front of her. A mist sprayed through the spears of light. Carl twisted around and covered his face. He stumbled past Chris and Alan, hacking as he tried to get away. Aida followed him and pushed the mist toward Alan, who tried to block the spray—but not well enough, because his yells came next. The boot came off Chris's neck, and Alan took flight, coughing and spitting with Carl across the parking lot, the two of them falling over each other and moaning. Chris covered his face, but he could feel the sting in his own nostrils, and his eyes started to boil.

Aida called his name, and he struggled to find his feet. She grabbed him by his shirt and practically dragged him into the passenger seat then reversed and peeled away with squealing tires. Chris spat and rubbed his burning eyes. Aida opened the windows. He let the air wash his face, moaning and crying beneath the sound of the wind and the combustion of the motor.

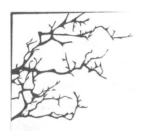

Chapter 10

Aida glared at the drenched form of Chris as she sprayed a stream of water into his face with the backyard hose. *How could you do this, Chris?* On his knees in the grass, he squeezed his eyes closed. He resembled a wet dog. She was glad that Frank had built the fences high enough in their backyard to keep the neighbors from seeing her at that moment. Aida could still feel adrenaline burning through her like napalm. Her hands still shook. She'd never been so scared in her life, and if she hadn't been able to control herself, she might have shot and killed those men. Remembering the bear spray in the car door had been nothing short of a miracle.

Her fear had boiled into anger. Chris had put her and Shannon in harm's way tonight. *He deserves the pain.*

Chris sputtered and coughed as he wiped mucous from his nose.

"How could you pull this shit, Chris?"

He lifted his face out of the water. "Ah, my eyes. Is this even helping?"

Aida rinsed his face again. "You'll be fine. Stop whining. Take off your shirt. It's covered in the spray."

Chris removed his shirt and revealed his pale chest and flat stomach. Goose bumps crawled across his bony arms. Aida gave him the hose again.

He shot snot from his nose. "Was that mace?"

"Bear spray."

"Why would you use that on people?" Chris scrubbed his eyes. "Burns so bad." Chris sat back and kept a hand over his eyes.

Aida tossed a towel on his lap. "Better than me shooting those guys. I *should* have called the police." She'd been hoping to find Chris wandering around Anchorage by himself. Aida had even pictured herself driving up to him while he was walking the sidewalk. She'd have told him something like, *If you don't get in now, you're never allowed back in my house.* Instead, she'd followed the tracker to a parking lot, where the two men were beating him on the ground. She should have called the police then, but her motherly instinct triggered instead. She laid on the horn and got out, thinking the men would take off. When the two guys didn't back down, she grabbed her gun. If she hadn't reined herself in, she might have shot them both dead. If she hadn't defended herself, they could have beaten her up and maybe even hurt or taken Shannon.

Chris continued to moan. "Does Frank know about this?"

That's all you can think about right now? "Why were those men beating you up?"

Chris toweled himself off then draped the towel over his shoulders. His blue eyes leaked tears, and red rings had formed around his eyes. "I..."

Aida sensed his hesitation. "Don't you dare lie to me."

Chris glared at her. His hair was askew. "You know why."

"Don't be coy with me, Chris."

Chris muttered, "Drugs."

Aida paced about the grass. "So apparently, you didn't like living with us."

Chris shivered and stared at the ground. "I do like living here."

No one else cared if Chris lived or died except for her. He'd blown the best chance he had. She could hardly stand to look at him. "Then why did you break the rules? What was the last week for, huh? Honestly, how could you do this to us?"

"You don't know—" Chris started to yell something, but he held back. "I'm sorry, okay? I'm sorry." Chris sniffed and held the towel close. "Can we go inside? I'm freezing."

"You heard Frank. One strike and you're out." She hooked her thumb toward the street.

"I think between getting my ass kicked and you bear-spraying me, I've been punished enough tonight." Chris spat on the grass.

Aida speared a finger at Chris. "There's the Chris I remember. I was wondering when you'd play the victim card. I must have been out of my mind thinking I could handle your bullshit. Oh, and thanks for stealing two hundred dollars from my purse, by the way."

Chris sat cross-legged on the grass and brushed his wet hair back. "I just wanted to sleep." He focused on Aida's eyes. "Did you tell Frank? Are you going to tell him?"

"He'll know soon enough."

"You're just going to toss me out? I have nothing." Chris motioned a hand away from the house. "What do you think I'm going to do out there? You're forcing me to steal, and then I'm going to start using again."

Aida balled her fists at her sides. "You did this, Chris. Not me."

Chris was shivering in a wet towel and nursing his fat lip. There was a red mark on his cheek, and his eyes were hollow. "So give me another option. Help me out, Aida."

"Check yourself into rehab."

Chris raised his voice. "Not happening."

"Well, then I'm through trying to help you." Aida listened as a commercial plane made its descent into Anchorage. "You can stay the night, but tomorrow, you're out of my house."

Aida shut the hose off and went inside to check on the baby. Shannon slept in her crib in the room adjacent to her own. The white-noise machine purred in the dim light. The room and her daughter calmed Aida's nerves. Somehow, Shannon had been immune to the events of the night. Aida envied her.

Chris's footsteps creaked as he came back inside and closed the door of his room down the hall. Aida left Shannon's crib behind and went to her own bedroom, where she switched on the lights, clutched her cell phone, and sat down at the small desk that she and Frank shared. He would be fast asleep up at the slope. He wasn't going to let this slide, and he shouldn't. Having Chris in the house was already a strain on the marriage, and Frank had limits. He didn't deserve to be put through all this. Chris couldn't stay there anymore—that much was certain. Even in Anchorage, he could get himself gummed up in trouble. Putting him back out on the streets in a foreign city would be dangerous and downright cruel. She could buy him a flight back to LA, but then he'd definitely slip back into his habit. She sighed in the quiet of the room.

He'd gotten through the physical withdrawal and was practically home free. She had been planning to bring him to a therapist. But now that he'd broken the rules, helping him was off the table. She'd planned to take Chris to see Max and help out at his cabin that week—so he could get out and exercise in nature, see Alaska a bit.

Aida scratched her scalp. She thought of Max toiling away on his remote property. He'd said she could bring Chris down for a day. If she tried, she might be able to get him to take her brother for longer. If Chris was out of their house, Frank would be satisfied, and Max needed someone to help him around the cabin. She wouldn't be abandoning Chris completely. The chances of success were low, but leaving him with Max would still be better than tossing him out on the street. And if he couldn't last on Max's property, she could at least feel like she'd done everything she could. All of that depended on Max allowing Chris to stay.

Aida called Frank's work number.

"Hey, babe. Something wrong?" Frank's mystified voice was breathless and confused. She'd woken him.

"I'm sorry for calling so late, honey," Aida said.

"It's fine." Frank smacked his lips. "What's up? Everything okay?"

"We're all fine. But it happened, like you said it would."

Frank groaned. "What did he do?"

"He snuck out a couple hours ago. I used the tracker and followed him. I caught him trying to get drugs by the strip club. Two guys beat him up. Chris has some scrapes and bruises, but he's fine."

Frank sighed. He was pissed—of course he was pissed. Frank had known all along that Chris wouldn't be able to stick to the rules. He'd been right, as usual.

"So where were you? Who watched the baby?" Frank asked.

"Shannon was in the car." Aida cleared her throat. *You're not going to like the next part.* "I had to use bear spray on the guys to get them off Chris."

"What? You what? Aida! That's... are you okay?"

She imagined that Frank's eyes were bulging. It took a lot to shock him, but she'd seen the face before. "I'm fine. It did the trick, and I got Chris out of there. The guys ran off."

"Why didn't you call the cops?" Frank paused. "I'm beyond pissed, hon."

"It happened so fast. I didn't have time." Aida pressed the phone to her cheek, paced over to Frank's closet, and opened the door. She grasped a hanging sweater and rubbed the wool on her cheek, wishing he were there.

Frank blew a long exhalation. "Well, Chris is getting the boot, obviously."

No surprise there. Aida closed the closet door and eased herself onto his side of the bed. She would have to start to steer his anger. Aida lowered her voice. "I don't disagree with you." "Why don't I feel like you're with me?" Frank asked.

It made her sad to think he thought she wasn't with him. They were a team, but Frank had to be forced into being flexible sometimes. "I have an idea."

"Aida, we talked about this. We *agreed* on this. We aren't going to change our minds now that he broke the rules. He's an addict, like it or not. He's chosen drugs over family. We're not going to be able to change him."

Frank was practically pleading for her to be logical. But Chris was her only close family member not six feet under, and they shared a bond of sadness. *Sometimes, you have to ride out the dysfunction.* "I agree. I don't think *we* will be able to change him. Not in Anchorage. Not at our house..."

"He broke the rules."

Aida rested her back on the cool wooden headboard. She released her ponytail and brushed her hair. "Frank..."

"Aida, he's not your problem anymore. You have to let him go." Frank's voice was harsh and urgent.

Aida examined the tan carpet. He was probably right. She should just let Chris go. Her life would be a lot easier. But the guilt would haunt her, and knowing that fact meant that she couldn't let him go. "Okay, all right. I listened to you. Now, please listen to me."

"Aida—"

"Frank, listen to what I have to say." They had argued plenty in their marriage. She and Frank had strong opinions, and they could both be stubborn. Aida knew how to wear Frank down, but overall, there was an emotional cost to trying Frank's patience. She didn't want to push him too far away, but there were times when he needed to shut up and listen to her. Now was one of those times.

"Fine," Frank said.

"Max." Aida said the name and gave it time to sink in. "Max can take Chris."

"You're going to unload him on Max? Don't you think he's had enough to deal with? It would be downright cruel to do that to the poor guy."

"You didn't see Max when I saw him. He needs someone out there with him."

"Honey, I think he would probably shoot Chris. I'm only being honest. I think Chris would piss him off, and Max would snap. We can't do that to him. He's our friend."

Frank had a point. Max had flashed a bit of anger, and his panic attack in the operating room had added to his instability. "Frank. I'm worried about Max, and I'm worried about Chris."

"So you're going to consolidate them into one spot?"

Having them both in one location would be helpful. The possible outcome of her idea was starting to make sense. "It would do them both good."

"This is crazy, Aida. You've got to—"

She slid off her bed, stood tall, and swung her free hand for emphasis. "Frank, you of all people know that people can change. I changed."

"This is different."

"It isn't different. Chris and I grew up in the same house. He chose drugs. I chose cutting myself." She hated that she was leveraging her problems to validate Chris's behavior. "I understand how you see this. I don't want this burden, Frank, but like it or not, he's my problem."

Frank gave another long sigh. "And Max agreed to this?"

Each sigh out of Frank meant she was getting him to cave. He wasn't a complicated man. He was loyal and hardworking and good—to a fault. He was her anchor against the current. "Max said I could take him down for a day."

"Well, there you go. That's not a solution."

She chewed her lip and scratched the surface of their desk table with her fingernail. "Okay. We'll leave it up to Max, then. I'll take Chris down tomorrow. If Max agrees to take him, he'll stay. If not, I'll take him to the airport and send him back to LA for good."

"I'll never understand why you try to so hard to help the worst people."

She pressed the phone to her cheek. "Frank, do you agree with that?"

"Yes, fine, fine. Now, can we talk more about you bear-spraying some guys?"

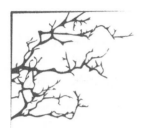

Chapter 11

Max opened his eyes and stared at the white truck cap just a couple of feet above his nose. The cap covered the truck bed and sealed him in against the weather, but sometimes, with all his supplies stuffed around him, he felt as if he were lying in a coffin. He could have set up a tent, but he didn't want the comfort, so instead, he slept in the truck bed every night on a thin bedroll on top of the raised wooden platform with only a wool blanket for warmth. The bed was stuffed with tools, building materials, clothes, and sealed containers of food and water.

Every waking day was another punishing reminder that he got to live while Julia had been reduced to a pile of ash. Max struggled to find the motivation to keep going. Once he got out of bed and back to work on the cabin, he was usually able to bury his emotions, but in the mornings, his thoughts grew like thorny brambles. They pinned him to his narrow bed and dissected him. The cold air washed his organs, and his body became raw. *Today might be the day.* The truck cap offered a small window to his right that was streaked in rainwater, and he could smell the soaked soil and wet moss. The sky was swathed with light-grey clouds, but they didn't seem to have any fight left in them.

His chest became heavy, and his eyes welled up. "I miss you, Jules." Tears slid down his cheeks, and he didn't bother to wipe them. His heart stuttered with a sudden downshift, and he turned to his side to curl up and grasp his rib cage. "I miss you so much." He sobbed and shuddered in the quiet of his truck.

He sniffed. "What's the point?" Silence was his reply. *I'm no good anymore—I gotta end this.* He'd thought of plenty of ways to do it, and he kept circling back to hanging. He had some thick rope that would support his weight. If he was going to hang himself, he wanted to be surrounded by the peace of the woods. The problem was that the trees around his property were mostly spruces and birches. All the branches were weak or too high up, and he wasn't committed to climbing them. He'd never realized how hard it was to find a strong, low-hanging branch on the Kenai Peninsula.

Max cleared his throat, blinked back tears, and hastily pushed himself out of bed. He shuffled onto his tailgate and slipped on dirty work pants, a long-sleeved shirt, and steel-toe boots. He wiped his damp cheeks and glanced up the hill at the many timber joists, supported by beams and concrete piers, that would eventually bear the weight of the floor and everything in the cabin. He'd had to get creative in his rigging to lug and set the beams. The cabin was coming along, but there was still much more to do. Being alone was a massive disadvantage.

His cell phone rang in the truck cab. Max listened to the chirp of the ringer. The sound brought him back to his former life—calls from work, friends, and a wife who needed him. The ring was unnatural compared to the tranquility of his property and annoyed him enough to get him to answer. He moved to the driver's door, ducked inside, and answered the cell phone.

"Hello? Max?" Aida said.

"Yeah."

"How are you?"

"Fine."

"Good. Good. I hope I didn't interrupt you. Can you talk?"

He was in no mood to talk, but he didn't want to be mean to her either. "Yeah."

"I'll just get down to it. You remember how you mentioned you'd take my brother Chris for a day to help you with the cabin?"

"The guy addicted to painkillers?"

"He's off them now. I helped him through withdrawals, and he's on the mend."

"Okay," Max said.

"Well, Chris is, uh... he, uh... he can't stay here anymore, Max. He snuck out to try to score some pills last night and got beat up in the process."

"Okay." The idea of an addict trying to score drugs wasn't a big shocker, but Aida's tone was. She seemed desperate and scattered, completely unlike her normal self. Her brother must have pushed her to her breaking point. From what Aida had said, after her parents died, she had basically raised Chris.

"There's no easy way to say this, but can you... take him? I know you said you'd take him for a day, but I'm talking about long-term—a month, maybe two or three."

Max rested his back against his truck. He could use the help if he was going to finish the cabin, but this kid was coming with baggage, and Max was in no shape to deal with another person. He could barely handle dealing with himself. He wanted solitude, and this Chris guy would take that away. Aida was a good woman, but this was a monster of a favor, and he could only wonder how she'd come to even thinking of asking him. "Aida..."

"I know. I know. Chris keeps refusing rehab, and we have to kick him out of the house, and I don't know what to do. Frank wants him gone, and I know if I kick him out, he'll probably get back on drugs until he ends up dead in a gutter. I don't want that to happen, but I don't know how to help him. I just... I don't know what to do." She voiced her defeat with her sullen tone.

Max scratched his scalp. It disturbed him to hear her lose her composure. He could understand her sadness. Max studied the cabin and pictured another person helping him raise some heavy frame-work. He could at least think about the idea. "I'm not agreeing to anything, but what kind of arrangement did you have in mind?"

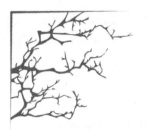

Chapter 12

Chris woke to Aida barging into his room. He covered his face with the comforter. Her hand latched onto his shoulder, and she shook him none too gently.

"Get up. You've been in bed long enough. We're going out."

He moaned into the pillow then yawned and stretched his back. His face and body still ached from the previous night, but oddly enough, he didn't hurt as badly as when he'd been dealing with the worst of the withdrawal. His head was clearer, his appetite had returned, and he'd even managed to finally get a good night's sleep.

"Where?" he asked.

Aida sat on his bed. "You haven't seen much of Alaska yet, so I figured we would spend the day down south on the Kenai Peninsula—just you and me, brother. Our neighbor Jen is watching Shannon for me today. I thought we could go for a hike. Fresh air will do you a world of good."

She seemed to be back to her enthusiastic self. Chris sat up. *Hiking?* "I thought you... were kicking me out."

"I talked to Frank. We decided that you could stay until he comes back. When he gets home, we'll discuss it more."

Chris wasn't sure what could have changed her mind. It seemed like an odd stroke of luck, but he didn't want to spoil his chance at staying here. "Okay. Okay, so hiking. Do I need to bring something?"

Aida stood. "Bring yourself."

Although all his backpack held was a gray sweatshirt, he brought it with him because he figured every hiker needed a backpack. Chris settled into the passenger seat, tipped his hat high, held his cheek, and watched the buildings of Anchorage rise and fall. Before long, the road opened up to marshlands, mudflats, and tidal waters. The Seward Highway wound along the coast, wedged between sheer cliffs of slate-gray brittle stone on the left and the ocean to the right. When Chris gazed ahead, he could see traces of snow on the jagged peaks, and Aida pointed out glaciers. He'd never seen a glacier before and had always pictured them as icebergs, but these were more like ice fields that filled the gaps between mountains.

Aida parked at a turnoff that overlooked the water at the inlet she called Turnagain Arm. She pointed out a pod of beluga whales as their backs broke the water's surface. Several people had stopped to watch as well—some squinted, while others peered through binoculars. The sunshine warmed the nape of Chris's neck, and the heat drifted down through his cotton shirt. A yellow-and-blue train ran below him beside the water. The beauty of the train gliding beside the shimmering water and the jagged mountain peaks in the background wasn't lost on him.

Aida continued driving him south, crossing over several rivers. As he glanced down at one chalky river, he saw men wading and holding long-handled nets in the water. "What are they catching down there?"

Aida glanced at the netters below. "Hooligan. They're kind of like sardines."

"Taste good?" Chris put his elbow against his door and glanced over at Aida.

"They're oily, but when Frank smokes them, they're delicious. We'll panfry some too. Later on in the summer, we catch fresh salmon and halibut—so good."

"Well, look at you, miss fisherwoman. I never knew you were so outdoorsy." Chris smiled at her and poked her side.

Aida swatted his hand away and offered a half smile. "I've changed, little brother. People *can* change, you know. Frank, he grew up here. He's taught me to fish, to use a gun..."

"Hard to believe that it was my sister saving my ass there last night. You should have just left me. I never wanted you or Shannon getting dragged into my problems."

"When I saw those two hurting you, I just lost it. Instinct kicked in, and before I realized it, I had the gun in my hand. That was my first time pulling a gun on a person, and I'd like it to be my last time." Her tone grew serious.

They were quiet for a while. Chris scanned the short beaches and the long mudflats below the highway. Two large birds—eagles—seemed to be fighting each other. "Hey, I want to check this out." Chris pointed out his window.

Aida parked the van, and Chris rushed to the guardrail.

"Is this the first time you've seen eagles?" Aida asked as she joined him.

"We don't have a lot of eagles in LA. At least, not that I'm aware of." Chris sat on the guardrail and watched the two bald eagles hop about the mudflats, taking flight and then fighting over some morsel of food. It reminded him of a time he saw two homeless guys fighting on the sidewalk, locked onto each other over something stupid.

Aida whistled a choppy birdcall.

Chris gave her a wry face. "That's not what eagles sound like. They make more of a piercing screech." He cupped his hands around his mouth. "Like this—*awoah*!"

Then one of the eagles made a choppy whistle sound similar to the call Aida had made.

"I'll be damned," Chris said.

"That sound they put on TV is actually a red-tailed-hawk screech. I prefer the real eagle calls myself." Aida got back in the van, and Chris followed.

"This is good. I'm glad you've taken me down here, sis," Chris said once they got back in the car. *Hopefully, this little bonding time will smooth over last night's fight.*

Aida smiled. "There's still a lot more to see, little brother."

They put the ocean behind them and drove past marshes dotted with dead standing barkless trees, then they moved into the green mountains littered with towering spruce and hemlocks. Long avalanche lines were engraved down the mountain faces. Snow still clung to the peaks and lined the slides and scree fields of the passing ranges. They passed rivers and ponds. Chris caught sight of a fly fisherman knee-deep in water, casting his line upstream into a glacial blue river. The man's line whipped in a circle, and his fly landed at the edge of the current. Chris imagined his own hand gripping a cork handle and how, with a sharp flick of his wrist, he would send the line shooting ahead of him.

"I have this friend." Aida's voice plucked him from his reverie. "I mentioned him to you before. He's... well, he was a doctor at my hospital. We used to work together. The best surgeon I've ever known." Aida's voice became solemn.

"He's not a doctor anymore?" Chris asked.

"He's taking time off—he lost his wife. Point is, he's a brilliant man, and he's choosing to live a simple life down here."

"Probably the only life you could live down here: *real* simple."

"We're going to drop by Max's property to say hi," Aida said, raising her voice.

Chris propped his sneaker on the glove compartment and chewed on his thumbnail. "It's your car. Take it wherever you want."

At a junction beside a lake, they turned right onto the Sterling Highway. The "highways" would probably only be considered back roads in California. Aida seemed to be getting quieter the longer she drove. She worked over her bottom lip with her front teeth. She usually did that when she was nervous. *Is she scared of me?* She probably had a right to be. He'd gotten her and Shannon mixed up in his life the night before, and she'd seen a side of him that he'd never wanted her to see. It made him sad to think that she might be nervous around him.

"Hey, cut it out. You'll chew your lip off."

She rolled her eyes. "Okay, Grandma."

"She used to say something else. What was it? I can't remember. Is that bad?"

Aida smirked. "She used to say, 'Worrying won't make the grapes grow.'" Aida did a good imitation of Grandma's old-timer voice.

"Yeah, that's it!" Chris laughed. "What were we growing—a vineyard or some shit?"

"Language," Aida said.

Chris stomped the floor with his other foot. "Oh, come on, Aida. I swear. There could be worse things, you know."

"You need to set a good example for your niece."

"Be more like Frank? No, thank you." Chris crossed his arms.

Aida raised the pitch of her voice. "I love my husband. He's been with me through hard times."

"What do *you* know of hard times? *I* know hard times." Chris tapped his own chest.

Aida glanced at him. "Well, if I had called the cops last night, you probably would have been *doing* hard time in jail."

She was goading him. Chris spun on her and pointed. "Ah-ha! There's Frank's voice. Well, thanks for saving me, sis, but if you'd really wanted to help me, you could have given me some meds to help me wean off. Instead, I went through a week of hell and couldn't sleep. You could have at least gotten me some sleep meds instead of driving me back to painkillers."

"You're clean, Chris. Don't you get that? *You* made the choice to try to score drugs last night—not me. The hard part was over, but you went and ruined everything."

"Don't pretend you know what this is like. You have stuff going on for you up here to make you happy, but I've got nothing." Chris slapped his palms down over his knees and faced the window. They passed a smashed porcupine on the side of the road.

Aida said, "You've got me and your family—that's more than a lot of people. You've got Alaska. Seriously, look at where you are." Aida gestured to the window. "People spend their entire lives trying to get here."

Chris rolled his eyes. The beauty of this place didn't change him. For years, all he'd had was pills to keep him happy. Now that he was clean, he realized how pathetic he really was and how little he had—no friends, money, or aspirations. He was a nobody, and the sheer size of Alaska just reminded him how small he really was.

"Kenai Lake. I mean, just look at it, Chris," Aida said.

A large lake dropped down to their left. The lake's glacial turquoise water was choppy with small whitecaps. The road followed the lakeshore for a bit until they crossed a bridge over the water. The bridge seemed to serve as the headwaters of the river. They followed the river, which now slithered on their right, parallel to the road. Aida continued down the highway past several cabins, outfitters, and business fronts. A silver rowboat appeared through the trees with two fly fishermen casting over the sides. The rower worked hard to keep the boat straight as the anglers watched their lines.

Aida scratched her hairline. "Oh, it's June eleventh already, huh? Today's opening day for fishing on the Kenai River. Those are drift boats."

The next time the river came back into view, there was another drift boat, this one black. The rower had ditched his oars and wielded a net as the boat drifted in the current. Another silver boat rested along a gravel bar, and several more fly fishermen cast from the bank. One of them fought a fish, his fly rod bent over while a tail splashed at the surface of the water.

"He's got one," Chris said under his breath, putting his fingertips to the window.

"What's that?" Aida asked.

"Nothing." Chris focused back on the road as the scene vanished behind thick trees. "Okay, fine. Tell me about these 'hard times' you had."

"Forget it."

"Come on." Chris straightened up in his seat. "You're the one who wants us to bond."

Aida held Chris's stare with her blue eyes—Dad's eyes. "I had a lot to deal with. I was in college, not much more than a kid myself, when I had to look after you and Grandma and Mom."

"Not that Mom lasted long." Chris kept his tone even. Mom had only been a widow for a month before she killed herself. Chris was twelve when he became parentless. Because of Grandma's dementia, Aida had been the main one to fill the parent role.

"You wanted to know about hard times, huh? You didn't have to mop the blood—Mom's blood. And let me tell you, when you slice open your carotid artery, there's plenty to go around."

Chris silently watched the passing trees. He and Aida had never talked about this in any sort of detail. "I didn't know you had to do that. I figured the coroner or something…"

"You figured wrong. I had to deal with the funeral and explain to everyone how Mom had managed to kill herself."

"Okay, I get it. You made me feel bad. You happy? But at least you never had to sleep on the street."

"You chose to sleep on the street! You've always had a home. Like right now. You have a home, and you go and break the rules when it gets too tough. You're only screwing yourself over."

Chris sighed. "Whatever."

"Yeah, whatever, whatever." Aida brushed her hair over her ear and eyed him. "You can't run forever, Chris."

We'll see about that.

Eventually, the river and the mountains fell behind them, and the land began to flatten. The trees appeared stunted, and the land became marshy. Chris dozed, and when he woke, his sister had broken away from the highway and was driving on a gravel road. He closed his eyes again.

He woke again with a jolt. One of the van's tires had dipped into a pothole. The road was partially washed out, and the van tossed dust in its wake.

Chris yawned. They'd been driving for over two hours. "Where are we going?" He rubbed his eyelids.

Aida focused on the road, steering in jerks to keep the van's tires on solid ground. "Max's property is a bit off the grid."

"Clearly," Chris said.

Aida drove for several miles, and the gravel road switched to a dirt road with deep cuts and rivets carved from truck tires. The only houses were small slapped-together shacks and cabins that appeared uninhabited and had signs that stated, NO TRESPASSING. There weren't even any telephone poles in sight.

"Seriously, where are we going?" Chris sat up, scanned the woods, and eyed his sister.

She bit her bottom lip again and drove the car around a protruding rock. "Almost there. My friend Max... he might not talk a lot."

"He one of those voice-box smoker guys?"

"No, he can talk fine, but he..." Aida rubbed her temple. "Well, he's been out here by himself for a little while."

"Sounds like a real nut job," Chris said.

"Don't say that! Max is a good man. His wife passed last month. Show some respect."

"Honestly, Aida, I don't really care about this guy or his dead wife."

He'd half expected her to put up a fight. Instead, she went silent and turned in to a dirt driveway. She put the car in park. Chris scanned a plot of land. There wasn't much to the place save for a wooden platform constructed on a small hill and a green Ford truck with an extended bed and a white fiberglass cap parked at one side of the property.

"Hang in here a bit. I'm going to see if he's around." Aida stepped out of the car, marched down the short dirt drive, and disappeared over the hill.

Chris flipped his leg over the opposite knee. He felt bad for Aida. She was only trying to help. When Frank got back from the slope, Chris would have to deal with him. Frank would probably be more pissed off than normal. Chris had broken the rules, and he'd have to work to get back into Frank and Aida's good graces. Aida, he could probably win over, but Frank wouldn't be folding so easily. Chris inspected his gray Converse shoe. He toyed with the sole. The bottom was coming off, and he flapped the white lip. *If these shoes could talk.*

A few minutes went by, and Aida reappeared from over the hill. Her cheeks seemed somewhat faded, and her eyes were weary. She got back in and started chewing her bottom lip again.

"We out of here?" he asked.

"Yeah." She started the car.

"Good. You find your friend or whatever?"

"I did." She buckled her seat belt and regarded the sun visor. "Oh crap, I forgot to give Max some mail." She held an envelope. "Do you think—"

"Yeah, I got it." Chris accepted the envelope.

"Great. He's over the hill there."

Chris stepped out of the van. The smell from the campfire and the scent of cut wood mixed with spruce needles. He ambled over to the raised wood platform, which stood on the highest point of the land. The cleared property was probably the size of a college football field. He listened as a chainsaw chewed up a tree at the edge of some thick woods. The popping and cracking of wood followed. The tree fell, ending with a *swoosh* and a crash.

Chris noticed Aida driving back the way they had come and spotted his backpack on the ground where she'd parked. He watched her as she drove away. *What's she doing?* He glanced down at the envelope and flipped it over. Small inked letters read "TO CHRIS."

She's going to leave me here. "No, no, no!" Chris chased after the van.

Aida sped up. Chris ran down the dirt road and squinted against the dust. He jumped potholes and sprinted as fast as he could. His bruised hip and ribs radiated pain, but he pushed on as Aida kept driving away.

"Wait!" Chris pumped his thighs but soon lost sight of her. He kept running anyway. His lungs burned, and sweat ran freely down his face. Despite his aching body, he ran, yelling for Aida to stop. The engine was all he could hear, and after a minute, he could no longer hear that. Chris slowed as cramps began eating holes in his sides. His mouth became dry, and his lungs begged for air. He trotted for a minute longer then gave up, bent over, and grabbed his knees, the wrinkled envelope still in his hand.

Chris threw the envelope in the dirt and stomped on it. He paced small circles, swearing at Aida and Alaska. His yells were absorbed by the surrounding forest. Chris sat on a rock beside the road and held his head in his hands. He remained that way for almost half an hour. Branches clattered behind him, followed by the sound of leaves being crushed underfoot. Chris spun around. A bull moose stood twenty feet behind him. The oil-drum-sized body rose high off the ground, covered in brown hair that had dark streaks. The moose's long face angled sideways as it stripped a branch with practiced ease. Chris had never seen a wild animal that big or that close. The antlers were spread wide, and Chris's instinct told him to run. Instead, he froze. The large eye gazed down on him as the moose stripped another branch and stepped closer.

Sweat trickled down his back, and he covered his mouth. The moose shifted its hooves as it chewed the leaves. He waited for the massive creature to make a move, but the moose seemed more interested in his meal than in the human in front of him. Chris got to his feet and backpedaled, stepping on Aida's letter. He bent over and retrieved it then retreated down the road toward the remote property. He glimpsed back where the moose had been and put his hand over his heart, which hammered his chest. Chris opened the letter.

Chris:

I'm sorry I had to leave you like this. I hope in time you will forgive me for deceiving you, but remember that you deceived me and the family as well. We thought we could help you in your recovery, but it's clear that even in Alaska, you have ways of finding drugs and trouble. I know it seems that I'm being harsh, but I don't think you see how your actions hurt the people around you.

Chris rested his hand on his sore hip. Aida had planned to leave him there all along. She was unloading him on some guy's property in the middle-of-nowhere Alaska with nothing. Chris kicked a stone on the dirt road, and it bounced off into the undergrowth. He continued reading.

I've been in contact with my good friend Max Fitwell, who has agreed to take you on as a helper for his property. As I told you, Max was a doctor that I worked with. His wife died last month, and he's left the hospital to build a cabin on his land. Max is very knowledgeable and will treat you fairly. You could learn a lot from a guy like him. He will give you food, and you'll have a place to sleep, which I guarantee will not be as nice as your room here in Anchorage. You can still get in touch with us through mail. I will write you. This is it. This is your last chance, Chris. If you stay clean and out of trouble and prove to Max and me that you can change your ways, then you may return to our house in An-

chorage in time. If you can't handle this, then you're on your own, and you're not welcome back in our home or our lives. The decision is yours.

Aida

Chris scrunched the letter and stuffed it in his pocket. *Just fantastic.* He had to hand it to her—he hadn't seen this coming. Now he had to prove himself to this Max guy. Chris glanced back toward where Aida had driven. He could head back to the highway and try to hitchhike back to Anchorage, maybe beg for change on the streets for a while and try to save up for a plane ticket to get back to LA. But in the end, he'd only be panhandling just to fly back to another place to panhandle.

Chris studied the washed-out dirt road to Max's property. He could try to see what this guy was like. Max might not be all that bad. Then again, he could be worse than Frank. Chris groaned and stood in the middle of the dirt road with his hands on his hips. *Fuck me.*

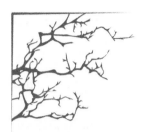

Chapter 13

C hris stayed in the middle of the road and considered investigating the other scattered shacks and cabins they'd passed, but the No Trespassing signs made him imagine they belonged to shotgun-happy hillbilly types. He came to the conclusion that he could at least go see what this Max guy was like and what sort of living situation he had. Chris went back to the edge of the property where Aida had first parked, scooped up his backpack, and watched a bearded man—who had to be Max—load a chainsaw into the back of his truck. The extended truck bed had two small berths built inside on a raised wooden platform.

Max collected a long ax then paused and examined Chris.

Chris stared right back. Max's navy-blue long-sleeved shirt and tan work pants were covered in sawdust. He waved Chris over then hefted the ax over his full shoulders and walked back up the bluff where he was building.

Great. This is just great. I get to hang out with Paul Bunyan. Chris trailed behind and watched as Max moved to a large stump littered with chips and cuts. Max moved a sledgehammer and a metal wedge out of the way, sank the ax head into the stump, and proceeded to a pile of cut sections of tree trunk.

Chris approached him. "You're Max, right? Aida's friend?"

Max eyed him. "Yup." He bent over to pick a log from the pile.

The log was cut from a tree maybe a foot in diameter. Max stood the log on top of the chopping block. He hefted the ax, started his swing, then stopped. "You chop wood before?"

Chris hadn't, but he didn't want to give Max the satisfaction of knowing that. "Sure."

Max offered the ax to Chris.

"No, I'm all set. You go right ahead." Chris wasn't about to provide free labor or a free show.

Max shrugged, hefted the ax again, and brought the head down. The wood split and tumbled away. Next, he cleaved the halves. Max bent down to collect the split wood. He hugged the pieces and cast an eye on Chris again before depositing the wood on a growing stack ten yards downhill from the blackened fire pit.

Max went to another pile that was covered in a tarp and came back with a bundle of older firewood and kindling. With his arms full of kindling, he kneeled down by the fire pit in his stained work pants.

He seemed to be demonstrating his actions as if he were training Chris for a job. Chris's arms remained crossed, but he watched as Max began building a structure with the small bits of wood.

"Going with the teepee or log-cabin method?" Chris wasn't an experienced camper, but he had seen some survivor shows on TV.

Max handed the kindling to Chris and moved away from the pit.

The kindling was in Chris's hands before he could refuse. *Any idiot can get a fire going.* Chris set his backpack aside and squatted down. He inhaled the stale scent of the black charcoal and started building a teepee. The pieces were too small on one side, and the teepee toppled. "Damn it! Fucking teepee."

"Log cabin," Max said and went back to chopping wood.

This guy isn't exactly a chatterbox, is he? Chris built up a pile of kindling by stacking the pieces over each other in a square. When it was high enough, he said, "You have some newspaper and a lighter or something?"

Max moved to the other side of the fire pit and collected the tan dead grasses. He balled the dried pile into a nest and handed it to Chris.

Chris placed the nest in the center of his log cabin. "You're not going to make me bust a coal here, are you?"

Max fished out a lighter from his pocket, which he tossed to Chris.

Chris lit the ball of dry grass, blew on the flames, and added more grass until he registered the first pops of the kindling. Soon, the fire was licking the whole pile of kindling. Max slid cut logs beside the fire, and it wasn't long till the bigger logs began popping.

Max rolled a large stump over by the fire. "Take a seat if you want."

Chris sat down and gazed at the flames that shifted with the light wind. From this part of the property, he could see the scope of the cleared land. Surrounded by trees and without another property in sight, he couldn't remember ever having been so deep in nature. Sleeping in city parks was one thing, but this was full-on camping, and he'd never done much of that growing up. Aida had said Max had been out in the woods for some time, and Chris could only wonder if he was some sort of hippy type or a redneck—or maybe a mix of both.

"I saw a big moose down the road when Aida..." Chris hesitated. "When she dropped me off."

Max used the chopping block for a seat on the other side of the fire.

"I want to know when I can get out of here." Chris held a poker stick, which he stabbed into the burning logs. Aida hadn't mentioned how long he would have to prove himself here. A week wouldn't be a problem, but after a month, he might just take his chances and hitchhike back to downtown Anchorage.

Max shrugged and watched the fire. "Depends on you. I'm not keeping you here, so if you want to leave, you can go ahead and save us both the trouble. You decide to stay and keep your nose clean, then that's what I'll tell Aida."

Great. "Not a big talker, are you?"

Max shrugged again then wandered over to the truck. He came back with a metal stand, a pot with water, cooking utensils, and a plastic bag filled with vegetables. Once the wood burned hotter and the coals were glowing, he placed the metal grill stand in place and sliced carrots and potatoes, which he dumped into the pot.

Max added some hunks of meat along with a packet of powder, and soon he had a bubbling beef-and-vegetable soup. He whittled something while he waited for the soup to cook.

When Max handed Chris a bowl of soup, he also gave him a crude spoon that he had cut out of the small stick. Chris shook his head. *Just a couple of cavemen out here.* He grabbed the wooden spoon and ate ravenously. The vegetables were soft, and the meat was tender. Thin strips wedged themselves between his teeth. His appetite had definitely returned since he'd gone through his week of hell. Chris slurped the remainder of the bowl and licked his lips.

When Max finished his soup, he dropped his carved spoon in the fire.

Chris did the same. The sun marched against the western treetops.

Max stepped away from the fire, gave Chris his back, unzipped, and peed in the grass. Chris slapped his palm to his forehead and dragged his fingers down his face.

When Max had zipped his pants back up, Chris said, "Aida mentioned you would have a place for me to sleep."

On cue, Max beckoned Chris to follow.

Don't make it be in the truck bed with this hairy mute. Chris gathered his backpack and trailed behind.

Max opened the back of his truck and pointed at the raised body-sized bed frame on the right side of the truck bed. There was a sleeping bag and a pillow waiting to be used. The smell of musk and body odor slipped into Chris's nostrils. *Of course.*

"Where do you sleep?" Chris asked.

Max gestured toward the left side, where there was a wool blanket and a balled-up jacket. "Gave you the only pillow."

Max offering a pillow as if it were a precious thing was laughable. Sleeping this close to Max would be like sleeping in a homeless shelter. "This truck run?"

"It runs." Max's tone and expression remained flat and uninterested.

Chris collected the sleeping bag and the pillow from the bed, opened the driver's-side door to the cab, and tossed them onto the front bench seat. He faced Max, who was still standing at the tailgate. "I don't get to choose a lot here, but I can pick where I sleep."

"Sleep wherever you want, kid." Max waved Chris off and crawled into the truck bed.

Chris detected a hint of disdain in Max's voice. He certainly didn't appreciate being called "kid" either. He closed the door and noted that the keys weren't in the ignition or under the visor. The seats in the back of the cab were buried under more sealed totes, tools, and clothes. There was a subtle odor of oil lingering in the cab.

The truck's suspension squeaked every time Max moved. Sleeping in a truck probably wouldn't seem as bad if he hadn't enjoyed the cushy queen-sized bed at Aida's house. Between getting his ass kicked and getting tossed into the woods with this hermit, Chris hadn't really had a chance to reflect on his situation. He peeled off his ball cap, stuck it in his pack on the floor, and examined his face in the vanity mirror. He picked at the flaking scab on the bridge of his nose and rubbed the cut on his bottom lip with his teeth. He brushed his fingers through his messy ash-brown hair and broke through split ends. *I'm a mess.*

His mood and thoughts had been erratic after withdrawal. Aida had dumped him here because he'd pushed her too far. He'd made promises, and he'd broken her trust. He could admit it now and could practically taste the bitter guilt. He'd fucked up. Exhaustion had pushed him, and he hadn't found the strength to fight back. Sobriety brought back the reality that he was a loser. His blue buddies had covered for him for years, but without them around, he could only see himself for who he was—which, it turned out, was nothing special.

Chris yawned and put the mirror back in place. Max's steady rhythmic breathing rose and fell in the truck bed. He didn't seem to really care whether Chris wanted to stay or leave. He seemed numb to the world and wasn't likely to be an easy read. *I'll see where this goes.* Chris didn't have a lot of options, but for the moment, he had a full belly and a place to sleep—which still beat being homeless in LA. With heavy eyes, Chris curled up in the sleeping bag and gave himself over to sleep.

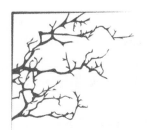

Chapter 14

C hris woke the next morning with the sun pouring through the truck windshield and the sound of water splashing. He peered out the passenger-side window and immediately wrenched his eyes away and covered them with his hand. Max was buck naked and scrubbing himself in the rigged-up shower that fed off the rain barrel.

"This guy doesn't give a shit about anything," Chris muttered to himself. He lay back down and waited for Max to finish. The rain barrel's design was actually pretty ingenious. Max had hung a green tarp to catch rainwater and rigged a hose at the point where the water collected and fed down into the barrel. The shower was primitive, but it worked.

The next time Chris sat up, Max was wearing work pants and another long-sleeved plain T-shirt. Chris watched him in the rearview mirror as he gathered items from the truck bed. Max had crow's feet stamped next to his eyes. He was fit and thin. His arms and chest were lean muscle, and his shoulders were like softballs. Max seemed to share the mentality of an ant, a mindless drone. He strode by with a French press and a few other items in a tote bag and didn't acknowledge Chris watching him.

When Chris came out of the truck, the first thing he reached for was the coffee. It tasted like wet dirt, but he ended up draining several cups. Max had made himself a light breakfast of toast, hard-boiled eggs, and a plastic bag of blueberries. He offered the same spread to Chris.

Chris rested the blue coffee mug down on a stump and watched Max clean the dishes. "I have to shit." Chris made a quick scan of the property. There was the fire pit, the cabin platform, several piles of wood and materials covered with tarps, and the truck. The rest was woods. "Where do I do that?"

"Woods." Max pointed at the surrounding trees. He retrieved a garden trowel with a roll of toilet paper around the handle and passed it to Chris. "Bury it."

"This isn't going to work, man," Chris said, a hard frown bringing his eyebrows closer together.

Max walked toward the platform.

"Come on, talk to me," Chris whined.

Max waved him off and continued to the far side of the platform.

Chris yelled at his back, "I'm not an animal! I'm going to need better than a hole in the woods!" He would have kept yelling, but his body didn't want to wait. He hastily snatched the toilet paper and hand shovel and scrambled off into the trees.

A short while later, Chris came back from the woods, shaking his head and grumbling under his breath. Max put a long-handled shovel into his hands and motioned for him to follow. He led Chris along the back of the property. Whenever a slight breeze swept through, Max paused, put his hand up, then glanced at the cabin platform. He settled on a sparse tree section about a hundred feet away from the cabin site. Then he pointed at the ground.

"You want me to dig here?" Chris asked. "Wait, is this for an outhouse?"

"Yup."

"How deep?" Chris stabbed the grass with the shovel blade, testing the soil.

"Dig a square four feet deep, four feet wide."

"You're going to help me dig, right?" Chris leaned against the long upright handle.

"Nope."

"Fuck that! That's not fair." Chris held Max's listless stare. "I'll dig the hole if you build the outhouse."

"We're both building it."

Chris eyed the woods where he'd had to dig a hole for his previous shit. He didn't enjoy squatting with his bare ass pressed against a tree trunk's rough bark. "Fine, but you'd better be working on that thing while I'm digging." Chris started ripping and tossing grass and soil with the shovel.

Max wandered away, but Chris kept his eye on him as he dug. Max removed a tarp and unveiled sawhorses, a gas generator, ladders, and dozens of boxes of screws, nails, nuts, bolts, power tools, and manual tools sitting on piles of rough-cut lumber and plywood. He set up the sawhorses, and soon the squeal of a circular saw sliced through the air. Max made more cuts, then he used the drill. Chris kept digging, knowing that at least he would have some basic comfort once they'd built the outhouse. While he dug, his tender bruises from the beating nagged, but the annoyance was small. He wiped sweat and welcomed the spitting rain that came for a few minutes. The wooden handle worked his palms tender, but he kept digging. As a kid, he'd helped his dad build and fix things around the yard, but he wasn't used to physical labor.

An hour later, Chris was about done when Max started bringing over some fabricated pieces. Max stopped and inspected the hole.

Still standing in the hole, Chris stabbed the shovel into the hard soil and left it there. He brushed the dirt from his hands. "I'd say it's good."

"Four inches deeper," Max said.

"Yeah, I forgot, because you have measuring sticks for eyes."

Max seemed impervious to the sarcasm and tossed Chris a tape measure that had been clipped to his pocket. Chris checked the hole's depth, which, no matter how he measured, was four inches shy of the four feet Max wanted. Somehow, Max had been able to eye-ball the hole and see that it was four inches short. *Bastard got lucky on that one.*

Max dragged over more pieces of box framework.

When Chris had gotten deep enough, he glanced at his dirty shoes and breathed heavily. "I feel like I just dug my grave. I'm taking a break." Despite feeling dog-tired, he admired the impressive hole that would be able to put up with a lot of shit.

Max pointed at the truck. "Food and water in there."

Chris pushed through the smell of man musk and motor oil inside the truck bed and opened several totes, which stored dried goods, canned food, and basic ingredients. He chewed granola and nuts and sipped from a gallon of drinking water. He found a medical kit and checked to make sure Max wasn't close by before opening it. Inside were the basics and over-the-counter junk. He closed the medical kit up and put it back. He could only wonder what he'd do if he found painkillers in there. Part of him thought he'd be able to say no and stay sober, but he knew there'd be a voice tickling his ears and urging him to just try one.

Under Max's bed, he spotted a polished wooden container no bigger than a lunch box. Chris peeked inside. It was a plastic bag of ashes. "Oh shit." He closed the lid with a clap and returned the box to where he'd found it, double-checking that Max wasn't anywhere close by. Chris would have bet anything that the ashes were Max's wife.

When he finished eating, he ambled back over to the outhouse site. Max had placed a large box made from two-by-fours and plywood inside the hole to shore up the dirt walls and keep them from collapsing. Over the hole, he'd placed a square base of four-by-fours and, on top of that, a layer of plywood for the floor with a space cut at the back.

"That's all there is? I thought it would be more complicated than that."

"Just a box on top of a hole." Max pointed at the wooden two-by-four. "Here, screw this in."

Max held the taller support framework while Chris used the drill, or tried to. He stripped his first screw. *Fuck.*

"Put your weight into it next time." Max handed him a hammer to remove it.

Chris removed the screw and pressed down harder with the drill. The rest of the screws zipped into the wood snugly. After they finished the framework, Chris held up the plywood walls, and Max began drilling the pieces to the frame. Max used the gas-powered circular saw to cut the excess. Soon they had three walls with space for a roof to be attached.

They took turns with the power tools. Max continued his strong, quiet act, only speaking when something needed explaining. Chris wondered what was really going on in Max's head. There was something curious about Max—he expressed little emotion and was generally unfazed. Max cared about his work but didn't seem to give a shit at the same time.

They constructed a roof and ventilation then added a door. Inside the outhouse, Chris and Max went to work crafting a seat. Chris stepped back as Max started to cut out the hole for it, but then Max set the jigsaw on the wood. "You do it."

Chris's cuts so far had been rough, but nothing that Max couldn't fix. Chris swallowed and started. He braced his body against the tool and got it going then guided the jig blade in a slow circle. When he finished, he admired his clean cut. Chris turned to see Max's expression, but he was gone.

When Max came back, he cut wood for a seat and handed Chris the power sander. Chris had never used most of the power tools before, but as he used the sander, like the rest of the tools, he got a good feel for what it could do. He'd been watching Max closely. Chris sanded the seat and gave the wood soft curves. Max screwed a stick of wood to a part of the frame and added a toilet paper roll. He rigged a bungee cord so that the door could be clipped closed either from the inside or from behind as a person walked away. They used a junk piece of plywood for a lid to cover the seat and attached it with soft hinges.

When Chris had zipped in the last screw, he let the toilet-seat cover fall. "Done!" He stepped outside and hooked his thumbs in the belt loops of his jeans as he examined their work. It was by no means pretty, but the outhouse appeared sturdy, and he'd be able to test out its functionality the next day. Chris smiled.

Max moved away and stowed all the tools and scraps under the tarps. He offered no sign that he shared Chris's enthusiasm about having an outhouse. Aida had mentioned that Max might not be talkative, but so far, he seemed downright robotic. Chris wondered if he was that way normally or if he was still hung up on losing his wife. Either way, he could have at least shown a bit of gratitude for Chris's help.

When night moved in, Max got a fire going. They reheated the soup from the day before. Chris flexed his raw hands, touching the blisters. He glanced toward the outhouse. "That looks pretty good, doesn't it?"

Max nodded without glancing up from the soup he was stirring.

Chris's eyes were fresh and wide open even though he was exhausted. "Really, I mean we built that in a day. I haven't built... hell, I haven't built anything before. It's easy once you get going. I can start to see designs in my head when I get to thinking about it." He sucked on a splinter in the webbing between his index and middle finger. "No more shitting in the woods for me." He studied Max, who seemed entranced by the fire. "What's your deal, huh? What's your story?"

Max gazed into the flames. According to Aida, Max's wife had died, but that didn't give him an excuse to ignore Chris, especially since he'd clearly let him come here.

Chris kicked the dirt at his feet. "Are you an asshole with everyone or just me?" His voice cracked as he said, "I might as well be alone out here." He glared. "This is fucking bullshit, and you know it!"

Max put a finger to his lips, then he gazed at the sky.

This guy is so damn weird. Chris swept his gaze across the sky. He couldn't recall a night with so many stars. The fire heated his legs, and the sound of the coals popping mixed with the thrum of insects. As he gazed across the stars, he spied the only constellation he knew, the Big Dipper with the North Star, and connected the points to form an image, like an architect filling in the gaps of a blueprint. Chris released a heavy sigh that carried away some of his resentment. A shooting star streaked across to his right. Max was an oddball, but he was also the one who would tell Aida when Chris was ready to go back to Anchorage, which meant Chris would have to learn to deal with him—at least for the moment.

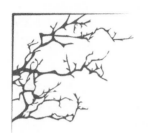

Chapter 15

Max woke and again stared at the white truck cap. He thought of his wife. *How absolute and endless death must be for her.* He wondered if it was lonely in the afterlife—if there even was an afterlife. *No one knows until they know.* The thought of her wandering about some ephemeral black landscape brought a tear to his eye. *Does she miss me as much as I miss her? Why am I making her wait?* Living was a cruel twist of a knife, and his wife was feeling the pain. He needed to find his way back to her. The sound of Chris's snoring drifted into the back of the truck. Being with Julia was more important than babysitting an ex-junkie and keeping promises to Aida. Julia was his everything, and he needed to be with her.

Max collected his clothes and got dressed outside the truck. He hesitated and glanced into the truck cab where Chris slept. Max had placed his keys in plain view on the tailgate. Chris could use the truck once he was gone. Max whispered, "Sorry, kid, but I gotta go."

Chris needed more than Max could offer anyway. Max strode over to the woodpile and gathered a bag with long bolts, nuts, and washers. He hefted an eight-foot four-by-four and collected a drill with a long bit and a wrench. The thought had occurred to him the previous day when they were putting together the outhouse. It was simple. Since he couldn't use any of the tree branches to hang from, he'd simply make his own branch. He could find two trees that were close to each other and connect them with a four-by-four.

He passed the newly constructed outhouse. Chris had been helpful and had figured out quickly how to use the tools. Under someone else's guidance, he might make a good apprentice for one trade or another.

A faint wind disturbed trees and tossed Max's hair about as he entered the grove. It didn't take him long to find two Sitka spruces that were suitable. At about six feet apart, the scaly trunks were both about a foot in diameter. They would be more than adequate. Max dropped the tools and materials and went back to the property. He strode over to the fire pit and removed one of the logs he had used for a seat. He rolled it down the hill toward the woods.

Using the wobbly log as a ladder and reaching as high as he could, he drilled a hole straight through the tree. Then he did the same to the other tree trunk. The drill made some noise, but surrounded by trees, it wouldn't be enough to wake Chris. Max drilled similar holes through the four-by-four and went to work threading bolts through the cut wood and trees then secured the wood with washers and nuts. He studied the beam that extended between the trees. It was overkill if anything. The climbing rope could support his weight and then some, so he wouldn't have to worry about surviving. He tied a hangman's noose and secured the rope around the beam. Using his knife, he sawed through the long tag end and slipped the knife into his pocket. He tested the noose and lifted his weight on the rope for a moment. It held him easily.

Max inhaled deeply and turned his back to his property. He viewed the grove of trees that were part of the dense woods. The smell of spruce needles mingled with rotting bark and fresh grass. The early sun had a clear shot and did its best to warm the earth. He listened to birds chatter as they flitted about, patrolling the forest. Every part of this place fed and contributed to the environment except for him. Working out here on a cabin for his dead wife wasn't helping anyone. He'd resigned his job as a surgeon. It was high time he quit living too.

Perched on the log, Max put the noose around his neck and cinched it tight. The rope wouldn't offer a drop, which meant he'd probably suffer till the end, which was what he deserved. Julia had suffered, and so would he. The rope was coarse against his skin. His heart flapped like a spooked quail. A chill ran across his arms, and goose bumps pimpled his flesh. He could feel sweat under his arms. He was afraid—afraid of the pain and the struggle and the black that would come. His guts chilled, but he knew he needed to go through this to be with Julia.

He glanced down at the log under his feet. *I'm coming, my love.* He kicked the log away. Max's eyes ballooned, and his throat closed as the wind was knocked out of him. The rope dug into his neck. His feet swung, and he struggled and kicked. His neck muscles burned. *No!* His hands grabbed the rope, but he couldn't lift himself above the noose. He clawed at the noose, but it was coiled tightly around his throat like a constrictor. His face cooked, and his vision blurred. He flailed for the beam above him, but it was out of reach.

Then something grabbed him and held him up. *Chris.* The young man wrapped his arms around Max's legs and lifted him, easing the tension off the rope.

"I got you!" His words were muffled against the blood rushing in Max's ears.

Max got two of his fingers under the rope at his throat and sucked in air. He reached into his pocket and brandished his knife.

"Wait, what are you doing?" Chris asked.

Max sliced through the rope. He fell, and Chris went with him. Max hit the ground and rolled over in the grass. He discarded the noose about his neck and lay on his back, breathing in cool air to try to relieve his burning throat. He coughed and wheezed.

"Could have warned me," Chris said.

Max didn't know if Chris meant about cutting the rope or trying to hang himself, but it didn't matter. Air mattered. He needed as much as he could get. "Water," Max said in a raspy voice.

Chris got to his feet and gawked down at him with spooked blue eyes. Even though his thin face was scruffy, he looked so young. His face had the pale complexion of a confused child, complete with a furrowed brow and a dumbstruck open mouth. "You want water?"

Max nodded, which added more gas to the ring of fire in his neck muscles.

Chris started to move away but rushed back. "You're not going to try to kill yourself while I'm gone, right?"

"Water. Now."

"Okay. Don't do it, though." Chris leaned over and grabbed Max's knife, which had been lying on the ground an arm's length away. He said, "Just to make sure," and hurried off.

Max lay there. He'd been so close. Death hurt. He'd gotten a taste, and everything inside him wanted nothing to do with dying. He actually wanted to live, a fact that took him by surprise. *But for what?* He didn't have anything to live for. Max kept breathing. The air cooled his lungs, and his heart started to calm down. *Fuck me.*

Chris came back, and Max tentatively sat up and accepted the gallon of water. The water soothed his throat. "Thank you." Words hurt.

"What the hell was that, man?" Chris's voice was mystified.

"Tried to kill myself." Max massaged his tender neck.

"Yeah, but why?"

"What do you care?"

"Seeing as I'm stuck here with you, I care a lot. You have to tell Aida when I'm ready to go back. If you die, that screws me over too. You going to try that again when I'm not looking?"

"Not today." Max coughed and closed his eyes as he regained his breath.

Chris sat down cross-legged two yards away with his back to a tree. "Good. One day at a time, right? Making some *real* progress here—and I thought I was messed up. Jeez, man. You've got some problems."

Max took another sip and pushed the water aside. He positioned himself supine on the grass. His neck was raw, but he'd gotten his wind back.

Chris said, "I'd just finished christening the outhouse when I heard something in the woods. Then I saw you kicking and hanging there."

Max would have been hanging dead if Chris hadn't acted fast. *Saved by a junkie.* Max's skin was tender, and his muscles were sore. Otherwise, nothing felt broken. There was going to be bruising where the rope had been. He wove his hands together across this stomach and lay with his eyes closed. *What do I have to live for, Jules?*

Chris sat on the stump across from him. "You want to talk about it?"

Max glanced at Chris. He didn't want to use his throat at all. "No."

"I get it. I get it." Chris plucked a blade of grass and split it in half.

"Thanks for doing what you did." Max's voice was raspy, but he needed to let Chris know.

"Hey, no problem." Chris kicked the grass and stared at the beam above them. "I, uh, I nearly died myself back in LA. Took too many pills and woke up choking on my puke. Scary feeling. I remember screaming in my head for help. I didn't want to die. I thought I was done until this housekeeper saved me."

Max had never figured that he and this kid had anything in common. He knew it would hurt, but he spoke anyway. "I thought I wanted to die—didn't realize until I was hanging that I wasn't ready yet. Maybe I need to see this cabin through to the end." Max gingerly got back on his feet. "All I know is that I'm taking today off."

Max lumbered over to the truck. He placed a tote of food and a half-empty jerrican he used for water on the ground for Chris and ducked inside the truck bed, where he opened a couple of cold packs from the medical kit. As he eased himself onto his bed, he positioned the cold packs on his neck and closed his eyes.

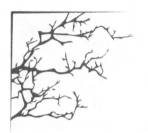

Chapter 16

Chris gathered the tote of food and the water container and sat down by the fire pit. His reaction upon seeing Max hanging there had been so swift that he'd surprised himself. He'd thought Max was strange but harmless up until that morning. The fact that Aida had left Chris alone out in the woods with a depressed head case baffled him. She must have known the guy was at least somewhat unstable.

It was Mom all over again. Chris could remember Mom's glazed eyes after Dad died. She was numbed as if by Novocain and as hollow as a rotten tree. A pharmacy of drugs flowed through her veins. Whenever he came to her bedside, Chris would hug her in hopes that she'd snap out of it, but she was always cold.

Chris wandered over to the cabin's platform. He examined the buried four-by-four posts and ran his hand along the wooden joists. He climbed on top and studied the skeletal platform.

They'd made the outhouse in a day. He wondered how long it would take to build an entire cabin. From this height, Chris could see across the umbrella treetops in all directions and had an unhindered view of the mountains in the distance. Their green slopes were still frosted with patches of snow. Since coming to Alaska, he'd realized how any given view could be a postcard. The beauty was a stark contrast to his old LA life.

Chris went through the boxes and messed around with the various power tools Max had stored under the tarps. He pocketed a small Swiss Army knife and explored the edges of the surrounding woods.

He squared up to a tree and carved "Chris Olson" into the trunk with jagged letters.

The woods were pretty thick, and he didn't want to venture too deep, so after a while, he gave up. Throughout the day, he wandered over to the truck to watch Max's chest rise and fall while he slept. He snacked on food out of boredom and started a fire just to have something to do. When it got late, Max still hadn't emerged from the truck, so Chris doused the fire and went to sleep.

The next morning, Chris woke to the sound of a pan clinking by the fire pit. He spied Max making breakfast. Chris got up and smiled as he headed to the outhouse. He'd almost forgotten how it felt to have a nice solid shit glide out and drop into the abyss. One of his least favorite side effects of painkillers was the constipation.

Chris joined Max by the fire for a breakfast of hard-boiled eggs and canned peaches. "Feeling better today?"

"Yup."

"Want to talk about it?" Chris asked.

"Nope." Max handed a plate of food to Chris.

"Fine by me." Chris chowed down and poured himself some coffee. While Max went about cleaning the dishes, Chris sat there and smelled his shirt and armpits. He smelled like campfire, cut wood, and body odor.

As if on cue, Max came over and handed Chris a towel and a bar of soap on a rope.

"Thanks," Chris said.

"I'm heading to Soldotna to get some supplies," Max replied. "Will be back in a few hours."

"Screw that—I'm coming." Chris set the towel and soap down.

Max squinted at the wood-chopping stump.

"What? I want to check it out." After being bored all the previous day, Chris wanted to see what sorts of towns were close. He was by no means committed to staying on Max's property, so if there was a town close enough, he might take his chances there.

Max shrugged. "Okay."

He strapped bungee cords over loose items in the back of the truck, and Chris sat in the passenger seat while Max drove down the dirt road. The pace was slow. Eventually, the trees they passed thinned, and they traded the dirt road for the rumble of a gravel road. Occasional cabins dotted the area. Some were maintained, while others appeared to be dilapidated. After another five minutes, they came to a stop at the end of the road, which he noted was called Moose Run Road. Max drove the truck on the Sterling Highway, the paved main road where Chris had driven with Aida days before. He thought about her letter and her deception at leaving him there. He didn't like his situation, but he'd have to bide his time in order to prove himself and get back to Anchorage.

They drove the two-lane highway, occasionally passing small communities—a couple of clustered houses or a random store selling wood carvings. Adults and children alike rode four-wheelers parallel to the road. Eventually, Chris saw a sign that said "Welcome to Soldotna" with a fish under the letters, and a town materialized.

Traffic shifted, and Max drove down Main Street. Families stepped out of stores, while grizzled men decked out in hunters' camo congregated outside a hardware store. Everyone wore hats: mesh trucker caps, cowboy hats, and a few lids that looked like Indiana Jones knockoffs. The occasional girl appeared, usually a teen with greasy hair or a rugged woman in worn oversized jeans and a loose shirt.

Max's expression remained flat. He parked in a packed lot of a retail store called Fred Meyer. Once they were inside, Chris wandered away from him. Chris glanced over his shoulder and watched Max push a cart in another direction. He wasn't watching Chris at all. *He doesn't really care if I stay or if I go.*

Chris glanced at the door. *I can just leave.* He doubted Max would try to stop him. His wallet was empty save for a single dollar for snorting and his license. He'd already burned every credit card company. He had to hand it to Aida: she'd left him with very few resources.

Chris wandered the store. People loaded up carts with the usual bullshit, and families and friends chatted across clothing racks and sporting goods. Before Chris realized, he was standing in the pharmacy section. Sweat gathered in his palms and at the nape of his neck. He watched an old man with a gray cane take a stapled bag. The rattle of pills caused Chris to sniff and chew his thumbnail. He thought about following the old guy outside. He envisioned offering to help him to his car, where he'd swipe the bag of pills and take off running. In a town this small, Chris probably wouldn't get far. He'd probably end up getting shot over some beta-blockers or diuretics. He eyed the rows behind the pharmacy counter. He was so close to so many good drugs, but aside from jumping the counter and robbing the place, he was powerless to get to them.

Chris found Max in an aisle, reading the back of a quart of chain oil. Max put the bottle in his cart and kept moving. Chris followed him as he filled the cart with food and supplies.

After Max finished his shopping, they drove back to his property. That night, back in camp, Chris's mind was too occupied for sleep. He tossed about the truck cab. He began fidgeting with knobs and handles. His hand wandered over to the glove compartment. Chris peeked through the tinted window to the back of the truck to make sure Max was asleep. Max's shaggy head remained still, and his breathing stayed even. Chris opened the glove compartment. The pale moonlight revealed a stack of papers, a dead cellphone, and some scattered pens and pencils at the bottom. He leafed through the pages and was about to pull them all out but paused when his finger brushed a pad tucked within the pile. He lifted it out and under the dim light read, "Max Fitwell, MD." *His prescription pad!*

Max's breathing remained steady. Having the pad was good, but the pharmacy probably wouldn't give him narcotics freely. He need Max's DEA registration number, a failsafe to stop people like him from writing fake prescriptions with stolen pads.

Max grunted and shifted in the back seat. He smacked his lips.

Chris froze. Max's breath once again returned to normal.

Chris studied the pad. They usually only used the DEA numbers on narcotic scrips, which meant he could find the number, if he was lucky, by shading over the page. That would work as long as the last scrip Max had written was some kind of narcotic. Chris felt as if he were holding a single scratch ticket.

He grabbed a pencil and slowly shaded the prescription pad. He spotted the outline of Max's signature, a date, a name—Adam Marlowe, the patient—and an order of oxycodone. *Yes!* He was running out of paper, but there at the bottom was a set of letters and the numbers—the DEA number. *I got you, fucker.*

He tore off the shaded page and ripped out several more. He slipped the pad back into the glove compartment and hid the stolen pages in his pillowcase. Chris couldn't believe his luck. He'd been sleeping next to his answer the whole time.

THE NEXT DAY, CHRIS ventured over to Max, who was busy cutting and nailing a plywood floor over the joists and beams of the base of the cabin. After he'd recovered from trying to kill himself, Max had gone back to being an antisocial worker bee. *Time to be buddy-buddy with this guy.* When Chris offered to help, Max handed him a hammer. They worked together until they had a floor they could walk on. When that was finished, they assembled the first piece of outside framework then raised and secured it into place on top of the deck.

"I like this work. It feels good to see this cabin come together." Chris offered a smile.

"Yup." Max eyed the raised frame.

Chris flipped his hammer in the air and caught it on the handle. "Hey, when are we going to head back to town again?"

Max rubbed his beard and offered Chris two fingers.

"Two days?" Chris smothered a smile.

"Try again."

"Two... weeks?" The idea settled like a boulder on his chest.

"That's right," Max said.

That's way too long. "There's got to be more stuff you need. You're building a cabin!" Chris let the hammer drop onto the deck.

Max picked up the hammer and squinted against the midday sun. "Got someplace you need to be?"

"Yeah, Tijuana." Chris stepped down off the deck. "I'm taking a break." He left Max to his work and ambled about the edge of the cleared property. He kicked a young birch and broke some branches off a standing dead spruce. "I can't wait that fucking long."

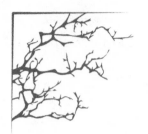

Chapter 17

Chris waited until sunrise the next morning then stole away from the property on foot. He trotted down the dirt road but shortly switched to a fast walk. He was huffing by the time he made it out of the woods and to the Sterling Highway. From time to time, he peeked over his shoulder, wondering if Max might come after him.

After about forty cars passed him, a black truck finally slowed and pulled over. Chris ran to the passenger side. An excited Labrador bumped his nose on the window and pawed the door.

The driver, a man in his forties with sapphire eyes and a shaved scalp, cracked the window. "Where you headed?"

"Soldotna."

"It's pronounced Soul-dot-na. The river's called the Keen-eye... it hurts my ears to hear you out-of-towners butcher it."

"My bad." Chris started to open the door.

"Ah, 'ey, hold on there, slick. There ain't no room in the cab. You can sit in the bed if you want." The man spoke with a drawl.

Chris eyed the grinning guy behind the dog. "Sure." He hopped into the truck bed and sat on a square of particleboard.

As the truck barreled down the highway, Chris patted his pocket, feeling the filled-out prescription paper within. He had copied Max's signature and the DEA number, filled in his own name, and requested thirty oxycodone—not so much that they might not have enough in stock to fill the order, but not so few that he would have to be back in a couple of days to refill. He smiled and embraced the early-morning sunshine. *Today is going to be a good day.*

He got dropped off close to Fred Meyer and weaved through the jam-packed parking lot. He hadn't expected it to be busy this early. The signage at the entrance reminded him that it was Father's Day, which had been an empty holiday at the Olson household after Dad died.

Although the main store was open, the pharmacy wouldn't open for another half hour. Chris ducked into the vacant bathroom. The fluorescent light above him flickered and wavered as he stepped across the sticky tile and in front of the mirror. The trick with pharmacists was to avoid suspicion. He couldn't look like a drug addict. He stripped his hat and the borrowed long-sleeved shirt, set them by the sink, then went to work on grooming himself. He scooped honeyed earwax out of his ears and washed off a layer of dirt, grease, and crusted salt from his face and hands. Using soap from the dispenser and paper towels, he vigorously scrubbed his armpits to mask his body odor.

A heavyset man came in, nodded to Chris, and squared up to a urinal.

Chris patted his pits dry and inspected himself in the mirror. His fingers traced his prominent cheekbones. His cheeks were still hollow, but his skin looked fresh, and his dark facial-hair scruff probably made him fit in more than stick out in Alaska. The shadows under his eyes were much more subtle than they had been—they had almost vanished completely. He couldn't remember the last time his eyes had been so clear. Chris combed his disheveled hair with his fingers and broke through his split ends. *I actually look pretty good.*

His thoughts drifted to Aida's letter. He'd read it several times and could recite the lines from memory. *"This is your last chance, Chris."* He could hear the penned words coming from her as if she'd said them. He'd had a good thing going at Aida's place, but as much as he wanted to blame Frank or Aida, he'd been the problem. *"If you stay clean and out of trouble and prove to Max and me that you can change your ways, then you may return to our house in Anchorage in time."* He didn't think that Aida knew the full extent of how depressed this Max guy was. Max would be dead if Chris hadn't saved him from hanging himself. Chris pitied the guy, but he had his own shit to deal with.

The urinal flushed, and Chris watched through the mirror as the man opted out of washing his hands and left. Chris tapped his pocket that held the forged prescription. Despite being tossed in the middle of the woods, he'd still found a way to score. His little blue buddies waited for him on the other side of that pharmacy counter to bring him back into their warm, numbing embrace. He missed his pills, and the thought of them tugged at his sternum. Sobriety had sharpened his senses, stripping the outer layer of his brain and leaving it raw. Clarity had turned his world sour. The way out was the way back. He'd take his pills, find somewhere to numb out, and just lie there—for days maybe.

Aida's words echoed. *"If you can't handle this, then you're on your own, and you're not welcome back in our home or our lives."* He didn't want to lose the only family he had, yet there he was. He'd already taken a few steps down the road that would lead him back to being a homeless addict sleeping on the ground. Back to choking on his own puke alone in a hotel room. Back to begging for change and chasing pills that were never enough. *This doesn't feel right.*

Aida's letter had ended with "The decision is yours." Chris could practically hear the warning tone in the words. He could feel his heart beat in his throat and throb in his hot ears. He splashed more water on his face and wiped himself dry with the rough paper towels. He spoke to his reflection. "I don't have to do this." The words were his, but getting them out in the open gave him the realization. He slung his shirt back over his head and brushed at the wrinkles. "One last time." His words were like cardboard.

Chris exited the bathroom and made for the pharmacy. There was one customer in line, an old woman in men's work pants and a plaid shirt, with a cloud for hair. The lady chatted it up with the pharmacist behind the counter, a drab-faced middle-aged woman with a bad case of rosacea, wearing a white lab coat and eyeglasses. Chris examined the forged prescription in his hand. If they filled the prescription, he'd still have to pay for it, which meant he'd have to find some items to steal. As busy as the store was, that day would be as good a day as any to shoplift some stuff then return them at customer service.

Chris wiped his damp forehead. This felt like cheating. Back in LA, he'd feared withdrawal, but now that he was clean, he feared sobriety. In the car ride, Aida had said, "Can't run forever, Chris." If she could see him now, she'd probably cut him out of her life completely. *What the hell am I doing here?*

"So that's everything you need, Mrs. Allister." The pharmacist gave the customer ahead of Chris a toothless smile, adjusted her glasses, and interlocked her hands.

"Thank you, dear." The old woman patted the counter then shuffled away, clutching her paper bag.

The pharmacist ushered Chris over. "How can I help you today? That a prescription?"

Chris's damp fingers were softening the prescription paper. "I, yeah. I..." Chris's cheeks became twin oven burners, and he blinked his watery eyes.

"You all right?"

He considered the prescription in his hand and extended the paper over the counter.

The woman eyed him and reached.

Chris withdrew the paper before she could snatch it. "Actually—I'm not going to do this."

"Oh. Okay." Her eyebrows and her voice shot up.

Chris peered beyond the puzzled woman at another pharmacist, who was filling a bottle with pills. "Yeah, sorry."

"No problem, young man. Is there anything I can help you with?"

Chris pursed his lips and shook his head. "You know, I think I'm okay."

"Well, that's good to hear." She snapped a finger and pointed. "Don't forget—today's Father's Day."

"Uh-huh." Chris pictured his dad with his military cut and dimpled chin. In his memories, Dad was always smiling with his gapped teeth. The memories themselves were warm but fuzzy.

Chris wandered away in a daze. *Now what?* His feet became light, and he meandered about the store without a purpose or plan. He passed the mechanical beeps of scanners at the registers, watched families fill heavy carts in the grocery section, and moved through departments.

He strolled the aisles and lingered in the sporting-goods section. A TV display played a short fly-fishing film, and Chris posted himself in front of the screen. The way the fisherman shot the fly line in a tight loop over the water was mesmerizing. The man cast a fly, and an underwater view showed a rainbow trout rise in slow motion and vacuum the fly into its gaping maw.

"You fly-fish?" The employee who asked was a short, rat-faced man who seemed to swim in his clothes.

"Huh? No."

"Oh, you're a spin fisherman?" The man spoke in an upbeat tone.

"I don't really fish."

"Well, you ought to. The Kenai is about the best place in the world to fish for wild trout and salmon. That's why we're so busy right now. The first run of sockeye salmon is here."

"Uh-huh," Chris said. *Get fucked, man.*

The employee turned away from Chris and waved to someone else. "I bet this guy fishes the Kenai, don't you, sir?"

Chris was dumbfounded to see Max, who regarded the salesman for a moment before locking his hard eyes on Chris.

The salesman moved on to another customer.

Max's pressed lips were masked by his beard. He drilled his stare into Chris's head.

How did he find me so fast? Chris stepped backward. He thought about running, but he had nowhere to go from there. He and Max had reached a stalemate, and Chris figured they both knew it.

Max put his hands on his hips. "Left a pretty clear set of tracks to follow to the highway. I figured the pharmacy might be a good place to find an opioid addict."

"I'm over that, man."

Max reached into his back pocket and revealed his prescription pad. He waved it in Chris's face. "Noticed a few pages missing—they number them, you know. I'm retired, kid. Kept the pad around for scrap paper—all it's good for."

Chris's jaw muscles tightened, and he locked eyes with Max. "I told you I'm over it."

Max crossed his arms. "No, you're not. Addiction doesn't just shut off. You'll always be battling it."

"I don't need advice from a suicide case." Chris tasted a growing bitterness in his mouth.

Customers poked about the section, plucking tackle off the wall displays and chatting to associates. Chris and Max stood a yard apart.

Max scratched his neck. "I have my own battles, sure. Some days I wake up, and it's like I have an anchor around my neck. Some days, it's like I'm falling off a cliff." Max sighed and shrugged. "Point is, I—"

"You going to tell Aida about this?" Chris lowered his voice. "If you tell her, I'll tell her you tried to kill yourself." He immediately wished he hadn't said it.

Max shook his head. "You have a lot of growing up to do."

"Screw you, man."

Max sucked his beard into his mouth and smacked his lips. "I'm through chasing around after you. I've got a cabin to build. Now, I could use your help, but I don't necessarily need it. So I'll be waiting in my truck in the parking lot if you want a lift back. If you want to dick around here, then be my guest, and best of luck. I'll tell Aida you left, and we'll be done with it."

"Whatever, man." Chris broke away and left the fishing section behind. He glanced over his shoulder. Max hadn't followed him.

Outside the store, Chris sat on a bench. A couple of minutes later, Max marched past him. He either didn't see Chris or wasn't making an effort to acknowledge him. Max made for his truck in the center of the lot, opened his door, and waited inside.

Several rednecks and wannabe cowboys eyed Chris as they entered the store. The sound of carts and voices collided and mixed with the mechanics and swoosh of automatic doors.

Chris slumped over and put his head between his knees. His baseball hat fell to the ground, where he let it remain. He massaged his scalp with his fingers then scratched with his nails.

Is this really any different from California? He'd sat on benches and had nothing to his name there too. The sun was as warm that day as it would have been in LA. The difference was that there were more people down there. Not that any of them really gave a damn about him. Friends like Jake didn't care about him. That was clear now. No one had been there when he'd been dying in the hotel room except for a spooked housekeeper. The only person who really wanted him around was Aida. It had always been Aida. He needed to fix this, or he'd probably end up trying to kill himself like Max. Like Mom.

"Daddy, why is that man crying? Is he sad?"

It took a second for Chris to realize the little boy was talking about him. Chris wiped his face and sniffed back mucous.

"Ben, that's none of your business."

"But why?" The young boy stopped ten feet away and stared.

"Benjamin." The father ushered his son into the store.

Fifteen minutes later, Chris approached the truck and got in on the passenger side. Max started up the truck and put it into drive. For once, Chris was glad for Max's silence.

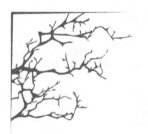

Chapter 18

Max put Soldotna in the rearview and drove along the lonely Sterling Highway with his silent companion. He'd driven that road hundreds of times over the years, and it had usually led him and Julia on some sort of adventure. Now, the road only led him back to his remote property with a messed-up kid who had no right being out there. In Max's peripheral vision, Chris held his cheek and peered out the window, which only offered a paint-stained sky hovering above a standing army of black spruces that seemed to go on forever.

Max yawned. It was a sleepy road most times. He could remember Julia being fast asleep in the same seat Chris now occupied. Julia had had that enviable gift of being able to fall asleep on command, and this road always knocked her out. He pictured how her braids spilled down her shoulders and remembered the earthy smell of her skin. Max could almost hear the sound of her parting lips when she cast smiles his way. He sniffed and blinked rapidly and concentrated on the road, which climbed a bit the closer they got to the mountains. As Max headed down Moose Run Road, Chris crossed his skinny arms and fixed his gaze on his beat-up sneakers.

When Max got back to the property, he parked and ascended the hill. Chris remained in the car, no doubt sulking. Max tapped his pocket and felt the truck keys. Unless Chris knew how to hotwire a truck, he was stuck for the time being.

Max made for the cabin. He'd meant to get a good deal of work done that day, but tracking Chris down had put a kink in that plan. When he'd spotted Chris in the store, he'd felt relieved at first. Instead of grabbing Chris by his neck and hauling him out of the store,

Max had hung back and watched him. Chris had gone to the pharmacy and waited in line. Max had been fuming. Not only had Chris snuck away and gotten the drop on Max, but he'd stolen from his prescription pad. Aida had trusted Max. He'd had to hold himself back while he waited for Chris to hand over the prescription to the pharmacist. Max was dumbfounded when, instead of giving her the prescription, Chis had shaken his head, buried the paper in his pocket, and promptly left.

Chasing Chris down had set Max back a few working hours, and it was nearly noon, which still gave him a good part of the day to work. He took up hammer and nails and promptly started in on a piece of framework. Nails sank into wood and brought structure to what had once been free air. He hadn't been working long before he noticed Chris coming his way. Max continued to toil but stopped when Chris stood below him with a flat expression on his scruffy face. He'd left his black ball cap somewhere, and his disheveled brown hair still held the shape of the hat.

His hands held his skinny hips. "You got an extra hammer?"

Max replayed Chris's words in his mind to be sure he'd understood him. "Yeah, sure. You can use mine. I've got to cut the next few pieces anyhow." He offered the wooden handle down to Chris, who grabbed it and lifted himself on top of the deck.

"I'm just knocking this piece—"

Chris grasped a handful of nails from the container on the deck and shoved them into his jeans pocket. "Yeah, I see what you're doing." He got down on his knees and sank more nails to secure the two-by-four.

Max let Chris be and headed toward the circular saw. "I'll cut the next pieces."

"Yup."

For the next eight days straight, Chris seemed to put his back into the work. He followed Max's directions and helped him piece together the framework for the cabin. Chris's demeanor remained calm and contemplative—and uncharacteristically rigid. He took it upon himself to build and erect a little tool closet closer to the cabin. Two posts held the cabinet above the ground. Plywood doors with hinges opened up to a row of hooks and nails. He organized the tools and hung them. When he finished the cabinet, he wrote "Halfway House" on the front in black marker. It was clever and certainly would save them time by positioning the tools closer to the build. Max wondered why he'd never thought of doing something like that. Chris had a natural talent for carpentry, and an ingenuity that he might not have been aware of came through in his craftsmanship. The sun offered long days in which work was abundant, and they each earned farmer's tans and red necks.

On an overcast morning, Max and Chris munched cereal across from each other at the fire pit. Chris's shoulders were slumped, and he had bags under his eyes. After breakfast, Max headed over to the skeletal cabin. He started in on a piece of framework, and Chris eventually joined him at the other end. Max eyed Chris as he knocked a nail connecting the two-by-fours. He'd nailed the wood together the wrong way. *What's he doing?*

Max came over and yanked the nail out with the claw end of his hammer. "It's supposed to—"

"I don't want to help you build your cabin." Chris dropped his hammer.

"It's not just for me."

Blood filled Chris's cheeks. "I don't want to fucking live here in the woods with you either. I hate it here. Don't you get it? I don't care about this. I'm just biding time till I can leave. Fuck this!" Chris gave Max his back, jumped off the platform, and marched down the hill. He trudged past the outhouse and stalked into the trees with no sign of stopping.

"He'll be back." Max turned back to the deck with a snap of his neck. A quick shot of pain clenched his neck like electricity. He grunted. His muscles had residual hurt from the suicide attempt, a reminder that he could still feel. Max examined the nail still lodged in the claw of the hammer. He loosened the nail and examined the warped curve. The bent metal reminded him of a fishhook. Using the hammer, he tapped the nail against the wood until it straightened back out, a habit he'd gotten from his father—a frugal man who hadn't been one to waste.

Max gazed at the woods Chris had disappeared into, which were now quiet. *Hope he doesn't go and get himself lost out there.* It was only a matter of time before a recovering city kid like Chris would break in this environment. Max knew he wasn't being a good host, but he'd never asked for this burden. He'd wanted solace, even though that had almost proved fatal. He wasn't really sure what he needed. He had the cabin to build, but at some point, that would end. It was probably a good time to find another project. Chris would no doubt prove to be one hell of a rebuild.

Max scratched his beard. His eye stung, so he plucked a few eyelashes then blinked away the blur. He released a long sigh and listened as the wind snaked through the dense wall of trees. He breathed in the scent of spruce needles and soil mixed with the treated wood. Life out here gave importance to the simple things. Chris hadn't quite figured that out yet. He was still busy fighting Max, Aida, and Alaska. Whether he liked it or not, Max was painfully aware at how he owed a debt to Chris. The kid had saved him when he'd been hanging in the grove, so Max owed it to him to try to find common ground.

He rested his hands on his sides and gazed off into the trees. He rolled the nail between his index finger and thumb. "He'll be back."

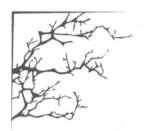

Chapter 19

Chris pushed through brush, and his sneakers popped sticks as he tore deeper into the woods. The light wind cooled his hot skin and rattled the tree branches. After Max had brought him back from Soldotna, he'd made up his mind to fix his attention on working on the cabin to show Aida and Max that he could change. The days were long, and his muscles were sore by the time he crawled back into the truck cab each night. He and Max didn't waste a lot of words as they both settled into their own thoughts and the work. Chris had found himself becoming drone-like, the way Max was, as he focused on the build. It didn't help his mood that he'd slept like shit the previous night. By the time he'd started to really fall asleep, the sun was casting its glare through the truck windshield.

Chris skirted around a pack of spruces. He and Max had made some progress on the cabin, but there was still a lot more to do. He'd probably be hammering the thing together for the next couple of months. And Max was basically getting Chris as free labor for all the long days. Max confronting him about the stupid backward board had been enough to trigger Chris's frustration.

As Chris trudged deeper into the woods, there seemed to be no end. He'd zigzagged so much to get around trees that he wasn't sure which direction he was going or how he'd find his way back.

"Who even gives a shit?" Chris said to the woods, and he kept going. He stepped around fallen trees and circled marsh areas, leaving his sneakers and socks thoroughly soaked. He sloshed through a foot-long creek and weaved between stunted trees. Chris snapped off dead branches and kicked patches of moss. He pushed through the fanning spruce branches and tore off their dangling cones. He kept pushing deeper into the woods while his rage sought a target—Max for making him work and live the way he did or Aida for leaving him there. Then there were his so-called friends, like Jake in California. *Fuck them all.* He broke more branches and plowed through brush.

Chris skidded to a stop at the edge of a grove of moss-covered spruce trees. A man stood in front of him. He pointed a huge revolver at Chris, who raised his hands and froze. Chris's breathing stalled, and his eyelids stretched wide as he stared back at the man, whose expression rippled from a frown to a soft grin within a second of registering Chris.

He holstered the revolver casually. "Sorry. You had me thinking you were a bear or moose charging through the woods like that."

Chris dropped his hands and exhaled. The skinny guy with the gun was in his twenties. He wore sunglasses that sat on a strong nose and wrapped around his lightly bronzed face. Paint-stained jeans were stuffed into brown knee-high boots that matched his T-shirt, which had the outline of a fish across the chest. He had raven hair that spilled down his neck and patches of black stubble smeared above his lips and across his rigid jaw.

"I told you," said a female voice.

Chris noticed a young woman crouching amid a crop of mushrooms. She tilted a cowboy hat up and held his gaze with deep-brown eyes.

"It's fine." His gut constricted, and his rib bones became icicles.

The girl plucked a mushroom out of the wet leaves, dusted off the dirt among the roots, and dropped it into a half-full plastic grocery bag. She pushed off her knees to stand. As she came over, Chris noticed the dark-brown boomerang scar that dug into her right cheek. *How'd she get that?* He shifted his gaze down to her brown boots.

She brushed her palms on her fitted jeans before offering her hand. "I'm Ethel, and this trigger-happy guy"—she nodded at her gun-clad Native companion—"is Roger." Ethel's big toothy smile glowed.

"Chris." He grasped her rough grip. He gave Roger a quick handshake then squared back up with Ethel. "Ethel, huh?" Chris somersaulted the name in his head. It was an ugly name for such a pretty girl.

"Yeah." She chuckled. "I get that face a lot. My parents told me I'd grow into it." She removed her cowgirl hat and brushed her pale forearm across her dark buzz cut before replacing the hat.

Does she have cancer or something? The buzzed hair and scar made her look like a punk-rock chick, but the cowgirl getup and boots didn't fit the part. She was quirky—that much, he could tell.

"What are you doing out here?" Roger asked as he studied Chris.

"I could ask the same for you guys." Chris had no idea if he was still on Max's land, but he figured he ought to defend it regardless.

Roger removed his glasses, and his dark eyes focused. His face hardened, and he tucked in his bottom lip. He hit his chest with his fist and stepped closer. "Oh, I see. Another white man trying to kick the Native off *his* land..."

Chris stepped backward. *Oh shit.* "No, I didn't mean that. It's not even my property—seriously."

Roger burst into raucous laughter and slapped a tree trunk. "Oh shit, his face... priceless." He turned to Ethel and mimicked Chris's shocked expression. Then he gave Chris a smile. "I'm just fucking with you, man." He wiped a tear from his eye. "Never gets old."

Ethel retrieved her plastic bag off the ground and brought it to Chris.

Roger put a hand up in protest. "Hey, don't show him those. It took us a while to find this spot."

Ethel came within a foot of Chris. "Please... he's not here for them."

The caps of the mushrooms in the bag resembled a sort of honeycomb maze. "What kind are they?" he asked.

Ethel, at least six inches shorter than Chris, peered up into his eyes, "Morels. We're hunting mushrooms. Roger's afraid you'll pick them all now that you know our secret spot." She pointed at the spongy-looking fungi that littered the forest floor.

Chris raised his palms. "They're all yours. Unless they're magic mushrooms, I couldn't care less." He smirked.

Ethel tilted her head. "These are better than magic mushrooms. Have you *tried* morels before?"

"Not sure."

Ethel stayed close to Chris. "So if you're not here for the mushrooms, why are you out here?" She glanced at his shoes.

Chris examined his soggy Converse sneakers. "Felt like going for a walk."

Roger rolled his eyes. "Well, that's a load of horse shit."

"Huh." Again, Ethel flashed a row of white teeth. "Where do you live?"

He hooked a thumb over his shoulder. "A little ways back there."

"By the look of you, I would say you're from the lower forty-eight." She winked.

Chris gave her a sideways smile. "California."

"I thought I smelled a touron," Roger said to Ethel and chuckled.

Ethel glanced at Roger with knitted eyebrows. "That's not nice."

"What's a touron?" Chris asked.

Roger wiped his eye with his shirtsleeve. "Touron: a tourist moron. I'm messing with you, man. Don't mind me. Probably just my ADHD talking." He leaned against a tree.

"I guess I live here now," Chris said.

"Have you spent a winter here? You a snowbird?" Roger asked.

Chris eyed Roger. "You've got a name for everything, huh?"

Roger shrugged.

"I've been here for a few weeks," Chris said.

"You here to stay? Where do you work?" Ethel dropped down and gathered another mushroom at the base of a tree. She examined it a few inches from her nose and dropped it into her bag.

"I honestly don't know how long I'll be here." Chris raised his hands and let them drop to his sides. "I'm helping this guy build a cabin back the way I came."

"What's his name?" Ethel asked.

"Max Fitwell. You heard of him?"

Ethel and Roger shook their heads.

"You're better off. He's a weird dude—trust me." Chris smirked and scratched his scruffy jaw.

"What's he charge you for rent?" Ethel asked.

"What?"

Ethel eyeballed Roger. "They have rent in the lower forty-eight, don't they, Roger?"

Is she patronizing me?

"They do—an arm and a leg in the big cities, especially California," Roger said.

"Well, he doesn't charge me rent, but I mean, I sleep in a damn truck."

"How about food? Max charge you for food?" Ethel asked.

Is she taking Max's side? "No, but I mean, it's soup and hard-boiled eggs and shit. Nothing special."

"Nothing special," Ethel repeated.

"I get what you're saying, but I mean, I'm not getting paid."

"The work that you're doing—is he forcing you to do it?" Ethel batted a fly away from her eyes.

"Not exactly." Max hadn't forced him to do anything so far, really, now that he thought about it. Chris had helped with the outhouse simply because he wanted a better place to shit. He'd helped with the cabin to show Max and Aida that he could be useful and change.

Max didn't tell him when or how long to work, and he hadn't forced Chris to do anything.

"Sounds like a decent gig," Ethel said.

She was right. On paper, it wasn't a bad deal, but sleeping in a truck in the woods was still a long way from his room at Aida's. And Max was unsteady at best.

"Well, what do you guys do for work?" Chris asked.

Roger puffed his chest. "I'm a fishing guide. Run a drift boat on the Kenai, and I do walk-ins and fly outs when I'm feeling frisky." He flared his fuzzy eyebrows.

"Now, that's a cool job," Chris said.

"It's hard work," Roger said, "but it's cool. I'll give you that."

"What about you, Ethel?"

She twisted her torso to crack her back. "Horseback-riding guide."

Chris pointed at Ethel. "See? Another cool job."

"It's a cheap way to fulfill my horse obsession." She examined her chipped nail.

"And this is... what? This is how you guys have fun up here?" Chris chuckled.

"It is," Ethel said flatly.

Roger was quick to add, "I mean, we do other stuff, like hunt and fish. Sometimes we go shed hunting."

"Shed hunting?" Chris's warped reflection was mirrored back at him in Roger's sunglasses.

"Moose antlers. They shed them, and if you can find them, they're worth some cash," Roger said.

"What do you do for fun in California?" Ethel asked.

"Well, I mean, there's always a party." Chris tried to think. Everything cost money—money he didn't have. *Pills.* "Beach... I don't know. You can do anything you want down there."

Ethel seemed to be searching Chris's face for more. It had been a while since a girl had shown that much interest in him. Ethel's questions and the way her eyes focused on him were intimidating, but she radiated a heat that he felt in his chest and cheeks. While Roger seemed friendly enough, he was probably more out to entertain himself, but Ethel seemed genuinely interested in what Chris had to say. *I wonder if these two are a thing.* He hoped not.

"You guys go out? Are there even any good bars around here?" Chris asked.

"I used to party, but I gave that life up." Ethel's tone became somber, and she brushed her scarred cheek.

"I work too damn hard to party. A bit of weed at the end of the day, and I'm good." Roger pushed himself off the tree he'd been leaning on and spoke to Ethel. "Let's move on to the blueberries."

"Good idea," she replied.

Chris sensed he was losing his audience, and on top of that, he was lost. It had been too long since he'd hung out with people his own age, and these two were interesting. He felt an urgency to bond with them and to impress Ethel.

"Can I come with you guys?" Chris asked.

"Sure." Ethel stuffed the stray bags in her backpack. "You'd probably die out here without us anyways."

Roger released a short laugh and started leading the way.

"Hey! I can handle myself."

She glanced down at his soaked shoes. "Of course you can." Ethel winked at him.

Chris couldn't remember the last time he had let himself smile so freely. It had probably been the last time he'd been high. He followed Ethel and Roger, who bushwhacked through moss-covered trees until they reached a clearing. They bent over and started collecting blueberries. Chris ate as many as he picked. The juicy morsels popped between his molars, and the sweet mush splattered on his tongue. Even though Ethel had a scar on her face and a buzz cut, Chris found himself drawn to her. The way she filled out her jeans reminded him it had been months since he'd been with a girl. Now that he was clean and sober, his body was telling him that his dick was more than a decoration.

While they filled bags with blueberries, Chris asked Ethel and Roger about themselves. He even ferreted out information about Roger and Ethel's relationship, which was purely one of friendship, although Ethel was quick to remark that Roger had tried to make a move on her once.

Roger stood up for himself. "I would never be able to handle you." He nudged Chris's shoulder. "Horse girls, man. They'll never love any guy as much as those damn horses." He scrunched his face.

Chris chuckled with Roger but secretly was pumped to hear that Ethel was single.

Ethel flashed Roger and Chris a coy grin that didn't reveal much. She stopped picking berries and faced Chris. "So why are you *really* up here in Alaska?"

Although she seemed to be seeing through him, he wanted to make her work for an answer. "Why do you want to know?"

"Because small talk is boring—I do it all day with the riding groups—and I have a feeling you're more interesting than you let on."

"Okay." Chris wasn't sure if she was complimenting him or insulting him. "I guess you can say I partied too much too."

"Alcohol?" Ethel asked.

"Pills. Painkillers." Chris popped a berry in his mouth.

"Are you an addict?"

It was rare to have someone ask so bluntly. There was a stigma to the word. People didn't want to believe that they were addicts... junkies. But he never saw the point in lying, unless it was the cops asking. "I've only really had a problem with painkillers, but yeah, I guess you could call me a former addict. I've recently kicked it."

"Thank you for sharing that with me," Ethel said with sincerity.

"No problem." *Doesn't hurt me any.*

"It takes guts, Chris. Really, I know."

He smiled. While praise from Ethel was amazing, he disagreed with her. It didn't take much to tell her the truth. He'd hidden his habit from Aida when he'd lived in LA, but he never wanted her to worry about him. He wanted to impress Ethel, but he'd learned from past relationships that hiding his habit only led to him getting kicked out, and he'd grown tired of lying.

"Now I'll share something with you," she said.

Roger eyed Ethel.

"I'm a recovering alcoholic." Her tone was subdued.

Chris grunted as he sat down on the dirt and rested his back on a moss-covered fallen tree. He wiped his blue-stained fingers on his jeans then focused on Ethel. "Huh. How long have you been sober?"

"Two years this month."

"Good for you," Chris said.

"Thanks."

Chris eyed the forest canopy. "I still miss the pills—the way they made me feel—or I guess just the way they numbed me out. On pills, I don't have to think about how crappy things are. I can float away." He smiled and sighed. "Now I feel everything." Chris swatted a mosquito away from his face. He watched Ethel squatting down as she picked her blueberry bush clean. He hadn't meant to swing the conversation back to him. "Two years sober. How'd you do it?"

"I fight it every day. I don't like the person I become when I'm drunk. I lose control, and that scares the shit out of me. Scares me enough to stay off the wagon. Plus, I've got friends for support, which probably helps the most." Ethel pointed at Roger.

Roger, who'd been quietly cleaning smudges from his sunglasses, gazed at Ethel. "We all have something."

"When's the last time you had pills?" Ethel asked Chris.

"When I got here. Like I said, it's been a few weeks." It had been years since he could boast that much sobriety. He was clearheaded now that he was sober. Memories of Mom, a few of Dad—he had plenty to want to forget. The pills had made the homelessness easier, giving him an escape from the boredom, but he wasn't homeless anymore. He had a place. He'd fought off his pill craving at the pharmacy, but the desire still remained, sitting in his brain like a glowing coal. He plucked a blueberry from the closest bush, popped it in his mouth, and tasted the mashed paste on his tongue.

Roger ducked behind a tree to pee.

"You should come to a meeting with me sometime," Ethel said.

"What kind of meeting?" Chris crossed his arms.

"Well, technically, it's AA, but we're not too picky."

"No, I think I'm good." Chris spat a blueberry casing out the side of his mouth. She wasn't the first person to ask him to go to meetings. The people working the shelters in LA used to come at him with the same offers. The way they brought it up made him feel as if they were trying to enroll him in a cult or something.

"Are you good?" She sized him up.

"I am." Although he'd never been to a meeting, he'd always pictured AA as a group of emotionally wrecked people. The thought of being trapped in a room full of recovering addicts made him uncomfortable. He had the sense that any person at a meeting would be a minute away from breaking down into a blubbering ball of tears.

"I was waiting for that," Ethel said.

"What are you talking about?" Chris asked.

Roger finished peeing and went back to picking berries.

"Wanted to see what it would take to trigger your defenses." She wiped her stained-blue fingers on a red handkerchief.

She was messing with him. Ethel was clever, probably smarter than him. He was both attracted to and wary of smart women. They had a way of seeing through him. His last girlfriend, Jane, had expected better of him. When she'd found his pills, she hadn't wasted time cutting him loose.

"Okay, no meeting. Hey, maybe I want an excuse to see you again." She grinned, a bit of blue staining her teeth.

Warmth spread through Chris's cheeks. He collected himself. "I'd like to see *you* again."

Roger stood up from his blueberry patch, rolled his eyes, and said, "If you two don't stop, I'm going to wash my mouth out with buckshot over here."

Chris held his smile as they continued the harvest. Soon, between morels and blueberries, Roger's and Ethel's backpacks were stuffed nearly full.

"These are for you." Ethel handed a sealed bag of blueberries to Chris.

"Thanks." Chris's finger brushed hers as he grabbed hold of the bag. "So, we should hang out sometime. You get days off?"

"Days off are kind of rare up here during the summer. My next day off is... next Wednesday. That'll be July second."

"What's today?" Chris asked.

"Monday," she said.

"Great. Okay. Anything in particular?" he asked.

"I'll think of something fun—outdoors, of course." She grinned, the scar curling with her cheek like a parenthesis.

"Sounds good." It had been a while since he'd been that close to a girl. He could feel the heat coming off her neck. He smelled lavender and moss. He could hear her wet lips separate as she smiled. He imagined kissing those lips... touching her pink tongue with his... pressing against her.

"We should get going," Roger said.

"Yeah." Ethel gathered her pack then glanced at Chris. "My truck's parked by the highway. We can give you a lift back to your place. What road is it off?"

"Moose Run Road. You know it?"

"I know it," Roger said.

Chris followed Roger and Ethel through the woods until they reached Ethel's white pickup truck. They tossed their backpacks in the bed. Chris sat in the back while Roger made himself comfortable in the passenger seat. Ethel drove down the highway, and Chris caught sight of his road when Roger pointed.

While Ethel navigated the potholes, Roger made the comment, "Not much out here."

When they arrived, Max approached from the top of the hill. There was a frown on his face as he studied the truck. Chris got out, and Ethel stepped out, too, while Roger stayed in the truck and dropped the passenger seat back to recline.

Max's frown vanished when he locked eyes with Chris, who escorted Ethel over to him.

"So you're Max?" Ethel asked.

"I am."

"I'm Ethel. The guy in the truck is Roger. I guide for Fred's Ranch in Cooper Landing. You know it?"

Max stroked his beard. "I know Fred. Good guy."

"I'm borrowing your helper here next Wednesday."

"Okay." Max's expression was as flat as it ever was.

"Wonderful. Whelp, nice to meet you, Max."

"See you." Max waved goodbye and headed back toward the cabin.

Ethel threw Chris a sly grin and whispered, "He's a peach."

"Oh, yeah. He's the best." Chris rolled his eyes.

"So I'll pick you up at seven in the morning next Wednesday." She got back inside her truck.

Chris put his hands on his hips and smiled. "I'll see you then."

When they were gone, Chris headed toward the cabin.

Max, using a magnet on a string, picked up stray nails hiding in the grass. When Chris approached, Max's eyebrows rose, and he stopped his task. He examined Chris with uncharacteristic curiosity.

"You seem like you want to ask me something. Have something to say?"

Max tucked his lip and shook his head. "Nope."

"Thought so."

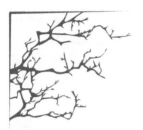

Chapter 20

The next day, after eating breakfast and a few of Ethel's blueberries, Chris watched as Max stalked toward the other side of the property and tossed aside the tarp covering some of the tools. He returned with a long knife dangling from one hand and a small wooden club in the other.

What's he up to? "What's with the knife?" Chris asked. "And is that a police club?"

"Going fishing. You coming?" Max carried on walking to the truck, where he drew out two dark broken-down fishing rods and inspected them.

Fishing? Chris surveyed the quiet property. *Nothing better to do.*

Max drove them down the Sterling Highway until they reached a gas station. He parked the truck. "Let's go inside."

"What for?" Chris asked.

"Need to get you a fishing license."

"Aw, man. I don't need a license. They never check for that sort of thing."

"Yes, you do need one." Max leveled his eyes on Chris. "We take conservation very seriously up here. You won't be poaching on my watch." He spoke slowly to emphasize the point.

"Well, I don't have any money."

"I'm buying. Let's get this done." Max stepped out of the truck, and Chris followed him into the store.

Inside, the old man behind the register and Chris took turns filling out lines on a pad, and in the end, Chris left with his out-of-state fishing license for the year. With that task finished, they got back into the truck, and Max drove until they reached a campground, where he paid the entrance fee and parked in a nearly full parking lot.

Chris watched Max reach under his seat and was dumbfounded when he lifted out a gun, which was in a chest holster. "Jeez, where did that come from?"

Max filled the steel barrel with large rounds. "It's just a tool. Better to be safe than sorry—and I keep the ammunition locked up, so don't get any ideas."

Me, get any ideas? You're the suicide case. "You think that's a good idea? I mean... you did try to... you know, hang yourself."

"Sometimes you make me wonder why I bother talking at all." Max strapped the huge revolver to his chest and tapped the barrel. "Let's get a move on."

The gun was about the same size as the one Roger had pointed at him in the woods—like something to use on an elephant. "Just saying, man."

Max having a gun after trying to hang himself struck Chris as a bad idea. Guns had never been Chris's thing, but after that close encounter with the moose his first day on Max's land, he could see the need. He'd seen signs warning about bears at the fee station, but it was hard to believe that a big grizzly would want to be around a place like this with a full parking lot and a frenzy of rednecks.

Max hefted a backpack and gave one of the two fly-fishing poles to Chris. He offered Chris a pair of brown rubber hip waders too. The floppy boots unfurled to reach his crotch. They seemed like something Captain Morgan would wear.

"You're trying to make me look stupid, right?"

Max's flat lips curled, creating the hint of a smile. He spun away and started hiking down the trail.

Chris stuffed the boots under his armpit, gripped his fishing rod, and hurried to catch up. Twenty minutes later, he said, "How far we walking, man?" He used the side of his hand like a squeegee to wipe sweat from his forehead. He dropped the rod, which clattered on the ground.

Max wasn't winded at all. He was lean and rugged and seemed built for this, while Chris was painfully scrawny and out of shape. Max bent down and gingerly gathered Chris's fly-fishing rod.

I'm fine with not carrying anything.

Max handed a water bottle to Chris, who gulped half the bottle.

Two men appeared farther down the well-maintained trail. They wore chest waders and boots, and as the two burly guys approached, the guy in front offered a "Howdy." The men both grinned and held sticks over their shoulders like hobos, but instead of bags, they each carried three fat silver fish swinging by their gills. The men had guns strapped to their chests as well.

Everybody's packing here.

While they shuffled past, one of them said, "The reds are in. Good luck, boys."

The two men continued on, and Chris eyed Max. "That's what we're fishing for? Red salmon?"

"Yup," Max said.

"I'll tell you right now that I'm probably not very good at this." Chris glanced at Max and then at a fern. He'd been excited at the idea of fishing at first, but now that they were getting closer, his confidence bailed on him. He'd never gone fishing before. It seemed like one of those things a father did with his son, and Chris's dad had never gotten around to taking him before he died in the war. Fishing for the first time as a twenty-one-year-old would probably be like having Max teach him to tie his shoes.

Max shrugged, slid his backpack over his shoulders, and continued on the trail. He led Chris another mile, passing dozens of people. Men and women toted guns, dragged coolers, and clasped fishing gear. Others balanced babies or cradled oversized camera lenses as if they were babies. *Why are so many people out here?*

Chris heard the waterfalls and hurried ahead of Max. When he got to a viewing deck, he leaned over the rail and admired the plunging cascades. The river was probably less than one hundred feet wide here, but the water moved like a car flying through a red light. The rushing water dove over rocks and tumbled down twenty feet or so into several plunge pools, creating a steady roar. His hot skin cooled as the mist drifted off the rushing whitewater and clung to his cheeks and forehead. Chris closed his eyes and tuned in to the sounds of the pounding water. When he opened his eyes, Max was leaning over the rail beside him. Max pointed at a pool below them. Chris squinted. There didn't seem to be anything special, although there were some dark-silver shadows within the glassy water. Then one of the shadows shot out of the pool like a javelin. The salmon glided over an explosion of white froth and stabbed into the water below another waterfall.

"Whoa, that's awesome!" he blurted. Another salmon leapt over a waterfall. The dark back and chrome scales flew through the air and splashed into an angry torrent.

Max touched Chris's shoulder, his disheveled-woodsman face softening. "Let's go."

Chris followed as Max rejoined the trail. Eventually, Max veered away from the main route and traded the open trail for a narrow goat path. Mud and wet rocks made the progress slow, even for Max. Chris skirted around piles of feces stuffed with berries. He asked about it, and without turning around, Max told him that it was from a bear. Chris scanned the dense wet greenery on either side of him. He didn't know much about bears, but he was glad berries were in the poop instead of bones.

Max kept on down the trail, and Chris hurried to catch up to him. At the bottom of a draw, Chris glimpsed the river again, flowing fast over rocks and around fallen trees. He shadowed Max, who ducked around brush and trudged along the muddy path until they reached a small clearing. Max unpacked and set up the fishing gear.

A bald eagle flew through the trees twenty feet above Chris and glided downriver. The eagle reminded him of when he and Aida had watched the two eagles duke it out on the mudflat outside of Anchorage. He kind of wished Aida could see him—constructing a cabin, picking berries with a cute local and a real Native guy, and now hiking through the woods to go fishing for salmon. She might actually be proud of him. If he did end up writing to her, he'd have plenty to say. He seemed to be surprising himself these days. Alaska was a strange place.

Dense green forests lined both sides of the river, but there at the bottom of the small canyon, the bank opened up with enough cleared space for some river access. A silver-haired grandpa in chest waders and a fishing vest was perched on a rock three hundred feet downriver. He concentrated while he swung his fly rod and slapped the water with weights and a fly.

Max showed Chris the rod and rigging—a burly rod and a chunky fly reel wound with yellow fly line and a clear line. The clear line had weights halfway down and a large black hook with red-and-white fly material tied off at the end. Max donned his hip waders and beckoned Chris to follow him out into the water. Chris slipped on his boots and waded into the water. Max made short casts, maybe ten feet out each time. The current grabbed the line and weights and bounced the gear along the river bottom, creating a constant bobbing and ticking of the rod tip.

Chris heard the squeal of a reel and tail slaps downriver and regarded the other fisherman, who was locked in a battle with a salmon. "We should wait to try his spot. There aren't any fish here."

Max pointed at the patch of glassy flowing water in front of them.

"I know, but there's nothing here."

Max produced a pair of sunglasses from his chest pocket and handed them to Chris. He pointed at the water five feet in front of them. "Take a look. You can go ahead and hold on to those glasses too."

When Chris gazed through the lenses, the shine off the water cleared, and he made out the blurred outlines of several gray shapes. "Those are salmon?"

"Yeah." Max cast ahead of the fish. The tackle ticked twice off the bottom, then the line stopped and went tight. Max jerked the rod. The shadowed shape turned, and the light shimmered across the scales on its side. A powerful tail motored the fish thirty feet upstream in two seconds. Max held on to the bent rod. The fish came to the surface and danced over the top of the water, shaking. Max swung the rod tip back to compensate. The drag of the reel whined, and when the fish gave slack, he worked the reel fast to catch up.

Chris marveled at how hard the fish battled and noted Max's concentration as he maneuvered himself and the rod. Max and the fish seemed evenly matched. *There's no way I'm going to be able to do this.*

Max deftly let go of the reel when the salmon made another run. The fish fought for its life but soon started showing fatigue while Max seemed rock steady. Max backpedaled toward shore and steered the salmon out of the fast current and into calmer water. He reeled the line tight, shuffled backward, and beached the fish.

Max moved quickly, dropped to his knee, and locked his hand onto the struggling salmon's tail. Removing the club from his belt, he brained the creature with force.

Chris recoiled and felt his eyes go wide at the sudden violent strikes from Max. The salmon shuddered and went still. Max removed the hook from its lip and made a quick slice with a knife in the gills, bleeding the fish. He put the salmon on blue stringer and secured the rope to a root beside the river. The fish still spasmed in the calm water, but it was most certainly dead.

Chris had understood that they'd be fishing for food, but he'd imagined it to be more civilized. He wondered if he could do this. He eyed Max with a fresh appreciation. *He's really good at this.*

Thanks to the sunglasses, Chris could see a dozen fish swimming right in front of him. His hands trembled. He hadn't experienced this kind of eager anticipation in a long time. His arms were light, but he moved close to Max. "Can I give it a try?"

"Yeah." Max pointed a bloody finger flecked with fish scales toward the rod that rested atop a cluster of wet gray rocks.

Chris grabbed the rod and stepped into the water. He clumsily messed with the yellow fly line on the reel line, which wrapped around the rod tip, while Max sat on a boulder along the shore and watched quietly. *I wish I could do this without an audience.* Chris hastily got the line under control and flipped the gear out into the current. The weights bumped and ticked across the rocks in the bottom. He did this several times. He yanked once but snagged on the bottom and nearly broke the rod trying to get the weights unstuck. Max showed him a technique to get the weights out of a snag by using an upstream angle. Chris resumed flipping, getting a better feel for the line and ready for a hit. He flipped the line about eight feet out. The weights skipped downstream, and the line paused. It went tight, and he jerked the rod straight up. A fish erupted, lunged headlong into the air, and splashed, and before Chris could think of what to do, it had broken the line and swum to the opposite side of the river. *That happened fast!*

He threw up his hand. "No idea what I did wrong there, but it got away."

Chris reeled in the line and examined the broken end. Max came over to him and rigged up a new setup in two minutes. Back in the water, he made a demonstration cast. He flipped it out, and when the line went taut, he set the hook low and to the right, instead of up as Chris had done. Another fish battled for its life. While Max kept the line tight to the fighting salmon, he showed Chris his technique.

"So keep the rod low?" Chris asked.

"Exactly." The fish got airborne then charged into the current.

"And hand off the reel... unless it goes slack, right?" Chris frowned.

"That's right." Max began to work the reel while his slitted eyes seemed to follow the fish.

"I can do that."

Max hauled the salmon in, bonked it, and added the catch to the stringer.

He makes this look easy. "How many can you keep?" Chris asked, staring at the stringer.

Max showed him three bloody fingers. "Three salmon a day per person." He handed Chris the rod.

A fish swam just a few feet in front of him. Chris stepped back toward shore and made a short cast. When he thought his hook was in the right spot, he yanked and felt the hook sink into flesh. The fish swam away, and the reel squealed. Chris glanced at Max, who shook his head.

The salmon was hooked sideways, but remarkably, it swam back to the water in front of him. Chris reeled the slack fast and, with a pull of the rod, dragged the fish in sideways until it flopped on the rocks. *I did it!* The fish flopped and hammered against the bed of rocks. He'd hooked the fish in its pale belly. He couldn't think of what to do next.

Max quickly grabbed the fish.

"Aw, man. I wanted to do that part. Hey! Wait, what are you doing?" Chris protested.

Max had grabbed the salmon by the tail and slid the hook out of its flesh. He was about to return the fish back in the water but twisted back when Chris said, "Aren't we going to keep it?"

"Not legal." Max pointed at the small hole in the salmon's side where the hook had been. "Have to hook it in the mouth in order for it to be legal." He slipped the fish back into the water.

Chris watched the river's current sweep by. "That's stupid. After I fought the fish, tired him out, then dragged him in. Doesn't make any sense."

"Don't count that fish out. Salmon can take a pretty good beating." Max retrieved the bottle of water from his backpack and swallowed a few gulps. He wiped his bearded lips with his forearm. "I can tell by your face that you're not convinced. Listen, I know some of these regulations may seem stupid, but trust me—without Fish and Game regulating these fish... they'd be picked apart by greedy men. I don't make the laws, but I sure as hell follow them. The same goes for you."

Chris sighed and waded back into the river, where he resumed casting. He had to step slowly because the river rocks were all covered in a thin layer of algae, making them as slippery as ice on a windy day. Three salmon swam into his hole, and he cast in front of them. This time, he waited for the line to bump a fish. After a half-dozen flips, the line stopped. He set the hook to the side, and the hook hammered into the fish with a thud. The fish tore away, and Chris kept the rod tip low and sideways. With the hook in the salmon's mouth, he was able to steer the fish. He walked backward in the water toward the bank.

His boot tread slipped on a large flat rock, and he went down. Freezing water filled his mouth and soaked through his T-shirt, waders, and jeans immediately. Chris held on to the rod but was aware of how the line had gone slack. He coughed water while still seated in the frigid shallows. He worked the reel like a madman and brought the rod tip back, relieved when he regained tension in the line. *I still got him!*

He pushed himself up with one hand and fought the fish with the other. "You're not getting away." Waterlogged, Chris scrambled over the rocks and flexed the rod to swing the salmon out of the main current. "No, you don't." Chris reeled and brought the fish back toward shore. He caught the sound of Max shuffling on the rocky shore behind him but kept his eyes on the end of his line, afraid to tear them away for fear of losing his fish.

Chris reeled more slack, and the fish tried to steam away, but Chris put more pressure on the bent rod and fought for every inch. The fish began to tire, and Chris had enough strength to hold on to the wet cork handle and haul the salmon onto the rocks. *I did it!* The silver body and white belly pounded on the dirt, battering itself in mud. "Yeah!" Chris dropped the rod and ran over to his fish. He used the club and hammered it hard on the head several times, which calmed it down. He quickly popped the hook out of its mouth and watched curiously as it went into death spasms on the ground. "I got him, Max." Chris turned and registered the scene behind him.

"Hey, bear! Get out of here, bear! Hey, bear!" Max's gravelly voice rang out. He had his back to Chris as he faced down three grizzly bears that slowly crept down the steep canyon cliffs fifty feet away.

"Holy shit!" Chris stared and felt his mouth go wide as the two bears closest to Max eased their bulk on clawed feet down the rocks. The two bears in front probably weighed three hundred pounds each. The bear behind those two, built like a tractor but covered in thick blond fur, probably pushed seven to eight hundred pounds. Their dark eyes watched, and their snouts pointed toward Max. The bears had somehow managed to sneak up behind Chris and Max and had boxed them in with the river at their backs.

Max gripped the revolver in one hand and waved at the bears as he continued to yell at them. He peeked over his shoulder and yelled,

"Hide the fish, Chris! And don't run. Whatever you do, don't run. They'll chase. Put the fish under a rock—somewhere out of sight."

Chris froze. He searched for a way out and saw the goat trail behind him.

Max glared at Chris. "What are you doing? Hide the fish!"

Chris eyed the three hulking grizzlies that were now about thirty feet away from Max. "Fuck that, man! Let them have the fish. Let's get the hell out of here." Chris's hands trembled, and he started to back away slowly.

Max held his ground and glanced over his shoulder. "Pull your head out of your ass and trust me! Hide the damn fish! Under a rock or something. Quick!"

Chris's soaked feet itched to run, and he wished he could slide himself under a rock. Despite those forces tugging at him, he moved his water-heavy waders, grabbed his dead salmon by the gills, and crept over to the stringer another ten feet down the riverbank. Chris eyed the bears, who were still focused on Max—the gun-wielding man yelling "Hey, bear!" at them like a lunatic. Chris's hands quivered as he hastily turned over a large wet stone and slid the three fish under it.

The two smaller bears had slowed as they investigated Max while the big mama rolled her massive shoulders and kept watch from behind the cubs.

"Hey, bear! Get out of here, bear. Hey, bear!" Max continued to wave his hands. "Come next to me, Chris. We'll try to push them back. If we hold our ground, they should keep away."

Should? You've got to be shitting me. Push them back? With what? A damn bulldozer? Chris had just done the bravest thing he'd ever done by not running, and now Max wanted him to confront three bears in the hopes that they didn't feel like ripping him to pieces? Max truly was crazy.

Chris wasn't about to hand his life over for a nut job. Again, he froze, crouched on the ground a few feet from the river. He eyed the goat trail. He could still make a run for it...

"If we make enough trouble, they'll leave." Max stomped his feet, kept his hands moving, and continued shouting at the three grizzlies.

Chris remained a dozen feet behind Max, crouched low.

The big cubs made grunts and little groaning noises. They seemed curious and playful as their noses wiggled and their eyes searched. They moved their brown bulk and claws over rocks and closer to Max, while the big sow sat back. Her eyes were fixed on Max, and she flapped her lips and made grunts of her own. She moved around a tree and squared her body.

One of the cubs clambered across a downed tree along the river, which brought it about ten feet away from Max. Max stood tall and waved his hands. He continued to yell—his voice became hoarse.

Max wasn't a pushover by any means, but he seemed small compared to the bears. Chris couldn't let him stand alone. He bit his thin bottom lip, swallowed, and got to his feet. He moved slowly toward the closest bear until he was beside Max. "Hey, bear." He got louder. "H-Hey, bear! Get out of here, bear!"

Together, they yelled and waved at the two cubs, who moved nonchalantly toward them while the sow hung behind them, her head low and her lips smacking as she weaved among the trees. The big cubs sauntered closer, and Max and Chris stepped back toward the river, their heels a few feet from the water. Then Max rushed a few steps forward and yelled while stomping the ground. The closest bear shied back and moved downriver along the bank. Max lifted and heaved a large flat rock, which clattered off more stones. He grabbed another rock and did the same. He didn't seem to be aiming to hit the bears but to get close enough to scare or annoy them. The revolver remained glued to his hand, but he seemed reluctant to use it.

"Shoot them or something!" Chris yelled.

"Not unless I have to." Max hurled another rock, and the bear danced out of the way then proceeded to sniff the stone.

Chris started throwing rocks, too, which the cubs chased as if it were a game. The heavy sow faced Max and growled. She traversed the steep incline. Her hulking body and massive shoulders propelled her as she climbed down the shallow canyon and toward the riverbank until she was about fifteen feet away.

The cubs had chased the stones into the water. One gave up and took to swimming in the current. The other cub joined in and bobbed downstream, spewing whining noises. The mama bear swung her blocky head toward the cubs then back to Chris and Max. She looked mean and almost seemed to frown at them as she breathed heavily. She huffed in their direction for a minute before she pointed her snout toward the cubs and nonchalantly gave Max and Chris her wide backside. She trailed the cubs and stepped into the river just a dozen feet downriver of them. The mama twisted her massive head once more toward Max and Chris, then she forded the river with ease. Once she got to the opposite bank, she followed her cubs as they floated downriver.

"Holy shit, man." Chris exhaled and ran his damp hands through his wet hair. "I can't believe that..." He slapped his side and pointed at the three bears. "That just happened!"

Max slipped the revolver back in his chest holster.

Chris remembered the grandpa fisherman. He ran into the river so he could see beyond the stands of trees along the bank. Downriver, he spied the old fisherman, who had moved even farther away. He was wading up to his crotch in the rushing main current and seemed focused on fishing in the water directly in front of him. Chris knew that when you were in the river, the rush of the water muffled other sounds, and at that distance, the old guy wouldn't be able to hear their shouts.

The two bears were still drifting along in the main current, but the fisherman didn't seem aware of them. If they stayed in the current, the bears would inevitably collide with him. "The guy. Hey! Max—the guy!"

Max frowned at Chris and rushed to the water and shaded his eyes as he squinted downriver. He lifted the gun back out of the holster. "Cover your ears."

Chris plunged his fingers into his ears and stepped back.

Max cocked the revolver and shot a round into the sky.

Even through plugged ears, the sound of the gun was a roar, as if the bullet tore through atmosphere on its way to space. The shot echoed through the canyon and beyond.

The old fisherman turned to look at the grizzlies that floated right toward him. He put a hand to his hat and hastily waded back to shore. The bears swam right past where he had been wading seconds before.

Chris unplugged his ears. Max pocketed the spent shell casing and replaced it with another round before he holstered the gun under his jacket.

"Did that really just happen?" Soaked from his fight with the salmon in the frigid water, Chris shivered as a chill swam up his back, and he rubbed the goose bumps that had spread across his arms.

Max uncovered the fish. He added Chris's salmon to the stringer and tied the rope to a tree root by the water. The strung-up fish floated in a small pool at the bank. Max must have noticed Chris watching him, because he said, "It's best to keep them in the water. Keeps them cold and fresh."

Is he really going to just shrug this off? Chris shook his head and gave Max a wry smile. "Yeah, sure, that's great—but how about we talk about our grizzly bear run-in instead?" Chris swung his hand downriver, gesturing toward where he'd last seen the bears.

"They came, we held our ground, and they backed down. Seems like a good result to me."

"That's not what I meant. Why didn't you just give them the salmon? Still have a death wish or something?"

Max closed his eyes briefly. "Okay, sure. So say I did that. We go ahead and feed those bears our salmon, and they leave us alone. Seems fine, right?"

Chris could sense by Max's tone that he was skeptical and out to prove something, but he didn't see Max's point. "Would have saved a hell of a lot of stress, don't you think?"

"Ever hear the expression *A fed bear is a dead bear*?"

Chris furled his lip and shrugged. It didn't seem to make any sense at all.

"If we feed the bears, then they get used to the free meals—they give up working for their food. It's training them to come to us for food instead of hunting and foraging. So they show up to every human they see, expecting to get food. They stop fearing humans. And what happens to all these fed bears that don't fear humans? Huh? Fish and Game comes and airs them out with bullet holes, yeah. This isn't a zoo. These are wild animals, and I don't want to see them all dead. They're important to this place."

The logic settled in. Chris nodded reluctantly. He rubbed his chilled arms. "All right. What do I know? I'm just a city kid."

"It's fine. Now you know, right?" Max's tone became flat again. "Remember when I said the rules and regulations were important? There's also a rule about feeding wildlife." Max moved close to Chris. He elbowed his wet shoulder gently. "Interesting technique, by the way—taking a swim while you fight a salmon." Max offered a wry smile and collected his fishing rod.

Chris rolled his eyes. Max's humor had caught him off guard, but the situation was kind of funny. The whole thing was just ridiculous.

Chris scanned the woods to check for bears. The lush greenery and trees of their small canyon seemed empty and quiet for the moment.

"One more red for me and two more for you. Let's get fishing." Max resumed fishing as if nothing had happened. He hooked a salmon and began another fight.

Chris wrung out his shirt and left it to dry on a rock. It took him an hour to catch another two salmon, but he got his limit.

Max unrolled a black mat from his bag and put his big knife to work. He scanned the river and the surrounding woods. "Whenever you gut and clean fish, be sure to keep your eyes peeled for bears. A lot of the time, that's when they show up."

He demonstrated how to filet the fish. When he finished, he handed the knife to Chris for the next salmon. Chris slid the sharp knife behind the gill and pectoral fin then glided the flat of the blade along the spine.

Two of the fish were females, which Max called *hens*. They were loaded with orange egg sacks, which Max plopped into a mason jar. He bagged the meat and tossed the salmon carcasses back into the river.

Chris frowned at Max as he flung another carved-up salmon into the current. "Won't those attract more bears?"

Max was about to throw another carcass into the river but stopped. "The carcasses are supposed to end up in the river. All the salmon that swim up here will spawn and die."

Chris pointed at the river. "All these salmon are going to die?" The thought had never occurred to him. He didn't remember learning about those kinds of things in school, but they interested him. The fact that the fish were all swimming to their deaths was kind of sad.

"Every single one. Their carcasses are important to the ecosystem. Everything eats them—the gulls, eagles, and bears. The trout eat their flesh and eggs, too, which is why they get so big around here.

Not only that, but the salmon carcasses add nitrogen to the river and the soil on the banks so that the trees and plants grow and the roots hold the banks together."

While Max cleaned the gear and washed his hands in the river, Chris donned his damp shirt and kept an eye out for bears. He was still chilled, but the sun helped keep him warm. Max packed up the fish and the rest of the gear, and Chris collected his rod and hip boots.

As they hiked back, Chris shifted his rod from one hand to the other. "We cooking these up when we get home?" *Did I really just call a truck in the middle of the woods "home"?*

"We'll cook two filets tonight and smoke the rest," Max said.

As he hastened his pace to keep up with Max, Chris said, "Hey, Max? I'm glad you're opening up a bit more."

Max adjusted his pack and was quiet as he followed the trail.

A little before dinnertime, they got back to camp. Max prepared the brine by mixing salt, sugar, and spices and caked it on some of the filets, setting aside the rest for dinner. He put the prepped fish in plastic containers and stowed them in what he called a "zeer pot," which was basically a clay-pot fridge. With cinderblocks and steel grates, Max constructed a chimneylike structure that he claimed was a smoker.

As Max went to work grilling the salmon, Chris asked, "Where did you learn to do all this stuff?"

"My father. I grew up in Alaska."

Chris wiped his palms on the pair of tan work pants Max had given him. "Yeah, but you became a doctor. You didn't live this way when you were working at the hospital with Aida."

Crouching, Max poked at the fish and added another small log to the fire.

"You got a house up around Anchorage?"

"Just north of downtown Anchorage, yeah. I have a house in Eagle River."

Chris had gotten Max to open up a bit, and he was genuinely intrigued by the question of how he'd come to live in the woods. Max had a great life going. Sure, he'd lost his wife, which was sad and all, but he still had a high-paying job and a house, which was a life Chris would have killed for.

"So why do you stay down here?" Chris asked. "You could just work on the cabin on the weekends or, better yet, hire some guys to do it for you."

Max examined his gold wedding band and stood up with the pan of sizzling filets. He set the cooked salmon on a rock to cool and, with a grunt, sat down across from Chris on a stump seat, the murmuring fire between them. "Can't do that. I need to finish the cabin. I'm not putting it off any longer."

Chris gave a long exhalation. "You're just stubborn—but not in a good way. Sometimes you have to know when to just give up and call it a day. Like that ring you keep staring at. Why do you still wear the ring if she's dead?"

"Watch your mouth, kid." The flames lit Max's menacing glare.

Aside from the crackling coals and Chris's heartbeat, the shadowy woods and the property became quiet. Chris sensed again how truly alone they were. There was no denying that Max was a lot stronger than Chris, and if he wanted to, he could overpower him. Chris was no fighter, and his beating in Anchorage by those two cement heads had shown that pretty clearly. Thinking back, he probably shouldn't have brought up Max's dead wife, but it was clearly Max's problem and the reason he'd tried to kill himself. He needed to get over her, but then again, Chris probably wasn't the right person to help. He didn't have the right words or background for any of this.

"I'm sorry. It's just—"

Max got to his feet and stepped over to Chris until he was standing above him, close enough that Chris could smell his musky skin. "You get this straight." Max's tone had bite. "Aida brought you here because you were being a deadbeat druggie. You don't know how good you had it. You've got people who love you. That's not easy to come by. Same goes for Frank. He's as good a man as any I've met, and he's fair."

Chris didn't have to be told why he was there, and he'd been called way worse than a *deadbeat*. Sleeping on the pavement had gifted him with thick skin. Even though Max was angry, it was refreshing to see him show some emotion. Chris didn't want to press his luck, though.

"Let's change the subject. Fishing today was fun. I'd be down for more of that... I might as well get the use out of this license, huh?"

Max's eyes shifted, and he remained awkwardly standing above Chris. He seemed unready to let go of the argument. "Yeah, fine." Max pointed his worn finger at Chris's chest. "Listen, no more talking about my wife. That's off-limits."

"I'll *try*." Chris grinned.

"Jesus, kid, you're practically begging me to kick your ass."

Chris stood up and met Max's stare. "If that makes you feel better, then be my guest, but don't forget who lifted you up when you were dangling from that noose."

Max winced and rubbed his neck as he shifted his gaze to the grove of trees where he'd made the attempt. He looked back at the cooked salmon, which was probably growing cold. "Fish is done. I'm going to bed." Max started off down the hill.

Way to change the subject. "Not going to eat?" Chris asked.

Max said nothing as he headed to the truck bed.

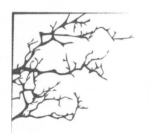

Chapter 21

The next day, Chris woke to the sound of Max sawing wood at the cabin and the smell of smoke and salmon wafting through the cracked window. A cloudy day didn't do much for Chris's motivation, so he lingered in the cab. He examined his hands. They were rough at the pads, and he'd already busted a couple of blisters. He watched Max, who seemed to have fallen back into his typical work-horse self. Ethel had brought up a good point the other day when she asked whether Chris was being forced to work. Chris really didn't have to lift another finger to help Max with his cabin, and Max would probably be happier for it—he needed to stay occupied with work to keep from offing himself.

This Max guy. Chris chewed a nail. Max had probably saved Chris's life with those bears. Chris would never have seen them coming. The bears had overshadowed the fact that he'd caught his first fish—three of them. He wished he'd gotten a picture so he could prove to Aida that he could fish. When Max had gone to bed the night before, Chris devoured the salmon. He didn't even bother with utensils as he ate the filets with his hands, licking each finger clean at the end. The fish tasted good. *Damn good.* Probably the best-tasting food he'd ever had. He'd never really cared much about what he ate, but somehow, those spiced, lemony chunks of seared fish had made him see food as something to be desired. He'd watched Max prepare the fish and figured he could probably replicate the meal from hook to plate if he tried.

Chris peered out the window past his bare feet into the forest beyond their makeshift shower. *There's something about this place.*

Each day on Max's land seemed like a shovelful of dirt that buried his memories that much deeper into the past. He still thought about pills and California. He recalled the nights sleeping on leather couches and the feel of the cheap recliner cushions in a hazy room with the steady buzz of a TV. He could hear the moans from a half-closed door where two of his friends were fucking, his good-night lullaby. He'd walk through parties in a blissful daze, a smile permanently stuck to his face like a refrigerator magnet. Sometimes, he'd meet a girl who wasn't that bad. Sometimes, she'd be almost good enough to set him straight. He chuckled and sighed. *Never* that *good*. Ethel had reminded him how much he missed women. He missed their soft skin and tight bodies. He needed to do something about this dry spell. Now that he was sober and alert, his emotions and urges kept surfacing. He'd already had to sneak out into the woods a couple of nights to jerk off.

Ethel wasn't anything like the past girls he'd been with. She was rougher and called his bullshit. She wasn't classically pretty like the tens that strutted along Hollywood Boulevard, but she had that pixie-in-the-forest kind of thing going for her. The buzz cut and her scarred cheek gave her a sexy edge to match her attitude, and he liked how she was so independent. He'd love to see what she had going on under those clothes.

Chris dug crust out of his eyes and pawed his scruffy beard. He glanced out the window to make sure Max wasn't around. The circular saw squealed from somewhere over the far side of the hill, but Max wasn't visible. Chris dropped the vanity mirror down. The face that frowned back was stranger and grittier than he could ever remember it being. His light-brown facial hair had taken root and spread like brown vines down his neck. A few nose hairs hooked outside his nostrils, but with his expanding mustache and beard, it didn't matter. His tangled brown hair poured over his ears, and his sideburns flared out. Amid all the brambles and dirt-stuffed pores, his eyes struck him the most—they were as white as the foam under a waterfall, with chunks of ice in the middle. They'd been cleansed. Chris glided his tongue over his grease-slick teeth and scratched a tooth, scraping off a smudge of white grime. His rugged appearance made it hard to believe that he used to be a pretty clean kid growing up. He didn't really miss the civilized look that much, and there was something liberating about letting his body do its thing. Chris was interested in seeing how full his beard would get. Still, he needed to at least be clean and not smell like wet socks if he wanted to have a shot with Ethel.

He stepped out of the truck and took a piss. Afterward, he stripped his borrowed clothes, hung them on the truck, and lathered his body with soap. He opened the spigot to the suspended rain barrel and hesitated before stepping under the frigid twist of water. "Oh, ah, ah, oh. Damn, that's cold!" His toes flirted with the wet grass as he danced under the chilled stream. The water splashed, and he wiped the filth from his skin as fast as he could. Then he toweled himself dry, dressed, and climbed the bluff to the fire. He smelled coffee. On the warm concrete blocks of the smoker, he found a cupful in his regular mug. Beside the coffee, in tinfoil, was a crude omelet stuffed with bacon bits and salmon.

There was movement at the far side of the cabin. Max had switched to the steady knock of the hammer.

Chris crumpled the tinfoil after thoroughly eating its contents then sipped the coffee from his log seat. He experienced a pang of guilt, as if he ought to be helping Max by that point. He quickly flung that feeling into the woods. No one could keep up with that man. Chris picked up the French press, topped off his coffee, and sipped from his cup as he viewed the progress of the cabin, which with Chris's help, now had several pieces of raised framework. The steady clap of wood probably meant that Max was putting together another section of framework on the raised platform. He would need Chris's help to lift and erect it—well, not really *need*, but Chris's help would certainly make the work easier. As good a builder as Max was, he could still use an extra pair of hands—or even a few extra pairs. Chris had often thought that a third or fourth guy would speed up the process.

He rinsed his coffee mug, stored it in the truck, and joined Max on the platform. Max squinted in the half-light at him. Chris couldn't think of anything to say, and Max wasn't talking, so Chris found another hammer and stuffed a handful of nails in his pocket. Together, they erected another piece of framework. By noon, they were both slowing down.

"Break?" Chris said.

Max knocked in the nail he'd been hitting till the head sat flush, then he dropped the hammer onto the floorboards. He peered up at the sky. "Sure."

Chris eyed the gray clouds. "I don't think those are rain clouds." When it rained with any sort of gusto, they usually ducked into the truck and waited till it let up.

"I agree." Max put his hands on his hips, his mouth hanging open while he flexed his jaw back and forth. They ate bread and dipped it in hot vegetable soup.

Max's frustration with Chris seemed to have carried over from the previous night. Max *had* taken him fishing, something he didn't have to do, and cooked salmon for Chris. He'd at least made an effort to connect with Chris.

Chris figured he probably should make an effort of his own. "Hey, Max, I'm sorry about last night."

Max studied the concrete smoker.

Chris added more kindling to the conversation. "Sucks to lose somebody, I know. I... well, Aida and I lost both our parents when we were pretty young."

Max got up and added two logs to the smoker's coals. "Thanks for putting the dishes and the food away last night." He shifted the logs into place. "Have to be vigilant with the food, or the animals will start showing up in camp."

"How did she die, man?" Chris asked. He needed to know about Max, but he wasn't really sure why.

Max pinned him with his eyes. "You're really pushing it, kid. Didn't we just do this last night?"

Chris sensed the woods go still as if an invisible weight blanketed the clearing. "Yeah, I tend to do that. I know I talk too much—it's one of my many problems—but I still want to know." Chris cradled the warm soup bowl on his lap with a chunk of bread soaking in the remaining slicks of broth. He extended his palm toward Max. "Getting mad at me isn't going to change that."

Max rubbed his temple and closed his eyes. "It's personal."

Chris scrubbed the last bits of soup with the heel of the bread and chewed with his mouth open. "I get that, but you already know my shit. My sister told you what I'm about. All I know about you is that you were a doctor and you know how to build stuff and live off the grid, but that's not who you really are. That's nothing, really."

"Why do you want to know?" Max asked.

Chris put the bowl down, rested his hands on his knees, and leaned forward. He gestured to the woods around them. "Look around, man. It's just you and me out here. We should at least try to get along. Does it really hurt that much to tell me a bit about yourself? I'll tell you about me. I've got nothing to hide." He let that sink in.

"My name is Max Fitwell, I'm thirty-six years old, I was a doctor—a surgeon—and then my wife died in an accident. We never had kids. Now I'm taking time away to build this cabin."

"Okay," Chris said, "but there's more to you than that, Max."

"What do you want from me, kid?" Max stepped closer to Chris, his pupils more focused than Chris had ever remembered seeing them.

Chris stood up. *What did I want out of this conversation again?* He wasn't sure what had gotten him started. Maybe he'd thought that Max would break down or leave some powerful insight. Instead, he was probably closer to throwing a punch. Chris had to say something to right this ship. "The truth."

Max exhaled through his nose. "I don't know what you are trying to get from this. I don't have a big existential reply for you."

Chris frowned.

"Existential. It means—"

"I know what existential means." Chris was pretty sure it meant *abstract idea* or something like that.

Max sat down and exhaled again, this time through his mouth. His shoulders slumped, and he spoke quietly. "Listen, I needed some time off when she died. So I took a leave. As simple as that."

"How long has it been?" Chris asked.

"A little over a month and a half."

He didn't get many opportunities to talk to Max like this and knew he should keep talking, but he didn't know what else to say. "So how did she die?"

Max's eyes were blurry, and his face became flushed. "I fucked up, okay? I'm to blame. If I could change places with her, I would, but I can't! She's gone, and this is all I've got." Saliva stretched from his lips as his words boomed across the property.

"Okay, okay. I get it." Chris peered at his shoes. Max's tone had shifted from flat to utterly defeated and desperate. He sounded uneasy, like a man on a ledge, and had the look of a kettle dancing on a burner. Chris's heart grew heavy. Max seemed truly broken, the same way his mother had been after Dad died. Chris lost any desire to ask further questions.

Max wiped his forehead with his forearm. He cleared his throat. "If you're through, I want to finish putting the outside framework up today."

Chris released a frown and said, "That's a lot of work." He was glad Max had offered them both a distraction.

"So we'd better stop talking and get to it."

Chris followed Max back to the cabin, and while they worked, he got to wondering how he could ease Max's burden instead of adding to it. Over the next couple of days, Chris wolfed down salmon in exchange for some hours working on Max's cabin. When their salmon supply ran dry, Max drove Chris back to the river, where they each caught three. Once they fileted the salmon, they packed up and hoofed their way back to the truck.

Scanning the thick woods on either side of the trail, Chris asked, "You ever go hunting, Max?"

"Of course," Max replied. "What? You tired of salmon already?"

"Huh? No. It's not that. I've just never shot a gun before. Might be useful, you know?"

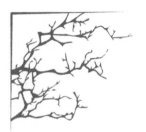

Chapter 22

In the morning, instead of a hammer and nails, Max brandished a rifle in one hand, a shotgun in the other, and a revolver holstered on his chest. To Chris, he seemed ready for war. Max set up tin soup cans on several stumps at the perimeter of the property and taught Chris how to shoot. After some tips, Chris found he could pick off the targets from a good distance with the rifle. The .44 snub-nosed revolver was another story. It was loud and heavy and had a hell of a kick. Almost all his shots missed the mark.

Max kept instructing him to reload the gun. "Have to get used to shooting the .44. If it comes down to it, this could be your last hope with a bear or moose in close quarters."

Yeah, right. Chris was certain that if a bear or moose came at him, he wouldn't have the nerve to point a gun at it, let alone be able to hit the damn thing with the .44. Chris's accuracy eventually improved, and he blew away several targets, but he still enjoyed the feel and accuracy of the rifle. The shotgun was just pure fun. The soup cans didn't stand a chance.

Max handed Chris another handful of shotgun shells.

Chris accepted them, grazing Max's fingers. "When are we going to shoot at something that moves?"

Max plucked out his earplugs. "It's harder to save a life than to take one."

"Who said that?"

"My dad." Max's eyes shifted to the dirt then back to Chris.

"Was your dad a doctor too?"

"Dad was an oil worker, kind of like Frank."

For a second, Chris was unsure which *Frank* Max was referring to. Chris's short stint at Frank and Aida's seemed more distant with each passing day. *I should really write to Aida.* He could still hear the hurt in her words. He'd been a real asshole. Part of it had been the intensity of his withdrawal, but plenty of the blame was on him.

Max pointed at Chris's chest. "The easiest part of hunting is pulling the trigger. The real work begins after you kill the animal." Max spoke low and with gravity. "You never waste meat. If you don't think the game will be retrievable, don't shoot. Maybe it's about to be too dark to see, or maybe the animal will fall off a cliff or run into a pond. Don't shoot. You only take the shot when you are a hundred percent confident that you will be able to take care of that meat. You got that?"

He was clearly laying a boundary, and the logic settled fine with Chris. "Fine by me."

Max said, "I don't believe any of that trophy-hunting nonsense. I hunt for the meat and according to state regulations. There's a Fish and Game regulation book in the truck. I suggest you read it."

"Yeah, yeah. So when are we going?" Chris asked.

"Today we work on the cabin. Tomorrow we get you a license and hunt for dinner."

Chris had found a discarded refrigerator calendar with a cheesy real estate agent's ad slapped on the top. Every night, before he passed out, he crossed off another day on it. His eye always gravitated to the circled date, July 2, on which he'd written, "Date with Ethel. Wake up early. Make it happen."

With six days left till his date, spending one day hunting worked fine for him. "Deal."

Max and Chris spent the afternoon on ladders as they nailed in rows of triangle rafters. Once Chris understood what to expect with each rafter, he and Max fell into a routine.

Chris kept a two-by-four in place for Max. "What are we hunting tomorrow?"

Max held a metal bracket and hammered a nail into the wood. "Snowshoe hares and squirrels are the only things in season right now." Max groped about his pocket for another nail. "How are you feeling?"

He met Max's gaze. Usually, Chris was the one asking questions. "A little tired from today, but fine."

Max nodded, still staring at him.

"You probably meant am I feeling any more withdrawals or cravings and shit, huh?" Chris sighed. "I'll put it this way: I feel much better than when I was in Anchorage."

"How long have you been taking pain meds?"

Chris shifted his hands on the rafter. "At least five years consistently."

Max knocked in another nail then asked, "Why do you take them?"

Chris let go of the wood, which now hung on its own. "I'm not going to make up some bullshit about a hurt back or something like that. They make me feel good. I don't have many things in my life that make me feel as good as the pills do. Being homeless sucks, you know?"

Max eyeballed the row of wooden supports. "I get it."

"That's it, Doc?" Chris frowned and tilted his head to Max. "Not going to condemn me? Tell me that the painkillers make me dependent or addicted? Kill my organs? Fuck up my brain?"

Max rubbed his beard. There were wood shavings still sticking to his scrubby hair. "No point in telling you what you already know."

Max sounded calm. The wrinkles around his eyes seemed to soften while his pupils locked onto Chris. Chris wondered if that was how Max had been before his wife died. He found it hard to see how this rough-cut caveman had been a doctor who went home every night to his wife and house in the burbs, but every now and then, he caught a glimpse of the man that Max had probably once been.

After putting in a full day's work, Chris sat on a stump and nibbled smoked salmon. He examined his sweat-stained shirt. He'd need to wash his clothes in a bucket before bed. He put the food aside and worked at a splinter in the saddle of flesh between his thumb and index finger—one of probably a dozen cuts, slices, and rough patches that littered his hands.

He drank some water and observed the framed building. They'd worked hard to get the cabin to that stage. It reminded him of the skeleton in his high school biology classroom. Soon they would cover it with patches of plywood, as if adding skin to sturdy bones. Max had no specific blueprint or even a drawing to follow. He seemed to know exactly what he was doing. He probably had a photographic memory or something.

Chris sucked a cut on his knuckle. The work wasn't extremely technical, and despite his odd habits, Max seemed to be a pretty intelligent guy. He had to be smart to have been a doctor. Chris wondered how long Max would stay out here and if he'd head back to rebuild his old life after the cabin was finished. He'd probably gone through a lot of schooling to become a doctor. It seemed like a waste for Max to throw all that away.

Chris would never be a doctor. He'd barely squeaked through high school and had been happy to leave academic life in the dirt. Sure, he'd worked some jobs but none that kept him interested. They were always sales jobs. Cell phones, cars, cameras, insurance... it didn't matter what crap he was slinging by the end of the day. He had the smooth approach and welcoming smile needed for sales. Eventually, he'd quit the job over something stupid and blow his savings on pills.

"Going to sleep." The coals popped, and Max glanced at the night sky. "We're leaving early for the hunt tomorrow. We'll be covering a lot of woods, so I'd get some rest. Go ahead and douse the fire when you go to bed."

Chris moved closer to the shrinking pulses of heat that warmed his legs. He gazed at the dark blue above. The clouds had passed, and the stars were unobstructed as they glimmered across his personal skylight.

With his tongue, he probed a flimsy chunk of salmon jammed between his back molars. He thought about the rush that came when he hooked into one of those chrome salmon—the squeal of the line's drag and the splash of the tail churning the water. He faced the pale wooden beams of the cabin bathed in moonlight. There was something about the people he'd met. Max, Roger, Ethel... *They don't give a shit about drugs, and why would they in a place like this?* Again, he scraped the tip of his tongue on the trapped salmon hunk.

He filled a bucket from the rain barrel and came back to the dying fire. He poured the water on the blushing coals, and the fire hissed at him. Smoke and steam plumed, and the light from the fire was snuffed out. Chris stood for a moment, breathing in the last tendrils of smoke and listening to a gust of wind filter through the spruce trees. His tongue found an opening, and he dislodged the fleshy sliver of salmon into his mouth's open space. He gathered the bit on the top of his tongue and launched it into the darkness with a fleeting *thwip*.

Chris smiled and shook his head. "There's something about Alaska."

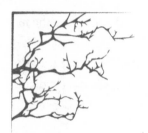

Chapter 23

"For some reason, I didn't think there would be this much hiking." Chris caught his breath and gingerly set the shotgun down against a tree.

Max had woken him at first light with a soft shoulder shake. During the long car ride, Chris had bounced in and out of sleep. By the time Max parked the truck at the edge of a calm forest, the sun was glaring down on him. Max handed Chris the shotgun and set out into the woods. Chris had trailed behind him for four or five miles through young trees and thick brush.

Max put his index finger to his lips and examined the dirt- and moss-covered ground that seemed no different from any other part of the forest. Chris hadn't realized how quiet a person had to be while hunting. That was great for Max, a man who thrived on silence, but Chris needed some chatter.

Max led him along a narrow path, which ran along the base of a ridge, and stopped when he reached the edge of a thicket. Peering through binoculars, Chris scanned the meadow littered with shrubs and thin trees. He focused his rabbit search on sections of the thicket, but after a while, that grew tedious. Aside from a few moths fluttering amid wildflowers, there seemed to be nothing remarkable about the place. With the barrel facing the ground, Chris toyed with the shotgun's safety switch.

Max whispered, "You stay put here." He fixed his gaze on the dense woods bordering the clearing. "Have your gun ready. If a hare comes out, it'll be quick. I'm going to try to rustle some bushes and make noise on their trails to see if I can scare one out into the open."

Max patted his orange vest. "I won't enter the meadow, but I'll yell if I see him heading into your range. Try to get 'em on the first shot in the open, but don't hesitate to take a second or third shot. Holler out to let me know."

Chris agreed to the plan but was fairly certain that they were wasting their time. Aside from a handful of birds, he hadn't seen any wild animals since entering the woods. Max moved off to the left, and Chris stood there, shotgun tilted down, safety off, finger hovering over the trigger. He watched the thicket for movement. Max had vanished into the trees. The warbles of songbirds and the rhythmic chirps and hums of insects were the only sounds. He examined the shotgun in his hands. Something inside him had changed. He'd put on some muscle in his arms, shoulders, and chest. He'd grown stronger and more awake. He'd been clean for longer than he could remember. Chris replayed Aida's words in his mind. *People can change, you know.*

A rapid popping of sticks underfoot sounded from off to the left. He surveyed the field for movement, but the low brush and scrub remained calm.

"Two rabbits coming your way!" Max said in his deep voice.

Chris shouldered the gun and slid his finger on the trigger. A sand-colored body sprang from the woods and, after two hops in the field, stopped and raised its nose to take a sniff.

The barrel exploded, and spray shot through the air. The rabbit flipped, and its white feet and underbelly somersaulted. Another hare came streaking out as well. Chris discharged the smoking shell and reloaded. The smell of gunpowder brushed his lips. The second rabbit booked it out of there like a hot blur. Chris swung the barrel and shot another burst. The shot was well short of the streak of fur that bounded into the thick scrub. *Shit.* Chris hastily discharged the second red shell casing and stared at the spot where the second hare had vanished. Crows cawed and fled their perches on urgent wings.

The second hare was long gone, but Chris could see the white fur of the first one, which still lay where it had fallen. Chris exhaled a shaky breath and yelled, "Got 'em!"

Chris shouldered the shotgun and approached the dead rabbit. Motionless and lying on its side, the snowshoe hare reminded him of a kid's stuffed animal.

Max appeared, dropped a backpack, and unfolded a knife.

"Not bad for a first timer, huh?" Chris stood tall and smiled.

Max wiped some sweat from his brow and smirked. "You did well, kid. You did well."

Chris examined the hare at his feet. A part of him felt a little sad about shooting such a cute animal. On the other hand, he'd already killed several salmon at that point, and a rabbit wasn't really all that different.

Max handed the knife to Chris and showed him how to field dress the rabbit. Chris cut where Max told him to, and he was impressed at how easily the hide separated from the pink skin. It was like unzipping and peeling off a wetsuit. Max demonstrated how to cut away the organs.

Max tossed Chris two bags, one for the pink fleshy body and the other for the hide. "Get enough hides, and you can make a hat. I usually save the fur for fly-fishing material."

Chris remained quiet throughout the whole process, as if he would be disrespecting the dead rabbit by talking. In reality, he understood that, like the salmon, it had simply changed from a living thing to food. He and Max had even used old grocery bags for the meat.

Chris and Max packed up and hiked back to the truck. When they got home, Chris watched Max slice up the rabbit meat and disperse the chunks into a stew with sliced carrots, onions, and potatoes. Max mentioned his desire to set up a garden so he wouldn't have to rely on the vegetables in town.

Chris figured that growing fresh veggies made sense, but it would also mean that Max would have even less time with civilization. Max didn't seem to relish going to town on their food or supply runs, but Chris figured it was healthy for him to at least see other people—even if the interactions were forced.

Chris bit into a chunk of rabbit, and his molar scraped a hard lump. He rolled the lump on his tongue then spat it onto his plate. He picked up the object and examined the tiny metal ball in the fading sunlight.

"Number six shot," Max said in between bites. "Sometimes you can't get it all." Max spat, and a metallic pang rang off his plate as well.

Chris smiled. Max smiled back.

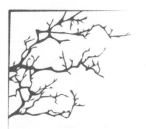

Chapter 24

Wednesday arrived, and Chris waited at the end of the dirt drive for Ethel. Part of him wondered if she would even show up at all. He should have asked for her phone number. He hadn't expected to meet a girl his own age out here in the middle of nowhere. A lot had happened since he'd met her and Roger in the woods that day. She could have easily forgotten that she'd made plans with him. For Chris, this was the day he'd been waiting for, but for Ethel, it was her only day off, and coming all the way out to Max's land wasn't exactly convenient. Still, he hoped she remembered.

The large granite rock next to the drive had a scoop that made for a perfect chair. He sat down in it, breathed the cool morning air, and listened to the forest. A songbird played a fast, high-pitched melody. Another bird chattered a response even deeper in the woods. Chris tried to locate the closer bird among the ferns and moss-covered tree fall, but it was no use. The young forest filled with a mix of soft and hardwoods was like a packed church where limbs spread like hands reaching for God and a space in the sun.

There was a revving sound of an engine in the distance. As the noise grew closer and louder, his heart picked up the pace. Chris leapt off the rock and stared down the road. Ethel's white truck appeared. *She actually came!* Ethel drove until she met him in the road. Chris didn't try to hide his smile as he opened the passenger-side door.

She wore a purple T-shirt, and her fitted jeans were stuffed into brown boots. Her hair—what little there was of it—was freshly buzzed, giving her head a pleasant curve. Her lashes were darker and thicker than before, and a touch of mascara made her brown doe eyes pop. She grinned back at him with her large teeth, the scar on her cheek curving. "Still alive, I see."

"I am. Collected a couple stories too."

Ethel pointed at a thermos in the cup holder. "Hot tea?"

"I already had coffee." He cracked his fingers. "So what are we doing today?"

Ethel swung the truck around and headed back out to the main road. "You'll see."

"Hey, how old are you, by the way? I never asked." Chris imagined her to be older than him.

"Twenty-four."

"Okay, only three years older than me." Chris didn't care much about age when it came to women, but there was a chance that she might care about being too old or too mature.

"Planning our life together, are ya?" Ethel slid him some side-eye and a smirk.

"What? No, come on."

"When you aren't getting embarrassed anymore, I'll stop." Ethel poked his shoulder.

He tried to smother his smile. "It's too early for this. Really, though, what are we going to do today?"

"*You'll see.* Good things come to those who wait."

"You don't know me that well." Chris chuckled. He wasn't exactly the most patient guy. If it were up to him, he'd probably suggest they skip the date and head back to her place. Then again, he didn't want to risk scaring off the one girl who had shown any interest in him.

"Yeah?" Ethel raised one eyebrow.

"Hey, I don't know you that well either, but I'm interested. What about you... are you interested in me?"

"He asks the girl who drove forty-five minutes to pick him up on her only day off..."

Chris rubbed his scruffy jawline. "Good point."

"Here, try these on." She grabbed a brown pair of rubber boots from the back seat, the same brand that Roger had been wearing the other day and that she wore now.

He kicked off his ratty Converse shoes and slipped on the boots. "They fit great—plenty of room. Where'd you get these?"

"Someone left them at my place a while back. They're yours now," Ethel said, keeping her eyes on the road.

"You serious? These are really nice!"

"After seeing you with those wet sneakers out in the woods the other day, it seemed like you could use a pair. They're Xtra Tuffs. They call them the 'Alaskan sneaker.'"

"Thank you, Ethel. That's really nice. I'm serious."

"No problem. They'll come in handy today."

Although she wasn't willing to tell him the plan, he figured they'd probably be doing something quirky along the lines of mushroom hunting. He hadn't noticed any fishing or hunting gear in the car, so he could only wonder at what she had in mind. They went through the small hamlet of Cooper Landing. At the outskirts of town, Ethel drove into a small community at the base of the mountains.

When she reached a tired cabin, she backed her truck up to a trailer with a green raft that sat at the end of the driveway. "This is my friend Leeroy's place." She stepped out, and he followed. Ethel grunted as she lifted the trailer tongue and connected it to her truck ball with a heavy *clunk*.

She's strong. "Ah, so this is what we're doing."

"Uh-huh." Ethel closed the trailer latch and connected some wires.

Chris inspected the raft. He ran his fingers along the thick, rubbery material and grasped the rope that was lashed about the circumference. A set of oars was shoved under a rower's bench. Rafting was yet another thing he'd never done before. He enjoyed wading in the river and fishing, and rafting seemed like yet another badass thing to do in Alaska. And Ethel was proving to be a badass herself. Without Roger around, Chris would probably have plenty of opportunities to make a move, and it seemed like a romantic place for a date.

"Does Leeroy know you're taking his raft?"

She snapped on the safety chains. "It's interesting how your lower-forty-eight side comes out sometimes."

"I mean, anyone could just show up and take it." Chris patted the raft.

"And go where?" Ethel's hands held her sides, and her eyes were focused on his.

"Could sell it."

"To who?" she asked.

"Well—"

"That kind of thing doesn't happen here. We're the biggest state, but there are hardly any roads and even fewer people."

"I guess you're right."

"Let's go," she said.

Back in the truck, with the trailer in tow, Ethel drove him back toward Cooper Landing.

"We're going to row down the Kenai?" Chris asked.

"Ding. Ding. Ding."

Chris grinned and crossed his boots. "Sweet." It made him think of the drift boats he'd seen on the Kenai when Aida had brought him down to Max's about a month earlier. The idea of rowing down that glacial water stirred his heart.

Ethel drove by the turquoise waters of Kenai Lake then back over the bridge, which she explained was *the headwaters*, where the Ke-

nai River began. When they got to a boat launch, Ethel parked at
the top of the ramp. Chris could see how the river stretched at least
the length of a football field across to the opposite bank. The river
moved along at a relaxed pace. In the driver's seat, Ethel waited as a
guy in chest waders dropped his aluminum drift boat into the water.
He slipped the boat off the trailer with practiced ease and guided it
to shore, where a group of people wearing waders and red life vests
waited. The guy secured the boat, got back in his truck, and drove
the empty trailer back up the ramp. He waved at Ethel as he passed
by.

"Know him?" Chris asked.

"Everyone knows everyone here," she said.

Chris had never really known a place like this. The idea of trust-
ing everyone around him and feeling safe felt foreign.

Ethel drove the truck and trailer up the hill a bit then reversed
down the long ramp, her eyes shifting from one rearview mirror to
the other as she worked the steering wheel until the trailer wheels
plunged into the water. She parked the truck and kept it running,
and he hopped out. Chris watched from the ramp as she jumped onto the trailer.

Ethel quickly released the straps. Her hands moved with purpose.

"Can I help?" he asked. She worked so fast and efficiently that he
couldn't see her needing him fumbling about, but he had to ask.

She grabbed the bowline and shoved the raft into the river. Ethel
handed him the bowline. "Pull it up to those rocks. I'll be right
back."

Seeing how calm the water was, Chris didn't have to work hard
to hold onto the raft. He guided it beside the drift boat and watched
as Ethel drove the truck and rattling trailer up the ramp to the parking lot.

The guy with waders and a couple of puffy pink flies stuck to his chest came back and helped load his people into the drift boat. "Okay, Margaret, there you go. Great! All right, everybody comfy? Any allergies or medical stuff I should know about? Last chance at a civilized bathroom. Any takers? Okay. Well, remember—if you pee in your waders, you have to clean them. Trust me, it's happened be-fore." He smirked at Chris, revealing prominent dimples.

Like the family of four on the drift boat, Chris grinned dumbly. The guide was cheesy, but that kind of positive attitude went a long way with people.

"Now, Jimbo already slipped me a hundred bucks to put him on the biggest fish, but if anyone wants to outbid him, well, a guide's wallet is always open." He pushed the boat off the rocks and leapt over the rail, and his hands latched onto the handles of the two black oars. "*Row, row, row your boat, gently down the stream*—too early for singing? Come on, guys. It's a beautiful morning, and we're going fishing!"

Ethel walked down the ramp in her brown boots. She tugged a white spandex long-sleeved shirt out from under her purple T-shirt. Instead of her cowgirl hat, she had slipped on a purple trucker hat. She had an athletic body, and every part of her looked solid. He wanted her for himself. *Why is she single? Is it the scar?* He'd have to try to figure her out.

"What are you staring at?" Ethel asked.

"Just waiting for my fearless guide," Chris said.

"Oh, yeah? Well, step on in, and put on your life vest—it's in the cooler."

"Do I need to?" Chris asked.

Ethel dipped her fingers into the water and flicked droplets to-ward Chris. "The water's coming off a glacier. You wouldn't last five minutes in there."

"Hmm."

Inside the raft, he popped open the cooler and slipped on the vest, which carried a faint odor of mildew, a smell he'd always liked for some reason. Ethel snapped on her own life vest, shoved them off into the river, and sat in the rower's seat. She slid the beefy oars into the locks and began rowing.

The current chugged at a leisurely pace. White origami-like birds that Ethel called *terns* hovered on paper wings and dove to the surface to pluck small, unsuspecting minnows. The subtle splash of the oars dipping in and out of the water blended with the creak of the oarlocks. He spotted an eagle as it landed on a tree on the far bank. To his left, several mountain peaks loomed, while to the right, a ridge ran parallel to the river.

"This was a good plan—great place for a date," Chris said, hoping the word *date* would get her thinking about him in a romantic way.

"I figured we'd cover a good stretch of water today and maybe see some animals. Just wanted to get on the water. It feels so good to not have to take goofy tourists on riding tours."

Chris lay back on his plastic seat and sighed. *Feels great to be out here.* "Do the views ever get old?"

"Sometimes, when I have to worry about money or things get tense at work... that's when I forget. But on days like today—my own time—I see how beautiful my home is." She brought them to the center of the river and slid the oar blades out of the water. "You want to learn how to row or what?"

He rubbed his palms together. "Sure."

She patted the bench beside her. He sat down on it. He caught the whiff of mint from her breath and was close enough to see the stray freckles under her eyes. For a second, he considered making a move—only inches from her lips—but he cast off the feeling. He would wait for the right time. Things were going well, and he didn't want to risk scaring her off.

"Pick up the oars."

He grabbed the heavy oars and manipulated them as if they were giant chopsticks.

"Brace your feet against the cooler." Ethel's voice was soft and calm. "Okay, now we're going to work on back rowing—no, that's front rowing. Yeah, there you go. Don't dip the oars so deep in the water. Small, shallow strokes—whoops, you're going the wrong way. Don't worry, you'll get the muscle memory. Keep going. Bring the handles in closer. Yeah, okay. Now switch and front row. Takes a second to figure it out, huh? We've all been there... okay, there you go. Keep doing that. Don't forget to push with your feet."

He fumbled around the calm river and worked through the awkwardness. Once he got the hang of it, he began propelling the raft farther downriver, where the current moved a little faster. He spun the craft around and toyed with the maneuverability.

"You pick stuff up pretty quick, huh?" Ethel said.

"Well, I wouldn't trust me with any rapids, but yeah, I think I can handle the slow water."

"You'd better take your seat back, then, because there's a class-two rapid coming up soon."

Chris gazed downriver. It still seemed relatively calm, but he was glad to offer up the oars, because in his inexperienced hands, they were heavy and cumbersome. His muscles were inflated and tight but in a good way. He gave up the rower's seat and shifted to the plastic chair closer to the bow. He swiveled to watch Ethel. Her strokes were small, and she deftly guided the raft in the fastest lines of current. He'd always found confident women sexy, and Ethel's take-charge attitude was just another thing that attracted him to her.

Chris spotted several drift boats ahead, anchored in the current, with fly fishermen casting beside them. "Hey, Ethel, don't take this the wrong way, but how come you're single?"

"Hmm, didn't expect that."

"Well, you're pretty and smart and strong..."

Ethel rolled her eyes and avoided looking in his. She fanned her fingers out over the oars as if to push his compliments away. "Okay, okay, enough of that."

"All I'm asking is how come you're not taken."

She frowned and kept her eyes downriver. "I've had boyfriends. And I've dated guys, but none of them worked out."

"Why not?"

"Do you wish they had?" she asked.

"No, I'm glad. I mean to say that I'm glad you're waiting for a good one." He wouldn't consider himself a good one, but he had his moments. He hadn't dated or been in many relationships that lasted, and he was sure none of the women he'd been with would call him a *good one*. He was probably more of a fixer-upper, but some girls liked that about him.

"Who says I want a good one?" She cocked one of her eyebrows.

For a second, he wondered if she was serious, but judging by her slightly sarcastic tone, he bet that she did want a guy to treat her right. "Well, you *deserve* a good one. What do you want?"

She could pretend to have thick bark, but he sensed a softness there. Underneath the haircut, scar, and verbal sparring was a kind and gentle girl. She even had an eagerness about her, as if she was becoming more and more ready to reveal herself to him if he just asked the right questions.

She chuckled. "You're sweeter than you want people to believe, aren't you?"

Chris shrugged.

"I've kind of taken a *siesta* when it comes to dating and love. Getting sober and healthy was my biggest concern the last couple of years. Guess I'm waiting for the right guy... something real." She peered into his eyes for a second then switched her gaze back to the river.

"So, about your hair..." Chris chuckled.

She quit rowing. "I'm not a cancer patient if that's what you're thinking. I shave it with a trimmer. I just... I don't know, I just like my hair this way." She removed her hat and rubbed her hand over her head.

The more Chris gazed at her fuzzy round scalp, the more he thought the haircut actually fit her face. They settled into quiet. Ethel rowed around a drift boat, and they exchanged waves with a boatload of old fly fishermen in cowboy hats who flipped their lines and puffed on cigars while their guide examined a tangled rat's nest of line.

The raft rounded a bend, and Chris spied the rapid—a funnel of water that dropped down several feet in elevation. Ethel guided the raft as the tongue of waves spat water over the lip of the bow. Chris held strongly to the edges of his seat and laughed and whooped as he dodged the icy water. The raft and Ethel handled the waves easily.

The river picked up speed and narrowed, but Ethel seemed at ease at the oars and let the current carry the raft. "Tell me a story, Chris."

"A story? About what?"

"About you."

He rummaged through his brain for a good one, something that would impress her but show that he was a good guy. He kept picturing himself doing drugs at parties, sleeping in shelters, and passing out on beaches. He couldn't think of one story worth telling. Sweat gathered at his hairline.

"How about from your childhood?" she asked.

"Um, I didn't have the best childhood. My dad died in the Iraq War, and my mom... she died later."

"I'm sorry to hear that."

"I'm over it." He hoped he sounded strong and that she wouldn't dig any further. Thinking about sad stories would distract him from the present, which was turning out to be far less depressing.

She toyed with her life-vest zipper. "Any siblings?"

"One older sister, Aida. She lives in Anchorage with her family. She's the one that invited me up here."

"So just you and your sister. Okay, what was it like for you guys growing up?"

He'd try to give her a quick glimpse of his life, and hopefully, it would appease her. "Well..." He shot through the memories. "I'll be honest. After my dad died, my mom kind of gave up too. Aida and my grandmother would try to get my mom through each day, but after a month or so, she... well, she killed herself. I was twelve at the time. Grandma helped out, but she died too. My sister did her best to try to raise me after that, but she wasn't that much older than me. So I spent as much time away from home as I could. I used to hang out at the scrap yard. I'd sit in engineless cars and smashed trucks and read comics or do my homework—although I only did that when I was really bored. I wish I could tell you I had some good stories, but I was kind of an outsider in school—in my family."

"It's okay." Ethel rested the oars under her knees and let the raft drift along in the current. They'd reached a wide stretch of river that moved swiftly but without whitewater, rocks, or any rapids to avoid. Ethel didn't seem concerned about the river. Instead, she seemed fixated on Chris. She smacked her lips. "I've got a story for you. Like you, I also have an older sister. I'm the baby too." Ethel cleared her throat. "So one day, when Glenda and I were kids—yeah, she got a *marvelous* name too. As I was saying, we were eight and ten and playing in the woods close to our home—we lived up north in the interior near Denali back then. We were gathering moss, leaves, and sticks because Glenda wanted to make fairy houses. So while we were out there, Glenda suddenly screamed and dropped the bucket full of twigs and whatnot. When I looked up, six wolves were watching us. We moved to run, but there were more wolves behind us. We were surrounded."

This must be how she got her scar. Chris nodded for her to continue. "What happened?"

She grinned. "Glenda and I climbed a tree and waited until they left."

Guess not. "Jeez... you guys were lucky."

"Yeah, but here's the thing: if the wolves had wanted to attack"—Ethel shook her head—"we would never have gotten the chance to climb the tree. They would have been on top of us before we even knew it. I think they were curious. They watched us while we were in the tree, and we watched them right back. The whole moment was surreal. You could tell just by their eyes that they were intelligent."

"You win," he said.

"It wasn't a contest." Ethel started working the oars again.

Chris eyed the hooked scar on her right cheek. "So do you mind if I ask about your scar?"

"I'm kind of surprised you didn't ask sooner."

"Well, I don't... you know—" Chris stammered.

"I took a wine glass to the face. It tore into my cheek."

"Damn." Chris squinted and drew in a quick breath through clenched teeth.

"I know. I was a mess back then." Her finger traced her scar. "I was twenty-one at the time—same age as you are now."

"How did it happen?"

Ethel eyed the river and put the oars to work. "Well, it happened at a bar... no big surprise there. They said I started a fight with this girl. I still have no idea who she was, but apparently, I grabbed her by the hair. So in the mix of it, she glassed me and took off. Luckily, Roger was there, and he hauled me to the hospital. I don't really remember any specifics."

"That's a rough night," Chris said. Her story made him think of the night he'd nearly died in the hotel room. He might not have a scar to show for it, but the thought of how close he'd come to drowning in his own puke still scared him. The conversation, like the raft, drifted for some time. Ethel gave him facts about the river and showed him eagle nests at the top of huge cottonwoods. Swallows chased bugs across the river's surface like miniature fighter jets. Ethel pointed out a hooded merganser duck with a train of ducklings blending into the sandy cut bank. She let Chris row some more, and he improved. The trick was getting in the right line and knowing when to start rowing away from fallen trees and rocks. They passed by another boat launch and entered a wildlife refuge thick with trees and untouched by roads or buildings.

Ethel rowed around another bend and pointed at a cluster of boats and fishermen along a gravel bar. "See Roger's boat? The black one there at the end."

Sure enough, Roger was knee-deep in the water with his waders and big sunglasses, helping a client with her fishing gear. It was cool to see a familiar face out on the river.

As they drifted by, Ethel yelled, "Hey, Roger, you getting 'em?"

Roger nodded and lowered his glasses. "Is that Chris?"

Chris waved. "Hey, dude."

Roger glided over to his boat and held up a stringer of four fat salmon. "Sockeye slaying today, baby! There are still a few fresh reds left in the run."

Two of the salmon were already blushed with rosy scales and hooked snouts. Max had told him about how the fish transformed the longer they were in the river. Their streamlined chrome bodies changed as they grew closer to death. The males grew prominent humped backs. Their faces turned green, and their bodies flushed red, which gave them their nickname. In their short lives, they were born into the river then matured in the ocean only to return to the same river and the same gravel bar where they were born. With their bodies falling apart, they spent their final days and energy spawning before forfeiting their heartbeats to become part of the river.

Chris had started his own change by moving to Alaska. The homeless addict scraping by for his next bag of pills seemed like a different guy. He'd struggled to let that guy go, and there was no place for him up here. Chris was actually proud of the things he'd done. He'd learned to build, fish, hunt, and use tools, none of which would have seemed possible months earlier but, up in Alaska, had become second nature.

Ethel smirked and rowed away from a fallen log as the current swung them around the next bend and out of sight of the fishermen. "Roger's a good guide. He's got the right personality for it."

"I like him. He's the first Native I've met."

"He's probably not the best ambassador for the Athabascans, but he's a good guy and a *very loyal* friend."

Roger had been there to help Ethel the night she earned her scar, so it didn't surprise Chris to hear her talk about him the way she did. He'd probably been there for her plenty over the years.

Chris dipped his fingers in the frigid turquoise water. "So how are we going to get back?"

"I called a shuttle company when I parked the truck. They brought my truck and trailer to the next boat launch."

"Smart."

"I'm prepared." She maneuvered the raft around a submerged rock.

He needed to do something. Ethel seemed so certain at all times, and he figured it was a good time to throw her off. He moved back to sit next to her on the rower's seat and grabbed her face and kissed her. Her lips were warm, but she cut the kiss short.

"Whoa! Whoa there, cowboy." She snapped her head back. Her eyes were the widest he'd seen them.

"Sorry." *Oh man.*

"I don't—I was not expecting... where did that come from?" Ethel's mouth hung agape, and she blushed.

"That was kind of the point." He scratched the back of his neck.

"Yeah, I get it, but I'm the type of girl that likes to take it slow... I'm still getting to know you."

"Do you like me?" Chris asked.

"I still don't know you that well. We're... what?" She checked her watch. "Just over two hours into our first date."

"Well, get to know me." The boldness started to rebuild inside him.

She pulled over to a gravel bar. They stepped out onto the river rocks, and Ethel hauled the raft safely onto the shore. She came over to him and stopped a couple of feet away. "I'm sorry for overreacting. You just surprised me, Chris. It's been a while since I've been on a date—and I'm clearly rusty."

"I like you, Ethel. I've never met a girl like you. You're beautiful, and hell, I want to kiss you again—like, right now." Something—raw emotion or raw passion—swelled inside him. He wanted to kiss those warm lips again, to hold her. She was unlike any girl he'd ever known. They shared tough pasts, problems that were behind them, that had made them both stronger.

Her eyes searched his face. "I like you too. You're kind of like me." She stepped closer. "It's not that I don't want to kiss you."

Fuck it—I'm going for it. Chris moved in again and brought her close. He had her warm lips again, and this time, she pressed back. She opened her mouth, and they kissed. He kept kissing her, trying to make her see how much he wanted her and how much he wanted her to want him... how good it felt. He was as hard as the rocks under his boots.

He cradled her face and kept her close after their lips separated. There was longing in her eyes. He was almost certain that she wanted this as much as he did.

Ethel tore herself from his grasp. She wandered a few steps away, tapping her fingers to her chin and humming as she strode along the shore. She sat down on the smooth gravel. "I think we should slow this down a bit."

He came over and sat beside her. *What's wrong?* All he wanted to do was tear off her clothes and fuck her brains out right there on the rocks. Now that he was off pills, his horniness had shoved its way to the front of his mind. "Okay, whatever you're comfortable with."

She rubbed her temples and seemed to watch the river slithering past their boots.

"Is something wrong?" Chris asked.

"No. I need some time to think about this."

"I mean, it didn't feel bad to kiss me, did it?" Chris crossed his legs and nudged her with his shoulder.

She smiled. "No, that felt good. *Very* good." She patted him on the shoulder. "You're a good kisser, Chris, although a stick of gum might help your cause."

Chris chuckled. "I live in a truck." He leaned in again and rubbed his nose on hers.

She pecked his lips and quickly backed away. "Last one. Sorry, but I'm the girl. I make the rules."

Chris sighed and tossed a pebble into the river. "Okay."

"Hey, don't feel bad. You're the first guy I've kissed in two years. That's an accomplishment."

Two years sober and two years without a kiss. She wasn't kidding about a long time. No wonder she's so hot and cold. "Yeah, yeah, yeah." He brushed his rough cheek. His beard had reached the scratchy phase.

Across the river, on the opposite bank, a young grizzly bear appeared and honed in on a salmon carcass on its gravel bar. The skittish bear didn't seem to pay either of the humans any mind, and with several hundred feet of swift current between them and it, Chris and Ethel were able to sit and watch the blond bear chew its salmon lunch. When the carcass was picked clean, the young grizzly ducked back into the woods on its side of the river.

Chris glanced at Ethel's brown eyes. "Still seems crazy to me that there are just bears all over this place."

"Yeah, that was a cute little guy. You should see the bears on Kodiak Island—they're huge." Ethel stood and offered her hand. She lifted him easily.

"You're strong."

"Oh, come on. You're not *that* heavy."

She rowed the raft down the river until they reached another boat launch. Chris helped Ethel load the raft onto the trailer and strap it down. She had seemed to regain her confident self, and even though Chris still wanted to hold her close, it was important to show her that he could keep his composure and respect her boundaries. There was a different dynamic now that they had shared a kiss. She wanted to take it slowly, and as much as that was the last thing his body wanted, Chris had plenty of time—he could stick it out. Knowing that Ethel was actually interested in him had given Chris an energy that would help get him through.

Ethel drove him back toward Max's land, and they made small talk until they arrived there. From the passenger seat, Chris scanned the quiet property. The truck was there, but Max must have been on the far side of the property or taking a dump, because he wasn't visible.

Chris pressed his fingers to his red forearm. He'd gotten some color that day. He glanced down at his new boots. "I had a lot of fun today—seriously. I haven't enjoyed myself that much in a long time."

Ethel gave him a brief coy glance. "Same here."

Chris stepped out of the truck and came over to her open driver's-side window. He considered leaning in for a kiss but thought better of it. He'd probably get further with Ethel by showing he could in fact contain himself.

"When can I see you again?" he asked.

Ethel stared at her steering wheel for a moment. Then she faced him. "There's an AA meeting Saturday night. Do you want to go with me?"

He wanted to see her again, but AA... *Is this a trap?* "I'll think about it."

"You'll think about it." Her tone was matter-of-fact.

"Yeah. I mean, I don't know if I want to go to a meeting, but maybe we could hang out on your next day off like we did today."

Ethel started the truck and put it in reverse.

He stepped back. "Hold up. Wait a second!"

The truck whined as Ethel backed out of the drive.

Aw, fuck me. He ran to the truck. "Hey, wait! Wait a second."

"What?" She kept backing away from him with her eyes trained on her side mirror and the trailer. She pressed her lips together, and a frown broke between her eyes.

"Fine. I'll come. I'll come. Jeez."

She stopped the truck with a skid. "Great. I'll be by for you Saturday night. Six o'clock sharp." Ethel put the car in drive and drove away from the property.

Chris caught her looking back at him in her side mirror, smiling. His choice had apparently made her happy. That time, she'd caught *him* by surprise. Ethel wasn't going to make this easy for him. Somehow, she'd gotten him to agree to go to an AA meeting, although the promise of being there with her had been the real bait. Things were changing faster than he had imagined they could. All he could do was roll with it, because he wanted to see her again. He didn't expect a girl like her to be normal, and he sure as hell wasn't normal either.

He found Max standing over a pot at the fire pit. Chris muttered to himself, "No one up here's normal." He stuffed his hands in his pockets and wandered over to see what Max was cooking up.

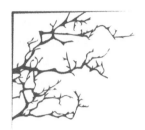

Chapter 25

The next day, Chris and Max grabbed some groceries in town. Chris added a box of mints and deodorant to the cart. Max went to the post office on the way back. He was only inside for a few minutes, and when he came back, he handed Chris an envelope from Aida. Chris had been giving Aida the silent treatment since she'd dropped him off at Max's, but if he knew her, she'd keep reaching out to him even if he didn't reply.

He wanted to read the letter without Max around, so he tucked it into his pants and ignored it until Max had driven back to the property. Then he went to the outhouse and opened the letter. The first thing he found was the picture of Mom and Dad at Christmas—the one he'd thrown at the wall during the worst part of his withdrawal. Chris blinked and sniffed and gingerly stuffed the photo into his jeans pocket, then he began to read the letter.

Dear Chris,

How are you? Shannon is fine, but she misses her uncle. Frank wishes you well from the slope. Is Max treating you okay? He'll mail any letter for you, and I hope I hear back from you soon.

I thought a lot about our last conversation in the car—about when we were kids—and it's hard for me to even remember life in those days. I know Grandma and I were poor substitutes for Mom and Dad. You probably hardly remember Dad.

He did remember his father. The pills had helped Chris cope with the loss of his parents and the sadness that came with it. He could remember the times before Dad was deployed—a Halloween when Dad had dressed up as Frankenstein, or the time he'd shown

Chris how to ride a bike without training wheels, or when he'd chased down the ice cream truck for blocks just so that Chris could get an ice cream sandwich. Those little moments were still in Chris's mind—they'd just been put away in a box for a while, thanks to his little blue buddies.

Chris angled the letter to get more light in the dim outhouse.

He loved you so much, Chris. I remember seeing you guys together. You two were destined to be best buds. I can even remember sometimes getting jealous that you had his attention.

I don't blame Mom for the way she became or for leaving us alone. Losing the love of her life... I think I see it even more now that I have Frank. If anything were to happen to him, I'd fall apart too. I feel that way about you too, Chris. You're my only brother, and I love you. I know you're a good guy—I even see some of Dad in you. To be honest, that's part of why I wanted you to be down there with Max. He needs someone to talk to, and being alone is never good after you lose someone.

Chris used to be mad at Mom, when he was too young to fully understand why she had killed herself. Aida was right. She was always right. Mom had been sad, and sadness had a way of killing good people. Aida was more correct than she even knew. Max did need Chris—he'd be hanging in the woods if Aida hadn't brought Chris to live with him. Max had let the sadness get to him. People fucked up. Good people died. And sadness was a son of a bitch. He knew that.

You had said that I should be mad about how we were raised. I was mad for years. It hurt my relationships with men. He may not seem like it, but Frank is an extremely loving husband and father. He taught me how to love again. I didn't make it easy for him. I used to fight with him, sometimes about the stupidest things. I never told you, but I used to be a cutter—it was my way of dealing with our parents' death. Now, I have to live with the scars. I'm telling you this so you can know that people can change. I did.

The fact that she admitted to cutting surprised him, but he wasn't surprised that she used to hurt herself. He could remember several times in high school when he'd caught Aida pinching her leg in a way that seemed painful. She probably thought no one was watching. She'd been quick to brush it off, but the image of her hurting herself had always stuck with him.

Aida had certainly changed over the years. Change had practically become Chris's motto since leaving LA. He shook his head and studied the plywood walls of the outhouse. "Here I am, reading a letter from my sister in an outhouse that I built in the middle of nowhere, Alaska. Change is an understatement," Chris said out loud.

He squinted to read the rest of the letter.

You're family, and we want to have you close to us but not until you're ready to let your old life go and start anew without drugs and without anger. When you're ready, we'll help you start that new life. That means finding a place and a job, but not until you've proven to us that you're ready.

Max has been keeping me updated on you. He's said some good things—that you're a big help around the cabin and that you are a hard worker. However, I was sad to hear you'd taken off to Soldotna with Max's prescription pad. That was a step in the wrong direction. You've got to prove to us that you're ready, Chris. Make the change—for yourself. I hope you write back to me.

Love,

Aida and your family

"That's bullshit." Chris could feel the back of his neck starting to warm. Max had been keeping tabs on him all along. Chris had always thought it was just Max and him out here. It turned out that Aida might as well have been with them the whole time. With letter in hand, Chris shoved the door to the outhouse open and listened as it snapped back closed behind him. The glare of sunlight hurt his eyes, but he marched up the slope toward Max, who was on a ladder amid the cabin's rafters.

"Hey!" The waves of heat moved to his chest and his legs.

"Something wrong?" Max asked.

Chris's heartbeat quickened as he scrambled onto the deck and approached Max. "Yeah. You. What the hell, man?"

Max frowned. "You're going to need to be more specific."

Chris held the crumpled letter and waved it at Max. "I didn't realize you'd be giving Aida a daily report on me."

Max rested a long bolt on the flat top of the ladder and stepped down two steps. "Calm down."

"Fuck off, man!" Chris unchained his voice. Max needed to know he was pissed.

"Once a week." Max's tone remained steady and deliberate. "I call Aida once a week to let her know you're alive and what you've been up to. That's the extent of it."

Chris's eyes became slits. "Were you planning on telling me about this?"

Max stepped down the ladder to the deck. "Aida told me she would let you know. Sounds like she did in that letter you keep flailing about. We thought you'd be a bit more grown up than this, though. Guess we were wrong."

Chris shoved his index finger in Max's face. "You're an asshole, Max."

If Max felt threatened, he didn't show it.

"What if I tell her you tried to hang yourself, huh? Yeah, they'd probably cart you off to live in a padded room. Serves you right."

Max crossed his arms. "Get that finger out of my face before you lose it."

Chris laughed dryly and didn't back down. "Oh, is that a threat?" His face became hot, and his pulse beat like a boxer working a speed bag.

"A fact."

Chris pushed his finger to the inch between Max's eyes. "What a tough guy you are. You know, I kind of wish I didn't save your life that day." Stirred on, Chris pushed his finger down hard against Max's forehead.

Max had his hands on him before Chris could blink. Chris watched helplessly as his feet left the deck. He fell down hard on his shoulder against the wood. He struggled to get up, but Max was too fast. Chris was pinned down on his belly, and Max had Chris's right arm bent backward behind him. The arm radiated pain.

"Argh."

Max held him down with his weight and with a firm voice said, "Calm down."

"Fuck you."

Max pressed, sending splitting pain from his shoulder up his arm.

"Argh. Okay. Okay—stop!"

"Are you going to listen, Chris?"

"If you let me go."

"I'm going to hold you here for a minute," Max said, "in case you're not getting it. I'm sorry I didn't tell you. I honestly didn't think it would be a big deal. Aida needed to know you were okay, so I agreed to give her a call once a week. What I told her was based on what *you* did. She knows you didn't get drugs at the store, but she knows that you snuck off to find them. She knows that you've been helping me and have been doing some good things too. She cares about you. We should all be so lucky to have someone who cares as much as she does."

"Let me go!"

"I will after I tell you one last thing." Max leaned close to Chris's face.

Chris could feel Max's hot breath touch his ear.

"You can go ahead and tell whoever you want that I tried to kill myself. I won't deny it. Maybe they'll put a psych hold on me. Maybe they'll put me away. Your call, kid."

Max released his grip, and Chris struggled back to his feet. He caught his breath, and he could feel that his cheeks were flushed. He dusted flecks of wood off his shirt. The shoulder that Max had been holding was sore, but otherwise, he wasn't hurt. Max had moved quicker than Chris could even follow. He'd always figured Max was strong, but he'd never expected him to be that fast.

This time, Max pointed at Chris. "And if you put a hand on me again, I'll do more than restrain you."

Chris flung a hand in Max's direction. "I freaking poked you."

Max rested his hands on his hips. "I don't care."

"You going to go call Aida and tell her about this too?"

"Why don't you tell her yourself? She wants to hear from you, Chris. Write her a letter, or give her a call—that way, I don't have to be the middleman anymore."

He'd been planning on writing her back, but he was too bitter to give her or Max the satisfaction.

"What did you expect, Chris? If you want to get back to Anchorage, you're going to have to prove yourself. It's going to take some time, but you know, I actually thought you'd been doing a good job... up until about a minute ago."

Chris didn't know what to say. His anger was fading fast, but he still resented Max for tossing him to the ground. He shouldn't have gotten in the man's face, but he'd felt betrayed.

Max scratched his nose with his knuckles. "I've known Aida much longer than I've known you. She's a good person—too good."

"I know my sister," Chris said with a flat voice.

"So are we good, or do you want to fight some more?"

Chris could get mad, but he was no fighter. The anger and adrenaline had abandoned him, and the wind cooled his clammy skin.

"You know, I could use some help adding these bolts to the rafters." Max hooked his thumb over his shoulder.

Chris released a long sigh and rubbed his forehead. "Fine."

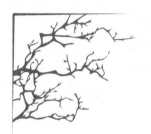

Chapter 26

Chris and Max made slow progress on the cabin the following day, due to the onslaught of pounding rain. Chris still hadn't written Aida back, but he'd been thinking of things to say to her. He figured he would wait until the scuffle with Max had blown over.

The weather improved by Saturday, and Max and Chris were able to put better working hours in on the cabin. Chris cut out early to shower, apply deodorant, and brush his teeth vigorously. When he'd mentioned that he would be going to AA that night with Ethel, Max had appeared taken aback. He'd wished Chris good luck and hadn't said much more about it. Chris figured it would at least be something good for Max to report to Aida, which could help his case. He was at the will of Max when it came to what he told Aida, which meant he would have to be more mindful of his attitude and actions. The situation wasn't ideal, but it was all he had. On the plus side, with Ethel entering his life, things had just started to get interesting.

Chris sat by the fire and rubbed his fingers through his scruffy beard as he waited for Ethel to arrive. Stepping up to go to AA with her would probably help Chris's case with Ethel too. He planned to try to kiss her again, and hopefully, that would lead to more. If all went well, she wouldn't cut him off or push him away. Chris shook his head. *Worrying won't make the grapes grow.*

Ethel arrived, and as they drove away from the cabin, Chris said, "Sorry, I don't have anything nice to wear." He examined his wrinkled jeans and the best long-sleeved shirt in Max's collection. He'd combed his hair with his fingers so that it flowed to the right. A mint dissolved in his gum line. Chris was proud of his beard, which made his small chin seem more pronounced.

Ethel fiddled with the radio dial. "First of all, this is Alaska, the worst-dressed state in the nation. Second of all, recovering addicts are the least judgmental people you'll ever meet. So wear whatever you want as long as it's practical."

"Well, you look nice."

She wore a plaid shirt with a large belt buckle and jeans. Her fuzzy head was visible—her woven straw cowgirl hat was in the back seat.

"I smell like a horse barn—I had a full-day riding tour today. One of the horses stepped on a hornet's nest." She showed off a pink welt on her arm.

Chris leaned in close to her neck and sniffed. She did smell like horse, but she'd tried to cover it with a fresh floral scent. *That's a good sign.*

"Approve, California boy?" She nudged his face away with her shoulder.

"You're all right." Chris paused. "Hey, this isn't going to turn out to be a cult or something, is it?" He'd never been to an AA meeting before, but he'd always imagined them to be sad and awkward. He wondered if any of the people at the meetings had done hard drugs. If they were all alcoholics, they might think he was far worse off than them because he'd fucked around with opioids.

"Yes, Chris." Ethel bulged out her eyes and put on a fake smile. "We want you to come and join us. Drink the punch—it'll make you see the truth!"

Chris gave a dry laugh. "Please don't ever make that face again."

"Scared you, huh?"

"It kind of did."

Ethel steered the truck around a pothole. "Don't worry. I was nervous my first time coming to AA. Think of it as free therapy. You don't have to talk—it's pretty informal. Most people don't say much at their first meeting. Actually, it's nice to have company for once. Roger would never go to one of these with me."

"What do you want to do after?" Chris asked.

"There's a place I want to show you."

"Sounds good to me." Chris reclined in his seat. "Will they care that I'm not an alcoholic? I mean, I'm not saying I don't have a problem, but my thing is more with painkillers than booze, really." Chris scratched the corner of his lip.

Ethel slowed the truck and took her eyes off the road. "Are you worried about this?"

Chris rubbed his damp palms on his jeans. "Nah, I'm good."

"You don't have to say a word if you don't want to," Ethel said. "Trust me."

Ethel parked in front of a drab two-story building. Chris balked once he started walking with her toward the front door. *This doesn't feel right.*

She grabbed his hand. Her hand was rough but her touch delicate. She held him with her gaze just as she'd done the first time they met. "Listen, you don't have to come in if you don't want to. It's pointless for me to force you."

It had been ages since a girl had held his hand affectionately. Her eyes were deep brown with flecks of gold and, like her hand, only offered comfort. He could run—she'd just offered a way out.

Fuck it. Chris started walking again and twisted his fingers until they were laced with Ethel's. "I'm fine, but I hope that what you have planned for later is more fun than this."

Inside, a perfunctory welcome greeted them, and he listened to some loud banter among the clusters of people milling about the white-tiled floor. The place looked like an office break room and had a sharp bleach odor.

Fifteen or so people were gathered, and Ethel introduced Chris to some of the motley group. A few rugged men with beards and beer guts mingled on either side of a heavyset woman with a washed-out blond perm and the biggest boobs he'd ever seen. She introduced herself as Dee and grasped his hand firmly, scraping his skin with her manicured nails.

"Fresh blood!" Dee gave a raspy smoker's laugh, and her smile revealed a missing a molar. "I'm just playing with you, honey. We won't bite. Ain't that right, Ethel?"

Ethel smiled back. "Oh, he knows, Dee."

Dee had the energy and ready laugh that made you want to laugh too. Either her attitude or her planetary tits seemed enough to draw the bulk of the men into her orbit.

After a few minutes, the group took seats in the ring of chairs. Chris sat beside Ethel and made himself small. He wanted to avoid eye contact, but it was nearly impossible, given the circle of eyes around him. His plan was to keep his mouth shut and ride this out until it was over. He sat with folded hands and pressed lips and settled in as an observer.

An older woman with short hair, a wrinkled forehead, and wire-framed glasses spoke. "As most of you know, my name is Janice, and I am a recovering alcoholic going on six years now."

They clapped.

Chris's shirt became itchy. He made a note of the exit.

"A friend I hadn't seen in years recently asked if I'd meet her for a drink. Well, I made sure that drink was coffee, because I'm okay with being a coffee addict." That granted her a few laughs. "I find it helps to let people know sooner rather than later that you're a recovering addict, because it sends a message that you care about yourself and tells everyone that offering you drinks is a bad idea. Have I mentioned how good it feels to be six years sober? Hallelujah!"

Janice seemed upbeat and lively, and Chris found himself liking her. Her words made him think about how Ethel had told him the first time he met her that she was a recovering alcoholic. It had been helpful to know at the time. He tried to picture Janice drunk and slurring on a bar top somewhere. Then he imagined Ethel the same way. He wasn't any better than them. He'd been as bad, or worse, when he got into pills.

Ivan, a man with a silver mess of hair and thick lenses, stood and told a story about drinking and operating construction equipment on a jobsite. He'd been fired, but instead of hitting the booze harder, he made a change and joined the AA group.

A guy named Yuri stood. He was new to the group and spoke with a Russian accent, retelling how he'd acquired multiple DWIs. He said he looked forward to getting his life back and was thankful that he'd quit drinking in time to avoid a jail sentence. His eyes were misty, and Dee, who was sitting next to him, patted his back when he sat down.

Everyone applauded. Chris's body loosened up a bit. The people who were talking were doing so on their own. It wasn't as if there were a line and he was next.

Ethel stood. "Hello, everyone. Most of you know me. I'm Ethel, and I'm an alcoholic. I used to be a party girl, and I made my share of bad decisions. I hurt the people around me. My family disowned me, I lost most of my friends, and I couldn't hold a job or a relationship." She took a deep breath and continued. "One night, I shared a bottle of tequila with this guy I'd met at the bar. He was a North Roader, and he brought me back to his trailer. It's hazy, but I remember somehow I got ahold of his revolver." Ethel's hands were shaking. "I emptied the rounds except for one. I remember spinning the chamber, and I can still feel the weight of the barrel against my temple. I can picture myself as I cocked the hammer... when I squeezed the trigger." A tear slid down her cheek and along her scar.

Jeez. Ethel was only standing there because of luck. Hearing her talk made him wish he'd known her then so he could have stopped her. It was hard to imagine her doing what she was describing. She always seemed so strong. She'd come a long way.

"I'm still here today. The sound of the hammer falling was my rock bottom. It scared me. I got out of there." She sniffed and wiped her cheeks. "I'm glad to say now that I'm two years sober. I have friends, a job... I still get urges to drink—even the smell of alcohol tempts me—but I stay active to avoid the lure. I keep a good stock of tea and keep going to this group."

She was about to sit down then stood back up. "Oh! There's some good news. My sister called me this week. I hadn't heard from her or any of my family in years. She's going to try to arrange a meeting with my parents." Ethel viewed the ring of people and smiled. "You guys have been a huge support for me when no one else around gave a damn if I was alive or dead. Thank you."

Chris and the rest of the group clapped, and Ethel sat down. He couldn't help staring at her strong nose and ready smile. Her cheeks were rosy. He found it hard to believe that a girl as happy as Ethel could have been capable of putting a gun to her head. But there it was—she'd laid herself out to this ragtag group. Just standing up and telling these people her story made her one of the braver people he knew. The smiling faces and the willingness of these people were amazing. He felt a tug in his chest. *I should do it.*

The room went quiet. Janice asked, "Anyone else have something to share?"

Chris glanced at Ethel again. She searched his face with her big brown doe eyes. Her mouth curled at the corner, and her eyebrows lifted slightly. *Aw, fuck it.* He stood up and scanned the faces. All eyes were on him.

"Hi, I'm Chris. So, I'm new to Alaska. I'm from California. I, uh, I'm friends with Ethel here. She told me about how everyone here is nice and stuff." Chris cleared his throat. "So, I do drink alcohol, but it's only one of the problems I've got going. My biggest addiction has been painkillers. I've been taking pills for five years now." He scanned the ring of faces that watched him. They were flat, expressionless, normal, even kind. "I've never done hard drugs like heroin, although there have been times I wanted to. I mean, not that there's really a difference between pain pills and heroin..." *Man, what am I talking about here?* "I'm sober now and have been since I came to Alaska. Well, that's a lie—since I came down to the Kenai Peninsula, so I'm a little over a month sober." Chris came up short, searching for more to say. The quiet in the room became oppressive.

He glanced down at Ethel, who was smiling. She made little encouraging nods.

Janice said, "Chris, thank you for sharing. Why have you chosen to quit your addictions?"

"I wanted to quit because..." At first, he hadn't really chosen to quit. He'd simply been removed from the pills. He'd made his true decision at the pharmacy that day. He'd found new desires to pursue—food, fishing, Ethel. Pills had fallen farther down that list. *But why do I want to quit? Well, mostly...* "Because I'm tired. Yeah, I'm tired of needing something so bad—no matter what the cost. I'm not me when I'm on pills—I know that. It's just a chance for me to leave, take a vacation in space, to step away. I've been staying in shelters, sleeping on beaches and under bridges... it's a shitty way to live. I've been in and out of jobs and relationships. I'm fucking tired, you know? Sorry for swearing." Chris shook his head. "I want to quit because I think I can do better and feel better. Plus, there's this girl." Chris's cheeks got hot, but he glanced at Ethel anyway.

She grinned up at him.

He sat down as they clapped. *Whew. Fuck me.*

Later, as they sat in Ethel's truck after the meeting, she said, "I'm surprised you talked on your first day."

That makes two of us. "I wanted to surprise you," Chris said, rubbing his passenger-seat cushion.

"There's something about you." Smiling, Ethel drove out of the parking lot and headed east.

Maybe she was planning to take him back to the river, or maybe there was a cozy spot in the woods that she knew about. Even better, she might be taking him back to her place, which was his favorite idea.

"So what do you think about me, knowing I was the drunk suicidal chick at the bar, huh?"

"It means we have a lot more in common than I thought."

"Damaged goods?" she offered.

"Yeah." He laughed. "You and me, we're damaged goods."

As they cleared civilization and continued on the highway, Chris asked, "Where are you taking me anyway?"

"You'll see." She gripped the steering wheel with her left hand while her right hand held the seat cushion.

I could have bet money she'd say that. Chris reached for her right hand. He half expected her to swat him away, but she didn't. Instead, she laced her fingers with his and squeezed. *She really is something special.*

The flat land of stunted spruce trees unfolded on both sides of the road. He spotted a female moose grazing in a ditch. Ethel drove farther into the mountains, which shot up on either side of the road like the spikes on a king's crown. The Kenai River wound parallel with the road, and they crossed the bridge in Cooper Landing.

Ethel veered off the highway onto a dirt road. She switched to four-wheel drive and took a narrow tractor road. Tree branches swept the sides of her truck while roots made the suspension rattle. The steep road ended at the top of a cliff. Ethel turned the truck around so that the bed faced the valley below and parked.

"Hey, make sure you put the emergency brake on. We're on the edge of the cliff here," Chris said with his head out the window. There was nothing behind them but an exposed cliff. No one was around, and it didn't seem likely that anyone would be bothering them, given the difficulty of the ride up.

"You know, it's cute how you worry." Ethel left the truck windows open and the radio on. A country song was playing—a guy singing about tractors, beer, and cornfields. Chris thought about suggesting they switch to another station, but it was on a preset, which meant that either she liked country, or it was the only station that came in around here.

She shimmied onto the tailgate, and Chris joined her. His sneakers hung a couple of yards from the edge, hundreds of feet above the main road. *That's one hell of a drop.* Kenai Lake rippled with light past the road. The glacial blue waters below were choppy as a steady wind funneled through the valley and the snow-streaked mountains beyond.

He slid closer to Ethel and wrapped an arm around her warm back. His heart beat fast, and his throat went dry. His chest got heavy. Ethel didn't say or do a thing.

"Hey," Chris said.

She turned, and with his left hand, he caressed her scarred cheek and moved in close. She met him, and they kissed—softly at first, sticking to each other's lips. Then Chris pushed harder, slipped his tongue in her mouth, and welcomed the gentle padding of her tongue. They breathed through their noses, and he cupped her head and guided her back onto the plastic rivulets of the truck bed. She kissed him and grabbed the front of his shirt. Chris's hands moved to her chest, and he released several strained buttons from her top. His fingers unhooked her bra, and he groped the soft mold of her breast. Chris pressed his body down on hers and kissed her neck. His knees hurt from the bed liner, but he ignored the annoyance. His dick pushed hard against his pants. He let her know by rubbing it against her thigh. She backed her lips away from his.

Ethel used the flat of her hands to push him off. "Wait, wait, wait." She caught her breath.

"What? What is it?" Chris asked, immediately wishing he'd been able to hide his irritated tone.

"Believe me, I'm into this, but I have to tell you something—before we go any further."

"Whatever it is, I'm fine with it," Chris said. *Is there another guy? Maybe she's married. I don't even care at this point.* He kissed her, and she obliged him then turned away.

Her face wore a frown. "I have to tell you something, and you might not be so eager." She fixed her eyes on his.

Chris groaned and met her brown eyes. "What is it?"

She slid out from underneath him and buttoned her shirt. "I want you to know that I like you, Chris." She held his hand. "And I want to be with you like this *really* bad."

"So what's the problem?" Chris asked, just shy of pleading.

Ethel exhaled. She glanced at her fingers. "When I was drinking, I was at a low point in my life. And I was with a lot of guys. None of them loved me or cared for me, but I didn't care."

Chris licked his lips. His stomach grew heavy as if someone had dropped a cinderblock in his belly. *I don't like this.*

"All right, here it goes. I have... herpes—there, I said it. I have genital herpes. It's for life, and I can't cure it, and I understand if you never want to see me again. I get it. I had to tell you." Ethel's eyes focused on her hands as she spoke.

Shit. "Huh. Not what I thought you would say." He knew every word would probably haunt him for a long time, so he spoke slowly. "So could I... you know, wear a condom and be fine?"

She shook her head and said quietly, "I wish it were that easy, but there's always a chance. Condoms help, but they aren't a total guarantee."

Worth the risk? What am I thinking? I don't want to get fucking herpes. I'm this close to getting laid, though. "Even if it's not, like... a breakout or whatever?"

"Nothing's a hundred percent. If we have sex, you could get herpes."

"What about kissing?" *We already did that. Oh man. What if I already have herpes?*

"Kissing is fine. It's only genital herpes."

That's a relief. Fucking herpes. Even the word made him cringe. *So blow jobs would be fine, right? Better not ask. She's about ready to cry as it is. Fuck! Damn. I knew it was too good to be true.* "I don't quite know how I feel about this. I like you, Ethel, but I need to think about it if that's okay."

Her eyes were taking on water. "Yeah, it's fine."

As they drove back, Chris was more than grateful to listen to the country music belting out lyrics about the Bible, Friday nights, and fishing holes. Other than that, the ride back remained quiet and seemed to take longer than the drive up. He tried to think of something to say, but he was fresh out of words. All he'd wanted was to have her, all of her, but his feelings had been spoiled. *Is it that big a deal?* Even though it wasn't life-threatening, sleeping with her meant he could get herpes and end up in her situation. At twenty-one years old, he didn't imagine that his next girlfriend—Ethel or someone else—would be his one and only. If he got herpes, he could be locking himself to Ethel for life. Or if they didn't work out, he'd have to explain to every future new girl that he had herpes and hope that she would be willing to stick around. Chris didn't have a lot going for him as it was. Add in some herpes... that might mean the end of his dating life forever.

Ethel dropped him off at sundown. He glimpsed her sullen face, and the thought of what was beneath her jeans bubbled up in his brain: an image of hundreds of shiny red bumps filled with pus. He bit his lip hard to deflect his thoughts. "Listen, Ethel, let me think about this for a bit, okay?"

She nodded, tight-lipped. He patted her hand, but she pulled away. *Is she mad at me?* There was a chance that this would be the last time he saw her. Part of him thought that might even be for the best.

Ethel sniffed. "There isn't a meeting this coming Saturday, so next Saturday, two weeks from now, I'll come by at six o'clock. That ought to give you enough time to think. I'll show up here. I won't get out of my truck. I'll just come here and wait. You can come with me or not. If you don't, I'll stay out of your life."

Chris grasped for words. "Okay. Good night, Ethel." *Great, that really helps.*

"Night," she said.

After he closed the door of the truck, she drove away. Chris watched her leave. He stood there even after she had vanished from sight, too confused to process much more than the smell of Max's dinner—rabbit stew again.

When he climbed the hill to the fire pit, Max glanced up from the pot he was stirring. "How was AA?"

"AA actually went well."

"Everything else okay?" Max was staring intently at Chris, and his brow was furrowed in the waning light.

Chris ran his hands through his hair and raked his scalp. With his hair askew, he said, "Tell you the truth, I'm still working the rest of the night out in my head. I'll let you know when I figure it out for myself."

"Fair enough." Max sipped from the wooden ladle. "Soup's just about ready."

Chris ate a small bowl then slipped into the truck and struggled to find sleep.

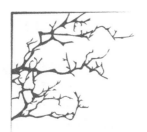

Chapter 27

The next day, Chris and Max went to work hammering treated plywood on the cabin under the hot sun and cloudless sky. Chris had struggled to hold onto sleep in the night. Thoughts of Ethel and her herpes buzzed around his mind like horseflies. When he pictured Ethel, he pictured her rowing down the river with a confident smirk on her face or staring intently into his eyes before he moved in to kiss her soft lips. She was by no means an ordinary girl. He didn't mind her scarred cheek—it was actually kind of cool. He didn't even care about her buzzed hair—it gave her an edgy punk look that suited her. The only thing stopping him was her herpes. Mouth herpes seemed like it wasn't so bad, but she'd specifically said "genital herpes," which made him imagine revolting images. He didn't know enough about it and suddenly wished he had the Internet to find out more. There was Max, who'd been a doctor. Chris wasn't sure about opening up to him, although after the scuffle the other day, the two of them had come to a truce. They were back to business as usual, and Chris wasn't complaining, because building the damn cabin at least kept his mind occupied.

The plywood walls went on quickly, and they even got the roof covered. There were only a few tricky cuts around the windows. Then Max rolled out Tyvek paper and showed Chris how to staple fasteners and tape the material. Chris and Max worked straight through lunch, and by the end of the day, they had finished the Tyvek and even added rain guards.

The cabin had transformed from a project to a hollow living space where Chris was able to stretch out instead of curl up like a human cashew in the cramped truck cab. He and Max went to town the next day and bought a door, windows, a couple of vent covers, and rolls of insulation. They installed the windows and door, and once the cabin was sealed, they began adding the insulation. Chris took little pleasure in the days they spent cutting and screwing sections of drywall and doing the tedious mudding and sanding. However, the final product gave the cabin a sense of place, making it a home. Now that the cabin was safe from the elements, Chris started sleeping on a cot in the single bedroom, while Max continued to sleep in the truck bed.

Chris had tried several times to write a letter to Aida in the quiet of the cabin. The sentences he came up with were like scattered thoughts. One of his letters was apologetic for his actions in Anchorage, while another mentioned how he'd tried hunting and fishing and how he'd never known that he liked all that sort of outdoor stuff. The words never came out right, and the letters all sounded forced, as if he were writing a book report. Each time, he ended up frustrated to the point where he crumpled the paper and tossed it into the fire. Between finding the right words for Aida and deciding whether or not to see Ethel again, Chris sought out distraction.

One night over the fire, he said, "When we fish for salmon, we're using a fly reel, but it's not really fly-fishing, right?"

"It's *flossing* salmon, a fancy term for closelining them in the face with a hook—glorified snagging," Max said and even chuckled.

Like the cabin, Max had gone through subtle changes. The smiles and laughs were still rare, but they came, often when Chris least expected. But while Max's attitude toward Chris had improved, Max himself still had his moments. A few days back, Chris had woken and glanced out the cabin window to see Max outside at the edge of the woods, staring off into the grove of trees where he'd tried to hang himself. He didn't know whether Max was contemplating another attempt or just lost in thought. Chris had made it a point to stomp around, and when he glanced back outside, Max had moved to the fire pit with a couple of logs.

"Yeah, it's snagging, but salmon fishing's for meat," Chris said.

"No other reason to fish for sockeye salmon than for meat," Max said.

"So they fly-fish trout for meat as well?" Chris asked.

"Sport mostly. Trout is pretty much catch and release around here."

"What's the point of fishing if you're not going to keep the fish?"

"Do you like paintings? Sculptures?" Max asked.

"I don't know." Chris remembered when he'd stared at a concrete statue by the beach once—a mermaid. She was beautiful, and he couldn't take his eyes off her. He remembered even crying at the sight, but of course, he'd been high off his ass at the time.

Max gazed into the fire. "For me, fly-fishing is art. The act of casting the line and presenting a fly while standing in water is enough enjoyment on its own, but there are few things more beautiful than fighting a cunning rainbow trout. The reward is holding the delicate body of a creature made perfect by time and water. Think of them as Fabergé eggs. Think of the moment when sunlight is trapped in the silver, pink, and green scales as the fish leaps above the surface or as the rainbow streaks through a current. You don't eat art unless you have to."

"Never knew you were so poetic, Max."

"I'm no Henry David Thoreau."

Chris didn't recognize the name but figured he was some writer.

"If you wanted to learn to fly-fish for trout, I could take you tomorrow—unless you have plans with that Ethel girl." Max gave Chris a knowing look and poked the fire with a stick. "Seems like a nice girl."

"She's cool." *Except for the herpes.* Chris had been crossing off days on the small calendar, and he still had a week till Saturday, when

Ethel would show up. He struggled with whether he should take her as she was or if it would be better to just let her go, so he'd just avoided making a decision, but as he crossed off days, he knew he would have to do it soon.

"Then tomorrow it is." Max slapped his knees and got up to leave. "Bright and early."

Chris thought about asking him about herpes, but the moment didn't feel right, and Max slipped away. Somehow, Max had become a sort of father figure for Chris. As good as it was to have someone to confide in, it was also pathetic that this strange man in the woods was all he had.

The next morning, Chris and Max drove for an hour and set about hiking to a pond. The trail was steep with plenty of switchbacks. The few times they stopped to rest, Chris would stuff the light fly rod under his hot armpit and wipe moisture from his brow. He noticed wet stains slashing the back of Max's gray shirt when he slipped off his backpack. Max seemed pretty rugged, but like Chris, he still sweated and bled. Chris had become aware of his own body, especially whenever he worked on the cabin or hiked. His legs had grown stronger, and his lungs seemed to be holding more air. His soft muscles had a bit more firmness these days, and he barely noticed the cuts and bruises he accumulated daily. His palms were rough, and his hands and cheeks were leathery and tanned. He tugged at his beard, which, like his messy brown hair, could have used a trim.

Chris kept up with Max until they reached a pond not much bigger than a public swimming pool. On the opposite shore, Chris spotted a black bear the size of a Labrador retriever as it worked over a berry patch. The black bear seemed skittish and bounded away when it caught wind of Chris and Max.

"Hey, let's chill for a minute." Chris rested the fly rod on the ground and lay back on the grass.

Max settled cross-legged on the grass a few feet away and rummaged through his backpack. "We can have a bit of lunch before we start."

He handed Chris a water bottle and a plastic bag stuffed with cornbread. Max hadn't needed to take Chris to the pond—the rainbow trout were catch and release, so he and Chris weren't there for the meat. *Max brought me fishing for fun.* The realization made Chris think maybe Max did give a damn about him.

Chris bit into a chunk of cornbread and spoke between bites. "You seem like a guy that enjoys his solitude. So why did you tell Aida you would take me on at your place?"

Max sipped water and wiped droplets from his mustache. "Aida and Frank have always been good friends. When a friend asks a favor, you help them out. That's how it is up here."

"Still, you didn't know me. Any night, I could have stolen a knife and slit your throat while you were sleeping. I mean, of course, that's not me, but you didn't know."

"I suppose that could've happened." Max's voice remained monotone.

"Or I could have taken off with your truck."

Max smirked. "You wouldn't get very far. Phones travel faster than tires." Max plucked a piece of cornbread from the bag and bit down on the flaky yellow chunk.

"Good point."

Chris lay on the grass and eyed the whipped-cream clouds. He wondered if Ethel could see the same clouds as she was off guiding clients on horseback. He imagined himself kissing her again on the tailgate, laying her down, the feel of her firm body and the sound of her urgent breathing. Then he thought about the moldy truth of her herpes. If he was going to make a decision about whether to see her again or bail, he needed more information.

"So you're a doctor, right?"

"Was."

"So... you'd know about... most medical stuff?"

"Spit it out, kid."

Chris sat up and faced Max. "What do you know about... uh... herpes?"

Max stopped chewing and eyed him, his gaze drifting toward Chris's pants. "Do you need to get checked out? Is that where this is going?"

Chris waved his hands. "No, no, no. I'm clean, I'm clean. I'm good."

"Okay, I'm listening," Max said.

"I mean, if someone has herpes—a girl—what are the chances that a guy could get it from having sex with her?" Chris realized he was being too obvious and that Max could put together why he was asking, but he didn't know any better way to get answers, and he was committed at that point. He was betraying Ethel's trust, but if any-one could keep quiet about medical stuff, it was Max.

Max drew a breath. "Well, there's protection: condoms, antiviral pills... I'll assume we're talking about genital herpes, which is trans-mitted from skin-to-skin contact."

Chris scratched a bug bite on the top of his hand. "Okay, here's what I'm trying to get at. Is it possible to have sex with a girl that has genital herpes and not get it?"

"Obviously, a person would want to avoid sex during an out-break, but if there aren't any symptoms, you—or *the guy*—could take an antiviral and wear a condom. With those precautions, I'd say the odds of contracting herpes during sex are low."

"Good to know." *Better news than I thought.* Still, it would only take one time having sex to be stuck with herpes for life.

Something about Max's calm voice and explanation put Chris at ease. When Ethel had first told him, he'd been so unprepared for the news that his mind got him thinking herpes was as gross and deadly as Ebola, when really it was just a bunch of bumps that came and went. The issue that still worried him was the permanence of it. If he got herpes, he might never be able to get another girl to go out with him again—not that he'd ever been a great catch in the first place, but add an STD to the mix, and his chances with women would only get worse.

Max cleared his throat. "Obviously, there are other ways to have sexual intercourse that don't involve genital-to-genital contact."

Chris chuckled. "Oh, really?" He laid the sarcasm on thick.

"Just saying."

"I got it. Thanks." *Another good point.* He didn't have to have sex with Ethel right away, although every part of Chris had wanted her like crazy. Sobriety made every feeling come back stronger, and his horniness was no different. He wanted Ethel, but he could always wait to have sex with her. There were other options.

A silence settled over the pond. Chris broke the quiet. "How did you know your wife was the one? I mean... no disrespect, but I just wonder about Mrs. Max Fitwell. Was she as hairy as you?"

Max's face tightened. "You don't let up, do you?" Chris was about to talk, but Max put up a hand and said, "Julia was..." He sighed. "You ever hear of Doctors Without Borders?"

"Yeah, they travel around the world and help third world countries and stuff."

Max nodded. "I always wanted to join, but once Julia and I got together, I kind of gave up on that dream. Julia wouldn't let me give up on it. She convinced me to go. Said she'd wait. We'd only been together for a couple months, and neither of us was getting any younger, but she said if I got called overseas, she would wait for me, however long I was away. I signed up the year the tsunami hit Southeast Asia. I'd never been out of the country before, let alone to Malaysia. I met people over there. You want to talk about loss? Those people understand loss. I remember one old woman that said something to me I'll never forget. After stitching a wound on her hand, I asked her what happened to her and whether her family was okay. She looked at me with empty eyes. Her only response was 'Gone. All gone.' I learned later that her husband and sons had all been killed—her house had been demolished and her village leveled. This was a human being with absolutely nothing left but her shirt and her body."

"Jeez." Chris had always figured he had it bad, but that lady truly had nothing to live for. He had a lot in comparison. He had Aida, Shannon, and even Frank. He'd had a place to live in Anchorage, although he'd fucked that up. Still, the cabin had a roof, and he had a cot to sleep on and Max to talk to. And there was always Ethel. It wasn't much of a life, but it was something worth holding onto.

"You don't forget those people. Their faces stay in here." He touched his shaggy head.

Heavy shit. "That's a hell of a story, but I was asking about your wife—about Julia."

"She's gone, Chris. What's left of Julia are memories, and they're mine to keep."

"Respectfully, I think that's a load of bullshit."

"You sure got a mouth on you." Max's eyes became slits, and his features hardened.

"There are worse things than swearing," Chris said.

"I'll tell you this: Julia made me a better man. A good woman can make you a better man."

Chris glanced back at the clouds, which had thinned out. He imagined Ethel's warmth as he held her hand. He thought of her earthy smell and blushing scarred cheek as he moved to kiss her. Ethel didn't judge him for his past and his habits, yet he was judging her for hers. Her face and voice had reflected her hurt, and he'd let her drive off feeling, no doubt, like an awful person. She didn't deserve that. No one deserved that. He could put his horniness aside to spend more time with her and see where things went. *Fuck, it's just herpes.* He'd overreacted, which was clear to him now, but at the time, he'd only thought of himself.

He was annoyed by how often Max was right—which was most of the time. Ethel made Chris feel better about himself in a completely different way from any of his past relationships. She made him want to be a better man.

Max pointed at a distant eagle slowly circling the sky hundreds of feet above them. "Did you know eagles nest for life and mate for life?"

"I didn't," Chris said.

"Julia was my mate. After I lost her, I lost who I was. You don't feel right living in a home you built for two—his-and-her sinks, her half-dozen different shampoos and conditioners in the shower, loofas... and sleeping alone on a king mattress doesn't feel right."

"Yeah, I forget you're more of a truck-bed kind of guy," Chris said.

"A man doesn't need a lot of space," Max said.

"So what happens if an eagle loses its mate? What then?"

Max sniffed and cleared his throat. "It will eventually find a new mate."

"Any plans to go find yourself a new mate?" Chris asked.

Max could survive out in the woods, but it wasn't healthy. He needed people, and Chris figured part of Aida's plan all along had been to give Max someone to talk to. Eventually, Max would need to get back to his house in Eagle River or at least to a town, because if he stayed out in the woods, he might give the noose another try. People needed people, and Chris wouldn't be staying with Max forever—that was for sure.

"The only plan I have is to finish the cabin. It was our dream ever since we bought the land." Max sniffed, cleared his throat, and blinked rapidly.

"Building a new nest, huh?"

"Something like that." Max grunted as he lifted himself off the grass.

"You know, you should..."

Max's wet eyes were fixed on the ground, and he put his hand to his chest. He made a grunting noise, and his cheeks became a deep red.

"Are you okay, man?"

"No. Give me a minute." Max strode toward the water's edge. He combed his hands through his hair, which left his greasy strands sticking up so that he looked like a mad scientist. Max paced along the shore of the pond with his hands on his hips and his head down. His chest heaved, and his breathing was urgent. He was muttering to himself, but Chris couldn't make out the words. Minutes rolled by, and Chris could only watch.

Chris couldn't help but think that Aida would know what to do. All the talk about Julia must have set him off. That had to be why Max worked himself to exhaustion. Building the cabin kept his mind occupied. Chris figured, in a way, that he was probably a distraction, too, but the good kind.

Chris grabbed the fly rod and got to his feet. "We came here to fish, right?"

Max lifted his head and stared at him through blurry eyes.

Chris offered him a fake grin. "You're going to have to show me how to set this thing up because I don't have a clue how to work it."

Max frowned at Chris and wiped his face with his forearm. Chris's words seemed to have broken the spell. Max unstrapped the chest holster bearing his .44 revolver. He eyed the gleaming barrel.

Chris froze. *What's he going to do with that?*

Max came over to Chris and pushed the holstered gun into his hands.

"What do you want me to do with this?" Chris said slowly.

Max wiped beads of sweat from his forehead. "From now on, you carry the gun. We'll move the rest of the guns and ammo into the cabin with you."

"You really trust me?"

"You saved my life, Chris, so yes, I trust you. And frankly, I don't trust myself—not as much as I used to."

Chris donned the holster, securing the gun to his chest.

As Max's panic faded, he gradually switched back to his old self. He set about rigging the fly rod and reel. He showed Chris how to manipulate the fly line and how to cast the leader—a clear tapered line with a small dry fly that Max called a Parachute Adams.

Max pointed out dimples in the pond's surface. "Those are fish rising to eat. Land your fly by those."

Chris's technique and casts were pathetic at first, but the more he toyed with the line, the better he became. A few fish even swiped at his fly, but each time, Chris freaked out and set the hook too hard or was too slow. Max fed him tips, and Chris kept trying. He landed the fly next to a few dimples on one cast and waited, focused on the tiny white puff, like a dandelion seed, that rested on top of the water. A fish rose. Its dark face broke the surface, and Chris set the hook with a quick but gentle tug of the fly line. The trout shook and fought, and Chris's lightweight rod bent and bounced. He stripped the jumbled line and managed to maintain enough tension to keep the fish hooked. The small rainbow trout jumped several times and gave violent headshakes under the surface. When Chris steered the fish close to shore, Max showed him how to handle the writhing body. With wet hands, Chris gingerly cradled the rainbow trout at the water's surface. At only seven inches long, the small life in his hand gasped for breath. A lateral pink stripe seared the body, and black freckles dotted the green scales. *It really is beautiful.* Chris glanced at Max, who explained how to release the fish.

Chris managed to catch a few more trout. Each time, the anticipation of the bite gave him a new high. Wondering whether the fish would eat the fly or turn away at the last second made his hands shake. When the mosquitoes got hungry, Chris and Max packed up and started hiking back to the truck. On the trail, Chris bent down to examine several big tracks. Each imprint was in the shape of a coffee bean.

"Moose tracks," Max said.

"That's what I thought."

"I go on a moose hunt every year—it's my favorite meat, and there's plenty to go around. Used to share a lot of the moose meat with Aida and Frank, since I always ended up with more than my freezer could hold."

"I'd eat moose," Chris said as they continued hiking down the trail. "Hey, Max, I'm sure you already figured it out, but when I was talking earlier, well, it's Ethel who has herpes. So please don't tell anyone."

"I got that, yes, and don't worry—I'll keep quiet." Max stepped around a slick of mud. "So what are you going to do?"

"I like her. I liked her the moment I met her."

"So what's the big deal?"

Chris was silent as he hiked through the darkening wood. Any argument for not dating Ethel seemed flimsy. The herpes really wasn't a big deal. As Chris hiked alongside Max, his shoes felt lighter, and the path seemed wide and clear.

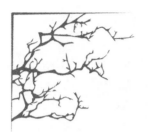

Chapter 28

M ax and Chris fell into a new daily routine. They woke at sunrise and worked on the cabin until lunch then went fly-fishing for the rest of the day. Chris graduated to fishing in creeks and rivers, where he learned different techniques for drifting flies in the current and the correct way to strip and swing flashy streamers. The trout started to get bigger. He caught Dolly Varden as well, silver fish that Max explained were similar to bull trout. With yellow lips, fins like scythe blades, and pink dots about their silvery sides, the dollies were as beautiful as they were stout. All the while, Chris kept crossing days off until his next meeting with Ethel.

One morning, he woke to the rising sun pouring through the bare window of his makeshift room in the cabin. Dust particles waltzed in the light. He squinted at his calendar. The day was Thursday, which gave him two more days to cross off before Ethel arrived to take him to the AA meeting Saturday night.

He rolled over on his cot and gazed outside. Chris's eyes stopped just below the tarp-covered wood-and-materials pile. A bull moose was standing tall and swinging a massive rack as it peered at the property. At about a hundred feet away, the giant eyes—cue-ball orbs with dark pupils—slowly scanned the ground. The moose dropped his head and munched grass. With the sturdy cabin walls between Chris and the moose, the animal really wasn't any sort of threat, but it got him thinking about how Max had mentioned that he killed a moose every year. Max had said it was his favorite meat, and Chris figured that the moose wandering onto the property was basically a gift. *This big fella would make some good meat. We wouldn't even have to pack it out.* He'd even be able to give some to Aida.

Chris glanced over at the truck. He couldn't tell whether Max was still sleeping in the truck bed or if he was maybe inside, waiting for the moose to wander off the property. In the corner of the cabin's common room, Max and Chris had made a crude gun rack that balanced the rifle and shotgun. They had placed the revolver and the boxes of ammunition in a crate that rested just below. Chris padded over to the gun rack on bare feet and lifted the rifle from its perch, then he bent down and grabbed a handful of rifle rounds.

He crept back to the window of his room and inched it open. The moose's head stayed down as it grazed. Chris slid the bolt back and pushed the round into place. He rubbed the sleep out of his eyes, peered through the scope, and waited for the head to come back into view. Adrenaline pumped through him with every heartbeat.

The moose lifted his head and offered up a large profile. Chris slid his finger on the trigger, aligned the crosshairs with the moose's head, and squeezed. The gun went off—the moose's body fell first, and the head followed. Dead weight collapsed to the ground.

Chris set the rifle on the floor and put his hands over his ringing ears. He stumbled out of the cabin and made his way to the moose. There was a faint calling of his name. He fingered his ear canals and listened as Max yelled his name again, louder. Chris stood over the huge body with dark-red blood oozing from the hole in the skull. The tongue hung out, and the legs folded and twisted. As he stared at the moose, he didn't feel victory—only curiosity as to how one bullet could take down such a massive creature. He touched the antlers.

Max entered Chris's field of vision. He was coming from the truck. His normally flat expression was twisted into a knot of muscles. Hands balled at his sides, Max stalked straight for Chris, wearing a sharp frown that could have split wood. Chris stepped backward and put his hands up. Max jabbed his fist into Chris's cheek.

Chris grabbed his face as he fell over and landed on top of the dead moose. The animal's still-warm body and coarse hairs rubbed the skin of Chris's arms. He pushed off the moose, and Max jabbed him again. Chris felt his jaw click and shift as he bit into his cheek. He almost fell again, but Max's hands were there to stop him from falling. *What the fuck? Why?*

"How could you be so stupid?" Max yelled. He punched him in the chest.

Chris bent over yelling, "I'm sorry. I give up, I'm sorry."

"You damn coward. Fight back!" Max yelled.

Chris peeked past his fingers. Max's eyes were open wide, and his lips were tucked under his beard.

"You had no right killing that moose," Max said, his voice taking on a harsh growl. He shoved Chris backward.

Chris recovered. "Fuck you, man!" He leapt for Max's throat, but all he caught was another punch. As he absorbed the blow, which struck his cheekbone like a wooden mallet, he kicked blindly and connected to something soft. Then he spun around and started swinging. Chris felt the sting of another jab to his cheek, but he pushed through it and swung a punch that connected to Max's jaw. Chris followed with a jab to Max's chest then landed another punch that ricocheted off Max's shaggy head.

Max kneed him in the stomach, which sent Chris to the ground. He moaned. His body radiated pain and wanted him to stay down, but his mind stirred him to get back on his feet. He was more than the homeless junkie that everyone thought they could kick around. He was stronger than they all knew. Chris scrambled back to his feet and ran Max through like a linebacker. They fell into a pile of chopped wood. Max howled, taking the brunt of the woodpile to his back, but Chris bore down on top of him and hammered fists into Max's face. Max blocked, but Chris was relentless, swinging and pounding, trying to get through and connect to flesh. His temples throbbed, and he continued to swing his arms and elbows like a go-rilla. Max shielded his face and punched Chris in the stomach, pitch-ing him to the ground. Chris found his feet at the same time Max did.

They stood a couple of yards from each other, both breathing raggedly. Max had a welt on his jaw, cuts on his cheeks, and a trickle of blood coming from his mouth.

"Why are you doing this?" Chris barked. He gasped for air.

"Because you killed a living thing with no regard for the rules. I told you how important the rules and regulations were." Max point-ed at the dead moose. "This moose is not in season, and you don't have a moose tag. That makes you a poacher. You can go to jail for this!"

The blood ran from Chris's face. *Shit.* He hadn't thought about the rules and regulations—he'd just seen the meat. "This is your so-lution? Beating me up?" he yelled.

"When you do something bad in this world, you'd better be ready to pay for it."

Chris still burned hot with adrenaline, although his rage had be-gun to subside. He walked a few steps and abruptly puked in the grass. That was the first time he'd ever fought back in a fight. When he'd snuck out in Anchorage, he'd let the two fake drug dealers kick him around like a soccer ball, but this time, he'd actually stood up for himself. He'd felt wronged and wanted to win. Now, as the reality of Max's words hit him, a bitter taste slithered across his tongue. He'd killed the moose without thinking about whether it was in season or if he had the right license. He didn't know any of the rules, which made him the asshole. He deserved the beating. *Fuck.*

Chris asked, "Are you going to turn me in?"

"Fucking hell, kid. You haven't really given me any other options here."

Chris shrugged. "I'm sorry. I really am. I just saw it and remembered how you said you like to get a moose every year. I didn't think."

"Stop saying you're sorry," Max said. "Sorry won't bring this moose back. I'm... I'm too angry to talk about this right now."

"Are we done?" Chris asked.

Max spat blood onto the ground. "Your work's just beginning." Max pointed at the dead moose. "We're not going to let that meat spoil. And you're going to do it all." He wiped his dirt-stained forearm across his beard and mouth. "I'll get the ropes and bone saw."

The hours that followed were the longest and most arduous Chris could ever remember experiencing. Max told him what to do and forced him to make every cut. Chris shifted the moose and tied the limbs to rocks and stumps. He'd skinned the rabbit, but that was nothing compared to the moose. Following Max's commands, he skinned the moose from the bottom lip all the way to the genitals. With his hooked blade, he punctured near the genitals, and after a few rips, a flood of blood and guts poured out of the carcass and rolled downhill. Chris's bloody hands cut away organs. He sawed through tendons and bone. The day was warm and cloudless, and sweat dripped off his nose and lips. Max pointed out every hair that stuck to the leg meat and needed to be removed. When Chris asked Max if they could take a break, Max denied him. Greenhead flies wheeled around Chris's head. He was too tired to fight Max or the flies. His blood beat in the welts on his face, his belly was tender, and his entire body was sore from his brawl with Max.

Despite the aches and pains, Chris kept working as Max voiced orders. Field dressing the moose was all about pulling and cutting. One hand constantly peeled while the other cut. Once he understood the bones to follow, he began using those as guidelines, as he'd done with the salmon. He flexed his cramped hands.

"Now cut that leg bone out. We're not going to be lazy and leave the bones in there. You're going to get every strip of meat off that's edible," Max said.

Chris clenched his teeth and grunted but continued cutting. With the back legs done, he already had large piles of meat spread on a tarp. *There's a shit ton of meat on these things.* He didn't know why he was surprised, based on the sheer size of the animal. He skinned and cut and stripped and sliced. The knife shaved bone, and his cuts became smoother and more meaningful. As the hours progressed, the bone piles grew, and the meat piles did too. Chris's cheek, eyes, and lip had become swollen from the punches he'd taken. He imagined his face looked as red as the tenderloin he'd just carved.

The ribs were the most tedious. He cut down each rib, peeled back, and cut again and again. The mountain of red meat he plopped down on the tarp kept expanding as one hour became two.

Max was standing behind him with his hands on his hips. Chris put the knife down. "Okay, I need to know. Are you going to turn me in? Tell Aida?"

Max frowned and let a long sigh slip through his nostrils. He stood stock-still, and Chris thought that he didn't intend to answer.

Max finally said, "I should. And you should turn me in."

"Turn you in for what?"

Max pointed at Chris's face. "I assaulted you."

Chris hadn't thought about the justice system working for him on this one. Max had thrown the first punch. He had assaulted Chris, although it didn't feel that way. Out here, by themselves, it was as if they had their own kind of law.

"I deserved it. I screwed up. I shouldn't have shot the moose. I was stupid."

Max held up a piece of plastic. "This doesn't make it right, but I'm forfeiting my moose tag for the season." He threw the tag into the fire pit. "And we're going to make sure every ounce of this meat is donated to the soup kitchen in Anchorage."

A cool sense of relief washed over him, but Max hadn't mentioned Aida. "What about Aida?"

"I'm not going to tell her. *You're* going to tell her, but not until we take care of this moose. Now, pick up that knife. You still have plenty more work to do."

He'd dodged the law, but he still had to deal with Aida. The first thing she'd hear from him since she'd dropped him off here would be him telling her about how he shot a moose out of season. *I'm screwed.* She'd cut him loose for sure. Max was ready to kick him out, too, which meant Chris was going to be back on the streets but, this time, in Alaska. Chris picked up the knife and got back to butchering the moose. When Chris had picked the carcass clean, Max ordered him to pack the meat in bags and then in boxes.

After that, Max said, "You have to burn the bones and guts next."

Chris added two dozen logs to the fire pit until he had a proper bonfire going. Max wrapped a handkerchief over his face like a bandit and handed Chris a shovel, which Chris used to scoop the guts and toss them into the fire. He fed the bones to the flames next. He tucked his nose under his T-shirt to ward off the stench of burning flesh and hair. His T-shirt was covered in blood and gut fragments and soaked in sweat. Eventually, he tore the wet fabric off, added the blood-soaked cotton to the fire, and worked shirtless. Max was relentless in his insistence that they burn every piece and make the fire bigger. The ribs and spine took the longest.

When that was done, Max told Chris to load the boxed meat into the truck bed. With the bed completely stuffed, Max opened the windows, and they drove into town. Despite Chris's worries about having to tell Aida about the moose and losing all the ground he'd gained up here, he was too beat-up and tired to stay awake. In the passenger seat, he fell asleep instantly.

He woke a short time later to Max shaking his bare shoulder. Chris gazed out the windshield to see a humble one-story house set back from the main road. The small house had a weathered barn attached to it with a painted Meat Processing sign nailed above the door.

"Stay here. I'll be a few minutes." Max's tone was low.

Chris rolled his window down for the fresh air and watched Max head into the barn. He didn't know what Max was planning here. If the moose was out of season, then the meat processor might turn them in or report them to Fish and Game.

Max was inside for about five minutes before he came over to Chris. "Okay. We're all set."

"So this guy's cool?"

"His name is Ted. He's an old friend. Now, get out. You've got a lot of boxes to lug."

With a heavy box of moose meat, Chris followed Max. Inside the barn was a hallway separated into several rooms. He was still shirtless, and the cold air chilled his skin as it emanated from the rooms he passed. Max led him to a cool room with stainless-steel tables, large scarred cutting boards, and a wall hung with knives and cleavers.

At the far end of the room stood a tall, bald man with a bulging stomach, thick arms, and a thick mustache. Chris assumed he was Max's friend Ted. With a bushy eyebrow suspended high and hard eyes fixed on Chris, the man offered him plenty of scrutiny. "Looks like someone had to tell you something twice, kid."

"You should see the other guy," Chris said, glancing at Max. Chris started to smile, but it made his face hurt.

Ted hooked a thumb to the back corner of the room, where plastic had been laid down. "You can stack 'em up over there."

Chris left the room to go get more boxes while Max talked to Ted about the number of sausages and steaks he wanted. Max seemed comfortable with the guy, which put Chris's mind at ease.

When Chris dropped the last box down, Ted regarded the stack then wrote something on a clipboard.

Max glanced at Chris. "That the last one?"

"Yeah," Chris said.

"Okay. I'll be out in a minute." Max turned back to Ted.

Chris caught his cue to leave and headed back to the truck. He was starting to close the tailgate when he noticed there was still one more box that he'd overlooked in the back corner. He wrangled the box and brought it inside. Right before he got back to the processing room, Chris recognized Ted's voice.

"Wife says she's worried about you, Max, which you know means that I have to worry about you too."

Chris stopped in the hallway and listened. He was curious about how Max would explain himself and didn't want to interrupt.

"I'm fine. Taking some time off... building a cabin."

"Cabin, huh? Been a while since anyone's seen you... since Julia... and you know, we just worry is all."

"Tell Laura I'm fine."

"She frets about everybody, Max. Listen, we want you to know that we know it wasn't your fault what happened. Julia was lucky to have you there that day. She's with the angels now."

"Uh-huh."

Ted's voice was hushed. "So you and I both know this moose ain't in season. What do I tell Fish and Game, you know, 'case they happen to come poking around?"

"Hit by a semi and left for dead," Max said.

Chris felt sour that Max was lying for him. Max followed the rules, but Chris had pushed him to this.

"That story isn't very sticky, Max."

"Best I've got. If you can think of a better one, be my guest."

Ted groaned. "I'll think of something, or maybe I'll just play with some numbers and move some weight around. Meantime, I better get a rush on this and get it all packed and frozen. There's no end of charities knocking on my door, asking for meat donations. I know just the one who will take it. Tell me, why are you covering for this little shit anyway?"

"Believe it or not, he's actually a good kid."

He really does care. Chris rubbed the goose bumps from his arms.

"Just keeps making stupid decisions. He's got so much to learn, but I'm not exactly the guy to teach him. He's been useful around the property—I'll say that much. Probably only a few weeks from finishing the cabin."

"Then what? You going back home? Back to work at the hospital?"

"Hell if I know, Ted. Just trying to get through the day."

"Good enough for me. I'll make sure this meat goes where it's needed."

"I owe you, Ted."

"Ain't nothing, Max."

Chris didn't want Max to know he'd been spying on them, so he quickly backtracked and waited outside by the truck. When Max stepped out the shop's front door, Chris showed him the last box and brought it inside. Ted was still there, and Chris stacked the last of the meat.

"Sorry. I missed this one."

"Hey, kid," Ted said.

Chris scratched his itchy jaw. "I'm twenty-one years old, man."

"Sorry. Hey, do me a favor and watch out for my buddy Max, okay?" Ted's eyes glistened softly, and his tone seemed sincere. "He's hurting—bad. I know he probably don't show it. Max is a good man, but grief is a tricky thing."

"How did his wife die?"

"He didn't tell you, huh?" Ted released a long sigh. "An accident."

Chris crossed his arms to warm his chilled bare chest. "Yeah, I got that." He rolled his eyes. "It's just me and him out there, and you and I both know he's not taking his wife's death well, so how about at least telling me how she died. Maybe it'll help me understand him better."

Ted sucked in his fat bottom lip under his mustache. "It was a hiking accident. They were at the top of a ridge, and Julia slipped and fell off a cliff. Max scrambled down to her and tried to save her, but it was no use. She was dead." Ted's eyes glistened. He pointed to where Max's truck was parked. "It wasn't his fault, but he probably blames himself. Max changed that day. Any man would. This ain't the same guy I knew. And I'm thinking that too much time in the woods might be taking its toll. So watch out for him—for me, okay?"

Chris didn't have the heart to tell Ted he probably wouldn't be around much longer, so he agreed to watch out for Max.

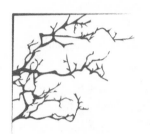

Chapter 29

While Chris lugged the last box of moose meat inside, Max retrieved the cell phone from the glove box. The phone had run out of battery, so he hooked it up to the car charger and let the truck's engine run. He had grabbed a spare shirt from the bed and placed it on the passenger seat. *What's taking Chris so long?* Max shifted in his seat and gazed toward Ted's weathered barn. The movement caused a sudden hot pain to surge from a muscle in his back. He massaged the tender muscle tissue along his spine.

Max replayed the moment when Chris had tackled him into the woodpile. Chris was stronger than Max had realized. He fought like an idiot, but despite his flailing haymakers, Chris had gotten the upper hand, and for a few seconds, Max thought he was going to get his ass kicked. He could still see Chris's wild eyes as they bore down on top of him and he clubbed Max's face with primitive instinct.

Max flexed his jaw and marveled at the new clicking sound. His anger from the fight had subsided, but he still dealt with a lingering headache. The pounding in his forehead had started when he had been ripped from sleep by the sound of the Chris's gunshot. He'd stumbled out of the truck and searched for Chris, yelling his name. The sight of the young man brought instant relief, but when he noticed the dead moose at Chris's feet, Max was thrown into a fast current of rage that swept him to a dark place.

Killing the moose was stupid, but Max's reaction had been downright idiotic. Now that he'd calmed down, he could rationalize the situation. The moose was dead, and no amount of punching was going to fix that. Plus, he wasn't teaching Chris anything by covering

250

the whole thing up. Max shook his head. He'd been foolish to think this setup with Chris would work. He wasn't any sort of role model, and he wasn't a therapist either. Chris had done well for a while. He'd helped with the cabin and the property, and he'd taken to fishing and hunting. Max was lulled into thinking that he was helping Aida and Chris out, but reality had hit him like an uppercut to the chin. He wasn't the right man for this job, and that day had shown as much.

A shirtless Chris appeared at the barn door and strode toward the truck. He seemed different from the scrawny, fragile kid Aida had dropped off. He seemed tougher and more aware than before, but that didn't change the fact that he'd broken the law and killed the moose. Max was hiding that fact from Fish and Game, but he couldn't hide it from Aida.

Chris got into the truck and sat down with his hands on his jeans. "Now what?"

"Put that shirt on." Max put the truck in gear and made for the Sterling Highway.

Chris slipped the navy-blue cotton T-shirt on and brushed the messy locks of hair off his forehead.

"Once the phone gets enough charge, you know who to call."

Chris sighed.

Back on the single-lane highway, Max drove in the direction of his property. "We lose reception here, but once we get through this pass, I'll pull over so you can make the call. When you're done, don't hang up. I want to talk to her."

Once they were through the mountains and the land started to flatten, Max slid the truck over to the edge of a ditch.

Chris grabbed the phone and dialed. "Aida? Hey, it's Chris..."

Max kept the truck in park and got out to give Chris privacy. He didn't need to hear what they said. He'd talk it over with Aida afterward. The highway was quiet with only an occasional car whistling by. Max sauntered over to the scrubby moss and the thin black spruce trees that grew off the road. The scent of gravel and needles blended with dark mud. He eyed Chris in the passenger seat about thirty feet away. He could hear Chris's tone but couldn't make out the exact words. His voice became louder and more urgent.

What a mess. Max knew he could have done more to prevent this. He'd thought keeping the guns in the cabin had been a smart idea. His panic attacks pushed him to a helpless desperation that scared him.

Chris's tone shifted to a murmur, then he lowered the phone. He stared out the windshield toward the highway. Seconds later, he stepped out of the car and rested the phone on the truck hood. With a long face and waterlogged eyes, Chris glanced at Max. "See you around, man." His voice carried defeat, and he started walking down the road in the opposite direction of the cabin.

"Where you going?"

Chris didn't answer but kept on walking.

Max picked up the phone. "Aida?"

"Max." Aida's voice was flat but firm.

Max glanced at Chris, who continued walking down the side of the highway. "So what happens now?"

"Chris told me about the moose and the fight with you. I'm pissed beyond words. I really can't believe it. I told him he'd screwed up for the last time. He's got to have some consequences."

"I mean, bringing him down here was kind of a consequence. It's no picnic."

"Well, now he won't have to worry about that anymore. I told him we're through and not to bother contacting me or Frank again."

Wow. He'd never known Aida to be so callous. "So that's it?"

"I'm sorry, Max. I really thought this could work. From what you've told me, he seemed like he was cleaning up his act, but I was wrong. I would have punched him, too, if I were there." Aida cleared her throat. "I was so happy to finally hear his voice. He never called, never wrote. He never fails to disappoint. I was just trying to—"

"Trying to help. I know, you always do. And you did. If you hadn't brought Chris here..." Chris was the only person who knew he'd tried to kill himself. The kid had made mistakes, but he'd done some good, too, and Max wanted Aida to know about it. "I'd be dead."

"What are you talking about?"

"Chris saved my life, Aida. I tried to hang myself, and he saved my life. Happened a couple days after you dropped him off."

"Max, I didn't know..."

Chris was a long way off by that point. He was a lonely figure on an empty highway. Max winced as he put his back to the side of the truck. He absorbed the heat coming off the truck engine as it mingled with his tender back muscles. "I was depressed, and with these panic attacks, I felt useless. Chris kind of helped me. I don't know how to explain it, but this dumbass kid actually helped me get through the worst of this."

"He's got to learn."

"I agree. But I don't think casting him out will help him any. He needs you in his life, Aida."

There was a long pause on the phone. "I'm sorry, Max, but I meant what I said. He's made his choices. Thank you for everything you did for him. He's not your problem anymore."

Max caught the sound of Shannon screaming in the background.

"Okay," he said.

"Sorry. Shannon's just as mad as I am today, and Frank's up on the slope. I'll give you a call soon. Better yet, I'll come down to visit. And thank you so much for trying. Chris's got to find his own way now."

Chris's lean body was blending into the distant road.

"Yeah." Max hung up and got in his truck. He chucked the nearly dead phone into the glove box and started the engine. When he checked his rearview mirror, Chris was too far gone to see. He wouldn't have trouble catching a ride. Alaskans were good about helping people out. He figured Chris would make for a city. There was the small coastal town of Seward to the south, but being unfamiliar with Seward, Chris would probably head to Anchorage. Max viewed the empty highway ahead of him that led back to his property. Without Chris, he would certainly have his solitude. The cabin would take longer, but he had nothing but time. No one needed him, and he was free to give himself back to the cabin. Max drove his truck out of the ditch and headed back to the property.

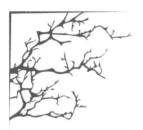

Chapter 30

C hris walked because it was all he could do. He touched his tender cheeks and lips. A bruised face wasn't going to help him get a ride. He'd finally pushed Aida too far. He was mad but not with Aida or Max or Alaska. He was angry with himself. He'd fucked up and spoiled a good thing. He'd been spoiling every good thing that came his way since he'd come to Alaska. All his mistakes had led him to this road, walking alone, with nothing but pockets full of lint and regret.

"Guess that's it with Ethel." Chris kicked a piece of gravel, and his eyes traced the long road ahead that wound into the mountains.

When he checked behind him, he wasn't surprised to see that Max's truck was gone—no doubt headed back to the peace of his property. Aida didn't want him, and now Max could finally be free of him too. Life was easier with Chris not around. His lower lip trembled, and his eyes got heavy. He'd have to get back to Anchorage. He'd have a shot at bumming for change. Maybe he'd find some pills and do what he did best. His blue buddies would welcome him back with open arms. *Fuck it. What's it matter anymore?*

Tears raced down his tender face, and he began whimpering. A few cars passed him by, but he didn't bother to try to hitch a ride. No one wanted to deal with a crying nobody walking down the road. Chris walked because he could do nothing else. He let the tears flow, and he followed his feet as they trudged through the dirt and gravel.

A sudden chirp of a car horn to his right tore Chris's eyes away from the ground. Max had pulled his truck over on the other side of the road. He waved Chris over and said, "Get in."

Chris shook his head. "I'll just mess something else up, man. If it's not this, it's the next thing. Sooner or later, everyone kicks me to the curb."

"Aida's mad. Madder than I've ever seen her," Max said.

"No shit."

"Wants me to let you go."

Chris shrugged. "She's usually right."

"She'll come around."

"I don't know."

"I need your help."

"No, you don't. You're better off without me. You, Ethel, Aida..." Chris was short of breath.

"You through?"

An RV barreled down the highway from the west. It moved to the center of the road to give Max's truck some space, and the weathered driver offered a momentary snapshot of a bewildered face before he and the RV passed, leaving a trailing wind that slapped Chris's damp cheeks.

Chris glanced at the long road ahead of him then at Max, whose eyes remained fixed on him from out the driver's window. "I'm tired, man. I'm just so damn tired of it."

"Me too, kid. Me too."

For some reason, he didn't mind that Max called him *kid*. Chris sniffed and crossed the road. He approached the passenger side of the truck. Max leaned over and unlocked the door, and Chris got inside. He sat down and let the warm cushions absorb him.

His eyes were heavy with water, so he didn't look at Max. Instead, Chris closed his eyes and asked, "Where we going?"

"Home." Max swung the car back around and headed toward the cabin. He switched the radio on while Chris let himself cry.

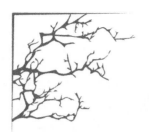

Chapter 31

After Max took Chris back home, they spent the remainder of the day cleaning up around the property. Max had decided to move the guns back into the truck with him, and Chris didn't argue. Chris went to bed early without dinner, and before he fell asleep, he thought about how he'd never been so tired in his life.

Chris opened his eyes at sunrise the next morning. He was stiff from his knees to his neck. His hands felt as if they were filled with leftover porridge, and his face remained swollen.

He shifted his frame on the cot. He reached into his backpack, found Aida's last letter, and retrieved the photo. His parents smiled at him. Mom and Dad became harder to bring to life in his mind—with every pill he'd snorted and every year that passed, their images had grown fainter. One memory hadn't aged, though. One memory was stuck on him like a birthmark.

Their childhood home's doorbell rang. "Doorbell, Mom," Chris had yelled to his mother, who was in her room, but Aida squirmed past him, and they both ran down the stairs, bare feet sticking to the polished wood, faces grinning as they jockeyed to be first. At sixteen, Aida was a couple of inches taller, but at twelve, Chris was quickly closing the gap. Aida won the race and hauled open the door. A man with shiny boots and a dark uniform stood in the doorway. For a second, Chris thought it was his dad. The man didn't smile. His face was serious.

Aida spoke up first. "Hello. Who are you?"

"Is your mom home, kids?" the soldier asked.

"Yeah, sure. Mom!" Aida yelled up the stairs.

"Be right down," their mother called.

Chris examined the soldier's heavy jaw, clean-shaven cheeks, and rigid brown eyes. He had wrinkles running along his forehead and at the creases of his eyes. Chris didn't remember seeing him at any family cookouts or holidays. "Are you friends with my dad?" Chris approached, unafraid of the man, who was wearing Dad's uniform.

The soldier examined Chris, and his stiff features loosened for a moment. Chris sensed his mother coming down the stairs behind him, and the soldier shifted his gaze to her.

When Mom was halfway down the staircase, she froze. A bewildered expression crossed her face.

The soldier removed his hat. "Ma'am, I'm Sergeant Daniel O'Keefe."

Mom's skin went white, and she sat down and covered her mouth.

"Mom?" Aida said.

The man stepped forward through the doorway. "I served with your husband, Ryan. He was a friend—"

"No! Please, no!" their mother yelled, the veins stuck to her neck like shallow roots. Her wild eyes were fixed on the soldier and her hand outstretched to shield herself.

"Where's Dad? Did something happen to Dad?" Aida asked, her voice rising.

Chris shifted his stare from Mom to the soldier. The air seemed heavy, and fear bubbled in his stomach. "Mom, what's going on?" Chris's voice cracked.

The soldier spoke directly to Mom. "Ryan's Humvee was on patrol. They hit an IED, a landmine, on the outskirts of Baghdad. He was killed in the line of duty at twenty-one hundred hours last night. I'm sorry for your loss."

Chris put the words together in his mind. He started shaking. He studied the man's face through blurry eyes. The soldier's serious expression held steady. Aida ran to Mom, who lay crumpled on the steps. Mom's face became dull, and her eyes seemed lost. Aida sobbed into her shirt, while Mom's mouth hung open, not speaking, as if someone had ripped out her battery.

Chris felt as if the roof were collapsing down on top of them. He ran. He ran down the hall and through the kitchen and burst out the back door, where his bare feet flew through backyard grass. He recognized Aida's voice screaming his name from the house. He hopped the wooden fence Dad had put up and kept running. Neighborhood kids watched him with interest, but no one tried to stop him. He crossed lawns and made it to the sidewalk. The sun boiled down on him, and hot air filled his lungs and cooked his cheeks. By the time he reached the playground at the park, his sobs had made it so hard to breathe that he had to quit running. He collapsed onto a bench, where he'd cried to the point of exhaustion. About an hour later, Aida had found him and brought him back home.

In the empty cabin, Chris sat up on the cot, blinked back tears, and sniffed. He found a pen and paper, and with a piece of plywood as a hard surface, he got to work writing.

Aida,

I know you don't want to hear from me, and I don't blame you. I've messed up a lot. It's been one screwup after another. I should have reached out to you before all this. I did try writing to you, but I'm no good with this kind of stuff. I don't even know if you'll open this letter, but in case you do, I wanted to tell you I'm sorry. I really am. I've put you and your family through a lot, and it wasn't fair. I won't give you excuses.

I've learned a lot since coming here. You should see me. I'm a regular Bob the Builder. The cabin is coming along. Max knows his stuff, but sometimes we butt heads.

It gets real quiet down here, and I think a lot about stuff. Remember how you used to take me rollerblading at the beach, and we'd always stop at the comic store? You took me everywhere back then. Must have been hard on you. You were too young for that shit.

Max is kind of like Mom sometimes, so I think it's good that I'm here to keep an eye on him.

I used to be angry at Dad for dying. He was what kept us all together, wasn't he? Man, I wish I could remember him better.

I'm glad you're happy, sis. I really am. I hope you and my niece are doing well. I guess the same goes for Frank too.

P.S. Again, sorry for all the trouble I caused.

Chris folded the letter and slid it into the pocket of his jeans.

Chris crossed off Thursday, July 14 on his calendar. *One more day.* He'd made a star out of July 16, when he would be meeting with Ethel. He patted his puffy cheeks and lips. "Hopefully, she doesn't like me for my looks." The swelling in his face had gone down some, but the skin was still bruised and tender to the touch.

He slipped on the boots Ethel had given him. He'd retired the gray Converse shoes as the boots were far more practical. Chris draped a towel over his shoulder, exited the cabin, and stretched his sore bones. He unzipped his pants and spent the next minute splashing urine on the grass. He yawned and wiped his bleary eyes as he trudged down to their rain-barrel shower. He noted Max's soft snoring from inside the truck bed as he passed.

Chris cracked the rain barrel's spigot, stripped, and stepped into the frigid cascade. With his hands, he worked the water into his greasy hair and over his face. The water ran along the curve of his back. Showers woke his senses better than coffee these days.

Early on, Max had given him work pants, a few pairs of underwear, balled-up socks, and several plain T-shirts. When the clothes got too stinky or crusty, Chris would hand-wash them and hang them to dry. Back in the cabin, he eyed the pile of wrinkled clothes under his cot. *It's getting to be about that time again.* Chris slid on the last clean shirt and the jeans that still had the letter he'd written to

Aida in the pocket. He would ask Max for an envelope and a stamp and hopefully be able to mail the letter to Aida that day. He didn't know what good it would do, but he wanted to at least try. Chris gathered the dirty pile of clothes. With a bucket, a stiff brush, and a few squirts of soap, he scrubbed the socks, underwear, and work pants. He rinsed the suds off the wet clothes next, and after wringing them out, he hung each over a makeshift drying rack made from thin tree branches that Max had shaved clean of bark.

Chris eyed their woodpile, which had dwindled since the bonfire. He built a log-cabin fire and got the wood cracking and popping in a couple of minutes. He was hungry, but the food was in the truck where Max slept, so instead of feeding his quaking stomach, he rolled a section of a cottonwood and placed it on the chopping stump. With the ax in hand, he split the thick log into smaller pieces of firewood. He stacked the pieces then chopped another log. He noticed that Max had gotten up and was taking a shower.

With no logs to split, Chris retrieved the chainsaw from the truck and proceeded to the edge of the property. He'd observed Max fell several trees. There was nothing too hard about it. He considered waiting for Max to finish showering to see if it was okay but then thought better of it. Chris had been living on the property with Max for more than a month, and Max had never had a problem with him using power tools. Max seemed to trust him, and Chris's carpentry skills had improved drastically. The chainsaw was just another tool, and there really wasn't much difference between cutting treated wood and cutting a tree. Chris gazed among the trees for a likely candidate. He moved toward the edge of the grove where Max had tried to hang himself. The four-by-four remained in place between the two trees about fifteen yards into the woods. He remembered the sensation of panic when he'd spotted Max kicking and fighting for life. He'd never pictured himself as the take-action type, but he'd changed a lot since LA.

The grove was dense, and Chris didn't trust his skill with the chainsaw enough to negotiate all those treetops and branches. Instead, he eyeballed the furrowed trunk of a hemlock in front of him. It was one of the many that ringed the cleared property at the edge of the grove. The tree was as wide as a telephone poll and already leaned toward the cleared property. He wouldn't have to worry about it hitting the cabin, as the top was too short to meet the distance. He knew from watching Max that the fall side was the side to notch.

He primed the gas and got the engine to turn over in three pulls. He pressed the trigger, and the chain screamed while the engine whined. He let off, and the small engine settled into a rhythmic idling. The smell of exhaust mixed with the scent of spruce needles and moss. Chris angled his cut down to make the notch. As the tree-pulp fragments sprayed his shirt and pants, he wished he'd bothered to put on glasses or earplugs. Gloves would have been nice too. His hands were damp.

The following day would be Saturday—marking a whole two weeks since Chris had last seen Ethel. He regretted how he'd handled the situation and wanted to tell her that he didn't care about the herpes. They didn't have to have sex right away. They could get to know each other. There was plenty they could do in the meantime. He wished he'd been able to think about all that back when she'd told him. Instead, he'd been an ass. Part of him wondered if she'd even show up.

Chris backed the chainsaw out of the cut he'd made and started another one angling up toward the first. He was pleased to watch the V block of wood fall away. *Perfect.* When Ethel arrived, he would be waiting, smiling. He'd greet her with a kiss and hug and then more kisses. They'd go to the AA meeting, and maybe he'd talk some more, then maybe he'd take her down to the river to fish. She'd like doing that kind of thing.

He repositioned himself on the other side of the tree as he'd seen Max do. At full throttle, he blasted through the tree toward the point of the notch on the falling side. With his left leg bent out and away, he positioned to a better angle and continued cutting through the trunk. Chris shifted his grip on the handle while he still held the trigger, and the saw bucked and came back toward him. *Oh shit!* The glimmering steel bar fell and punched down on his bent leg. The spinning chain ate into his inner thigh, tearing into his leg.

His pants and skin shredded, and the chain chewed deep. Red insides unfurled as if he'd hacked into a salmon. Chris yanked the bar out, released the trigger, and dropped the saw to the ground. It took him a dumbfounded moment to register what had just happened. Chris stepped backward only to lose his balance. He fell flat on the ground, and the back of his head hammered down on a tree root. Dazed, he screamed and yelled for Max. From his back, he fumbled his hand down to his leg, and when he brought the fingers to his face, they were drenched in dark blood. His toes and his cheeks went cold. His eyes opened wide, and he lay back. *Oh God. Oh my God.*

A hand shook his shoulders. Max was kneeling beside him. He had a deep frown on his face—the grim face of the soldier who had shown up at his door so many years ago to tell them Dad had been killed in action patrolling some far-off desert. Chris pointed behind Max to the tree as it started to fall. Daylight was swallowed by inky black.

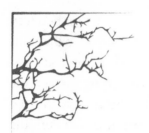

Chapter 32

The sound of the chainsaw starting followed by its chugging idle made Max pause while he toweled himself off from the shower. *What's Chris doing?* He listened to the engine whine, which meant Chris was putting it to work. Max wrestled his pants on and cinched his military belt closed at the waist. He grabbed the first long-sleeved shirt he could find and slipped it over his damp torso.

"Is he cutting down a tree?" As he tied his boots, he heard a scream.

"Max!" There was terror in Chris's voice.

Not good. Not good. Max ran to the sound of the idling engine. Chris was lying flat on his back amid a snowfall of wood chips wrapped around the base of a nearly severed hemlock. The orange chainsaw lay beside him on the ground. Chris's hands were painted with blood, and he was moaning. Max killed the engine and bent to Chris's side. His thigh had opened up, and blood puked from the open wound. Max stripped his shirt, balled the gray cotton up, and packed it into Chris's wound. The blood soaked through the cloth quickly. That rate of blood loss meant that the spinning chain had probably lacerated or severed his femoral artery.

Hot blood soaked the shirt and painted Max's hands. *It's happening again. It's happening again. Julia. Chris. What do I do?* Chris's grimacing face and dazed eyes passed over him. Max couldn't breathe. His chest tightened. He couldn't breathe. *This is what happens. Everyone dies. Everyone dies. Jesus, no, no, no, please.*

His ears registered a new sound. *Crack! Pop... pop... pop, pop, pop, pop...*

Chris lifted a hand to point behind Max.

The tree! The tree was falling toward them. Max lassoed Chris by the armpit and dragged him out of the way just as the trunk fell and settled to the earth with a heavy thud.

Max quickly reapplied pressure to Chris's leg with the soaked shirt. Chris's pupils went north, and with a shiver, he shut his eyes. His body went slack. Max touched Chris's thready pulse, relieved to find him only unconscious.

During his first year of residency, Max had learned a trick from his mentor, an orthopedic surgeon and former marine who had said, "When shit goes sideways and everyone's counting on you, there's something you need to do. Something you won't find in a medical book—outside the normal ABCs."

"What's that?" Max asked.

"Stop and take a breath."

"That's it?" Max had expected something more technical or profound.

"When they're screaming and your next move determines life or death, remember: you will always have a moment to take a breath."

Max focused on Chris. His eyes were closed, and his skin was pale. Max's hands glistened red as they pressed down on the wet cotton covering Chris's wound. Max closed his eyes, drew a breath in through his nostrils, and released a shaky exhalation through his lips. *I got this. Like before. Like I used to be.*

Max undid his military belt and wrapped the webbing above the wound. He ratcheted the belt tourniquet as tight as he could. When he checked the wound, the bleed had slowed but not stopped completely. Chris had already lost a lot of blood, and if he didn't get to a hospital soon, he'd bleed out. Max tied the soaked shirt around the wound and lifted Chris off the ground.

Shirtless and with warm blood oozing onto his chest, Max carried Chris to the truck and maneuvered him into the passenger seat.

Max grabbed a ratchet strap from the truck bed, slid the webbing around Chris's wound, and tightened the strap above the belt to make a stronger tourniquet. He elevated Chris's legs by placing them on the dashboard and buckled him in. *The phone.* His shaking hand reached into the glove compartment. He tried to turn the phone on, but it was dead. *Shit!* He hastily plugged the phone into the car charger, started the truck, and drove off down the road at a fast clip while the stuff in the truck bed clanged and was tossed about.

When he got to the end of Moose Run Road, he turned the phone on and checked for a signal. *A couple of bars. Good enough.*

"911. What's your emergency?" a woman asked.

"This is Max Fitwell. I'm a doctor—"

"I know you, Max. It's Carolyn Ball."

"Carolyn, I'm en route to Soldotna Central Peninsula Hospital with an unconscious twenty-one-year-old male. Patient has suffered trauma by way of a deep laceration to his left leg—and what looks like a femoral bleed." Max checked for a pulse and breathing. "He's got a weak pulse and shallow breathing. I applied pressure and a tourniquet. I'm en route about fifteen to twenty minutes out from CPH. I'm driving west on the Sterling Highway in a green truck with a white cap over the bed. I'm driving as fast as hell and could use some cops to clear the road for me."

"Okay, Max. I'll get the Soldotna Emergency Department on the line, and I'll get police to meet you on the road. We'll get an ALS intercept started."

"The way I'm driving, I'd beat the ambulance intercept to CPH. Here, patch me through to the Soldotna Emergency Department."

"I'm doing that now." There was a short pause.

Max pinned the accelerator down and crossed the double solid lines to pass a rusted pickup. Back in his lane and with the phone cradled in his neck, Max felt Chris's neck for a pulse and was met with a subtle tapping against his fingers. *Stay with me, Chris.*

"Hey, Max, it's Sean. Tell me about the patient."

"Sean, patient is an unconscious twenty-one-year-old male who suffered trauma to his left leg. A chainsaw opened up a ten-inch laceration—femoral bleed. Open airway. He's breathing and has a weak pulse. I applied a tourniquet, which slowed the bleed. He's in my truck on the way to CPH. We're fifteen minutes out, maybe less."

"When did you apply the tourniquet?" Sean asked.

Max passed another slow car, and the driver blared his horn at him. "Five minutes ago," Max said. "He's shocky. We'll need plasma bags. I'm going to call and get the blood type, allergies, and medical history from his sister."

"Here, give me the number. We can call her," Sean said.

Max needed to call Aida himself. Chris might die right there in his cab, and she was going to need to hear this news from a friend. "No. I got this, Sean."

"Okay, I'm prepping the team. We'll be waiting for you and your patient outside the ED. Call back with the plasma type."

"Who do you have for surgeons?"

"Terry McDowell is here, and we're calling Alice Tenor—she lives close."

For a second, Max pictured himself scrubbing up and getting in there, but Chris would be no better for it. Chris's heart was running short on blood. This was going to come down to minutes, and Max would only get in the way. He was doing his part by driving Chris as fast as he could to very skilled doctors. He knew Terry and Alice. Terry was rock steady both physically and mentally. Alice had some of the best hands he'd ever seen. Both of them had dealt with plenty of trauma victims down here in the Peninsula.

"I'll call back with the blood type and history."

"We'll be ready for you. Drive safe, Max."

Max was on the ass of a big rig. He beeped the horn and flashed his lights. There was virtually no shoulder to the single-lane highway, so the drivers couldn't move aside. Max had to pass every car. The road was starting to curve, but when he peeked around the tractor trailer, he didn't see any cars coming. Chris's lips and face were pale. *Hemorrhagic shock.* He'd lost a bucket of blood. Max pushed down on the gas and crossed the double solid lines while he whaled on the horn and made to pass the big rig. His truck was slow to pick up speed on the turn. As he leveled with the front of the tractor trailer, the driver flicked him off and hit his air horn. Instead of slowing down, the truck driver sped up to stop him from passing.

Get out of my way, asshole. Max kept the gas pedal pinned and squinted at the road ahead. The sun hit the narrow chrome frame of the motorcycle driving toward him. *Oh shit.* Max beeped and glared at the trucker. "Let me pass, you prick!"

The truck driver mouthed a "Fuck you."

"You want to measure dicks?" Max grabbed the revolver under the seat and pointed it at the trucker.

The driver hit the brakes and backed off while Max slid over into the right lane just as the motorcycle roared past.

Max kept the speed up and barreled toward Soldotna. He called Aida next. "Aida, it's Max. Don't ask questions—I need Chris's blood type stat."

"He's O positive, same as me."

"Does he have any allergies? Or medical history?"

"No allergies. As far as history, he's an opioid addict, but he's been reasonably healthy other than that. What—"

"There was an accident. I know you said to let Chris go to find his own way, but I wanted him to stay. He was using the chainsaw this morning—it cut into his left leg. He's unconscious and has what looks like a femoral bleed. I got to him quickly. He's got a tourniquet on the leg, but he's shocky. I'm driving him as fast as I can to Central Peninsula Hospital right now."

"Is he... going to make it, Max?" Aida stammered.

Max glanced at Chris. He had elevated Chris's legs to help manage the bleeding by jamming Chris's boots between the dash and the window. Blood dripped down onto the seat and floor mats. Chris's head bobbed with the road. Max checked for a pulse again and was relieved to find a weak tap. "I'll take care of him, Aida, I promise, but I got to go. Call CPH if you get any more history. And get there as soon as you can. I have to go."

He called Sean back with the blood type. Two police cruisers were waiting by the Soldotna town sign. Max slowed down, beeped, and waved. The cops flipped their lights and hit the sirens and led him through the traffic lights all the way to the emergency department doors. Sean was there with several techs and nurses. They lifted Chris out of the truck onto a stretcher. His face was bone white, and his body was limp. Max abandoned his idling truck and followed the stretcher inside.

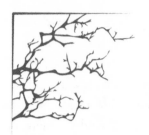

Chapter 33

Aida hung up the phone and rested it on the counter. She slid the pan off the burner and clicked the switch off. She'd been scrambling egg whites when Max called, and his message had gone off like a flashbang grenade at her feet. A subtle ringing bloomed in her ears. The ringing grew louder, and her heart knocked against her chest with a manic beat—as a nurse, she had a habit of noting her own symptoms whenever they arose. Nausea and blurred vision came next. She had the sensation that she was floating away from her body. Her eyes darted from the kitchen counters then to Shannon, who was sitting in her high chair, reaching out with her tiny hands for Aida. Shannon's eyes were wet and filled with concern. Her cries raked against Aida's ears.

Aida needed to do something. Chris was dying, but she could hardly move her body. *I did this.* The thought was irrational and stupid, but something inside her knew there was truth to it. She'd been furious with him, and she'd been caught off guard when he'd called her about the moose and the fight with Max. She'd let him have it. Her last exchange with Chris had been to banish him from her life. Now he was dying or maybe even dead from blood loss. She had to do something.

Shannon's screams were muffled against the overwhelming ringing. Aida could feel her circuits overload, and one by one the fuses in her brain popped off. A sickening numbness spread through her. She pinched her thigh through her jeans—softly at first, but she increased the pressure to try to feel the pain. She needed more. Aida examined the bulletin board by the fridge. The cork was peppered with tacks that could stab and scratch her skin and give her another stripe to go along with the old scars on her leg. *I'm over that.* The last time she'd cut herself had been years before she and Frank were even married. But now, it felt like the only thing she could do to control the cyclone around her. The sweet pain would help give her focus, a short-term medication that could manage her symptoms.

Shannon wailed and shifted in her seat. Her little hands worked to get her out of the chair, but she was helplessly stuck, so she was using her voice. The blood flooded Aida's ears. *Chris is going to die, and I practically condemned him.* Guilt leveled her, and she used the granite island to keep herself vertical. Aida gazed at the knife block within her reach, which was filled with gloriously sharp blades.

She needed to call Frank. He was her support, her best friend, her soul mate. With him at her side, she could rule the world. She sat down on the stool, slipped a heavy knife out of the block, and set it on the counter. The light slid up and down the blade as she admired the angles. She slid her jeans down to expose her thigh. She touched the scar tissue—her zebra stripes—as if preparing a patient on an operating table—but this time, she was the patient, and she had no need for anesthetic. Her breath hastened. As she brought the knife closer to her thigh, her heart churned even faster.

Shannon pounded the plastic tray in front of her, and tears and snot dripped down her face. Aida brought the cool blade to her skin and rested it above the last scar. The cuts were like the marks a prisoner made on a wall, etching down the days to freedom. Aida bit her lip to prepare for the pain.

Shannon screamed and begged for her touch.

No! Aida tossed the knife into the sink with a clatter. She blinked, and tears fell down her warm cheeks. She hauled her pants back up and buttoned them. *Never again.* She wasn't that person anymore. She'd changed into something better. She was a mother, and her baby needed her. Chris needed her. People counted on her because she was reliable. She was on point—a badass in the operating room and a fighter for her friends and family.

She gathered Shannon as the ringing in her ears began to fade. She wiped her daughter's face and held her tight. "Shhh. Mama's here, my baby. Mama's back. I'm sorry. It's okay. Shhh."

Chris needed her. She needed him too. Soldotna was about one hundred fifty miles away and about a two-and-a-half-hour drive, but it was less than half that distance as the crow flew. She needed to fly down there. Fortunately, she and Frank had several friends who piloted small planes. Aida called Tim first, but the call went straight to voice mail. She called Mark next. He picked up after two rings.

"Aida! Long time. How are you?"

"Mark, hey. Listen, I have an emergency. Shannon and I need to get down to Soldotna ASAP. Are you in town? Could you fly us down? Like, right away?"

"Whoa. Uh, yeah... well, I'm actually looking out the window at my plane right now. You said Soldotna, so, yeah, sure, why not? Weather's actually prime right now. I'll get her fueled up and prepped. When can you be here?"

"Ten minutes."

"No kidding." Mark grunted as if he'd lifted himself out of a chair. "Okay. Yeah, I'll be ready."

Thirty minutes later, Aida was inside the cockpit of Mark's four-seat single-engine Cessna, flying over countless trees and lakes. She sat in the back next to the baby's car seat and shifted Shannon's earmuffs.

Mark glanced over his shoulder, and Aida's worried face reflected back at her in his aviator sunglasses. Mark's tinny voice in the radio of her headset said, "We'll get you there, Aida."

"Thank you." She could only wonder how much blood Chris had lost before Max applied the tourniquet. She imagined Chris unconscious on a table as doctors worked on him. *I'm coming, little brother.*

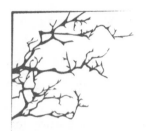

Chapter 34

Dad's voice broke through the red pain. "Whoops. Oh, Chris. Hey, Chris! Are you okay?"

Chris had tumbled down the granite steps in the front of the house. His palms were scraped raw against the stone, but this paled in comparison to the pain in his leg. "Ouch! Daddy!" His chubby calf was smeared with blood, which dripped from his knee. The hot sting worsened the more the air touched the cut. This wasn't supposed to happen. This wasn't how his knee was supposed to look. It scared him to feel the warmth coming out.

"Aw, I'm sorry, Chris." Dad was standing over him. He bent down until he was at eye level. "You're okay. You're okay now."

The sting burned hot, and the tears came. He wailed and pushed his face into Dad's polo shirt. "It hurts. It hur... hur... hurts, Daddy!"

Chris's eyes shot open. Several masked faces bobbed over him. He didn't recognize any of the faces, but he read concern in the frowns splitting their eyes and the concentration in their gazes. He was surrounded by machines, scrubs, and tubes. Light glared down at him, and urgent voices circled his head. He was in a hospital—an operating room. They moved him onto a table, and a searing pain wracked his leg and ricocheted against the walls of his skull. He was too weak to fight the pain, and it overwhelmed him. He was so tired. He closed his eyes.

Dad's heavy arms held him close, and his big hand patted Chris's back. "Cheer up, cheer up. It's only a scrape. Here, let Dad kiss it better, okay? Can Dad kiss it better?"

Chris wiped his tears with his chubby forearms. "Nuh... nuh... no." He wanted to be strong like Daddy.

"It will make it feel better. I promise."

"Oh... oh... okay." Chris had to work to catch his breath in between sobs.

"Well, first I have to blow some magic on it. Are you ready for me to put some magic on your cut?"

His dad leaned over the red cut, puffed up his cheeks, and blew lightly over the scrape.

Chris's eyes opened. An oxygen mask had been placed over his mouth and nose. Latex gloves with blood on them flashed in front of his face. A nurse pressed down on his shoulder, pinning him to the table. Needles and IVs and pain—his head was cloudy. He was too weak to move. He could feel his body losing the fight. His eyelids became too heavy. He struggled, but they came back down.

"Still hurts, Daddy. Still hurts."

"Well, of course. I haven't kissed your leg yet." Dad kissed the skin above the scrape on his knee.

"Still hurts."

"The magic takes some time to work. It's a little better already, right?"

"A little."

Chris could feel his body losing power on the table of the OR. He couldn't open his eyes anymore. *I don't want to die.* The thought floated in Chris's head and became fragmented, like shattered ice, then melted and evaporated into the darkness of his mind.

Dad planted a kiss on his forehead and rubbed a calloused hand through Chris's wavy hair. He lifted Chris off the ground effortlessly. Chris's hand grasped the skin on Dad's sunburned forearm. Dad carried him up the steps and into the house. He was going to be all right. He was with Daddy.

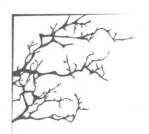

Chapter 35

After he handed off Chris to Sean and they'd whisked him to the OR on a stretcher, Max trailed behind them and tried to stick close. He wanted to be in the OR, gloved and gowned, even though he knew full well that this wasn't his hospital. A stern-faced nurse put herself in his way and declared that she didn't care who he was—he would wait like everyone else in the waiting room, or she'd call the police.

Max moved his truck out of the emergency area. He was shirtless, with arms and chest caked in crusty blood. No wonder she wouldn't let him in. He crawled into the back of the truck, hastily grabbed a rag, soap, and a gallon of water, and scrubbed himself clean in the parking lot. He slipped on the first shirt he could find and rushed back to the waiting room. He badgered the receptionists about updates, fully aware that they didn't know squat. He told them he was a surgeon. They wanted to see his credentials. He told them he didn't have them on him. They asked him if he was related to Chris. He said he wasn't. They told him to wait. He waited.

Chris hadn't crashed yet, but it was likely to happen. They needed to fix the artery quickly, fill him back up with blood, and pray his heart could handle the rest. If he survived, there was a good chance he would lose the leg. He'd definitely have muscle damage and possibly nerve damage too.

Max again wished he could be in there. He wasn't doing anyone any good being stuck in the waiting room. He refused to sit down and resign himself like the rest of the scattered people in the chairs. One man with silver hair, wearing a grease-monkey suit with "Eddie" ironed onto the chest, was reading a magazine, but he methodically checked the clock on the wall every minute as if to confirm that time really was moving forward.

A young man with a face etched in misery eyed the leaking bag of ice on his swollen foot. Rubbing the young man's back and whispering to him was a motherly woman who monitored the hospital staff like an osprey.

Max circled the room and chewed his thumbnail. The phone rang in his pocket. He fished it out and answered.

"How is Chris?" Aida asked.

"Aida. No news yet. He's in the OR."

"I'm at the Soldotna Airport. Come pick me up."

She'd flown down here. He'd never expected her to get to the hospital so quickly. "On my way." Max hung up and cast a glance at the reception area. He didn't want to leave, but Aida needed to be with Chris. "I'm going to be back in twenty minutes with his sister. Okay?"

The aging woman gave him a half-hearted wave.

The airport was no more than ten minutes away. Max sprinted to his truck, punched the keys into the ignition, and drove to get Aida. When he arrived at the airport, Aida was waiting out front with a bulky bag over her shoulder and Shannon in her car seat. Aida's lips were pressed tight, and a deep frown cut into her eyeglasses. Her auburn hair, cinched off in a ponytail, seemed wilder than usual, but her eyes were steady and focused on Max. One of Frank's good friends from childhood, Mark, was standing alongside her, his face tight.

Mark opened the passenger door of the truck and, with a knowing glance, said, "Take care of them, Max."

When Aida moved to come inside, she froze, her eyes fixed on the seat. "Jesus."

Max followed her eyes to the glistening blood soaking the passenger seat. Max put his hand up. *Shit!* "One second." He reached behind his seat into the truck cab, grabbed a loose towel, and spread it over the passenger seat.

When Max tried to help Aida install the car seat, she shooed him away and told him to turn the airbag off. She finished securing Shannon and climbed into the middle seat. Before she'd even buckled, she said, "Drive."

Max followed orders and headed back to the hospital. "Aida, I know—"

"All that matters is that Chris is okay. That's all that matters." Aida brushed some hair out of her face. Her feeble voice was underpinned with strength and determination.

"I got him to the hospital as quick as I could. I don't think he severed the artery completely, but it was bleeding bad, which made it hard to tell. The good news is that I got the tourniquet on pretty quick. If he lives through this, he might lose the leg."

"I just need him to live." Aida sighed and wiped tears away from her eyes. "What docs are working on him? Do they have plasma?"

"They had plenty of plasma, yes, and Terry and Alice are working on him. You know them, right?"

"I do. They're good. That's good." Aida pinched the bridge of her nose. "So it was a chainsaw?"

"After the moose and the call with you, I let him go like you wanted, but when I started to drive away, I just couldn't go through with it. I like the kid, Aida. Like I told you, he saved my life."

"I'm not blaming you for this, Max, but can you tell me again how this happened?"

Max stopped the truck at the red light then turned onto the main drag. "He woke up before me. Must have wanted to add more firewood to the pile, so he took it upon himself to get the chainsaw while I showered. He's usually pretty good with power tools—you should see him. I know he'd seen me cut down trees before, but this was his first time with it. Must have lost control, or maybe it bucked on him. I got to him just after. I put pressure on the wound and used my belt as a tourniquet."

Aida winced, and Max knew she had to be imagining the chain chewing through her brother's leg. They crossed the bridge over the Kenai River. Aida's eyes were closed, and she massaged her temples.

When they arrived at the hospital, Max dropped Aida and Shannon off at the entrance. He parked the truck then hustled inside, where he spotted Aida at the counter, speaking with Admissions. She cradled Shannon close to her chest with her left arm, rocking her, and clutched a plastic bag and a pacifier in her right hand.

When Max joined her, Aida said, "He's still in surgery. No news yet."

He eyed the plastic bag.

"They gave me his stuff." Aida popped the pacifier back into Shannon's mouth and offered her to Max. "Can you hold her for a minute?"

Max hesitated. It had been a long time since he'd held a baby. "Uh, yeah, okay." He gingerly accepted the squirming baby and held her close. She made little mewling noises and sucked and worked her pacifier.

Aida held tight to Chris's belongings, and they moved to sit down. Max eased into the chair beside her, looked past Shannon's droopy eyes, and peered into the bag on Aida's lap. He spotted Chris's brown boots and a ziplock bag with a wallet and a blood-stained envelope inside. The rest of the clothes Chris had been wearing probably weren't worth saving. Even sitting beside her, Max could smell blood and wood chips emanating from within.

Aida unsealed the ziplock bag and pulled out the envelope. The blood had stained through to the letter inside. Aida unfolded the letter and squinted as she read. Max shifted his grip on Shannon. Aida's name was at the top of the handwritten note. He didn't attempt to read what it said but watched Aida out of the corner of his eye.

She put a hand to her lips. "Am I bad person, Max?"

"No. Aida, you're the best person I know. I'm not just saying that."

"I want Chris to know that I forgive him. I only hope I can tell him that myself."

Max wanted to tell her that she would get that chance, but he didn't want to get her hopes up. Chris was going to need to be a fighter to get through this, and even then, a person could only lose so much blood.

Aida stared at the sealed doors of the emergency department. "It's so strange to be on this end, you know?"

"I know. I hate being stuck here. I feel so damn useless. But at the same time, these guys are good. So at least Chris is in capable hands."

Shannon tried to get out of Max's grip, and when he held her tighter, she started making noise.

"I think she wants her mama."

Aida wiped her eyes again and collected Shannon. "Shhh. Mama's here, love. I know... shhh."

The next hour was a lifetime. Max's insides had been replaced by a guitar string winding tighter and tighter. Finally, Terry McDowell pushed through the doors of the emergency department. He looked at Max and then at Aida with an expression that Max figured Aida and he both knew well.

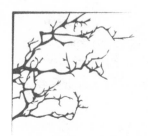

Chapter 36

The lights were dim, and the curtains were drawn. Chris found himself lying on a hospital bed. His head was slightly elevated. His eyes were heavy, and he was drowsy. A fog lingered in his head. Someone had covered him in a blanket. A nurse with dirty-blond hair in a bun examined a fluid bag hanging from a pole to his right. She pressed buttons on a machine attached to the pole. Tape lashed the needles and tubes stemming from his right arm. He was tethered to monitors and fluid bags. He was dressed in nothing but a thin hospital gown.

The chainsaw. My leg. With the blanket over him, Chris made to move the blanket aside. The nurse stopped him.

"Hey, easy."

All Chris could manage was "My leg."

She examined him with caring green eyes. "Here." She brushed the blanket aside.

A wave of relief washed over Chris when he saw he had both his legs. His left leg was heavily bandaged and compressed right above his knee.

"We've got it immobilized for a bit to keep you from ripping out the stitches."

He was relieved when he spotted his toes. He tried to wiggle them. *Pain!* He closed his eyes and grunted until the throbbing faded. He fell back asleep.

The next time he woke, daylight was coming through the windows. Aida was by his side, holding his hand.

"Hey, sis."

"Hey, Chris. Welcome back." She had tears in her eyes. "I'm so happy you're okay."

Keeping his eyes open required significant effort. "Me too. How's my leg?"

"It's going to take some time to heal. You'll need rehab. The muscles and ligaments were torn up pretty good."

"I feel like shit." Chris's voice was haggard. His head was loopy. It seemed like forever since he'd had painkillers, and he suspected he had some sort of opioid swimming laps in his veins.

Aida brought a jug of water with a thick straw to his lips. He tried a couple of small sips.

"That tends to happen when you almost die. You lost a lot of blood, little brother." Aida put the jug down on a tray.

"The chainsaw bucked on me." He closed his eyes and exhaled. He could remember the fear of seeing it mow through his leg with his blood and tissue caught up in the chain.

Aida clasped his forearm. "Max told me. He put a tourniquet on your leg and drove like a madman to the hospital. He saved your life. And from what he's told me, I guess that makes you guys even now." Aida shook her head and blinked back tears. "All that matters to me is that you're okay—both of you."

Chris opened his eyes. "Where is Max?"

"Shannon was getting antsy, so he took her for a walk through the hospital. They're making the rounds."

Chris nodded toward the fluid bags hanging above his right shoulder. "Pretty elaborate way to get some painkillers, huh?" His smile came with a wink. He winced.

Aida patted his head and smiled, wiping a tear from her eye. "Not if I have anything to say about it."

"Only joking." Chris sighed. "What have they got me on? Stuff is strong."

"Morphine for now, but they're going to wean you off."

"Fine by me. It actually makes me feel nauseous." Chris released a weak laugh.

"I like your beard." Aida leaned over and pinched the hair on his chin. "It suits you."

Chris brushed a hand through his scrubby facial hair. "Keeps me warm."

Aida waved a bloodstained folded-up piece of paper. "I got the letter you wrote me, by the way."

"Meant every word."

"I forgive you, Chris." Aida tossed her leg over her knee and stared into his eyes. "I was so scared I would never be able to get the chance to tell you that. Now I feel like I'm lucky to have the chance."

"Thanks. I know I made some stupid mistakes—up in Anchorage, with the moose and Max and—I mean, look at me. I'm a mess."

"I'll take what I can get, little brother."

Chris looked into Aida's bleary eyes. Her auburn hair was frizzy. There were bags under her eyes, and her brow was furrowed, but she smiled despite herself. Even though she'd been mad at him, she'd come anyway. Whenever he was in trouble, she always came.

"You remember the day when we found out Dad died?" he asked.

"The soldier at the door. Yeah, I'll never forget that day."

"Me neither." Chris sniffed as his eyes grew heavy. "But that's not the part that I'll remember the most. I'll always remember how I ran out of the house and ended up alone on the park bench. But it was you. You were the one who came and found me and brought me home."

Aida hugged him, and he did his best to hug her back. They held each other for a long time then let go.

Max stepped into the room, cradling a yawning Shannon, who was rubbing her face on his chest. Max's eyes flicked to Chris then to Aida. He whispered, "Probably past her bedtime."

He gingerly handed Shannon off to Aida, who placed his niece into her car seat and covered her with a blanket. Max came over to Chris's side and inspected the bandaging on his injured leg. His face seemed brighter than before, and there was a new warmth coming from him.

"What's the prognosis, Doc?"

"I'll let your physician explain it to you when he comes around."

"No. I want to hear it from you."

"Okay. Well, you're extremely lucky. You lost a lot of blood, and you could have easily lost your leg, but the surgeons here are good—they're used to trauma like this. They fixed the tear in your femoral artery and reestablished blood flow in time to save your leg. Then they cleaned out the debris in your wound. They reattached your torn muscles and ligaments after that and stitched you up."

Chris regarded his leg, which was bandaged tightly just above his knee. "Damn."

Max put his hands on his hips. "Yeah. You're on antibiotics. While you heal up, they'll want to monitor you for infection and blood clots. My guess is you'll be out of here in around two weeks if things go well. You also took a good whack to the back of your head when you fell, which probably gave you a mild concussion."

Chris touched the gauze taped to the back of his head and massaged the lump underneath. He pictured the way his head had hammered the ground when he stumbled. "So am I going to have a limp or anything?"

"You'll have to give your muscles and ligaments some time to heal, then you'll have crutches, but you should be able to walk normally again with some physical therapy. With the nerve damage, my guess is you'll probably lose a bit of feeling around the injury. Again, you were incredibly lucky."

"It's going to be an impressive scar. That's for sure," Aida said.

Chris beamed with pride at the idea of a scar slashing his thigh. It reminded him of Ethel's scarred cheek. He glanced out the window as the sun peeked out just above the trees, half-smothered by a rolling cloud bank.

"Hey, what time is it?" Chris looked from Max to Aida.

Aida said, "It's late, ten thirty already."

"Wait. What's today?" Chris asked.

Max said, "Saturday."

Ethel! Chris's mouth opened. "Oh shit! No, no, no. I was supposed to see Ethel today." Stuck in bed, all he could do was point at Max. "Oh man, Max, you need to tell her I'm in here. Please, man, can you get her to come and see me?"

"Where does she live?" Max asked.

"I don't know. I don't have her number either. Shit." Chris winced.

Max put his hand up for Chris to stay still. "Fred's Ranch. She said she worked for Fred. I'll make some calls and let her know you're here."

"The sooner, the better, man. I was supposed to go to AA with her today. Damn it. Tell her I wanted to go with her, and explain what happened for me. Please." He imagined her arriving at the property, waiting in her car for him, and leaving without him. She probably assumed that he had rejected her, but she had to know that he wanted to go with her. He wanted to hold her and kiss her and spend more time with her. He didn't have it all worked out, but he knew he wanted to be with her, even if that meant not having sex for a little while. Max had to find her and let her know he hadn't meant to stand her up.

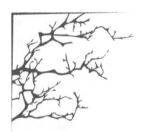

Chapter 37

As Max drove away from the hospital, he called Fred's Ranch. He knew Fred through Julia. She'd always loved going down there to scoop out the barns and help exercise Fred's horses. Fred told him where Ethel lived in Cooper Landing and gave him her cell phone number, but he said that she didn't get service at her cabin. Max tried her cell anyway, but the call went straight to voice mail. Chris had been so eager that he get in touch with her, and time seemed important. Max got into his truck and drove to Cooper Landing.

It was dark when he arrived at her small cabin, which sat on a quarter-acre parcel of land at the base of a mountain. Her truck rested quietly beside the small home. Max got out and made straight for the door. When he knocked, she didn't answer. A faint light lit the room within.

"Ethel, it's Max. I need to talk to you." He peered through the clear space in the curtains and spotted something on the floor.

He squinted and saw Ethel facedown on the floor. There was a long dark stain beneath her. *What the hell?*

Max tried the doorknob. No good. "Ethel!" He whaled on the treated pine with his fist.

The door still didn't move. He stepped back and kicked it. The lock gave, and the door swung open, and Max stepped inside. The scent of liquor filled the room.

He got down on his knees and patted her back. "Ethel!"

He put his face by her lips. His heart beat in his throat. Then breath brushed his cheek. *She's alive.* He patted her back harder. "Ethel."

She was still clutching an open wine bottle in one hand. Max looked closer and realized she was lying in a puddle of pinot noir. She muttered some incoherent words. Her eyes fluttered, and she seemed to be coming to. He scanned her, but aside from a stained shirt, there were no obvious injuries.

"Are you okay? Are you hurt?" The curtains were all closed, and several liquor bottles were strewn across the floor. "Talk to me, kid."

Her eyes opened and closed lazily. A smile crept on her face. "Fine, I'm fine. I was just enjoying a little drink." Her voice carried a heavy slur, and she chuckled. "Would you like some, Max? You seem like a guy that could use a good drink." Ethel giggled again. She hiccuped, covered her mouth, and laughed some more.

Max eyed the stain on her shirt, which appeared to be wine, but given the last few days, he wasn't about to take any chances. "Ethel, Ethel, look at me. Are you bleeding at all? Are you hurt anywhere?"

Despite the buzz cut and scar, Ethel had a pretty face, but at that moment, her confused expression was overly exaggerated, and her skin glistened with alcohol. She reeked of hard liquor, and her white shirt was soaked and stained dark red. She peered down at her shirt, grabbed the fabric, and wrung out the wine onto the floor. Ethel stripped the shirt off and chucked it toward the cabin's small kitchenette.

Max caught a view of her pale stomach and bra. He didn't see any obvious wounds or injury. He averted his eyes. Fortunately, she only appeared to be drunk. Max got up and moved toward her bedroom, rifled through her dresser, and grabbed a simple blue-cotton shirt.

He joined Ethel back on the floor and slipped her head through the neck hole of the shirt. She managed to work her arms through the sleeves herself. Max lifted her by the armpits and dragged her over to a small couch.

Ethel giggled and said, "Wee!"

At least she's a happy drunk. "What happened here? Aren't you in AA?" Max squatted down next to the couch to meet her at eye level.

Ethel squinted at Max. Her head bobbed from side to side. "No one wants me. I thought my sister was going to help... I haven't talked to my parents in so long... I miss them... but they still want nothing to do with me. My mom and dad, they think I'm a lost cause—a drunk!" Ethel raised her voice and yelled at the roof, "Well, here I am! You happy?"

She locked eyes with Max and stared as if she'd just recognized him. "Where's your buddy Chris? Huh? I went to see him. I waited in my truck." She hiccuped. "He doesn't want me either." Ethel's voice dropped down low, and she eyed the wine bottle on the floor.

"That's why I'm here, Ethel. Listen, Chris got hurt—an accident with a chainsaw. He's in the hospital."

"What?" Ethel closed her eyes and was still. Max counted four breaths by watching her chest rise and fall. Then her eyes flew open. "Wait. Oh, oh no. Is he okay? Max, is he okay? Please." A sudden clarity and concentration returned to her eyes.

"He lost a lot of blood, and he's going to need some rehab, but they're taking good care of him at the hospital. He should be okay. He told me to tell you that he wanted to go with you to AA."

"I thought... I thought he didn't come because of... wait... he said he wanted to come to the meeting with me?" Ethel's voice carried an unsteady rhythm.

"Yes, he said he wanted to come, but he got hurt, and he's in the hospital."

"I have to go see him. I... I... have to. I'm too drunk. Damn it. Two years I've been sober. I can't believe—I... ah!" Tears sprang forth, and she buried her face in her hands.

Max stepped closer and crouched down to her level. "Listen, Ethel. We all screw up sometimes—we're only human. Let's pour out this booze and put you to bed."

"Thank you. Ah, I'm so stupid." She struck her head hard with her palm.

Max grabbed her wrist before she could hit herself again. Her face was wrinkled and damp.

"You can still change, kid. You're young. You've got your whole life to fix your mistakes." The words were as true for Ethel and Chris as they were for him. When Julia died, he had chosen to see the world as a cold, lifeless, meaningless place. He'd cut himself off to float across a numb landscape. Detaching himself from support had been a self-inflicted wound, and taking his own life was almost inevitable. Then Chris arrived, and the world Max had run from had been thrust back into his life. He traded the numbness for anger, fear, and moments of levity. He began to remember that helping people, being a doctor, and caring were coded into his DNA. The cabin was nothing more than a mausoleum or a pyramid—a tribute to Julia. Max had thought himself broken and useless, but it wasn't true. *Alone in a cabin with a drunken girl I hardly know is a strange place to have that revelation.*

"Thank you, Max. Really, thank you."

Max poured out the bottles of liquor and wrapped them in a garbage bag, which he threw into his truck. Ethel puked into a bucket several times, and Max was there to help with water and a damp cloth.

"Ethel, listen. Do you have any friends close by that could keep an eye on you?"

"Roger. Two cabins... up the road."

Max went up the road and roused Roger from his sleep. When he explained the situation, Roger put on his shoes and followed him back to Ethel's place. He promised to take care of her.

In the dark of night, Max headed back to the hospital. The car ahead of him was going the speed limit, which was fine. Unlike the previous day, he wasn't racing to save Chris's life. Max listened to the thrum of the truck's tires, and his mind wandered. *Is this what it's like to be a dad?* He ran a hand through his thick hair. If Julia were still alive, she'd be able to handle this better than him.

He peeked at the night sky. "You seeing all this, Jules?" Unlike him, she had been equipped to be a parent. Compared to a room full of kindergartners, Ethel's and Chris's problems would have been crumb cake. "I really wish you were here." He pressed his lips together and reclined his head. "Don't worry about me, okay? I think... I think I'm going to be all right."

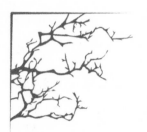

Chapter 38

C hris woke in the night when the nurse checked up on him but passed out shortly after that. The next time he woke, the orange sun was bursting through the shades of his room in the ICU. Despite the drugs in his system, his stitched leg throbbed. Aida and Max occupied two chairs about ten feet to his right. Aida was asleep, using Max's shoulder as a pillow. Max's eyes were sleepy, but he was awake.

"Ethel?" Chris whispered so as not to wake Aida.

Max nodded. "She got your message."

"And?"

"She wants to see you."

"Good." Relief came as if he'd been underwater and had just breached the surface. He lay back and let his thoughts get absorbed into his pillow. He was swept off to sleep again.

When he woke next, Ethel's face appeared at his door like a dream. She was ghostly pale, and there were bags under her glassy eyes, but her sharp gaze focused on him. He waved her over. She came to his bedside and clasped his hand. He squeezed her cool hand.

"Let's get some coffee." Max helped Aida out of her chair.

Aida, who'd still been sleeping, regarded Ethel and Chris with a perplexed expression. Max scooped up Shannon and ushered Aida out of the room.

Chris peered into Ethel's eyes. There was a soft sadness there. "I'm sorry I'm late."

"I think they'll give you a doctor's note." Ethel smiled. "Are you okay?"

"Come closer," Chris said.

When Ethel leaned in, Chris kissed her hard and strong and held her there. When they separated, he whispered, "I don't care. I'm sorry I even had to think about it. I want you, Ethel. That's all I care about."

Ethel's tears dripped onto Chris's cheeks as they kissed. She shifted her gaze to the floor and sighed.

"What's wrong?"

She frowned and shook her head. "I fucked up."

"What? How?" Chris asked.

Ethel sniffed and backed away a step. Her eyes searched the room. "It all kind of hit me at once, you know. I got a call from my sister. She'd been trying to arrange a meeting between my parents and me." Ethel's voice broke. "They said no. They still don't want anything to do with me. My own parents..." She sobbed then sniffed hard. "And then I showed up at your place, and you weren't there. In my mind, no one wanted me. It was stupid."

He'd hurt her. Guilt grabbed him by throat, and his chest became heavy. "It's okay. Hey, it's all right. I'm here. I want you." It worried him to see her so vulnerable.

"I'm more mad than anything. I fucked up. Two years of sobriety, and I pissed it away. I got drunk last night."

"Hey, it's okay. Hey, seriously, listen. I blew it too." Chris hooked his thumb in the direction of the hanging bag of morphine. "They loaded me up with painkillers in here. So I messed up too." The pain in his leg was legitimate, but he wanted to get off the drugs as soon as he could. He'd been through withdrawal already, and he didn't want another round of that hell. He'd done too much good to be drawn back in by addiction. "Let's start over, huh? We'll keep each other sober together. What do you say?"

Ethel came close and used the sleeve of Chris's hospital gown to wipe her eyes. He kissed her scarred cheek.

She grinned through her tears and beamed. "We really are a couple of royal fuckups, huh?" She sniffed and rubbed the bedrail.

"Yeah, all the best people are," Chris said.

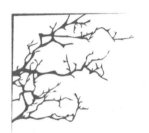

Chapter 39

After a couple of days in the ICU, Chris was transferred to a normal room. The nurses assisted him with range-of-motion exercises for his leg, and they weaned him off the painkillers, which helped clear the fog from his head. After a few days of being stuck in bed, Chris made his first attempts to hobble around with crutches. He struggled to put any weight on the leg and was quick to tire. Although his progress was slow, he mopped up the sweat and bit through the pain. The old Chris would have succumbed to the pain and fatigue and sought out pills, but now he recognized his own will and desire with clear eyes. His doctor told him that with some physical therapy, he could expect to be walking normally again in four to six weeks. According to the doctor, the fact that Chris was in shape would help with his recovery. Chris was glad all the hammering and hiking had paid off.

Max showed up daily to check on him. After Chris complained about being bored, Max gave him an instructional book on fly tying and a vise along with a bag stuffed with hooks, thread, and colorful materials. With time to kill, Chris was soon nimbly clamping hooks onto the vise and winding thread with ease. He began tying flies during the day in his hospital room. He got better over time, and soon he was tying dozens of flies a day: Copper Johns, Prince Nymphs, big articulated flesh flies, leeches, hoppers, wooly buggers, flashy streamers, and many more patterns. He filled several fly boxes and even developed a few of his own patterns. At first, the nurses were annoyed by the mess he made on his bed with the materials, but soon, word got around, and a few interested nurses and doctors had dropped in to watch him create flies. Soldotna was, after all, a fishing town.

Ethel came every night, often bringing him dinner or a plump bag of wild berries. When the nurses weren't around, she hopped into bed with him, and they held each other, kissing like teenagers. Chris was always sad to see her leave.

Aida and Shannon came down every few days and even brought Frank, who was back from the slope. Chris surprised himself by actually maintaining a few pleasant conversations with Frank, who, as it turned out, had had a few run-ins with power tools himself over the years. He shared a few of his scar stories. Chris figured Frank was the type of guy who grew on you with time.

He told Chris that after some discussion with Aida, they decided that if Chris wanted, he could live with them again in Anchorage. While Chris was happy for the news, the thought of being hours away from Ethel, Max, and the cabin didn't seem right to him. Frank and Aida both seemed surprised when he told them he'd have to think about it. Max had said he was fine with Chris coming back to the property and even mentioned that he counted on Chris's help to finish the cabin. On top of that, Chris wanted nothing more than to be close to Ethel. The life he'd sprouted down here seemed far more appealing than Anchorage.

AFTER TWO LONG WEEKS in bed, Chris's doctor gave him the okay to check out of the hospital. His leg was still bandaged and braced, but the wound had healed up enough, and his leg could bear his weight for short periods of time. He was off painkillers but still needed to go to outpatient physical therapy a few times a week in Soldotna for the better part of a month.

Although Chris had made up his mind to move back to the cabin with Max, Aida insisted on being the one to pick him up from the hospital. With Shannon and Frank at home, she drove Chris away from the hospital and back toward Max's property. Despite his eagerness to ditch the hospital gown for the tan work pants and blue long-sleeved shirt Max had given him, Chris found himself feeling tense as he scanned the wall of dense trees along both sides of the Sterling Highway.

Aida eyed him from the driver's seat. "You sure you don't want to move back in with us in Anchorage? It's an open offer, you know."

He got the feeling she had picked up on his nervousness. Life wasn't easy living out in the woods, but he couldn't forget the moments when he'd relished the earthy smells, the warmth of the fire, and the quiet peace.

Chris rubbed his beard, which had grown thick and bushy. It gave him a sense of pride and accomplishment. "I'll probably end up accepting that offer eventually, but I figure I owe it to Max to help him finish his cabin."

Aida's eyebrows jumped. Her hair was pulled back. Smile marks creased the corners of her eyes, and there was a glow about her cheeks. She looked younger and more refreshed than he could ever remember her being.

"I never really told you thanks," he said.

Aida glanced away from the road and at Chris. "You don't have—"

"Thanks for being there for me."

She put a hand on his shoulder. "Well, you're welcome. Dad would be proud of you, little brother."

"You know, I think he would." Chris smiled back.

When they arrived at Max's property, Aida said, "We'll be ready for you whenever you're done here."

With a crutch under each armpit, Chris watched Aida's van drive away again, although this time, he wasn't planning on running after her. He glimpsed Max chopping firewood to the right of the cabin. While Chris crutched his way up the rise, Max sank the ax head into the stump chopping block, wiped his forehead, and regarded Chris.

Spying the wall of wood stacked on either side of the front steps of the cabin, Chris shook his head. If it weren't for Max, he would have died two weeks earlier. The thought was sobering. The chainsaw bucking had been a horrific reminder of how quickly death could occur here. The beauty and remoteness of this place was also what made it so deadly. Yet he still found solace in the fact that all of his and Max's efforts had led to a nearly finished cabin. There was freedom in this place and a toughness that gave Chris a sense of pride that was stronger than any fear orbiting his heart.

From the outside, the cabin appeared much the same, as it was still covered in Tyvek that would need to be covered at some point. Chris was kind of surprised that Max hadn't gotten around to adding siding yet. The most obvious new addition was behind Max, just off the porch. The structure appeared to be a woodshed, which was stocked to the ceiling with firewood like an oversized box of matches.

Max stuffed the pieces he'd just cut inside the shed as Chris came over to him.

"You decide to go to war with the trees?" Chris asked.

Max smiled a toothy grin through his bushy beard. He pointed at the far side of the property, where Chris had nearly died and where Max had hung himself. The trees that had supported Max's noose had been cut down and removed. The whole grove had been cleared away for open soil, except for one solitary stump, which seemed odd by itself.

"I figured that particular grove of trees would be the perfect place to plant a garden."

"How did you get the stumps out of there?" Chris asked.

"Ripped them out with some chains and my truck. Had to blow up the stubborn ones. You missed quite a show."

"That would have been cool to see," Chris said.

Max dusted his hands off. "Well, there's still one more stump that's giving me trouble—same tree that put you in the hospital."

Now the mystery of the lone stump made sense. Max had saved it for him. Chris had to admit—ripping that stump out or blowing it to smithereens did sound fun. Even though Chris's own carelessness had gotten him hurt, he figured the tree still played a part in nearly killing him.

Since Chris was still on crutches, Max did the work while Chris observed. He drilled a deep hole into the stump then carefully packed the hollowed-out tube with black powder. He attached a long fuse from the stump.

Max pointed at the woodpile, which was one hundred fifty feet away. "We'll take cover behind that woodpile. You up for it?"

Chris took the lighter and eyed the end of the fuse. "Is this safe?"

"Don't worry. This is a slow-burning fuse. It'll take a while to get to the powder. Go ahead."

Chris lit the fuse and set the sparking line on the ground. As Max had said, it burned like a kid's sparkler.

"Let's go." Max ushered Chris toward the woodpile.

Chris did his best to quickly crutch himself over to the head-high stack. By the time they reached shelter, Chris was out of breath. He peeked through the gaps in the split wood and could see the sparks and hear the distant sizzle of the fuse. They waited a few minutes as the sparks crawled toward the finish line.

When the fuse had nearly burned to the end, Max told Chris to cover his ears. The spark reached the hole, and nothing happened. Then the stump exploded like a gunshot, splitting several ways and rocketing smoke and debris into the air. Bits of charred wood rained down around the blast site. The stump had been reduced to a smoking ruin. Chris and Max grinned like a couple of teenagers lighting off M-80s.

Chris wondered if all Max had done during his two weeks in the hospital was chop wood. Only when he went inside the cabin to sleep did he notice the changes. Every stick of wood inside had been sanded and stained and now shone with a polyurethane finish. The room still had a lingering chemical smell, but the cross breeze from the window in the kitchen and the bedroom kept fresh air moving. A braided rug rested on top of the finished floor in the living room, and a couch that Chris recognized as being formerly in Aida's house faced the wide window, which offered an impressive view of the western horizon. Against the wall was a small desk with a refurbished wooden chair. Chris assumed Max had gotten help from Aida or Frank in lugging the heavy stuff.

In the bedroom, Chris's cot had been replaced with a full-sized mattress with sheets, a fleece blanket, and a red-and-white quilt. The mattress sat on a hand-carved bed frame and headboard. A similarly crafted nightstand stood beside it. The room actually seemed like a bedroom. The kitchen area had a few pieces of refurbished wooden furniture: a table, four dining room chairs, and vintage cherry cupboards had been added, and a long counter with cabinets below ran the length of the wall. There was a stainless-steel sink, though when Chris opened the cupboard beneath it, he found a pipe that emptied into a five-gallon bucket. Little things were added, too, like blackout curtains and kerosene lamps. When he'd last been inside the cabin, it had seemed like a work site, but now it had the cozy feel of a home.

Despite the new comforts, Max still insisted on sleeping in his truck. Chris didn't like the idea of sleeping comfortably in the lone bedroom while Max resigned himself to the truck bed. He figured Max could at least stretch out on the couch in the living room.

When Chris called him on this, Max said, "If I sleep in there, I'll get too comfortable and lose working hours."

"You'll take the room back once we finish, right?"

"When we finish and you're healed up."

The next day, Max cleared the stump debris and put together some raised plant boxes in the former grove. Chris watched from the sidelines, leaning on his crutches. He wanted to help, but he'd be more in the way than useful. Max didn't bother planting anything since the fields were already flush with purple fireweed. He had explained that the fireweed was an early reminder that winter in Alaska was never too far off.

Ethel came by that night and joined Chris and Max at the fire pit. Sitting outside on the stumps, watching the flames, had become a ritual for Max and Chris. It was a good way to burn the brush and scrap wood as well as close out the day. Chris moved aside to let Ethel share his stump seat, and the three of them recounted the events of the day. Before long, Max decided to go to bed early and made his way for the truck. Chris and Ethel saw the obvious opening he had made, and they took full advantage of the night in the cabin.

At dawn the following morning, Ethel slipped out of Chris's bed and headed to work. All morning, Chris couldn't hold back his smile. After breakfast, Max drove him to physical therapy in Soldotna and dropped him off.

When Max came back to pick him up, Chris noticed several buckets of wood stain in the truck bed. Max asked if he wanted to help stain the siding. Chris was tired from his exercises with the physical therapist, but his desire to be useful again overrode his fatigue, and he told Max he could handle a paint roller. The sky was clear, and the sun offered her warmth, making it a perfect day for staining. Outside, beside the cabin's steps, Max set up sawhorses and laid out long slabs of rough-cut wooden siding that resembled long strips of bacon. Chris soaked a roller in the stain bucket then coated the thirsty rough-cut wood. When he finished a piece, Max would take it away to dry and add another for Chris to work on. Doing any work with the crutches was still awkward, and Chris's leg was tender and achy, but it felt good to be out of the hospital bed and to have a purpose again. He tolerated the pain, which seemed to be lessening with each passing day.

Chris rolled the brown stain on the new piece that Max had slipped on the sawhorses. He caught Max's eye. "You know, Max, I never actually thanked you for saving my life. Thank you, man."

"You did the same for me, kid."

When Chris had first shown up at the property, and Max had called him *kid*, Chris had thought Max was belittling him. But somehow, over time, Chris had started to like it. Lately, Chris found the word more endearing than condescending.

"So what's next for Chris Olson?" Max asked. "Think you can make a home up here in Alaska, or are you heading back to the lower forty-eight?"

"Well..." Chris scratched his beard. "There's not a lot left for me in California. Dead-end jobs and deadbeat friends—not one of those bastards gives a damn about me. Plus, it wasn't easy sobering up, and I'm not about to let myself get drawn back into hell again."

Max hauled off the finished piece of stained wood and swapped it for another piece of rough-cut lumber. "Seems like your sister and your family give a damn about you. Ethel's pretty fond of you too."

"Yeah, I noticed." Chris smirked as he finished his piece and moved on to another. "Guessing you noticed she stayed over last night. Do you care if she—"

"If she wants to visit you, she's free to do so anytime. You don't need my permission."

"Thanks, and who knows? After we finish this cabin, maybe she'll want me to move into her place." Chris winked and nudged Max's shoulder.

Max rolled his eyes and smirked.

"Ethel was telling me how Roger might be able to get me in with the fishing-guide community around here. Probably not for this season, but maybe I can get a job lined up for next spring. Getting paid to take people fishing? I could totally get down with that."

Max nodded. "I could easily see you being a guide."

"So what about you, Max? Seems like you have some choices to make too. Going to stay a hermit out here forever or head back home to Eagle River? Maybe give the doctor thing another go?"

"My first priority is to finish this cabin," Max said.

"Seems like we're getting there," Chris offered.

Max put his hands on his hips and stared at the cabin in front of him. "Looks that way. After we put this siding up and install the fireplace, it'll be just a matter of adding some finishing touches. I don't expect that the electric company will be out here for years, but there's plenty of hardwood on the property that'll make great firewood. It'll be a dry cabin, so until a well is dug, the drinking water will have to be collected from the natural spring down the road. Most people around here fill up there."

Chris eyed the cabin. "You've got yourself a fine place, built by some of the best craftsmen in the world."

Max cracked another of the smiles that lately were appearing more frequently.

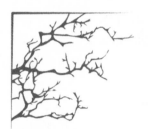

Chapter 40

Two weeks later, Chris and Max sat down for lunch across from each other at the cabin's kitchen table. Chris had whipped together a batch of tuna with mayo, which he sprinkled with black pepper. He and Max split a sleeve of Ritz crackers, and they scooped chunks of tuna from their bowls.

"Think there's still any fresh reds pushing up the river?" Chris asked.

Max worked over his teeth with his tongue. "Sure. We can go after this if you want. Might have to pick among the spawned-out zombie ones, but there might still be some good late-run fish to be caught."

Chris had noticed that the sockeye salmon had been changing color and shape the last time he'd gone fishing for trout. Their return to the fresh water of the river spurred a transformation. Their strong, tight bodies softened, their chrome scales switched to tomato red, and their faces turned green while their noses and teeth became hooked and warped. Still, they pushed farther up the river and into the creeks. They wouldn't give up until they found their spawn beds and pushed out eggs or milt. Only then could they finally quit fighting the river's current and instead join its flow downstream.

Chris collected the last bits of tuna with his cracker, ground the food in his mouth, and licked the fish oil off his lips. He rubbed his index finger on the table, following the dark wood-grain waves. He reflected on Aida's words: *People can change.* Chris had a beard and some more muscle, but the real transformation had been his finally shedding the numb, homeless junkie who'd roamed LA. He sponged up all feelings now, from the residual pain in his leg to his desire for something more with Ethel.

Max got up from his seat at the table, cleaned his dish, and slipped it on the drying rack. He sauntered over to the various fly-fishing rods hanging on the wall hangers that Chris had recently constructed.

Chris sat back and gazed at the cabin that he and Max had nailed and shaped into a home. They still had to pick up and install the wood stove that Max had ordered, but Chris could sense that his time at the cabin was coming to a close. Although Max hadn't told him any of his plans, Chris figured he would most likely move back to his house in Eagle River or someplace where he could stay busy and get back to work. Max, too, had made a transformation since Chris arrived more than two months ago.

"There might even be an early silver salmon or two in the river," Max said.

When Chris had been in the hospital, one of the male nurses had told him that the silvers, or *cohos*, arrived with the fall, sneaking in behind the second run of sockeye.

Max pantomimed pulling fly line. "You can strip streamers with your fly rod for silvers. They'll take a fly."

Chris cleared his dish and joined Max by the rods. "That's what I heard. I've tied some pretty good-looking streamers. I bet they'll work."

Max drove them to the river, and they spent the rest of the day walking the trail and peeking into every fishing hole, trying to spot fresh sockeye among the spawned-out reds. At the end of the day, Max managed to catch one red worth keeping, while Chris was overjoyed to land his first coho with a streamer fly of his own design.

The next day, Max and Chris set about installing the wood stove, which would be the last major project for the cabin. They maneuvered the heavy stove onto a raised brick-and-mortar foundation in the main room. The hard part was running the flue duct through the roof then adding the final Tyvek and metal around the chimney cap.

Around dinnertime, instead of convening at the fire pit, Chris built a fire in the wood stove. He and Max went outside to watch the smoke puff out of the chimney. Chris gazed at the cabin, while Max moved away to hang up the tools in the halfway house. If there were an exact moment to say that the cabin was done, this would be it. Of course, there was plenty more work to do, but for a primitive cabin in the woods without water or electricity, it was as finished as it would ever be. The building was well insulated and rigid, and Chris knew that it would be able to take the punches of winter and hardly even flinch.

The last time Ethel had stayed over, she had proposed having Chris move in with her once they were done. Although the thought of having each other so close was tantalizing, after talking it out, they both came to the conclusion that they might move in together eventually but not yet—it was too soon. Chris told her he planned on moving back to Anchorage. Even though he wasn't a fan of the city, there were plenty of places up there where he could work, and even if he just washed dishes, he would be able to save money thanks to the free room and board at Aida's. Then he'd be able to buy a car and visit Ethel every second he got.

Max came back over to stand beside Chris. "Even though the cabin's essentially done, there's still plenty more I could picture doing here. Still could use some latticework under the porch. A nice sunroof would let in more natural light. This would be a hell of a place to watch the aurora borealis in the winter. Next spring, the planter boxes should be good for vegetables—tomatoes, potatoes, carrots, lettuce, and hearty plants like those do well up here. There's enough spare wood to build a chicken coop. You can't beat free eggs. Always more work to be done on a place like this, but at some point, you have to call it done."

"I learned a lot here." Chris tapped his left leg. "Hard lessons to come by but stuff I needed to learn."

"I did too."

"I never met her, but I bet Julia would have loved this place."

Max rested a hand on Chris's shoulder. He kept it there and said, "You're right about that, kid. This was her dream, and I want to thank you for helping me build it for her."

Max's affection caught Chris off guard. He choked up and blinked back tears. He didn't dare look Max in the eye. He cleared his throat. "No problem, man."

Max kept his hand on Chris's shoulder for a second longer then let go.

THE NEXT DAY, CHRIS woke with the sun and made his bed, thinking about how Ethel had promised to come by that night. He shuffled out of his room. On the table was a folder with the penciled writing: "For Chris." He opened it and saw a note on top of a stack of papers:

Chris,

When you first met me, I was running out of reasons to wake up. The only thing that kept me going was this place. Then you came along and showed me that I can still have a purpose. I can still help people and save lives. I'm headed back to my home in Eagle River for the time being. Maybe I'll try to get my old job back. Or maybe I'll give Doctors Without Borders another go. Or maybe I'll just try something new. Either way, I'm excited to get back to work helping people, and I'm ready to get back out in the world.

I want you to have the cabin. It's as much yours as mine, and the same goes for all the tools and the land. I've included the deed and all the signed paperwork. Take the truck too. It's not a looker, but it has some years of living left. Kind of like me.

If you need a job close by, you can pretty much walk into any of the businesses in Soldotna. As long as you've got a pulse and a way to get to work, they'll hire you.

If you need anything, don't hesitate to get in touch.

Thanks to you, I still have life, so I'm off to live it.

Max

Chris put the letter down and leafed through the other forms in the folder. The pages all had Chris's name amended to the paperwork. It was hard to fathom. The property, the truck, and the cabin. *No one gives away gifts like this.* With fresh eyes, he gazed at the couch, the stove, and the cupboards filled with food and supplies.

"I'm a homeowner." Chris laughed at the ridiculousness.

He stepped outside on the porch and was greeted by the cool, crisp morning air. The porch offered a long view to the west, and he swept his eyes over the cleared land to see if Max was still around. He scanned the property—*my property.* The truck was still there—*my truck.* There wasn't any sign of Max.

He scratched his head and embraced the warmth of the sun. He couldn't wait to share the news with Ethel. This was all he ever wanted and more. "I have to be the luckiest son of a bitch in the world."

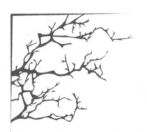

Chapter 41

Max crested the ridge and swept his gaze across the many green-and-yellow valleys ahead of him. The wind tore through the landscape and carried a sharp chill. He stood at the exact spot where Julia had stumbled. He glanced down over the precipice at the stark, terrifying descent. Max tried to guess her last thoughts, but he could only imagine them to be in the form of a feeling, and that feeling must have been pure fear.

He put his back to the cliff and walked to the other side of the ridge. The wind slashed at his bare face before it hurried off to the distant valleys below. He stopped at a rocky outcrop. An azure sky with only a few woolly clouds propelled him deeper into the wilds. Many of the trees in the valleys below had flushed with gold. Fall was always a short season in Alaska.

He unzipped his father's pack and pulled out the polished wooden box. He hugged the box tightly to his chest and patted the smooth lid. Tears had pooled at the creases of his eyes. He dabbed them dry with his shirtsleeve. "I'll always love you, Jules."

He tossed the contents into the wind. The plume of ash gave shape to the air as it tumbled and spread down the hillside to the ponds and forests beyond. With a harsh sniff and a swallow, he turned away and eyed the mob of jagged peaks in front of him. Max hefted his pack, tightened the straps, and continued walking. "Sweet home Alabama..."

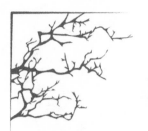

Chapter 42

The July sun warmed Chris's forearms with pulses of heat. He adjusted his chest waders and slogged to the edge of the fast water. That day was his first day off from guiding in over a week, and he was spending the afternoon fishing the same stretches of river he took his clients to. The difference was that he was casting light gear for trout instead of salmon. Roger had been the one to hook him up with the fishing-guide gig after Chris had spent the fall and winter working with an aging hunting guide and as a clerk at a Soldotna tackle shop. He was grateful to have a friend like Roger. He was even more grateful to have a girlfriend like Ethel.

Ethel had moved in with Chris, and the cabin stayed warm with her wrapped in his arms every night. They made love with ferocity and stayed awake kissing while the northern lights spread across the dark sky out their window. Chris had never imagined himself being so close with a woman, but during the long, dark days of winter, she kept him smiling. They kept each other sober and continued going to AA meetings. Ethel had even decided to give up trimming her hair and was letting it grow back. She evolved more each day. She was so easy to love.

Over the winter, Chris had hosted several dinners at the cabin with Ethel, Roger, Max, Aida, Frank, and Shannon. Max had taken temporary work at a small clinic in Anchorage. One night over dinner, Max was excited to break the news that he'd joined a volunteer medical organization based in India. When Chris asked when he was planning on returning to Alaska, Max said he didn't know. Chris couldn't help but smile at how Max carried a new energy about him.

The clean-shaven, bright-eyed man bound for India was so different from the Max he'd known the previous summer. In the spring, Max had rented his house in Eagle River and flown off to Mumbai. Chris imagined him over there in India, examining a kid with a broken bone. He missed having Max around, but he knew he was helping others and himself.

Knee-deep in the river with his rod clasped in his armpit, Chris scratched at his thick brown beard. He opened his fly box and selected a Prince Nymph. He inspected the pea-sized, dark-bodied fly wrapped in gold. White wings flared, and a copper bead head shone at the eye of the hook. Chris tied the fly to his line with an improved clinch knot, bit through the tag end, swung a roll cast, and dropped the nymph into a seam of current behind a fallen cottonwood. Through his polarized lenses, he glimpsed a grayish salmon and the brief ripple of green scales from another fish, undoubtedly a monster rainbow.

Adrenaline woke his senses. It had to be the largest rainbow trout he'd ever seen—a fish of a lifetime. He exhaled a shaky breath and bit his lip. He rolled another cast upstream of the fish, and this time, he high sticked the leader so the fly would pass through the current drag-free. The white mouth opened and inhaled the fly, and Chris set the hook. The fish peeled fly line off the reel as it streaked down river. *Shit!* Chris ran to catch up so as not to let the thin tippet snap. He charged through the water and flexed his rod toward shore, trying to steer the fish into the calm pool below him. The fish got airborne and leaped several feet out of the water, searching for slack, and Chris craned the rod tip behind him and reeled fast to keep the line tight. The fish made another run, this time upstream. Chris slogged through the water and moved closer to shore. He laid the wood to the fish and trusted the strength of the bent rod.

The rainbow suddenly charged him.

"Oh crap!" Chris buried his rod tip and line in the water, a trick
to add tension to the line, and reeled as fast as he could. He didn't
feel the fish anymore. Dread filled his heart. *Did I lose it?* When he
caught up to the slack, he was met with the familiar tug of the fish
and the violent bulldogging headshakes. Chris licked his lips and listened to the clicking as the fish worked his drag. The rainbow was
starting to tire, and Chris steered the fish out of the main current
and into his pool. At least thirty inches of rainbow trout still struggled and thrashed in the knee-deep water at his legs. Fat and heavy, it
was by far the biggest rainbow he'd ever caught—a trophy. He hastily shoved his rod in his armpit, grasped the fish's tail, and cradled
the trout by the belly at the water's surface. This rainbow was bigger than most of the salmon in the river. The leopard-spotted body
was splashed with green and a streak of pink. Yellow eyes with black
pupils searched, while the long kype jaw gaped.

Chris caught his breath. Even though the water was freezing, his
wet hands remained warm with adrenaline. He slid the tiny barbless
hook out of the thick lip and held the fish in the eddy's slow current,
letting water pass through its gills. He was reminded of how Max had
first taught him about catch-and-release fishing for trout, describing
the fish as "a creature made perfect by time and water." Chris lifted
the rainbow and planted a quick kiss on its scaly back before placing
it in the water. The trout stirred, brushed past his fingers, swam upstream, and became one with the river.

Acknowledgements

A big thanks goes to Red Adept Publishing's staff members, who were supportive and patient while I worked on this book. I want to thank my content editor, Alyssa Hall, for her ability to find depth in my characters. Thank you, Sarah Carleton, for being a helpful and precise line editor.

I owe a lot of thanks to my beta readers and writers in arms, Kelly Stone Gamble and R. W. W. Greene. I was lucky enough to have some medical friends with specific knowledge necessary for this story. Thank you to my medical squad: Alex Vellucci, Tyler Hanna, and Claudia Burns.

Thanks, Dad, for reliving a gruesome injury for the sake of authenticity.

I want to thank my MFA crew for your constant support. A big thanks goes out to my South Carolina writing group: David, Christy, Tim, Brigitte, and Austin.

Other friends who were kind enough to provide answers to my many questions are Marisa Cologgi, Jamie Hurley, and Ross Gagne.

Last but not least, thank you, Alaska. You continue to inspire us all.

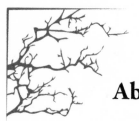

About the Author

David Rawding has a BA in English from the University of New Hampshire and an MFA in fiction from Southern New Hampshire University. He has been nominated for the Pushcart Prize, and his short stories have been published in numerous literary journals and magazines.

David spent three years as a fly-fishing guide in Alaska, worked several years at a non-profit for at-risk youth, was an online adjunct professor, and has a litany of other jobs in his wake. When he's not writing, he enjoys traveling the world with a backpack and a fly rod.

Don't miss out!

Click the button below and you can sign up to receive emails whenever David Rawding publishes a new book. There's no charge and no obligation.

https://books2read.com/r/B-A-FLYB-FOCT

BOOKS 2 READ

Connecting independent readers to independent writers.

Did you love *Redemption Grove*? Then you should read *Taking on Water* by David Rawding!

When James Morrow, a social worker, first meets Kevin Flynn, he suspects the teen is being abused. To learn more about Kevin's home life, he gets to know the boy's father, Tucker, who's a lobsterman. James is able to put his suspicions to rest, and the two families begin to form a friendship.When a kid at the local recreation center dies of an overdose, Detective Maya Morrow adds the case to the long list related to the drug problem plaguing the small New Hampshire coastal town of Newborough. But her investigation gets her much too close to the dangerous players.Both the Morrows and the Flynns are holding dark secrets, and when their lives collide, tragedy is inevitable.

Also by David Rawding

Taking on Water
Redemption Grove